Gathering Storm

RADICAL SOUTHS ▼

MICHAEL P. BIBLER and JAIME HARKER, editors

Radical Souths reclaims and reprints some of the most revolutionary works of Southern literature from the twentieth century. The fight for racial, sexual, economic, and political justice in the South has always been a homegrown struggle led by Southerners themselves, and Southern writers have always turned to the power of literature to bring those ideals to life. This series finally makes key texts from this radical tradition available to a wider audience, giving these voices of antiracist, queer, feminist, and socialist protest renewed urgency and authority.

A complete list of books published in Radical Souths is available at https://uncpress.org/series /radical-souths/.

A NOTE TO READERS

Some of the books in the Radical Souths series may contain racist, misogynist, queerphobic, or transphobic language, as well as graphic descriptions of sexual or racial violence, including assault, lynching, rape, and murder. But we the editors believe these scenes are never gratuitous. These books attempt to imagine ways to confront, challenge, and change these patterns of language and violence. And we feel that when the authors of these books choose to include graphic scenes, they do so to remind us exactly what is at stake in fighting the forces of domination and oppression. We invite our readers to approach these books with care but also with an open mind and a willingness to turn any potential shock and anger into action.

GATHERING STORM

A Story of the Black Belt

▼

MYRA PAGE

Foreword by Michael P. Bibler

The University of North Carolina Press
CHAPEL HILL

Designed by Lindsay Starr
Set in Sentinel by codeMantra
Manufactured in the United States of America

First published by The University of North Carolina Press in 2025.

Originally published in the United States by
International Publishers in 1932.

All illustrations by Juanita Preval, from the 1932 edition
by Martin Lawrence Limited.

Cover art: Ozark Mill in Gastonia, North Carolina, in 1908.
Photograph by Lewis W. Hine. National Child Labor Committee
Collection, Library of Congress Prints and Photographs Division.

Library of Congress Cataloging-in-Publication Data
Names: Page, Myra, 1897–1993 author | Bibler,
Michael P., 1971– writer of foreword
Title: Gathering storm : a story of the Black Belt /
Myra Page ; foreword by Michael P. Bibler.
Other titles: Radical Souths
Description: Chapel Hill : The University of North Carolina Press, 2025. |
Series: Radical Souths | Originally published in the United States by
International Publishers in 1932. | Includes bibliographical references.
Identifiers: LCCN 2025021695 | ISBN 9781469691084 cloth
alk. paper | ISBN 9781469691091 pbk alk. paper |
ISBN 9781469691107 epub | ISBN 9781469691114 pdf
Subjects: LCSH: Loray Mill Strike, 1929—Fiction | Labor unions—
Organizing—North Carolina—Gastonia—History—20th century—Fiction |
Labor unions—Southern States—History—20th century—
Fiction | Communists—North Carolina—Gastonia—History—
20th century—Fiction | Depressions—1929—Fiction | North Carolina—
Social conditions—20th century—Fiction | BISAC: FICTION /
Historical / General | FICTION / World Literature /
American / 20th Century | LCGFT: Novels
Classification: LCC PS3531.A235 G38 2025 |
DDC 813.52—dc23/eng/20250521
LC record available at https://lccn.loc.gov/2025021695

For product safety concerns under the European Union's General Product
Safety Regulation (EU GPSR), please contact gpsr@mare-nostrum.co.uk
or write to the University of North Carolina Press and Mare Nostrum
Group B.V., Mauritskade 21D, 1091 GC Amsterdam, The Netherlands.

Contents

Foreword

BY MICHAEL P. BIBLER

TWO DIFFERENT FIRST EDITIONS of Myra Page's *Gathering Storm: A Story of the Black Belt* were published in 1932. I bought my first copy, a paperback, from an online bookstore in the United Kingdom in 2008. The title page states that it was published by Martin Lawrence Limited in London, but the verso tells of another origin, in all caps but a smaller font size: "PUBLISHED BY THE CO-OPERATIVE SOCIETY OF FOREIGN WORKERS IN THE USSR" and "PRINTED IN THE UNION OF THE SOVIET SOCIALIST REPUBLICS." The almost khaki-colored interior pages have a pleasant weight and stiffness, but they are still somewhat pulpy, and the cover pages do not feel noticeably thicker. Although both red and black inks were used on the cover and title page, and the book includes eight illustrations by Juanita Preval, who also drew for the Communist publications *Daily Worker* and *New Masses*, this is not an expensive book. The curling paper on the spine lists the original purchase price of only two shillings, which,

Juanita Preval's cover illustrations for the 1932 UK edition of *Gathering Storm*, published by Martin Lawrence Limited (*top*), and for the 1932 US edition, published by International Publishers (*bottom*).

according to inflation calculators, equates to just under five pounds in 2024. And my copy, purchased so many years later, still did not cost much. When it arrived from London, the whole book was so saturated with the smell of cigarette smoke that I had to let it air out on a shelf for almost four months before the smell dissipated. Sometimes—quite wistfully, I confess—I picture the previous owner as a diehard Marxist revolutionary, a radical chain-smoking British beatnik in a tiny flat full of pamphlets and books, an invaluable collection of agitprop and theory that they later sold at insultingly low prices to offset bills in New Labour Britain or, even sadder, that their next of kin pawned to a book dealer for quick sale.

When I moved back to the United States, I bought another copy because the back cover of my paperback had torn off. Thankfully, this edition was not laced with a lethal dose of nicotine, but I was surprised to discover it featured a stiff (though still cheap) cardboard cover and different cover image. This time the title page identifies the publisher as "International Publishers, New York," but the verso is the same as in the British edition. I have since learned that the two different editions were both printed in the Soviet Union, probably to minimize import duties as copies were shipped to two different literary markets.[1] Otherwise, however, the books are identical. The cardboard cover makes the American edition a fraction larger, measuring five by seven and a half inches and three-quarters of an inch thick, but in both cases the physical dimensions and cheaper paper quality evidence a wish to make this Communist novel as affordable and accessible as possible to working-class readers. As C. Hartley Grattan notes in his review in the *New York World-Telegram*, *Gathering Storm* may well be "the first novel dealing with an American subject-matter, and seemingly addressed to the American public, to be printed in Soviet Russia."[2] And, as I like to demonstrate to my students, each copy fits easily in a jacket pocket or purse. This book was purposely designed to be carried by the common folk, with the goal of spreading its message to as many people as possible.

Indeed, an undated article by *New Masses* editor Mike Gold, included in Page's papers archived at the University of North Carolina at Chapel Hill, quotes a letter from "M.C.P." affirming that workers did share proletarian novels with one another:

> My copy of *Gathering Storm* is worn ragged and the same is true of Grace Lumpkin's *To Make My Bread* and Jack Conroy's *Disinherited*. They are read and passed on and returned to me only to go out again to a long waiting list. And who are these eager readers? A daughter of an East Side tailor, a clerk in an East Side grocery store, a driver for a laundry wagon, a telephone girl, Negro and white high school students.
>
> They have passed through fifty or more hands. Not a sectarian group. Some of them are just beginning to think at all, but they like these stories better than anything they have ever read before.[3]

Esther Lowell's review in *New Masses* begins with the same claim: "'Workers down in Birmingham [Alabama] like Myra Page's book, *Gathering Storm*,' one of the southern organizers told me."[4] Make no mistake: Page's novel is unabashedly a work of Communist propaganda, clearly aligned with the Communist Party USA (CPUSA) and Soviet government and aimed at spurring American and British workers into action. But I highlight the novel's materiality and publishing history to stress an important aspect of the text: namely, its interest in building a deeply intimate rapport with and among its readers.

For all the ways *Gathering Storm* wants to recruit its readers into a political ideology and movement, it is even more so a novel of persuasive feeling. Undeniably, being printed in the USSR gave this novel added political cachet at the time of its publication. But its interest in making emotional connections with readers plainly locates *Gathering Storm* within the wave of Depression-era American novels that sought to convey Communist ideas to a wider, more middlebrow readership as well as to the working-class readers M.C.P. describes.[5] *Gathering Storm* packages its ideals in an engaging, well-written narrative that helps readers understand and appreciate how the personal is always political, and vice versa. And it encourages readers to build sympathetic ties with others along and across lines of class, gender, race, and region as part of a truly diverse, interracial, international, feminist proletariat. If my British copy was owned by a chain-smoking radical, at least in my fantasies, the inscription in my American edition points to this intimate, and perhaps no less radical, feminist reading public:

Florence Shapiro
Sept 30, 1938
(Edith Welt's "going away present")

Maybe Edith was the tailor's daughter and Florence was the telephone girl. Or maybe they weren't from New York's East Side but the queerer, more bohemian Greenwich Village. Or maybe they were Black and white students or teachers who had joined the cause down in Birmingham. Or maybe they were roommates at Vassar or Smith, or housewives in a reading group in Columbus, Ohio.

Wherever the reader may be, *Gathering Storm* is not just an American novel printed in the Soviet Union but a novel specifically about the Black Belt of the US South. It is part of a remarkable group of novels inspired by the turbulent and

deadly strikes at the Loray textile mill in Gastonia, North
Carolina, in 1929. Critics typically identify five other "Gastonia novels": Mary Heaton Vorse's *Strike!* (1930), Field-
ing Burke's *Call Home the Heart* (1932), Grace Lumpkin's
To Make My Bread (1932), Sherwood Anderson's *Beyond
Desire* (1932), and William Rollins Jr.'s *The Shadow Before*
(1934). Burke (the penname of Olive Tilford Dargan) also
wrote a sequel entitled *A Stone Came Rolling* (1935), and literary scholar Suzanne Sowinska includes Lumpkin's *A Sign
for Cain* (1935) in this group as well.[6] I would add two more
works: the short story "Little Doc" (1935) and novel *Between
the Devil* (1939), both by the almost totally forgotten writer
Murrell Edmunds.[7] Of this group, Burke, Lumpkin, and Page
have received the most critical attention. And while Burke's
and Lumpkin's novels were reprinted in 1983 and 1995, respectively, it is impressive that Page's novel has received almost equal attention despite remaining out of print since its
publication in 1932.[8]

As historian John A. Salmond has documented in detail,
the Loray Mill in West Gastonia, North Carolina, was "the
largest [mill] in the whole South," and work conditions were
difficult and "increasingly unhealthy" as greater mechani-
zation translated into more work, longer hours, and fewer
breaks under what was known as the "stretch-out" system.[9]
In this system, which becomes a key point of contention in
the plot of *Gathering Storm*, workers were made to work longer shifts than they had before, and some were made to work
at night so that the mill would be in operation twenty-four
hours a day. In addition, the pay structure changed, so that
workers were paid according to how many pieces of fabric
were produced ("piecework rates") instead of getting paid
"wage rates" by the hour, which meant that they usually took
home less pay than before. To protest these stretch-outs,
workers across the South staged walkouts in record numbers,

especially in 1929. A fledgling but notable labor movement was already developing throughout the South and attracting attention from the CPUSA, as Robin D. G. Kelly has famously illustrated in *Hammer and Hoe: Alabama Communists During the Great Depression*. And in 1929, the newly formed National Textile Workers Union, which had deep connections to the CPUSA, decided to send agents to this new South of labor agitation, including New Englander Fred Beal, who went to Gastonia to help organize the strikes at Loray Mill.

While there had already been walkouts in the previous year, the Loray Mill strike that gained global notoriety began on April 1, 1929, and it quickly escalated into a violent confrontation between the strikers and management's forces of police officers, National Guardsmen, and vigilantes. Women were especially visible in the picket lines, and photographs of them grabbing the rifles of National Guardsmen circulated around the country. The CPUSA and other organizations then sent more people down to observe and participate as the mill bosses blamed Beal and his "Bolshevik associates" for fomenting the unrest—activating the "outside agitators" myth that always gets deployed when progressive Southerners push for change.[10] However, the mill protest was clearly more homegrown: Most of the strikers did not think of themselves as "the conscious vanguard of the revolution" but were "acting much more out of the tradition of spontaneous protest against real grievances that had animated the Loray weavers the previous year, for example, and would be seen throughout the Piedmont during 1929."[11]

As the standoff in Gastonia continued into summer, the fear and violence escalated. On June 7, the strike leaders staged a march in defiance of an antiparade ordinance, which led to a brawl with police. Some officers brutally targeted the women strikers, and Gastonia's chief of police, Orville F. Anderholt, was killed in a shootout between police and guards that the strikers had posted. His death spurred even greater violence and repression against the strikers until, in September, a group of vigilantes opened fire on a flatbed truck carrying workers to a union meeting, killing twenty-nine-year-old organizer, mother, and songwriter Ella May Wiggins. At the trial in February 1930, even though there were numerous eyewitnesses to Wiggins's murder, the jury deliberated only thirty minutes before finding all the suspected shooters not guilty. Wiggins's death and the egregiously phony trial gained international attention, and the CPUSA and other organizations helped publicize the strikers' cause further by circulating Wiggins's protest songs far beyond North Carolina. They are still being recorded and performed today.

Page did not visit Gastonia during the strike, but she had spent time there and in Greenville, South Carolina, in 1925 and 1926, conducting research for her dissertation in sociology at the University of Minnesota. In 1929, she turned that dissertation into a book-length account of the textile workers' conditions, *Southern Cotton Mills and Labor*. Prior to completing her dissertation, Page was already writing essays and stories for several leftist journals and magazines, including *The Crisis, Labor Age, Labor Defender, Southern Workman, Southern Woman, New Masses, The Communist, Daily Worker*, and more. In the early 1920s she had also worked as a labor organizer for the Amalgamated Clothing Workers of America and American Federation of Teachers. After these experiences in the field with working-class people, she grew to believe that her dissertation was too much of a "cold, removed academic piece" to win readers to the cause of workers' rights. And so, in *Southern Cotton Mills and Labor* she added personal, intimate material from her interviews and observations that she could not include in the scholarly work, trying to write "sympathetically about mill people and what they wanted to be" and "avoid academic language so that it might appeal to a working-class audience."[12]

When the Loray Mill strike broke out in 1929, Page decided to find more ways to make her writing connect with the very people she was writing about. She adapted many of her observations and characters from *Southern Cotton Mills and Labor* into *Gathering Storm* and added specifics from the strike in the last third of the novel, including Wiggins's murder and the trial. Rather than simply allegorizing Communist theory and doctrine in flat characters and plots, Page was trying to educate and inspire her readers on a more personal level. She sought to give them exactly the kind of stories they could identify with and see themselves a part of—the stories that M.C.P. claimed working-class readers liked "better than anything they have ever read before" and that Florence Shapiro and Edith Welt clearly liked as well.[13] After *Gathering Storm*, Page wrote a novel about an autoworker who emigrates to the Soviet Union, *Moscow Yankee* (1935), reprinted in 1996, and a novel about women in coal-mining country, *With Sun in Our Blood* (1950), reprinted in 1986 as *Daughter of the Hills: A Woman's Part in the Coal Miners' Struggle*. These books were published under her pseudonym, Myra Page, which she had adopted in the 1920s to avoid tensions with her parents. However, with the second Red Scare in the 1950s, Page needed to distance herself from her Communist associations and used her married name, Dorothy Markey, for her next two books: juvenile biographies about the scientists Charles Steinmetz and Michael Pupin, published in 1956 and 1963, respectively.

Myra Page was born Dorothy Page Gary on October 1, 1897, in Newport News, Virginia. Both sides of her family had emigrated to Virginia in the early 1700s, and both grandfathers had fought for the Confederacy in the Civil War, but her immediate family was comfortably middle class and relatively progressive for their time and place. Her mother was well educated and a talented artist, and her father was a doctor who, unlike most other white doctors, treated both white and Black patients. Theirs was a happy home full of art, music, culture, and books, and Page notes that her parents pushed against the conservatism of the Jim Crow South, even though, she says regretfully, they "never pushed too far."[14] Early on, she felt that her mother and aunts also did not do enough to push against cultural gender norms, but her parents still made sure that all four of their children went to college. Dorothy received bachelor's degrees in English and history in 1918 from Westhampton College in Richmond (now the University of Richmond), and in 1919, at her mother's encouragement, she began studying for a master's degree at Columbia University, taking classes with such luminaries as anthropologists Franz Boas and Melville J. Herskovits.

In college, Page strengthened her commitment to antiracist, progressive ideals while working with the Young Women's Christian Association (YWCA), which was explicitly devoted to empowering women and fighting for racial equality. In 1917, she invited Eva Bowles, an African American industrial secretary on the national YWCA board, to speak with the white students at Westhampton about racial integration and other topics, arguably the first interracial meeting at the college.[15] In the early 1920s, she worked as a teacher and organizer in Virginia, New York, New Jersey, and Pennsylvania. In 1924, she married John Fordyce Markey while studying for her PhD in Minnesota, and the two officially joined the CPUSA in 1925. The Markeys were very active in the party and traveled to the USSR in 1928 and again in 1931 on the same ship as Fred Beal, the CPUSA agent sent to help organize the Gastonia strike, who at that time was fleeing his dubious conviction for the murder of Police Chief Anderholt in Gastonia.[16] They stayed in the

Soviet Union from 1931 to 1933, during which time Page wrote *Moscow Yankee* and, with John, worked with "the world-wide underground movement against the fascists."[17] After World War II, they settled in Yonkers, New York, and raised two children. Page remained a member of the CPUSA until 1953 and later claimed that she had become disillusioned with the party gradually, not just because of McCarthyism. But she never gave up organizing and protesting: she traveled to the South in the summers to work with the civil rights movement and worked with the antiwar movement, women's movement, environmental movement, and other groups, until a change in her health compelled her and her husband to move into a nursing home in 1986, where she stayed until her death in 1993.

The Communist ideas that Page embeds in *Gathering Storm* are clear and accessible; yet, refreshingly, she never gets so didactic that she breaks the flow of her narrative. To those familiar with the history of the labor movement, however, her presentation of those ideas might look simplistic. She depicts very little of the factionalism that existed within the CPUSA and the larger labor movement—and that exists, for that matter, in any political struggle. She also does not dwell on the racism and sexism infamously built into the very structure of the CPUSA during this time; and she does not mention the atrocities and power struggles that occurred in the Soviet Union under Stalin's brutal regime. In the case of the famines and gulags in Soviet Russia, Page later insisted that she simply did not know about them: "The authorities showed us a Communist society in the best light possible, and I accepted what I saw at face value. Not realizing how much Stalin covered up, I trusted the Party." But to her credit, she also acknowledged that her own faith and idealism had practically blinded her to that negative side of the Bolshevik Revolution: "Looking back, I see that I didn't want to see it and I was wrong. I wanted to believe that the people in the Party knew what they were doing."[18]

However, *Gathering Storm* reveals a more positive component to Page's seemingly narrow idealism, for it is a novel of optimism and hope, not dogma. We follow her characters through their political awakenings as they hone their skills of critical thinking and community organizing. When the strike and the novel end, the protagonists take these skills and move on to escalate the fight for workers' rights across the globe. The heroine, Marge Gregory, is not "swept along," the novel's last paragraph assures us, but is "deliberately, joyously a fore-runner, a marshaller of the gathering storm." In this way, Marge resembles Page herself, who was, at least by her own account, a strong-willed force of nature in the party. She claimed, "I also rebelled and took discipline only when I chose to. We [she and John] made difficult members of any organization, particularly the Communist party. First, I thought a matter through and decided if it was right. If I spoke out, it was because I believed I was speaking for the right thing. I was for socialism and getting things done, but I didn't like this highly politicized business."[19] If *Gathering Storm* might seem too idealistic or tunnel-visioned, then, it is not *just* because Page is being propagandistic. Rather, her singularity of purpose is also a sign of Page's feminist determination to voice her own thoughts *despite* what else the party might say or require. Like her heroine, Page is not trying only to follow the party line; she is positioning herself as a "marshaller" of what she sees as "the right thing," thus hoping to inspire her readers to become activist "fore-runners" as well.

Gathering Storm follows the development of young Marge Gregory, originally Marge Crenshaw, who grows up working in the mills in Greenville, South Carolina, and eventually becomes a union activist and organizer of the Loray Mill strike in Gastonia. Two generations prior, Marge's family had been recruited to come down from the mountains to work in the mills, and her parents and grandparents teach Marge from a very young age how to analyze and critique the socioeconomic forces that keep them in poverty, particularly the unequal wages between men, women, and children—and between white and Black—as well as the discrepancies in wealth, health, and education between the workers and mill owners. Early on, in chapter 2, young Marge asks her grandmother, Old Marge, what can be done about these inequities, and Old Marge immediately gives her an answer that clearly fits the party line: "What we gotta do is fight for our rights. Like we done that time in Georgy [Georgia]. For more vittles'n more larnin' for our young 'uns." It is true that, later in the novel, activists from the North help organize the workers' personal observations and grievances into political protest, but Page emphasizes from the start that even the least educated workers of the South are not so ignorant that they cannot recognize and understand the source and nature of their exploitation.

Marge also learns from her family about the profiteering of industry and government during the Spanish-American War of 1898, a critique that Marge echoes when her husband, Bob Gregory, volunteers for the Great War (now known as World War I) and comes home shell-shocked, ill, and destitute. But most of her growing recognition of her place in the exploitative system of the mills, and of capitalism more generally, comes from her gendered and sexual understanding of her status as a woman. In addition to resenting the lower pay given to women at the mill, she sees the crowded millhouses filled with sickness and more children than the women can care for. She thus intuits sex as something "evil . . . that got you in the corner, and cursed you with extra mouths to feed." As she tries to avoid attention from boys, her family worries

that she's turning "quare," but eventually she finds she cannot resist her own love for Bob. Then a new terror arises
when Bob gets shipped overseas and Marge discovers she is
pregnant. In a storyline true to the period before *Roe v. Wade*
(1973), Marge desperately searches for a way to get an abortion while knowing that the upper-class women in town can
easily afford doctors for both contraception and abortions.
She even prays that the stress of having to keep working until
she gives birth will save her from having the child she knows
she cannot support. Of course, as soon as baby Roberta is
born, Marge is filled with unconditional love. But then, after
Marge has to return to work just two weeks later, she faces
sorrow and grief when Roberta dies from innate weakness
and malnourishment. Bob also dies not long after his return
from war, followed by their son, Bobby, thus linking Marge to
labor organizer Ella May Wiggins, whose most famous song,
"Mill Mother's Lament," captures the tragedy of losing four
children at the same time to whooping cough. As a Communist novel, *Gathering Storm* broadly narrates the problems
of class warfare and economic exploitation inflicted by the
propertied elite. But it is even more urgently a feminist novel
that examines and protests the social, material, and political problems specifically faced by women in this oppressive
system.

The problems of sex in this novel are not Marge's alone.
As a gruesome counterpoint to Marge's courtship with Bob,
Martha Morgan, a Black woman Marge's age, is raped and
murdered by the mill owner's son, Elbert Haines. Earlier,
Marge encountered Martha in a key moment of cross-racial,
"human to human" recognition, in which she fully realized
for the first time that Black women have a lot in life that's
"worser'n mine." In this brief flash of empathy and identi-
fication, Page invites readers to imagine the world of the
mills from Martha's perspective, not just that of the white

characters. After Martha's murder, her lover, Jim, retaliates by killing Elbert, which in turn prompts the white elites to launch a campaign of terror and lynching against the entire Black community. Structurally, this violence parallels the later violence inflicted on the strikers, strengthening Page's Communist critique of the interwoven systems of racial and economic exploitation in the Jim Crow South. But Page also does not subordinate race to class by conflating the events. She makes sure her readers are able to recognize the clear differences between the lynching and the backlash against the strike.

In her portrayals of Black characters and race relations, Page has been alternately praised for her sensitive realism and criticized for being too idealistic about their interactions with whites. But her harrowing account of Martha's rape and murder and its aftermath is brutally honest and sympathetic. Feminist critic Paula Rabinowitz writes that, whereas most feminist proletarian literature "premises rape as one element of bourgeois male perversity," Martha's rape compellingly, if tragically, illuminates how "racial and gender differences [are] inscribed on the body of the working-class black woman" differently than white women.[20] Page was a shrewd observer of what Black feminist scholars Kimberlé Crenshaw and Patricia Hill Collins defined almost sixty years later as intersectionality, and she took great care to highlight the complex ways that race and racism combined with gender, sexuality, and class to create uneven lines of oppression for Black and white women and men in the segregated South.[21] As always, Page's critique of systemic racism, sexism, misogyny, and class oppression begins in the crucible of an individual character's personal experience.

Page knew just as well as CPUSA leaders, who discussed it extensively, that unionizing the South would require cooperation between Black and white workers. And while it might seem that her Black characters in *Gathering Storm* are a little too quick to trust their white colleagues and embrace this interracial coalition, she also knew that white Southerners had more to unlearn. Thus, she devotes key parts of her narrative to her white characters' slow shift toward sympathy and understanding across the color line, with a particular focus on Marge's brother Tom, who goes to New York to find work. Chapter 20 offers a key moment when Tom realizes how deeply ingrained his racist programming truly is. But in keeping with everything else about this relational novel, his recognition arises from a deeply intimate moment with his Black friend George as they ride a train back down south to help organize the union at the mill. When George rests his hands on his white friend's knee and explains the pain he feels at returning to the South, it is hard for any reader, then or now, to miss the power of their affectionate touch as it helps dispel the "pizen" (poison) of racism, as well as what we would today call toxic masculinity and homophobia. And then Page immediately turns from the personal to the political. As the men's tender touch becomes both a symbol for the bonds of Marxist camaraderie and a sign of a new kind of masculinity, it also fuels the men's readiness for direct political action, with George affirming that "now [he knows] how to fight" the social, economic, and material causes of his personal pain.

Page also discusses this interplay between individual experiences and systemic critique in a 1929 piece for *The Crisis*, "Beyond the Color Line," which she wrote at the encouragement of W. E. B. Du Bois. The essay describes four important friendships Page had with African Americans throughout her life, all of which helped her to recognize the pain, trauma, and inequality caused by racism and which, importantly, led to her revelation that simply "changing men's hearts" was not the means by which "social relations would right themselves." Thus, at the end of the piece, she shifts from a discussion of intimate relations to a critique consistent with Communist ideology—albeit without naming it as such—as she learns that "the system [is] stronger than individuals" and that the solution is "changing the system itself."[22] "Beyond the Color Line" paints a rather simple picture of the evolving consciousness of a white liberal born into privilege. And with its almost paternalistic depictions of Page's four Black acquaintances, none of whom ever had the same rights or privileges as Page, the piece might not sit well with many modern readers. Likewise, modern readers will not fail to notice in *Gathering Storm* Page's occasional use of primitivist tropes and the racialized language of the 1930s, which might seem to compromise her antiracist aspirations. But these two works still stand out for their unflinching and honest attempts to fight racism in minds, hearts, *and* "the system." Page is highly unusual, even among proletarian writers, for speaking frankly to her white readers about her efforts to confront and unlearn what the white liberal Southern writer Lillian Smith would later call the childhood "lessons" of racism, sexism, and heterosexism—and for calling on her readers to undertake this difficult work as well.[23]

Altogether, as a partisan text, *Gathering Storm* deftly ties the political to the personal and explores intersectional lines of oppression at the level of the individual, all while offering a distinctly Communist analysis that seeks to leverage those personal experiences in the fight for systemic change. But *Gathering Storm* is also simply a good work of literature, with nuanced characterizations that humanize its characters and a compelling narrative that carries its readers along. In that respect, it easily holds its own next to, if not surpasses, more familiar proletarian novels of the Great Depression. One might even wonder how much *Gathering Storm* directly influenced John Steinbeck's later novel about a violent strike in California, *In Dubious Battle* (1936), as well as *The Grapes of Wrath* (1939).

But *Gathering Storm* should not be read only as a work of social realism. As a feminist novel focused on poor Southern white women, it follows in the paths charted by Elizabeth Madox Roberts and fellow Virginia writer Ellen Glasgow, one of Page's greatest influences. Clearly there is a strong affinity between this novel and *The Little Foxes* (1939), the wildly popular play and film by Lillian Hellman, famously a member of the CPUSA, that protested the greed of Southern elites and industrialists. And readers can also draw interesting connections to Katherine Anne Porter's representations of white womanhood in the South and Communist revolution in Mexico in *Flowering Judas and Other Stories* (1930).[24] Indeed, *Gathering Storm* also situates Page as an important and early voice among writers seeking to draw attention to poor white Southerners during the Depression, including Erskine Caldwell and James Agee. And finally, her critical attention to race relations and her attempts to write overtly sympathetic, anti-racist narratives puts her in close dialogue with important works of Southern African American writing, including Jean Toomer's *Cane* (1923); fellow CPUSA member Richard Wright's *Uncle Tom's Children* (1938) and "Bright and Morning Star" (1938), first published in *New Masses*; and Zora Neale Hurston's *Mules and Men* (1935) and *Their Eyes Were Watching God* (1937). Hurston's work in particular shares with Page's the anthropological influence of Franz Boas in their treatment of poor and working-class Southerners. In fact, just four years after Page earned her master's at Columbia, Hurston entered Barnard College and also studied with Boas. Coincidentally, Page was also born just six days after Mississippi novelist William Faulkner. It is worth considering how the Southern literary landscape starts to look different when we put the radical Page next to these prominent writers.

In 1930, between the publications of *Southern Cotton Mills and Labor* and *Gathering Storm,* twelve white Southern men who called themselves the Southern Agrarians published their reactionary, antihumanist, anti-Communist manifesto, *I'll Take My Stand.* In the same year, Faulkner published his first novel about poor white people, *As I Lay Dying.* In the context of Page's work, both texts demand to be read as responses to the anticapitalist protests that rocked the South in 1929, especially the Loray Mill strike. *I'll Take My Stand* was a conservative attempt to combat those protests culturally and ideologically. *As I Lay Dying* can perhaps be read as an attempt to capitalize on the sudden media interest in poor white Southerners and finally earn Faulkner some income as a writer—much as he claimed that he wrote his next novel, *Sanctuary* (1931), to make money. Thanks to the academic credentials of the Agrarians, their conservative understanding of the South drove the emerging field of Southern literary and cultural studies well into the 1990s, leaving radical leftist Southern writers like Page in the margins. Similarly, critics have traditionally used the experimental form of *As I Lay Dying* and other Faulkner novels to reinforce hierarchical divisions between high modernist literature and the social realism of writers like Page and Grace Lumpkin. But *Gathering Storm* offers a chance to rethink this landscape of Southern writing and put narratives of radical resistance back in the center.

Page gives us an example of this chance to reconsider the literary canon in the novel itself. In chapters 7 and 8, Marge's brother Tom turns her world upside down when he sends her a copy of Upton Sinclair's social realist novel *The Jungle* (1905). After reading it, Marge pesters the public librarian in Greenville to provide other works along the same lines.

Previously, the librarian had given Marge books by the popular Confederate apologist Thomas Nelson Page and books for girls such as *Three Little Women*.[25] When Marge asks for more books like *The Jungle*, the librarian rebuffs her with "horror" and "a fifteen minute monologue" before handing her a book entitled *When Patty Went to Boarding School*. Frustrated and disgusted, young Marge gives up on the library entirely: "What did all of this have to do with a cotton mill girl?" *Gathering Storm* is exactly the book that Page wanted girls like Marge to have access to. And with this reprint, her book will have a greater chance to inspire new readers.

NOTES

1. I thank Catherine Williamson for this information. Page explained that Alexander Trachtenberg, the head of the radical leftist International Publishers, "had the sheets set up in the Soviet Union through an English firm, so that back in the United States he played both ends by paying smaller taxes and printing bills." Christina Looper Baker and Myra Page, *In a Generous Spirit: A First-Person Biography of Myra Page* (University of Illinois Press, 1996), 116.

2. C. Hartley Grattan, "The Soviet Prints an American Novel," *New York World-Telegram*, December 27, 1932, box 16, folder 245, Myra Page Papers #5143, Southern Historical Collection, Wilson Library, University of North Carolina at Chapel Hill.

3. Quoted in Mike Gold, "Change the World!," box 16, folder 245, Myra Page Papers #5143, Southern Historical Collection, Wilson Library, University of North Carolina at Chapel Hill.

4. Esther Lowell, "Gathering Storm," *New Masses*, May 1933.

5. See Jaime Harker, *America the Middlebrow: Women's Novels, Progressivism, and Middlebrow Authorship Between the Wars* (University of Massachusetts Press, 2007), 115–46.

6. Suzanne Sowinska, "Writing Across the Color Line: White Women Writers and the 'Negro Question' in the Gastonia Novels,"

in *Radical Revisions: Rereading 1930s Culture*, ed. Bill V. Mullen and Sherry Linkon (University of Illinois Press, 1996), 120–43.

7. For more on Edmunds, see Michael P. Bibler, "Queer Antiracism and the Forgotten Fiction of Murrell Edmunds, a Southern 'Revolutionary,'" *Philological Quarterly* 90, nos. 2–3 (2011): 287–316.

8. Although this is not an exhaustive list of critical works discussing *Gathering Storm*, see Barbara Foley, *Radical Representations: Politics and Form in U.S. Proletarian Fiction, 1929–1941* (Duke University Press, 1993); Sylvia Jenkins Cook, *From Tobacco Road to Route 66: The Southern Poor White in Fiction* (University of North Carolina Press, 1976); Wes Mantooth, *"You Factory Folks Who Sing This Rhyme Will Surely Understand": Culture, Ideology, and Action in the Gastonia Novels of Myra Page, Grace Lumpkin, and Olive Dargan* (Routledge, 2006); Lisa Schreibersdorf, "Radical Mothers: Maternal Testimony and Metaphor in Four Novels of the Gastonia Strike," *Journal of Narrative Theory* 29, no. 3 (1999): 303–22; and James Mellard, "The Fiction of Social Commitment," in *The History of Southern Literature*, ed. Louis D. Rubin Jr., Blyden Jackson, Rayburn S. Moore, Lewis P. Simpson, and Thomas Daniel Young (Louisiana State University Press, 1985), 351–55.

9. John A. Salmond, *Gastonia 1929: The Story of the Loray Mill Strike* (University of North Carolina Press, 1995), xii, 1.

10. Salmond, *Gastonia 1929*, 26.

11. Salmond, *Gastonia 1929*, 27.

12. Baker and Page, *In a Generous Spirit*, 98.

13. Quoted in Mike Gold, "Change the World!," *New Masses*, n.d., box 16, folder 245, Myra Page Papers #5143, Southern Historical Collection, Wilson Library, University of North Carolina at Chapel Hill.

14. Baker and Page, *In a Generous Spirit*, 12.

15. Baker and Page, *In a Generous Spirit*, 31–32.

16. Later there was evidently a falling-out between the Markeys and Beal, as Beal tried to convince the FBI that Page was acting as a paid agent of the Soviet Union, which she was not. Baker and Page, *In a Generous Spirit*, 174–75.

17. Baker and Page, *In a Generous Spirit*, 135.

18. Baker and Page, *In a Generous Spirit*, 121.

19. Baker and Page, *In a Generous Spirit*, 99.

20. Paula Rabinowitz, *Labor and Desire: Women's Revolutionary Fiction in Depression America* (University of North Carolina Press, 1991), 90.

21. See Kimberlé Crenshaw, *On Intersectionality: Essential Writings* (New Press, 2019); and Patricia Hill Collins, *Black Feminist Thought: Knowledge, Consciousness, and the Politics of Empowerment*, 30th anniversary ed. (Routledge, 2022).

22. Dorothy P. Gary, "Beyond the Color Line," *Crisis*, May 1929, 153, 170–71. In Page's papers archived in the Wilson Library at the University of North Carolina at Chapel Hill, she remembers this essay with a different title, "Color-Blind," which does not, I think, reference the idea of "not seeing color," as the term often means now, but instead conscientiously acknowledges that she was blind to all the ways that color worked to control and limit the lives of the Black people she writes about, as well as her own mentality. Myra Page, "Color-Blind," 1931, box 3, folder 31, Myra Page Papers #5143, Southern Historical Collection, Wilson Library, University of North Carolina at Chapel Hill.

23. Page is very much a sociological writer, of course, while Smith uses a psychoanalytic frame to explain and fight white racism in her novel *Strange Fruit* (1944) and her book of essays, *Killers of the Dream* (1949). Smith, born just two months after Page in 1897, was also aggressively anti-Communist, especially in the 1960s. Nevertheless, these two white Southern women writers have much more in common in their exceptional attempts to deprogram the racist mindsets of their white readers in the South and beyond.

24. The short story "He" in this collection was first published in *New Masses* in 1927, suggesting further affinities between the two writers.

25. The bestselling Thomas Nelson Page was a fellow Virginian, but I do not know if he was related to the Pages in Dorothy Page Gary's—Myra Page's—family.

Gathering
Storm

I.

Down from the Mountains

"SURE, CHILE, I 'MEMBER IT like it was yestiddy. Though it's been nigh forty years since we come down from the Blue Ridge mountains to the cotton mill." Ole Marge's chuckle faded off into a sigh. Rocking her gaunt frame back and forth on the narrow porch of their company shack she peered down the yellow dirt street lined with dingy low-crouching houses. Behind them loomed the red brick mill, standing as if on guard. With a blunted match stick she carefully dipped herself some snuff out of a handleless cup gripped in one knotty hand.

"Tell me, Granny," Young Marge begged. "You know—what all happened." Her eyes, the colour of deep sea water, clung eagerly to the swaying figure in its black and white checks. There was nobody, she felt certain, in Row Hill or all of Greenville who could touch her Granny. Some in the village might call Ole Marge quare 'n with a tongue dipped in bitters.

They were just stick-in-the-muds, 'n her Granny too smart for 'em. Too smart 'n with a way all her own.

"I never saw the likes!" the old woman clucked her tongue. "Ain't you heerd that tale over'n over. I 'low you know it better'n me, by now.

"But every time it's new-like," her grandchild pleaded. "Every time you think of somethin' you left out afore."

"Wal—" Ole Marge squinted at the lowering sun. "I reckon I say it as shouldn't. But honey, you sure make as pretty a pitcher as sore eyes wanta see this side the pearly gates."

Young Marge, flushed with the close heat of a southern August, sat with her head thrown back against a worn post, her hands clasped around her raised knees. The Carolina sun flirted with the tiny patterns of her pink gingham slip, darted across her throat and sensitive face, woke to life the gold in her soft yellow hair.

"Only," her grand-parent ruminated, "you're a mite peaked-lookin'. That's what the spinnin' room's doin' to you." She spat vindictively. "Here you a bare fourteen summers 'n at work more'n a year!"

"Why, Granny, what's wrong with that? Everybody goes to work, a lot of 'em sooner than I done."

"I know, chile, I know. Who minds the law on cotton hills? But somehow I'd hopes in your case. An ole fool I was. Ain't I watched the mills long enough to know better? I'spose you were lucky, bein' a hand's chile, to get as far in school as you did. But a smart gal like you deserves an ejication 'n a chance."

The girl's hands gripped, her eyes clouded. The rocker squeaked mournfully back and forth across a loose board.

"I reckon," she answered slowly, "I got all the ejication I'll ever get. Onct a mill hand, allays a mill hand. That's what they say."

"Yah," the other muttered, "'n how can a hand get more ejication than to read 'n figger for 'em in the mill?" The rocking came to an abrupt halt. Ole Marge lunged forward to shake a clenched fist at the brick mill blocking the end of the street. "Dam 'em. They takes us young 'n makes us ole afore our time. They dumps us out, 'n we ain't good fer nuthin' but to feed off-a our chillen 'n wait around to die."

"Oh, Granny, doan say that. You *are* some good, a lotta good. What'd Ma do without you, cookin' 'n cleanin' 'n makin' our clothes? Why, it's only that its Sunday now that you're sittin' without mendin' in your lap. Besides Granny," her voice dropped, "what'd all of us do without you? . . . Why, I . . ."

Granny's hands were trembling. "I know, chile. But the mill ain't no call to treat us so. I ought to be in the spinnin' room, instead of you. But no, they wants quicker fingers than mine."

"Watch out, Granny, you'll spill your snuff!"

"Thar, now I've done it." A brown stream trickled off her cotton print onto the worn boards. "The ole hand ain't so steady as it was. This here is my one dress too," she mourned, "it's a sabbath, 'n no day fer washin'."

"Wait a minute, I'll fix it." Young Marge ran into the house, coming back with a wet cloth. First the brown streaks were wiped off the old woman's dress, and then from the boards. "There, you're nice 'n clean agin."

"You're a great one for neatness, sweet. But wait till you've a string of lil' uns a taggin' afta ya, to feed 'n clothe, on top of workin' at th' mill.

Marge tossed her head. "No string of lil uns fer me."

"Doan be so sure, missie. What the Lord sends, he sends."

"But we're forgettin' the story, Granny."

"So we is, chile, so we is."

"It was back ten year afta th' Civil War, wan't it?" Marge prompted.

"So it was." Ole Marge settled herself in her rocker. "'N I says to Hinry—your grandpa—I says, 'Hinry, what's that thar a-comin' up over the hill?' I was washin' in the yard behind our cabin, at the time, 'n had straightened from the tub to rest my back.

"Hinry was in the tater patch, pullin' weeds. He yanked himself up, 'n shaded his eyes with one long arm, to have a look. Your grandpa had 'bout th' longest arms 'n legs any man ever did have, I reckon.

"'Huh, now, I wonder,' he says, 'n leans over agin to pick some dried branches offa the plants. I could tell he was wor-rit with them plants. The sun was scotchin' up everythin'. If them tater plants died, there'd be nuthin' to feed us 'n the ba-bies. That made me sigh, 'n I rubbed so hard, I tore th' baby's shirt. 'Law'd-a-Maercy,' I said to maself, 'this ain't no time to be a-tarin'. It's the last stitch the chile's got.' I wrung out ma clothes, all the time keepin' an eye out for that man a-comin up the hill. Somehow I felt excited. 'Hinry,' I says, 'he doan stride like from round these parts. I 'low he's a lowlander.' At that, Hinry jerked hisself up agin. 'Hm,' he says, 'he doan bring no good tidin's I bet, nuther. Us poor folks is bad enuf off as it is, without no strangers round these ways.'

"'Kinda nice to hear some news, I figger.' I answers him. 'That last stranger now, he tole us all about the shootin' of the president. Mebbe this lowlander'd know how it all come out.'

"'Like as not,' Hinry grumbled, 'but he ain't no business messin' around these parts.'

"'Ma, who's a-comin'. Kin we go see?' It was them five little urchins, running from the cabin with not a stitch of clothes to cover their nakedness. 'Go back to bed, you lil' varmints,' I yelled, 'ain't I tole you to stay thar 'til your clothes git dry on the line?' But quick as a flash, Sal (that was your Ma), 'n your Uncle Jack (dead these many years), they was off down the hill, dodgin' behind trees 'n bushes." Ole Marge chuckled, while her listener rocked with glee. "Yessiree, while that thar stranger was a-climbin' up he diden know two pair of eyes was spyin' on him, 'n two young 'uns, as wild as mountain squirrels, was a-scurryin' along aside him. When he set down to rest a spell, they set, too. But he rest so much 'n clum so slow, Sal'n Jack got plum wore out, watin' on him. Soon as they was sure he was headed our way, they came tearin' home, to tell us, 'n git their clothes. I'd got down the switch, but this time they warn't a-scairt. I'd tech 'em.

"Sure 'nough, by 'n by, the stranger hove into sight. Hinry made forward to meet him, 'n find his business in these parts. He'd took the gun down 'n stood it behind the door, 'n me near it, with the chillen in their damp clothes, a-tuggin at my skirts. You know, mountain folk had learned to be keeful o' strangers. Never kin tell when it'd be government agents snoopin' on hill folks 'n jailin' poor men for turnin' the corn he couldn't sell, into moon shine." Ole Marge chewed her lip angrily. "What business of the govern-*ment's*, what we done with it, we never could figger. *It* doan care if we starved, but let us keep the wolf away by moonshin', 'n them laws come a-flockin' like birds of prey."

"Wal, to git on with the story. We soon found that this warn't no law, so we askt him in, to pass the time of day. 'N right well we passed it, too. That fella was full of news as a chicken is full of worms. 'N he was right sociable-like too."

"What'd he look like?" Marge reminded her.

"He'd soft hands, what'd never plowed or hoed in their life, 'n a winnin' smilin' way with chillen. He wore clothes the like we'd never seen afore—a black coat 'n trousers, 'n a white bossom short, 'n across his chest was a big silver chain, 'n on the end of it, the first watch we ever see. Atop his head, sot a big, black hat, with a broad brim.

"Afta we'd et our meal, the stranger got to tellin' us about the cotton mills, 'n what a fine chance thar was thar for folks like us. 'Why, ma'am,' he says to me, 'the houses is built of two rooms. They ain't jest one room cabins, with dirt floors. 'N thar's a water pump in each block.' 'That'd save a lot o'totin, Ma,' Jack put in. 'Hush up, Jack, speak whin you spoken to, or I'll box you 'side the jar.' But I was thinkin', how we had to tote all our water from the crik, two hundred yards, 'n in winter, with the ice 'n snow, it was a considerable matter. 'You know, the pay is good, too,' the stranger went on, 'two to three dollars a week, 'n the wimmen 'n chillen kin work too.' I was wonderin' why Hinry sot there, so gloom-like for. 'Whar's the catch in all this?' he spoke up.

"'Thar ain't no catch,' the stranger replied. 'You see, some of our city folks heerd how bad off the hill folks was since the war, 'n they be studyin' a way to helpen you, 'n theirselves at the same time. So they's buildin' the mills, 'n it's helpen everybody all around. It's a sin 'n a shame,' he went on, 'fer smart folks like you to be wasting away up here, when there's such opportunities down thar in the valley.'

"'Wal, things is right bad, I admit,' Hinry 'lowed, 'but I ain't aimin' to leave the hills. My pappy 'n my grandpappy lived right here in this cabin, 'n I was born here, 'n I reckon I'll die here. What was good enuf for them, is good enuf fer me.'

That made me plum mad. He allays was a stick-in-the-mud.

"'Hinry Marlow,' I tole him, 'ain't you shamed to set thar 'n talk so! Your folks and mine live and die ignorant 'n down-trodden. You want our chillen should be the same? Down thar in the valley thar's schools, so the stranger says, whar our chillen can get some larnin', 'n a chanct to live decent, not like pigs in a trough.'

"Hinry give me a sorrowful look. 'Marge,' he answers me, 'I ain't calculatin' on messin' up with the niggers. I fite to help git 'em free, for no man, white or black, should live in slavery. But I doan want to live near 'em. They brings bad luck.'

"'Niggers 'n white folks doan mix down thar, nuther,' the stranger said, 'each goes his own way, as I explained afore.' 'But they're too close,' Hinry went on in his stubbornest voice, 'up here we keep 'em out our hills, 'n that's whar I want to stay.'

"How'd granpa figger niggers bring bad luck, granny?" young Marge interrupted to ask. The old woman sucked in her lips, pursing her brows.

"Wal, to tell you the truth, chile, I doan know. Po' Whites sure have their share of bad luck wherever they go, niggers or no niggers. But the notion growed up, that somehow or 'tother it was the black man's fault. If they'd never been brought over here as slaves from Africy, or wherever it was, we'd never been made Po' Whites.

"But they didn't come of their own free will, did they?"

"Naw. The rich men brought 'em. Why the good Lord didn't punish 'em long ago, I doan know. But it 'pears like the Good Book got it backwards. The wicked flourish while the good perish from offa the face of the earth. But I never could study it out."

"But, granny, go on with the story."

"Well, I declare, here I'm ramblin' agin. Whar was we?"

"Talkin' with the stranger, about comin' to the mill."

"Now I recollects. Wal, we talked on a spell longer, 'til Hinry went out to the tater patch, 'n the stranger said as how he must make it over the hill, to spread the good tidin's further. He said he'd be back our way in three days. By then, if we'd made up our minds, we could jine him 'n the other families journeyin' down to the mill.

"The next mornin', afore sunrise, I made off to the closest neighbors we had. It was a good five hour's trip each way. I was hurryin' along when I heerd runnin' footsteps behind. Thar was that little Varmint, Jack agin, 'n Sal taggin' at the rear. I scolded 'em right smart, but my heart warn't in it, 'n they knew it, 'n diden turn back. Soon we was goin' down the trail, one on each side. I can shut my eyes now 'n see those hills in the mist, 'n feel the wet branches at our sides 'n faces.

When the sun come out over the mountain top, my troubled spirit leaped up, 'n I knew that come what might, we must go down to the valley.

"The stranger had passed by our neighbours, too, 'n they tole me they planned on goin' to the mill. Annie Totherow was mo' spruced up then I'd seed her since the last of their chickens tuckered out. 'You tell your ole man,' she says to me, 'that the good Jehovah sent this stranger to us. I prayed, Lord, send some-one from Macedonia to helpen us. Your people is dying' here in the hills, 'n the stranger come, an answer to my prayer.'" Ole Marge paused.

"Lookin' back on it now I doubt that Annie was right. Hinry allays said, it was the devil who sent that man, 'n I ain't sure but he was right, for onct. The company had sent the stranger, we found out later. Anyways, at the time I was right willin' to pass on what Annie said to Hinry. Finally, afta me'n Jack naggin' at him all that day'n the next, he come round to say, 'If the tater plants give out, we'll have to go. But I doan lak it. Po' folks doan git so much without thar bein' a hitch somewhars.'

"'It's jes' you figgerin' that anyone can read'n write must be a crook,' I tole him.

"Wal, I lay my plans agin those tater plants. Annie'd prayed 'em dead, but I wasn't takin' no chances. At high noon, when Hinry was gone with Jack tryin' to catch us a snack of fish from the crik, I watered them plants, 'n the sun did the rest. It seemed right unkind to the po' things, but they was dyin' anyway. 'N what kin you do, when a man's so stubborn? He'd never let me'n the chillens go down alone. He'd shot us all plum dead, furst.

"When he saw them plants, Hinry knew I'd tricked him. But a word's a word, so we made ready to come down. It diden take long, since thar warn't much to pack—a few blankets, a skillet, the shotgun, a couple of stools and table Hinry's made, 'n the feather tick that was handed down from my grandma's side, 'n what you'n Ruthie is sleepin' on at the present time. Hinry acted glum as a mule, 'n with Sal 'n the babies cryin', 'n us right at the pint of leavin' the hills 'n all, I began to feel droppy maself. But Jack kept cheery jumpin' around 'n tellin' us to hurry, or we'd be late to the cross-roads, whar we was meetin' the stranger 'n the others.

"Wal, jest as we was startin' out, we found Sal was missin'. 'You wait right here,' I says, 'I know whar she'll likely be, 'n I'll fetch her.' I drapt my bundles 'n give Jack the baby to hold, 'n run down the path back of the house to whar the rock juts out over valley. If you clum out on that rock, you'd git the best view of the valley on the whole of Smoky Mountain, 'n Sal'd stay thar by the hour, drinkin' in the sights 'n 'smell of the pines 'n wild laurel, 'n a-wistlin' with the birds. Shore nuf, she was thar, now, a-lyin' flat of her stomach, her chin propped on her wrists, a-gazin' so sorrowful-like, it sent a pain through my chest.

"'Sal, honey,' I says, 'it's time to start.' She clammered to her feet. 'Oh, Ma, doan take me from the hills. Lemme stay here.' Finally I had to carry her by force. May the Lord forgive me, if I done wrong to bring her to the cotton mills. 'Couse, Marge, your ma Sal was a changed chile, onct she was on the mill. Seems like the life went plum outa her, like a wild squirrel or a song bird put in a cage."

Ole Marge let out a long, whistling breath, and dipped a pinch of snuff.

"Were you too late to come down with the others, Granny?"

"Naw. We was a mite late, but they waited fer us. Annie stood thar, with her face shinin' like it allays done at revival meetin's. But all the three days it took us to git down to the valley, Hinry's face looked like he'd swallowed a green persimmon.

"So, lil' Marge, that's how we Marlows come down to the cotton mill."

II.

Into the Mills

"GO ON. GRANNY, DOAN STOP. What'd you find when you come to the mills?" Huddled over, hands clasped across her pumpkin stomach, the old woman rocked more rapidly, staring intently ahead.

"It's a long, bitter story, chile," she answered impatiently. "'n you know it too well, already. What's the need to git our-selfs all agitated over it on the sabbath, what's meant for peace 'n meditation?"

"All right, Granny. I doan aim to be over-urgin' you. Only—" Young Marge sat, basking in the sun, and biding her time. The rocker creaked back and forth.

"Thar is a reason, chile, why I should speak it all out—though I can't rightly make clear in my mind what it is." Her forehead screwed into tiny ridges, as she wrestled with her thought. "You're young. I ain't here fer much longer. I want you should know it all—all. Mebbe in future yars it'll come handy. Though I doan know." Still Young Marge waited. Crickets hummed lazily in a tree nearby.

"Wal," Ole Marge shifted her tobacco cud to her cheek, "as I was sayin', it seemed like the whole mountain side'd come down to the cotton mill. 'N from the beginnin' thar was trouble, 'n it's been nothin' but trouble 'n worriment ever since. As we clum down the second day, dog-gone if a black cat diden run across our trail. To his dying day, Hinry held out that that was a sure sign of what we was a-headin' fer."

"When we come to the mill, we found that stranger had lied a-plenty. Thar warn't no paved streets, no pump in each block, 'n no schools, 'n thar warn't no church, nuther. Alice 'n some of t'others was all broke up over it, but I worrit mo' about no schools. It was plain as day, the millmen diden mean to have no school, 'cause all the chillen, some no mo'n knee high to a grasshopper, was at the mill. What'd the mills care that we hands wanted our chillen should have an ejication, in the worst way?"

"But, Granny, there's a grade school 'n church now?"

"Sure, chile, sure. But they come later. It took many year of squabblin' with the boss-men to git 'em. 'N now we got 'em, what they amount to? It's mystifyin'. But doan take me off my story, honey, or it'll never git all tole. As I was a sayin', that stranger had lied a-plenty, but one thing he tole turned out true. That was, we all could work at the mill. We shore did. Me 'n your granpa, 'n Sal 'n Jack, 'n even lil Becky, though she warn't turned six year at the time. Hinry got him a job at night, so he could be to home with the babies in the day time while me 'n the three oldest was to the mill. Thar was no limits on hours, then. We went in afore mornin' light, 'n we worked til the bossman said stop. No whistle blew or nuthin', 'n the mill hands 'lowed as how the mill diden want the town 'n country folks roun' about to know how long we worked. Anyways, thar warn't no whistles.

"Wal they paid the mens two dollar and fifty cent a week, 'n they paid wimmen folks a dollar and seventy-five, 'n the chillen, they got tin cints; so all tole we had four dollar 'n fifty-five cints. At furst that seemed like a lotta money, 'cause up in the hills, month around we ain't had our hands on so much cash.

But when we come to pay the company the rent, 'n buy groceries at the company store, that money jes' natchally melted through your fingers. Look like at the end of each week, we owed the company stead of it owin' us.

"It's the same way now, Granny."

"I know, chile. Many things has changed, these forty year, but there's many things that ain't 'n that's one of 'em. Wal, to git on with the tale. Many got discouraged-like, 'n lit out fer the hills, or the lowland country, whar they'd come from. 'N as fast as they move out, the comp'ny agents brung mo' in. Thar so much movin' 'n confusion, it'd make your head dizzy.

"Hinry, he'n Sal wanted to go back, too. They was honeing fer the hills, that was plain. He argued, folks was too close here, livin' right on top of tother. Besides, the mill was unhealthy. But I was sot on stayin'. Bad as it was, the hills was as bad, or worser. *Thar warn't no goin' back.* I knew that. It'd be jumpin' from the fryin' pan into the fire. Thar'd never be schools or nothin' in the mountains. What we had to do was make the mill do what they'd a-promised, 'n take the chillen outa the mill'n put 'em in school, 'n larn 'em how to read'n write."

"Didn't you ever want to go back, too?" Reaching for a battered palm leaf across which was written in bold letters, "Patronize Us—the Finest Funeral Parlor in Greenville"—Marge began to fan vigorously.

"Not perzactly. Though onct or twice I come clost to it, after Hinry took to hangin' round with a crowd of mill hands 'n stayin' out Sadday nights. He'd allays been a good man 'n never lifted a hand to me or the chillen. But the village changed him. He took to drinkin' 'n carryin on with the rest. Chile, thar was such carryin's-on in them early days, it was like the Devil Himself was let loose on mill hills!" Ole Marge, like her ex-mountaineer neighbors, termed all mill villages "hills." And as hills they became known, although villages usually stood on flat stretches of yellow dirt, with ant mounds the highest elevation in sight. "Why it come to the place," she continued, "whar Regina Smith what lived in t'other half of the house with us, had to take down the shotgun to per-tect her chillen again her ole man. I doan want to pizen your young ears with it all. There's sure enough devilment on mill hills today, but this here hill of Back Row is a moral place. All folks here is got a good character. We mill hands seen to that. All we got was our good character, 'n we were gona hold on to that.

"Wal, the second winter we was to the mill, thar was a mix-up." A grin crept around Ole Marge's eyes, and lifted the corners of her mouth. "That thar mill agent brung some of the Allen clan to the hill. You know, the Allens what we Mar-lows'd feuded with goin' on five generations, we ain't gone mix with, down here. Thar was some rastlin' 'n shootin', one night, 'n lucky fer the Allens, the laws cleared 'em out of town afore they had to be took out, heels furst. One bullet near hit that mill agent in the seat of his pants." She chuckled, and slapped her thigh gently with her free hand. "The mill super called me 'n Hinry in, 'n we 'splained what had happened, 'n he tole us not to be so free with our gun afta this, but seein' we was good mill hands, he'd overlook it this onct. 'N from then on, the mill'd give orders to its agents, not to mix up no mo' clans.

"That summer, I lost both my youngest, 'n lil' Becky, too. How your Ma Sal managed to pull through, I doan know. The typhoid fever took young'n old by the dozens from the hill. It was sad days, 'n every summah since, it's been stinks, flies'n folks drappin' off from typhoid fever.

"Year followed year, 'n we tried many hills, but they was all the same. Then, in the 'nineties, we furst tried somethin' diff'rent." Her voice lifted, her faded eyes gleamed down at her companion. "Yes'm, we mill hands tried somethin' diff'rent. We was plum tired of seein' our chillen growin' up in ignorance, 'n bein' stunted at the mill. We was plum disgusted with starvin' 'n bein' treated like no-counts. So one day, we all jest walked outta the mill, 'n we tole the boss men we warn't gona spin nor weave no mo' so long as the babies was at the mill stead of at school, 'n we wanted mo' pay. The mill was stubborn, but we was stubborner. 'N the end of it was, we got a raise, 'n the hours was sot reg'lar, at twelve a day, 'n no chillen below tin years was to go into the mill. That meant privation for many, but as I said, we was stubborn. The ones what diden like it, could move on to tother hill. But plenty mo' wanted to move in. 'N that's how come your uncle Rem 'n Aunt Mary kin read n'figger, though your Ma never got to go, nor Jackie, nuther.

"By this time, mills was springin' up lak mushrooms, all over. No matter how fast they brun folks from the land, thar still warn't enough. So mills took to biddin' agin one another fer help. That give us mill hands a bit of a chance to better things. We went whar thar was mo' pay, 'n school fer the kids, or whar the hours was mo' reg'lar. You'd be serprised, how quick word'd spread, even in them days, that a mill'd put up a school or a church, or somethin'. So one way or t'other, we got our heads outta the mire, though we are still in it up to our waists. As I was sayin' things has changed, 'n agin they ain't.

"Thin Hinry up 'n got the lung trouble. What with the mill 'n drinkin' 'n all, he was jest nachally tuckered out. It was a sorrowful sight to see him, toward the end. He'd cry like a baby to go back to Smoky Mountain. But it was too late then, 'n besides, thar warn't no money or way to take him. The best I could do was to promise him to bury him up thar, by the cabin."

"'N did you, Granny?"

"Certainly chile, you knows I did. Everybody helpen to send him back. Thar was a collection, 'n ma cousin Ben

Simmons come with his mule 'n wagon, off'n his farm, 'n took Hinry's body up to the cabin. He was a whole week, comin' 'n goin'. If ever you go up to the far side of Smoky Mountain, near Look Out, thar you'll find the cabin 'n your grandpa's grave."

"Oh, Granny, I'd love to go! 'N to see the mountains. What're they like?"

"They's a right smart sight, chile. Still 'n powerful, with white clouds movin' round their tops. In the distance, they look sometimes blue, 'n sometimes a purple color. I'd like you should see 'em. The thunder storm's the best, when it goes a-rollickin' 'n a-rollin' down the mountain-sides, tearin' trees'n makin' the cabin reel 'n shudder."

"Gee willikins, I'd like that!"

"You shore would. Your Maw now, she was allays a queer chile, shy 'n quiet. But you," once more Ole Marge chuckled, this time with pride, "you are a chip off'n the ole block. . . . Shucks, here I am wanderin' agin.

"When your Ma was turned sixteen, she up 'n run away with that good-fer-nuthin', Herb Crenshaw. I knowed they'd been makin' eyes at each other, 'n I forbid him th' house. So they run off and got married. No good ever come o' it but you. Sal come home, 'n afta Gertie 'n Tom, you was born here, right into my arms. When you furst opened your eyes, it was on misery'n want, 'n guns a-poppin'. Not a good sign, but somehow I allays set hopes by you."

"What about the guns, Granny?"

"The war had broke loose—the one with Spain."

"Oh, tell about that. What was it like? It must be fun to live while a war's on. Teacher told us about it, bands of music, 'n soldiers, 'n flags flyin'—"

"Huh!" Ole Marge interrupted. "That's what it looks like aforehand. But when they's on, they's diff'rent."

"How diff'rent?"

"It's hard to tell, 'til you seen one. All I can say, it's jest mo' worriment, 'n fear, 'n a lotta killin' fer nuthin'. I lost your Uncle Jack in that thar war. He was no mo'n a boy, but he would go. He was sick of the mills, 'n they dazzled him with their talk."

"But he died to make the Cubans free, diden he?"

"That's what they said at the time. Spain was a tyrant o-pressin' the Cuban people, 'n they was revoltin' 'n wanted us what believed in liberty to helpen them. Then all the papers 'n talk was about 'Remember the Maine.'"

"Oh, that's what it says on that china battleship they've got, over to Rhoadses."

"A what?"

"A china battleship—a pintray, 'n catch-all."

The old woman grimaced. "Lemme git ma hands on that thing, I'll bust it."

"Why you feel thata way. Diden the Spaniards blow up that ship, with all on board?"

"That's what they said at the time, 'n everybody was het up to teach 'em a lesson. But, chile," she leaned forward and hissed out her words, "my cousin, your Great Uncle Nat was to that war, 'n he come home 'n tole us, it come out long afterwards, *that thar ship was blowed up from the inside!*"

"Oh, Lawsy! You mean—?"

"Yes-sir-ee. Twarn't the Spaniards done it a-tall. Furst, thar was a lot of furor, Nat said, 'n then it was hushed up. But Nat was shore it was govern-ment trickery, 'n that some rich men wanted that war."

"But, why?"

"I ain't clear on it. Nat used to say it was the sugar fields 'n cheap labor they wanted. But it was all hushed up so, 'n the mill made Nat clear off'n the hill 'cause of his talk, so I somewhat dis-remembah.

"Wal, after the war, the mills spread faster than ever, 'n the rich folks in town got theirselfs biggern'n bigger houses, 'n took to puttin' on mo' airs than a peacock. The way those rich folks look down their noses at mill hands'd make your blood bile. For we may be po', hard-workin' people, Marge, but thar ain't better blood or char-*ac*-ter in all of the two Carlynys than's on cotton hills, 'n doan you be forgettin' it."

"The story's nigh its close, now. You know the rest. Your Pa kept comin' back 'n jest stay long enough to leave Sal with another mouth to feed, 'n he'd be off agin. Sal was allays too weak-willed to drive him off for good. It's a good thing he ceased, or thar'd be mo'n you six chillen to tend the mill, not mentionin' the four Sal's buried already.

"So here we is, mill hands. Onct, a mill hand, allays a mill hand. Some tries to git way, or larn their young-uns a trade, but it doan come to nuthin'. They's got us, hand 'n foot. Why it's come to the place, its mo' looked down on to be a mill hand than to be a Po' White on the land. We're treated worser than nigger slaves."

Marge climbed to her feet, and throwing her arms around the huddled figure, gave her Granny a tight hug.

"Lawsy, honey chile, its sech a hot, stewin' day fer huggin'." Loosening her hold, the girl patted the tight little knot of grey hair which rested sedately on the crown of Ole Marge's head. Smoothing back the stray hairs, she said in a troubled voice:

"You shore hate the mills, doan you, Granny?"

"That I do, Lil' Marge, 'n I reckon I got reason. Ain't I watched 'em 'n slaved fer 'em this forty year? Ain't it swallowed up my folks, one after one—jest turnin' 'em into cotton cloth, at tin cints a yard? Look here when I furst come down, your Ma was a sprightly gal lak you, 'n me 'n your grandpa was hale 'n hearty. Though not too fat. Look at us, now. You Ma bent 'n draggin one foot after t'other, your grandpa gone long ago.

"'N now it's taken you. The boss-men'll feed them machines the gold outta your hair, the shine outta your eye, the quickness outta your fingers, 'n in tin year," her voice dropped, halted, "in tin year you'll look 'n feel like an ole 'oman."

The girl shuddered.

"But what we gona do? I gotta do ma share, ain't I? What with so many to feed 'n all—"

"Sure you gotta do your share," Ole Marge broke in irritably, "I ain't arguin' agin that. But what's your share, 'n what's the share of the boss-men's gals,' of Rebecca Haines, whose Pa owns this here Back Row mill? She rides around the city in a big car, wears fine clothes, goes to parties, 'n never does a lick of no-kind of work. She'n her Ma's got three nigger gals to wait on 'em, hand 'n foot. Soon the Haines gal'll go off to school somewhar, but she ain't nigh so smart 'n pretty as you. What's right about all that, I want to know?"

When young Marge didn't reply, she asked her over. "What's right about it? All over this hill thar's babies gittin' pellagry fer want of food the well-to-do give to their hogs. Look at your own lil' brother, Jackie."

Two small fists bore down on Granny's shoulder. "'Course it ain't right! But what we gona do? What we gona do?"

"I spun many hundred of yards of cloth in my time, but all I got to show for it is this here one dress," Ole Marge went on, unheeding. "'N thar's many a mill hand what's come off worser'n me, in their ole age. I'se lucky to be free of the po' house. Sure I hates 'em child, them 'n their soft hands 'n hard ways. They made their money outta us. If they warn't so rich, we'd not be so poor. Sure I hates 'em, 'n God forgive me, 'll go on hatin' 'em till I die."

"I hates 'em too, Granny. But what we gona do?"

"Come round here, child, whar I can look at you." Young Marge dropped on her knees in front of the rocker, her gaze searching the furrowed, stern face. "What we gotta do is fight for our rights. Like we done that time in Georgy. For more vittles'n more larnin' for our young 'uns."

The child spinner glowed. "If we only could! But—"

"Thar's a lot of mill hills, lil'un, ain't got no spirit. I spit on 'em. But you 'n your kind—you come from a fightin' people. Your great-grandpa was at King's Mountain when ole Cornwallis 'n the red coats was cleared out. Your grandpa fought to free the slaves. Nat 'n Jack fought in '98 in the war we was a-talkin' 'bout. The trouble was, they never fought in no war yet that brung nuthin' to our own people—the common, workin' folks."

"But that time in Georgy, Granny, the mill folks stood up for theirselfs, didn't they, 'n won too!"

"That we did. 'N what's done onct, can be done agin. That's how I figger. Sal, your Ma, now, she figgers diff'rent. She's lost all the spirit she ever had. She might as well be dead." Faded blue eyes glittered across the flushed set face and fastened on the girl's widening eyes. "You ain't gona lose the fightin' spirit, be you?"

"Naw, Granny."

"No matter what happens?"

"No matter what happens."

Leaning over, Ole Marge gathered her off-spring to her flat chest. "I doan know what's ahead for you. Mebbe you'll have to go through thick 'n thin."

"I'm willin'. If only—"

"It'll not be easy. But mebbe the way'll open up. It's your only chance."

III.

Escape

"WAL, IT'S TIME TO BE A-FIXIN' SUPPER, you-all." Sal's long, sallow face peered through the screen at the two on the porch. "No time now to be settin' 'n gossipin'."

The two Marges followed her stooped, round-shouldered back down the narrow hallway into the sweltry, dim kitchen. This was a place to be avoided as much as possible in the summer months. When the cold weather came, as the only warm spot in the house it served the family and boarders as a place in which to gather of an evening, after the day's work was over. The children played on the floor around the wood stove, Marge or one of the boarders read out the evening news and relaid the gossip picked up at the mill or company store. By nine o'clock all were ready for bed, except Gertie, who'd stay on with one of the men boarders, and catch her death of cold.

The kitchen's low boarded walls were darkened with soot, and a smooth path was worn on its floor planks by the tramp of many women mill hands back and forth across its surfaces these twenty years, cooking their meals, so that they and their men folks'd have strength to stand by their looms or spools another day.

To and fro the flies buzzed lazily. They, too, had worn a path. Theirs lay from the toilet, boarded in at the rear of the hallway, to the kitchen and back. The small insects could never quite make up their mind, so they were drawn back and forth between the smells in the hallway and the stale odors of food which brooded over the kitchen like some evil guardian spirit.

"Look at them flies," Young Marge exclaimed. "Whar's paper to make a swatter?"

"Here, chile. I do declare they've been lyin' in wait. Look, they's gathered around to give us a welcome. They kin smell mealtime a mile off," Granny snorted.

Smack! Smack! went the paper, as Marge's arm swung up and down, up and down.

"A fly at each stroke!" she exulted. "I'm settin' a record tonight."

"You're wastin' your strength," Sal grumbled. "You can whack all night 'n all day, but you'll never be done. I declare it's a sin 'n a shame, that's what it is, the comp'ny not a-fixin' these screens. Holes as big as your finger in the window screens 'n one the size of a half-dollar in the back door.

"Back in the hills, now we never had no bother with no screens'n sech doin's 'n we got along better. That thar stool now. I'd ruther have a out-house any day, what's not so close to whar you eat and sleep."

"The ole thing's allays clogged up, 'n stinks to heaven." Marge scooped up a handful of dead flies, and threw them out of the back door. "But try'n make the mill fix anythin'!"

"It ain't no use," Sal complained, "if you ask the sheriff too often, you jest git a bad name for nothin', 'n furst thing you know he'll be tellin' us to move on—"

"Like they done to the Joneses," Ole Marge nodded.

"What's that?" Sal paused, with spoon in air, "I hadn't heard."

Smack! Smack!

"Marge, do stop that thar whackin', so I kin hear Ma."

"This is how it come about. The Joneses roof begun to leak bad. Furst a li'l leak. They tole the mill sheriff, 'n he said as how he'd have it fixed right up. But he diden. He's that triflin'. Then, one night, afta everybody was in bed, sound-a-sleep, a terrible storm blew up. The rain jest poured down in bucketfuls. Miz Jones says as how she dreamed she was a-drownin' in a big lake, 'n goin' down the second time. So she screamed 'n grabbed her ole man round the neck, 'n that woke him up. He shook her wake, 'n thar they was, in a bed full o' water."

"Wal, I do declare!"

"Yes'm. Their bed was a li'l pond, with an edge of mattress round-abouts. The young 'uns was screamin', 'n when Mr. Jones clum out of bed to go to 'em, he slipped on the wet floor 'n sprained his ankle."

"Fer the land sakes!"

"They was all mad, 'n rightly so. 'N Miz Jones's got right smart of a tongue on her, 'n I reckon what she tole the mill sheriff the next day was a-plenty. She called him a No-Count, 'n he said he diden have to stand fer any of her cheek. So the outcome was, the mill give the Jones their time, 'n they moved on. 'N the mill had the carpenter fixin' the roof, afore the week was out."

"I seen the carpenter up thar a nailin' last Friday," Young Marge said, "'n wondered how come."

"So you see," Sal put in, "that's what comes of complainin' to the mill."

"That's what come of livin' in shanties owned by the comp'ny," Ole Marge retorted. "I'd rather have two sticks of my own any day than live under a mill roof."

"Oh, that mill sheriff makes me sick, he does." Young Marge swung her fly-killer viciously. "Allays spyin' 'n movin' folks out, 'n sayin' they's jest playin' possum when they's shore 'nuf sick. He thinks he's a somebody, jest 'cause he's the sheriff!" Smack! Smack!

"Marge, quit chasin' them flies 'n do somethin' useful," Sal scolded. "Here, take the buckets 'n git us some water from the pump. We're plum out. Tom, by rights is 'sposed to git it, but that good-fer-nuthin' ain't around. He never is, when thar's work to do. But he's always on hand when thar's eatin' or playin' to be had."

"Tom ain't sech a bad boy, Sal. You're too hard on 'im. Allays scoldin'."

"Now, Ma, you know it ain't right fer Tom to—" as Sal's voice began a crescendo, Marge grabbed the pails and rushed off. Ma's nagging was terrible! True, Tom was troublesome of late, since he got to runnin' around with that crowd of boys from Brandon, and makin' up to that light-headed Lucy Fields. But Ma's naggin' only made it worse.

Marge crossed to the water plug, which stood in the center of the block, and leaning over, began to pump into battered pails. What endless times she and her Ma and Granny before her had done this! The pump handle was worn smooth as glass, by twenty years of usage. The old thing groaned and shuddered with effort, as it sucked up a rusty-colored stream and spouted it into the waiting pails. Smaller streams trickled down the handle and up Marge's arm, splashed on her one dress-up dress that she'd worked overtime to buy and sat up nights to make, and formed puddles around her feet. Life in this hill was just full of aggravations like this!—small things in themselves, but when heaped together, they made a monstrous pile to tote in the mill and out. Seemed like the company was forever slapping you in the face and bearing you down.

A full pail in each hand, she started back to the house. Facing her were a row of houses, each one just like the next—gray, wooden boxes standing on wooden props along a stretch of yellow dirt which the once-mountaineers always termed a "hill." Three steps lead to a small porch and the front door. The only difference between the shacks was that some needed painting worse than others, some had more leaks and bugs than the rest, some were double and some, single size; and a number had a few pots of plants on the porch or flowers growing near the doorway. Granny had planted honeysuckle and Sweet William near theirs, and Marge could smell their sweetness as she walked toward the house.

The inside of the houses, Marge knew, were as much alike as the outside. Two rooms (or four rooms, if the family was a big one or took boarders like they did), a narrow hallway, beds, a few chairs and a long table. No plastering, no pictures, no books. These houses were as old and unchanged as the village pumps. The one new thing was the electric lights which the company had put in, when it added its power plant.

Back of the two hundred shacks loomed the red brick mill and its off-spring, the company store where groceries and notions were to be had. On the Main Street, which ran from the mill stood also the wooden church and grammar school which the mill had built ten years ago. Hedged in between stood the freshly painted houses of the boss-men and overseers. Marge had never been inside one of these, but she'd heard it said that there were six rooms, all plastered, with carpets on the floors, and running water. The mill super lived in a big house in town, while the owner and his family had a place outside of Greenville that Marge had sighted once, through the trees. Why, that house looked bigger than the mill itself, and the grounds around it took more ground than the whole of Back Row.

What would one family want with so much place! No wonder it took five darkies to keep it going.

"Now set the table," Sal greeted Marge, "'n soon Ma 'n me'll have things ready to put on. It's too hot to have much."

"Besides, thar ain't much to have," Ole Marge chuckled the sharp edge off her statement.

"Corn pone, 'lasses, 'n cole tea ain't so bad, Ma, 'n a helpin' of sauce fer the boarders."

Marge began placing knife, spoon and fork next to each plate. Whew, what a mess of dishes it always made! Glad it was Gertie's 'n Ruth's turn to clean up, tonight. Going back to the kitchen for the sugar bowl and tea, she broke the silence to ask:

"Ma, why is it, mill folks has it so hard? Does God plan it thisaway, or what?"

"Everything's God's Will, Marge. It's hard, but we'll understand it bettah by 'n by. Parson Brown saws we gotta bear our cross in patience, 'n re-sign ourselfs to God's mysterious Plan."

"Huh!" Ole Marge snorted, "I kin quote scriptures as long as any of 'em, Parson Brown not excepted, but I doan know how come they kin make it out God's plan, the way these mills is run. Seems like we done left God back up in them mountains. He doan feel at home in these here villages, the way they is, now."

"Ma!" Sal nearly dropped the applesauce in her astonishment. "You're blasphemin'. Religion is a comfort to the poor. It's all we got."

"Naw I ain't. Leastways, I doan mean to. I'm jest sayin' out God's truth. Now, thar's a text, for instance, 'Suffer the lil' chillen to come unto Me! fer of sech is the Kingdom of Heaven.' But does that mean fer the mill to suck in our babies—does it? One thing I do know, it says that it's harder fer a rich man to git into heaven than fer a camel to go through the needle's eye, 'n I sure believe that. But do Parson Brown ever say anything about it? That he doan. He doan never say nuthin' 'bout what matters. He sure ain't no model to copy, nuther, him'n his carryin's on!"

"What you mean, Granny?"

"Shut your mouth, Marge. Ma, I woan have you talkin' like this to the chillen! It's scand'lous to harbor sech thoughts, without your speakin' 'em out."

"Wal, I can't help seein' 'n thinkin' things these forty year. I ain't gone plum blind like some."

Sal turned on Young Marge. "Call 'em in to supper, 'n," she added, "doan lemme hear you ask no mo' sech fool questions."

Marge went to the porch and called, "Uncle Mat, Gertie, supper's ready."

The little Crenchaws, Billy and Sam, came running, falling over one another in their hurry to reach the table.

"Oh, do stop shovin' me, Billy 'n Sam," Gertie addressed her two small brothers, "'n take your dirty paws off the back of my good dress." Gertie, three years older than Marge, and almost as pretty, pushed the boys aside and slipped into her chair. Eleven-year old Ruth, who Ole Marge said took after Sal, sat on one side of Gertie, and Tom flushed and breathing fast from his rapid walk home slid into the empty chair on the other. The two little tow heads of Billy and Sam were hedged in safely between Sal and Granny, Uncle Mat took his place at the head of the table, a place he'd fallen heir to when Pa died, and the two young boarders, Harry and Ed, sat at his right. Young Marge's place was near the kitchen door, so she could slip out, when anything was needed.

"Hush up, Billy," Sal cautioned, "while Uncle Mat asks the blessin'." All heads bowed, while from Uncle Mat's thin mouth issued one long word, "Lor'makeusthankfelferwhatwebouttoreceiveamen." With a sigh of relief all looked up and fell to. For a while there were only the sounds of crunching bread and sipping tea, intermingled with soft, drawled phrases of "Ma, gimme some 'lasses," "Thank ye fer the corn-pone," and Uncle Mat mumbling through his dripping whiskers, "Fill my glass agin, will you Sal? 'n thank-ye kindly." Their first hunger appeased, the conversation brightened up.

"Ma," Sam piped suddenly, his mouth full of corn-pone, "What makes Harry look at Gertie all the time fer?" Amidst the general laughter, Harry blushed, and Gertie tossed her head. But Sal barely smiled. "Hole your tongue, Sam, or I'll box your jaw 'n send you from the table."

Will Gertie have him? Marge wondered. Hardly, her head's too full of notions from runnin' round with those town boys. She's hopen to do better by herself than that.

Harry hitched himself in his chair, and sought desperately to divert the conversation into other channels. "From what I heard tell over at the store, Tom, you'll not be goin' into the mill tomorrow?"

All eyes turned toward Tom. Eating ceased. It was his turn to blush. "Aw, doan believe everythin' you hear."

Sal's lips quivered. "What you up to now, Tom Crenshaw? Thar's jest one botheration afta t'other with you! What you done? Out with it!"

Tom scowled. "Nuthin', I tell you. The boss weaver come round fussin' bout the cloth, 'n I jest tole him it warn't our fault, the thread was runnin' bad."

"'N, accordin' to what I heerd, 'course I doan know," Harry was enjoying his role, "but what I heerd was, thar was mo' back talk 'n he tole you to mind your mouth or he'd give you your time."

"Wal, Tom Crenshaw," Sal stormed, "you got us drive offa one hill, with your sassy ways, 'n now you fixin' to git us turned off another? Speak to him, Mat," she addressed her brother-in-law, but rushed on, before that lank individual had finished clearing his throat and preparing what to say. "I wish your Pa was live. *He'd* know how to handle you, 'n your carryins-on. Your Uncle Mat hyar's not lost more'n three days at the looms in forty year, 'n I've drawed in nigh as long, only stoppin' when you chillen come. But *you*, with your triflin' ways, you'll bring trouble on us all, yit. Meddlin' round with that scatter-brained Lucy—"

Tom slammed his chair against the wall. "That's enough. I ain't no baby no longer, you kin scold lak you wan'. Mebbe you wan' to be shet of me? Wal, I tell you, I'm plum shet o'naggin'," and he flung out.

Sal slipped away in the direction of the bedroom, from which muffled sobs issued under the closed door. The rest of the meal was glum. Later, on the porch, Granny sidled up to Marge and whispered, "Doan worry, honey, it'll blow ovah like the other times."

When the dishes were done and Gertie and Ruth had joined the others on the crowded porch, "Les' have some music," Uncle Mat proposed. Ruth went for Sal, who emerged from the bedroom red-eyed but calm, bearing in her hand the key to the sacred room, the parlor. She unlocked the door and all trooped in, with the respect and awe appropriate to the occasion. This Sunday night ritual was, for Marge, the one genuine pleasure of the week.

The parlor was a room set apart, dedicated to the high dreams and frustrated hopes that Sal, Gertie, and the rest had of a nobler life—of "livin' like we was a-somebody, 'stead or jest millhands." It was hallowed by years of scrimping and planning that had made it possible. No matter how crowded the other rooms might be in which they slept and ate six days of the week this room—with its shellaced floor, its crayon, life-size drawing of Pa on the wall, its Family Bible, its two horse-hair-covered chairs, and wheezy organ, must remain inviolate, waiting for its Sabbath evening ritual. There were certain other rare occasions, when the parlor might be entered, such as when the mill social workers called, or a cousin came visiting from the country and you wanted to impress him with your grandeur, or when there was a wedding or funeral in the family. Otherwise, the door remained locked, and Sal hid the key where even Billy and Sam's prying fingers could not locate it.

There were not many families on Row Hill which could indulge their longing for such a luxury.

All gathered around the organ, except Sal and Ole Marge. Sal sat, half in the shadow, her worn hands, which twitched slightly, folded in her lap, her lips moving softly in union with the songs.

"Whar's the song book?" Harry inquired. Gertie located it back of the organ, and it was opened and duly placed on the rack. Marge could not read the notes, but played by ear, and the singers knew all the words and tunes by heart. But the singing could never begin without the song book.

Marge busied herself pulling out stops, and all was ready. When the Crenshaws had first purchased the organ from one of those agents known in the village as "loan sharks," on the five-dollar-down-one-dollar-a-week plan, Marge had busied herself trying out all possible combinations of the twelve stops, and picking out the tunes, until she and the others had been satisfied by the effects produced. By now she played with quite a little skill, "'n with the sweet touch," as Ole Marge put it, "that reaches out from music in the heart."

Beginning with "Yield not to Temptation, for Yielding is Sin," they sang all the old favorites.—"Wash Me and I Shall Be Whiter Than Snow," "Oh to be Nothing, Nothing Only to Lie at His Feet," "What a Friend," and "There is a Land." As they chanted the hymns, the harmonies stirred their souls with a mysterious beauty far beyond their humdrum lives. While

Marge's fingers slipped over the keys, and her feet pumped, first right, then left; Gertie's clear soprano soared above the rest, Ruth piped a husky alto, Harry rumbled around among the base notes, and the others sang "on the tune." But tonight, Tom's soft tenor, rounding out the harmony, was missing.

Billy and Sam, leaning a tow head at each end of the organ, gazed at Marge completely absorbed in watching her lips, and fingers, and timing their own with hers. Granny, watching them, thought, "The two lil scamps. Now they looks lak cherubs, but wait til tomorrow, 'n they'll be up to mischief agin. 'N I'll warrant there's tears a-ready in them hand-me-down thousands o' theirn."

As they sang "Shall We Gather at the River—the Boo-ti-ful, the Boo-ti-ful River?" and the harmonies rose and swelled, Marge felt some compelling force take hold of her and waft her away to parts unknown, where a gurgling stream bubbled through green fields, and everywhere were dancing lights. As Gertie's voice rang out, high and sweet, a shiver of delightful pain ran up Marge's spine. What happened to her when they sang, she couldn't explain, but it sure was sweet.

Ole Marge, singing with a vim, suddenly noted the quiet tears slipping down Sal's cheeks and splattering on her hands.

"Marge," Granny spoke sharply, "ain't it pretty nigh time we stopped?"

"Yah, we sung nigh through the book tonight," Uncle Mat agreed.

"'N ma legs'n back is nigh broke." Marge, coming to, stretched herself, "'n tomorrow's another day at the mill."

Sal went off to put protesting Billy and Sam to bed, Gertie and Harry lingered in the parlor, and wished Uncle Mat would have the sense to depart.

Marge found herself once more alone with Granny on the porch. By now the world had turned a soft blue, etched with purple shadows, where trees or shacks stood outlined against the sky. "The stars is bright tonight, ain't they Granny?"

"Uh, huh. Ma ole mammy used to say that meant the angels was a peepin' down at you. Jest her idee, I reckon."

Marge didn't answer. She was listening to the throaty creaking of the frogs, and busy with her thoughts. Granny, also busy with hers, sat quietly by, fondling the girl's hand between her own.

Presently Marge spoke. "The Bible's full of all kind o' things ain't it. Granny?"

"Uh huh, 'n I've taken perticular notice that each one quotes it to his own likin'."

Again there was silence. "You worryin' over Tom, honey?" Ole Marge ventured.

"Granny, can't you git Ma to lay off him some? . . . Hush, thar he is now." He had slipped around the corner of the house, and stood there uncertainly, pulling his overall strap into place. The straps were forever sliding off his slim shoulders, and he having to put them back.

"Hi, thar, Tom?" Marge called softly, "come up 'n set down. It's me'n Granny."

Tom slouched over. "Oh, it's you two ole cronies, is it?" His voice carried a relieved note, as he slid onto the door step.

"The singin' was pertic'lar good, tonight, Tom. I wisht you was thar."

"Ah, nobody missed me." He broke off. "I reckon you-all is sore at me, too," he began.

"Oh, no, Tom. Honest. Only—you know Ma ain't well. Her nerves is gittin' bad on her, 'n—"

"It'll go right hard with her, Tom, if we all has to move agin."

Tom shuffled his feet impatiently. "Wal, I guess I'm through 'round these parts. Be bettah all'round if I clear out."

Marge leaned forward. "Oh, Tom, you doan mean that? What's come ovah ya? You ain't been youself for weeks."

"I'm fed up, that's what, with this town 'n mill. All always the same. Granny knows. Workin', eatin', sleepin', 'n mo' workin'. 'N allays naggin' at a fella. Anyways, thar's nuthin' hyar fer a *man* to do!" Marge squeezed Granny's hand. She dassent laugh. But Tom, talking like that, and him only eighteen! "Granny," he went on, "how come you stood it all these year?"

"What else was thar to do?" Granny asked dryly.

"Oh, well, I guess it's different fer wimen." He jumped up. I guess I jest bring trouble. Reckon it's time I tried my luck somewhere else."

Marge saw him bend over Granny quickly, felt him brush past her with a husky, "S'long, kid," and he was gone. As soon as it had dawned on her, what had happened, she was off after him down the street, running and calling—careless for once of what the neighbors might say, "Tom, Tom." But he was longer-legged and faster than she, and was soon out of sight, altogether.

Panting and dusty, she walked slowly back up the dirt street, then circled to the house, on the chance that the Browns and Johnsons had not recognized her in the dusk, the first time, and that maybe she could save Ma the chagrin of having it said a child of hers was streakin' and hailin' down the streets on a sabbath night.

When bed-time came, there was still no Tom. Sal fumed and worried, but Ole Marge hid her concern. "Doan worry, daughter. No doubt he's spendin' th' night with th' Stern boy 'n he'll be home afta work tomorrow 'n things has blowed over."

THAT NIGHT, MARGE LAY in the three-quarters bed alongside Ruth, staring up into the dark, and pondering over the day's happenings—her talk with Granny. . . . What had come over

Tom? ... What did the years ahead hold for her and her family? Was Granny right, was there no way to leave the mill hills and get to be a-somebody? Was there no way to win more of their deserts? The girl's hands clenched and her eyes flashed out into the night.

The mill sure had gotten Ma. Marge tried to picture Sal as a little, carefree, mountain girl, bidding her hills and birds goodbye. She could not do it. It seemed impossible that Ma, a bent, old woman at forty-two, her mouth pulling down at the corners, stomach bulging, hands beginning to twitch, and her voice rasping and sharp, always tongue-lashing or complaining, could ever have been the little Sal that Granny described.

Then, clearly, it came back to Marge. Five years ago, when the Crenshaws had been on a Sunday School picnic in the woods, Ma had taken Marge by the hand, and left Pa and the others, and gone off into the country. The southern pines towered over them. The fragrance of pine needles underfoot filled the air. Far overhead the sunshine and blue sky showed in little patches, through the gently swaying branches. For a while the two walked in silence. Finally, near the edge of the forest, where the maples and oaks joined the pine grove, Ma halted and squeezed Marge's hand, motioning her to be quiet. "Listen," she whispered. Then Marge heard the soft twitter of birds, while the fragrance of the woods and fields crept in on her. Looking up, she was startled to see a change go over Ma. She could feel something quivering through her, and go lighting up her face.

Then Ma began to whistle and trill—soft, light, then louder, then softer again. Then she stopped, called again, stopped. From out of the woods came an answering call. Ma trilled in reply. "It sounds jest like the real bird," Marge marveled. Once more the songster answered, this time nearer. Back and forth the woman and bird called to each other, each time the bird's call drawing closer. Soon Marge beheld the feathered creature flitting into view, coming to rest on the branch of a great oak nearby.

"Look, Ma, look, it's a warbler," she whispered excitedly. Then as the bird flew away, Ma threw back her head and laughed like a young girl.

"Thar, chile, you've frightened him off. But never mind," she added, "it's time we was a goin' back, nohow."

As they walked back in silence, Marge had seen the sad look creeping back into Ma's face.

Marge, lying in the dark, wondered if she would ever see Ma happy like that again. She didn't believe she'd been to the woods since. The mills had weighed her down. Now, instead, Ma went to church services, and sang with a hearty mournfulness, and murmured, "Amen," to what Parson Brown had to say.

And Tom. Her devoted, fun lovin' playmate of a few years ago, now moody, takin' to corn likker with the boys, 'n turnin' into a No-count?

Marge could hear the clock ticking, mingled with the snores of Granny. She must go to sleep. Soon morning would come, and it would be time to start out to the mill.

But her mind kept working.

What was it all about, anyhow? Ma said it was all part of God's Plan, 'n if you trusted Him it'd all come out right some day (but would it?). The thing, Ma 'n Parson Brown said, was to have faith.

But did she, Marge Crenshaw, have faith? Not like Ma. Terrible doubts once more assailed her. She was wicked.

Ever since a little girl, she had worried under the covers over this appalling fact. She had never been converted away from Original Sin, and known herself saved—that experience the hymn book and the sermons told so much about. Sometimes, when all were singing, she'd know a few moments of exaltation, but it soon passed. God, what was God? Why couldn't she be sure? Feeling herself still a heathen, she shuddered. If God and Faith were not too real, pictures of Hell Fire and Brimstone were.

Marge had no way of knowing that hundreds of others in their early teens endure the same experience—struggle to square the world of realities around them with the ideas given them in religion, and failing hopelessly, tremble at the brink, daring not go on, until events force them. For ahead lie two ways—either that of clinging to reality and renouncing the traditional beliefs, facing the scorn and derision of believing neighbors and parents,—or, the other route of drowning thought, and thereby doing violence to an inner integrity of personality.

Marge, dimly realizing the immensity of her problem, wrestled unhappily, and feared. She felt so alone. Except for Granny. The sound of her tranquil snoring in the corner where she slept with the twins reassured the girl. Granny had hated all these years, and said what Ma called wicked things. Her religion didn't seem to bother her much. Yet God hadn't wrecked His punishment on her, any more than on believin' mill hands.

So, turning on her side, Marge slept. But her sleep was troubled by dreams of fighting machines and spinning frames that turned into dreadful creatures with long prying fingers that tried to poke into your eyes and chest. And Ma was calling, "Stop fightin' 'n pray," and Granny hissed, "Fight 'em, chile, fight 'em." Then Marge was fighting flies. Millions and millions of them buzzed around, biting her on the face and arms. Granny was yelling, "They're suckin' our blood," and to Marge's horror, the flies changed into the faces of the boss spinner, and the super, and the mill owner's family, and she was swatting them. Tom threw a Bible at them, and the mill super dropped dead at her feet.

"Marge, you're all in a sweat, 'n you been moanin' 'n tossin' somethin' awful." Ruth was shaking her petulantly. Relieved, Marge surprised Ruth by hugging her.

"Jes' had a bad dream, I reckon."

"Wal, doan have another. 'N do go to sleep."

That was right. Soon daylight would be here, and she'd have to mind her frames for eleven hours. She must sleep.

The next morning and evening came, and the next, and still no Tom, and no word from him. The following evening Bill Stern, Tom's pal, stopped Marge and told her Tom had sent word by him to say not to worry about him. He was all right. He'd gone north to work and to see something of the world. No use to look for him, as he was never coming back.

The Crenshaws had to accept this, like many another mill family has had to do, when their boy nearing his majority has decided to shake the dust of the hill off his feet, the mill lint out of his lungs and eyes, and go forth into the world, in the hopes of finding "somethin' asides work, eatin', sleepin' 'n mo' work."

IV.

Back Row

BACK OF THE MILL, alongside the railroad tracks and separated from the section of Row Hill where Marge lived by a field through which meandered a foot path, stood another group of company dwellings. In these fifteen shacks, huddled together and slanting toward one another as if seeking support, also lived families who worked at the mill.

This colony, known as "Back Row" and "niggertown," was barely two hundred yards from where the Crenshaws lived, in space as measured by the feet. But if the distance had been two thousand miles instead, Marge and the people on her side of the village and those on this could scarcely have known less about one another. For on Marge's half lived the white mill hands, while here in the dip by the railroad tracks, lived Negro families who also helped to transfer cotton fluff into cotton cloth at ten cents a yard.

The field of daisies and wild grass was like an invisible gulf which yawned between them, and which those on both sides took largely for granted, as the gulf had been there when they came into the world.

Only a few shacks were needed at Back Row, as the colored men and women were restricted to doing manual labor around the mill—hauling and cleaning cotton, washing the windows and sweeping the lint along the floor—and this required a scant two score hands. Back Row shacks were far poorer than those lying across the field. Two thinly-boarded rooms stood flat on the ground; a smoke stack of tin poked through each roof. In the rear there were two sets of outhouses, swarming with flies and hornets. Near the doorstoops of the shacks a few morning glories and sun flowers struggled up through the red clay, and little brown bodies in one-piece garments busied themselves, digging in the mud. There was one pump which all fifteen families used. In wet weather, the ground before the houses was turned into a small pond as the water filled the dip, while even in dry weather there were muddy spots, and shallow pools in the rear where dish water seeped into the ground, since there was no other place to throw it.

Early evening had come to Back Row with the same kind touch that it reached out to Marge's part of the village. Nature draws no color line.

Pa Morgan and his two youngest were sitting on their doorstoop, watching the fire-flies dart hither and thither across the fields, while Pa strummed his banjo and hummed under his breath. From inside came the sound of soft talk and laughter, as Ma and Marthy finished the evening dishes. When Ma laughed, her broad hips and generous bosom shook gently under her blue calico dress, and her black eyes flashed and sent dancing lights across to her companion.

"Thar, now, Marthy, we's all done, 'n can go outside. You shore is a help to your Ma, honey. I doan know what I'd do without you." She put an arm around the girl's firm shoulders.

"Why, Ma, you know I ain't leavin' you fer a long time, yit."

"Wal, mebbe, mebbe," she gave Marthy a teasing look. "We gals in our family allays marries young, 'n you're plum size fer your age. Look mo' like twenty than sixteen. 'N Jim, now, I 'low he's pullin' at the bit, ain't he, 'n pressin' you to set the day?"

Martha smiled back and lowered her eyes. "Quit your joshin', Ma. You know we ain't a-marryin' yit. Besides, Jim's got to git a raise, 'n we-uns mo' saved up afore we could start out."

"Wal, he's a good boy, up right 'n hard workin', 'n I ain't begrudgin' you to him. But I ain't hurryin' 'long the day, nuther."

The two joined the others, who sidled over to make room on the stoop. Ma took Charlie and Myrtle onto her lap, while George Johnson, from next door, crouched contentedly between Pa Morgan's knees.

"Ma," Charlie asked, "kin you tell what make th' fireflies shine thata way?"

"How many questions you kin think to ask, chile!"

"Myrtle says they got tiny lanterns, 'n Pa says they's jest made thataway."

"'N Pa's right. They's made like they's made, 'n that's the way the good Lawd intended 'em, 'n I recokon he knowed what he was a-doin'." Ma smoothed the wooly head.

"They sure is pretty, 'n that's a fact," Martha added.

"It ain't fire flies you's thinkin' 'bout, Marthy," Myrtle commented, "You's a-lookin' out fer Jim."

"That's him, now, ain't it, comin' cross the fields?" George slipped from his resting place and started on the run, holding Martha tightly by one hand.

"Evenin', folks, evenin'." With George on his shoulder and one arm around Martha's waist, Jim came toward the stoop, tempering his gigantic stride to the girl's slower one. His powerful shoulders and frame were outlined under his khaki overalls and shirt which were 'spankin-clean' fer visitin'. As he laughed, a throaty, pleasant sound, two rows of white teeth gleamed in the dusk.

"Howdy, Jim, howdy! How you all?" Ma Morgan greeted him.

"Howdy, Aunt Eillie, howdy, Uncle Ben." They were no relation to Jim, but this was the common term of affection used in this part of the country. "Oh, I'se feelin' furst-rate, right now," he gave Martha a gentle squeeze. "How's you-all?"

"Tolable. Tolable. Have a seat." Pa brought a bench from the shack. "It's been hot weather to the mill this week. 'N Miz Johnson, next door, has been complainin' the white folks' washin's this week was bigger than ever."

"Wal, that's too bad. Them mill folks up at Haines'es place must have sweated out of their white skins this week, too. How 'bout it, Marthy?" Martha worked as housemaid at the mill-owners' place.

"Yah, it's been hot all right, but Miz Haines 'n her gals, they lays in bed till afternoon, drinkin' lemonade 'n readin', 'n havin' us help to fan 'em; so the heat doan worry 'em much."

"You doan tell! They jest lazies round while you folks is slavin' fer their ole man at the mill. Wal, I guess we-all wish we could rest our weary bones thataway, some of these steamin marnin's. Ain't that right, Uncle Ben?" Jim pulled his pipe from his rear pocket and reached for a match.

"They's a good-fer-nuthin lot, out to all hours at night drinkin' 'n carryin'-on." Martha spoke so bitterly that Jim looked at her in surprise. "Anythin' botherin' you, honey?" She shook her head. "Naw, 'course not." Should she tell him, later on, about young Haines trying to put his arm round her, in the pantry, yesterday? A white rich man's son making up to a colored gal; no good had ever come of that. But she'd not tell Jim nor Ma, neither; for they'd make her quit her job and that'd mean Mister Haines'd turn the whole family offa the hill. No, she'd manage to keep out of young Haines' sight, after this, and he'd soon have forgotten all about her. She'd jest be a black pair of hands round the house, once more. That was the best way out of it. Martha shivered and slipped over closer to Jim's sturdy shoulder.

"Look, Jim, see what Marthy made me outta the corn cob you brung last week." Myrtle held up a crude sort of doll.

"Wal, that's nice, I do declare."

"How's it out your way, Jim?" Pa Morgan repeated his question.

"It's gettin' hard times in the country, Uncle Ben. My boss' temper grows worser 'n worser each day thar's no rain. Last year, the bo-wevil got the crop, 'n this year, thar's too big a crop all over the country, so he got no price a-tall. Us two hands he's feedin' scantier 'n scantier, 'n grumblin' so I ain't sure we'll get our next month's wages, out'n a tussle."

"This workin' fer a white man ain't no good. We ain't humans to Po' Whites. We's jest black faces 'n *hands*.

"Soon I'm aimin' to start out fer myself. How 'bout it, Marthy?" She smiled back, a dark flush gliding under her golden brown skin.

"Anotha couple of seasons in the field 'n we'll have enough saved up to go farmin', or—"

"You still aimin' to go farmin', Jim?"

"Wal, I is 'n I ain't. I was calculatin' on talkin' it over mo' with Marthy 'n you-all. I likes the land, 'n makin' things grow. But it's purty risky business, share-cropin', with white mens, 'n white laws. Fer the nigger, it's heads I win, 'n tails you lose, ev'ry time."

"Yah, that's right," Uncle Joe Johnson, appearing on the stoop next door in time to hear Jim's last sentence, broke in on the conversation.

"Evenin', Uncle Joe. Evenin', Aunt Polly. Come over 'n make yousefs to-home."

"How's you, Aunt Polly?" Jim inquired.

"Po'ly, thank the Lawd, Po'ly." Aunt Polly was always enjoying poor health and making the most of it.

"Jim, ma boy, you never spoke a truer word than jest now," Uncle Joe continued, "'n I reckon I got cause to know. Any farmer in the country of Macon 'll tell you thar warn't a one could raise mo' cotton per acre than what I could, 'n scare the bo-wevil 'n pests away so sartain. Me'n Polly 'n the chillen slaved year in 'n year out, 'n skrimped. But no matter, every time the reckonin' come, afte Mister Lemmons weighed the cotton, 'n tooken his half—"

"Why'd he do that, Uncle Joey?"

"'Cause, chile, he owned the place, 'n he furnished the seeds, 'n that was his payment. Wal, afta he tooken his half, he'd git out the bills, 'n add up, 'n subtract, 'n he'd say, he would 'Wal, Joe, afta buyin' your half the cotton at market price, you owes me thirty-five dollars balance, but we'll put that on next year's counting. Youse a good tenant,' he said, seeing me look downcast, 'doan git discouraged, mebbe you kin pay off, then.' Wal, next year, we skrimp some mo', 'n pull in our belts. We diden git the dress-goods from Mr. Lemmon's store we needed fer the chillen's clothes, so as not to run up expenses. 'N we worked harder than ever befo'.

"But, come the end of another season, 'n Mr. Lemmon figgered it out the same way. What's mo', we knew he was a-lyin. Even if me'n Polly coulden read 'n figger from the books, we had him read it out, 'n he said we'd buyed things, we nevah had. Shoes 'n piece goods, 'n 'bacy. But he woulden take no argument. Anyways, it ain't safe fer a nigger to give any back-talk to a white man in Georgy."

"Nor South Caroliny, nuther, Uncle Joe."

"No, as I tell Joey," Aunt Polly took her corn-cob pipe from her mouth, "the only way to git along with the white mens is to let 'em have their way. Leastways, to let 'em *think* they's havin' it."

"So," Joey continued, "finally we give up, 'n come to the cotton mills."

"'N you was lucky at that to git away," Jim broken in. "Now in Mississippi, from what my cousin who worked thar tells me, they holds the colored folks on the land by right of the law."

"So I heard tell. They does right start of that in Georgy, too."

"If they git away," Jim went on, "the landowner'n the govern-ment send officers afta the colored man with guns, They come to the next state, or wherevah he's gone to, 'n take him 'n his family back, 'n make them work out their debt. They's tied to that piece of land 'n the landlord for life!"

"What's that but slavery!" Martha exclaimed indignantly.

"'N that's what it is. But what kin they do?"

"When I grows up," young George announced, "it's gona be diff'rent. We-uns ain't gone let the white mens treat colored folks thata way!"

His elders chuckled at his cock-sureness, but Uncle Ben shifted the boy to a more firm position between his knees, and answered in a serious voice, "Doan laugh at the boy. Sonny, mebbe you's right. Mebbe you'n George here, 'n Myrtle'll live to see it diff-rent." A silence fell over the little gathering. Pipes gleamed in the dark.

"By the way, Miz Johnson, what's the news with your boy, Fred, what's up north? I heard down the way you done had a letter, I hopes," Aunt Polly inquired anxiously, "thar's nuthin' wrong?"

Ma Morgan brightened. "Fred's gittin' along tolable, thank-ee. He's got him a job loadin' ships, out of New York harbor. He says it's hard work, 'n ain't as reg'lar or as good pay as it might be. Costs a lot to live in the city, too. Fred says they hoist a flag on the dock when the ship comes in, 'n all the mens rushes down, 'n the boss picks out as many as he's needin' that day, 'n the rest go home."

"But Fred's so tall 'n strong 'n handy, I bet, Ma, he's picked every time!"

"But what if the blocks he's loadin' fell on him?" Aunt Polly spoke mournfully, "or what if he slipped off the wharf into that dark ribber?" Ma shuddered, but the others grinned. Martha whispered in her mother's ear, "Doan mind her, Ma, she's allays a-talkin' of death or misery."

George stirred restlessly. "How 'bout a lil' music, Uncle Ben?"

"Yes sir, give us some of your sweet stirrin's."

"Then move, son, so I kin have room." George slid from between the old man's knees. Uncle Ben struck a few chords. "What'll it be?"

"Swing Low," Myrtle asked. As they sang, dark figures drifted out from the other cabins and joined in the rich, swelling harmonies which blended, soared to a climax, dropped to a whisper, and then died away on a sigh. "Nobody Knows the Trouble I've Seen," crooned Aunt Polly, and the others chorused, "Oh, Yes, Lawd."

As song followed song, the figures swayed gently in unison with the rhythms, and became welded into one. It was as though a gentle wind blowing from the quiet sky across their toil-marked bodies struck chords in their throats and hearts, and awoke music which flowed out as naturally and irresistibly as clear water from a mountain spring.

"Let's sing 'Listen to the Lambs,'" Martha begged. There were tears in more than Aunt Polly's ready eyes when this plain minor came to a close.

Suddenly Ma's voice rang out, "Oh, I Know the Lawd, I Know the Lawd's Laid His Hand on Me."

"This one's fer Charlie." Uncle Ben announced, and struck the opening chords of "Steal Away to Jesus." Uncle Ben had told the children more than once how this song had been used by the Negroes, when still in slavery, as a signal for a meeting in the woods. Here, late at night, and far away from their master's plantations, they'd gather as they were forbidden to do, and talk of freedom.

"Pappy," Charlie angered by the tales of slavery days, had asked, "why did grand-pappy'n tothers stand fer sech doin's? Why diden they rise up 'n strike 'em dead, 'n git their freedom sooner?"

"Why Charlie," Aunt Polly broke in, in her quavering voice, "I'm serprised at you. Same as axin' why we doan rise up today. There ain't but one way to git along with white folks'n that is to let 'em have their way."

"'Course, when the war come, that was diff'rent. But afore that, what could the slaves do, when they scattered all apart, with no guns or nuthin' but their bare hands?" Uncle Joey ruminated. "The white marses had the guns 'n govern-ment'n everythin' on their side."

"Wal, Joey," Uncle Ben replied, "even with all that, I'm right glad to be able to tell Charlie, even with all the odds agin 'em, they did rise up, once in awhile. Men, even slaves, got to show some spirit, 'n not be like dumb beasts, like the marses wanted. Yes, chile, the slaves got desperate mo'n onct, 'n rise up, fought with shovels, pick-axes, or hoes, whatever come to hand. Mo'n one over-seer'n owner bit the dust. 'N the slaves strung fer it."

As the last bars drifted across the fields, Charlie, blinking at the stars, let out a contented breath.

One lanky boy did a slip-step and remarked, "Gee, wisht it warn't Sunday, so we could have some dance music, 'n cut some capers."

"Oh, woan you, Uncle Ben, jest this onct?" the boy's sleek-haired companion urged.

The older folks threw up their hands. "Land's sakes. What the young ones comin' to? Miseration'll come to you, yit, fer desecratin' the Lawd's day."

"Oh, it's only old fogies that believe like that. Now my cousin what's in Harlem says, Sunday night is one of the big nights."

"That's the place of the debil, nohow."

"Thar's too much jest workin' 'n worshipin' 'round here," the boy persisted, "'n too lil' fun."

"Boy," Aunt Polly poked her finger under his nose, "shut your mouth'n doan you say another word. The black folks gotta cling to their religion. It's one thing we gotta hold onto, that 'n our singin'. You'n your slick ways'n sinful talkin' ain't no place to be at Back Row, nohow."

"Come on, boys, quit your arguin'," Jim spoke persuasively. "Mebbe tomorra night Uncle Ben'll play fer you-all to cut the pigeon wing."

"Tomorrow night's no good. Everybody's too tire out, from workin' at the mill."

"That's right. Funny how it tells on a-body mo' afta a day's rest."

"Then how'bout Tuesday?"

"All right, Tuesday it'll be." Uncle Ben slid his fingers over the strings.

"Uncle Ben, play us, 'Let Ma People Go!'" George requested, "'n Jim, you sing it."

"All right, Georgie, 'n everybody in on the refrain." Jim drew in his breath and sang in deep-chested, ringing tones:

> Go down, Moses,
> 'Way down in Egypt land,
> Tell ole Pharaoh,
> To let ma people go.
>
> When Israel was in Egypt land,
> Let ma people go!
> Oppressed so hard they could not stand,
> Let ma people go!

Marge, walking back toward her house, following her vain chase after Tom, caught a faint echo of the singing as it floated across the fields from Back Row to Row Hill. When the last martial note had died away, Martha commented, "That's the best song we got."

"'N the truest," Pa Morgan added, "Moses lead the chillen of Israel, 'n we needs somebody to lead us."

"Whar, pappy?" Charlie inquired eagerly. "Whar'd we go?"

"Nowhar's, chile, perzactly. I mean lead us to the freedom we was promised."

"We's free-born, ain't we Uncle Ben?" George asked. "That's what Ma says, we's free-born."

The old man rested his banjo across his knees. "So we is, chile, but we ain't free yit. Pappy tole me how, when the news come that thar was a war fer freedom, all the slaves what could git away jined the northern army. Then, when finally the proclamation come, settin' 'em free, the colored people everywhar drapped down on their knees 'n thanked the Lawd 'n the federal govern-ment what brung this about. ... That was mo'n fifty years ago.... Yah, you'n me too, we was born in freedom, but we're slaves still. We's kept ignorant 'n dirt-poor, 'n the white man's servant."

"But—A Great Day's Comin' Bye 'n Bye," Ma Morgan threw back her head and the tones slipped from her throat like swallows on the wing. Soon the hallelujahs were echoing along the country-side.

"Lawsy, it's time we-all was in bed." Uncle Joey smiled around at his companions and rose to his feet. He and Aunt Polly were like Jack Spratt and his wife: he had all the fat and easy-going humor and she all the lean and melancholy. "Tomorrow mornin' thar'll not be a one but what's sleepeyed 'n slow to rise."

"Work, work, allays work," Miz Sparrow grunted, pulling her self to her feet. "Seems like I'se swept enough lint 'n dustin's from that mill to fill the sky."

Slowly the group broke up. Families returned to their cabins. But a few boys and their girls struck out for the fields.

Martha and Jim lingered on the door stoop for a few moments before he started back across the country-side to Farmer Brown's place. As he strode past corn rows and cotton patches that shone softly in the moonlight, his head full of dreams of Martha and their future life together in the cabin and fields, Jim's massive shoulders unconsciously lifted and he burst again into song. Lawd, the smell of the earth was good 'n clean! No mill life fer him'n his chillen. No matter what came, he'd stay by the land.

Everyone at Back Row was on hand Tuesday evening, ready for the frolicking. Even the moon was out, casting its fantastic, pale, glow over fields, shacks and whirling brown and coal-black figures. Buck and wing was in full swing. Black eyes darted, while teeth gleamed, bright-colored scarfs and ties, red bandanas and crimson dresses turned leery colored under the greenish-gold light.

The older ones sat on the stoops and kept time with their clapping hands or patting feet, as the younger ones danced back and forth, in and out, to the tune of Uncle Ben's banjo. The number ended amid cheering and shouts of "Once mo', Uncle Ben."

"Gentlemen," he announced, "git your pardners fer the Virginny reel." "Ladies, face your pardners." To the tune of "Oh, believe me if all those endearing young charms," played in rag-time, they were off, giggling and following Uncle Ben's called directions, "Swing your pardners," "Turn your pardners," "Back to back," and "Saschey."

"Now, cake-walk, Uncle Ben," they demanded.

"All right," and he struck up, "Turkey in the Straw," followed by "It's a hot time in the ole town tonight." The old folks laughed and clapped until the tears ran down their cheeks at the antics of their off-spring, bending, prancing, cake-walking until finally Pa Morgan's fingers were too cramped for more, and the dancers threw themselves laughing and out of breath on door-stoops, chairs, up-turned grocery boxes and the red dirt which glimmered like a purple carpet stretched in front of the leaning shacks.

AT FIVE O'CLOCK THE next morning people were stirring at Row Hill and Back Row. Dressing, washing, eating followed one another in rapid, wordless succession as mill hands, white and colored made themselves ready for another eleven hours at the mill. At quarter to six, the whistle blew, three blasts, then two streams began to trickle out of shacks and cabins—men and boys in blue and tan overalls, women and girls in one-piece calico slips, with many carrying sunbonnets. At five minutes to six, there was another imperative blast, and the stragglers began to run toward the mill and disappear within the gates. Then the old red brick building began to rumble like some hungry beast.

V.

Across the Miles

GEORGE BURST INTO THE ROOM where Aunt Polly was busy over her washtubs, scrubbing the dirt out of the white folks' clothes. She flung up her hands, holding one dripping garment aloft in her fright.

"Lawsy, boy, how you scairt me, bustin' in thataway!" Then, spying his expression, "What's wrong? Is it—"

"They'se wantin' you right away, Mammy," he caught his breath, "down at Perkinses."

Quickly she dried her hands on her apron, grabbed a few things and mumbling to herself, hurried off, the boy at her heels. He caught phrases, "Her time's come—that washin'll wait—Lawd-a-Mighty be with us this day—" Then, noticing George she said sharply, "Be off with-ya. No time and place for young'uns around." George disappeared in the opposite direction.

As she neared the Perkins' cabin, two women, relief on their faces, ran out to meet her. From inside came sounds of moaning. "She's in a bad way, Miz Johnson. Took sudden-lak, she was."

Grimly Ma Johnson set to work, and the other women followed her directions throughout the morning without a murmur of dissent. For Polly Johnson had brought more than one colored infant into the world without mishap, with prayers on her lips, shrewd eyes and hands busy meanwhile, carrying out the rites which her mother had taught her and which Aunt Polly had amplified by twenty years of experience.

Yet the hours passed, and still the woman on the pallet moaned and tossed. Ma Johnson beckoned to one of the women to come outside. Taking her apron, she wiped her dripping face. "By the sun, its high noon. Mill folks'll be comin' home fer victuals any minute now. Liza, you go down, 'n send 'em scoutin' fer a doctor."

Liza protested. "You know no white doctor'll evah come down hyar to Back Row. She's in a bad way, Ma, ain't she?"

"You tell 'em to tell the doctor it's life or death fer her 'n the young'un. We'll hold her on, 'til they comes. Tell the doctor it means operatin', 'n mo'n Polly Johnson kin do. It's in his 'n the Lawd's hands, now."

Liza groaned. Ma turned back to where Julie Perkins lay on her pallet. "This ain't no time fer groanin', Liza. Git a doctor."

The noon whistle blew, mill gates opened, and from one gate issued a stream of white mill hands hurrying home for a meal, from another, a shorter stream of colored folk. Liza grabbed Earl Perkins by the elbow. "Earl, run fer a doctor." She relayed Aunt Polly's words. "My Gawd, where'll I go?" and he was off. Quickly Liza sent others off in three different directions. Maybe this once, one of the four white doctors would come.

Back Row swallowed its noon-day meal in silence. A foreboding gloom settled over the cabins. This wasn't the first time that death had threatened Back Row, and there had been no doctor to fend off his approach to the sick one's bed. Moodily they returned to work.

The rumble of looms and spindles drifted into the sick room. Many a one, pushing cotton bins or sweeping up lint, was busy with thoughts of pretty Julie, tossing on her pallet.

Earl, sweat pouring from him, and panting for breath, stumbled into the room.

"Woan none come with you, nuther?" Aunt Polly spoke hoarsely. The strain was telling on her. Shaking his head, Earl walked over to the pallet. At the sight of Julie's pain-twisted face, he slipped down beside her, and began to sob like a child.

After a moment, Polly took him gently by the shoulder. "That ain' helping' Julie none, Earl. Brace up, 'n go heat me a big kettle of water." Obediently, he started off. Liza followed him out, and asked timidly, "Hadn't ya better go back to the mill? Plently o'uns to do here. Woan the boss fire ya fer stayin' off?" Earl, fumbling for the kettle, started over to the creek, so Liza went back to the sick room.

When Back Row folk returned home from work that evening, they found that Julie Perkins and her infant son were dead. What made it most bitter, all felt her death unnecessary. If a doctor had come in time, Earl wouldn't be there now in his shack, by two still bodies. So all felt.

Back Row followed the pine coffin Pa Johnson and Uncle Ben had made, in which lay Julie, in a white dress, her baby by her side, to the small cemetery, back of the country's colored Baptist Church. Here, the parson in a black coat and white vest, intoned sorrowfully, "The Lawd giveth 'n the Lawd taketh away." But Black Row knew that it was the lack of a doctor that had robbed Earl of his Julie.

Ma Johnson was a day late with the Haines' washing that week.

"Her girl who brought it said that Polly had been sick a day," Miss Haines studied her polished finger-nails. "But of

course, I know she was lying. They're all a trifling lot, 'n can't
be depended on. Probably, there was a picnic, or some frolic.
But Polly's a good washwoman, so I usually overlook things.

"By the way, don't you think, Eleanor deah, I should have
a new evening gown for the club dance, this Saturday? One
can't afford to appear twice in succession in the same dress."

"COME ON, CHARLIE, LET'S go to the crik," Myrtle's tightly
braided pigtails popped up and down in an excited way.

The creek flowed through a shaded lane of over-hanging
trees. Birds trilled lazily as Charlie and Myrtle sat on the
bank, and contemplated the cool mud oozing up between
their dusky toes.

"Look," Charlie pointed, "there's two lil' white kids
a-comin' this way." He had spied Billy and Sam on their daily
trip for a wade in the creek.

"Uh-huh," and Myrtle pushed the wooden craft she had
fashioned out of a stick with its twig mast and scrap of pink
cotton sail, further out into the stream.

For a while the four paddled around in the water, in opposite directions. Billy and Sam eyed Myrtle's small craft en-
viously. Theirs had no sails. "Mebbe we kin make sails too,"
and Billy tore a square from his ragged shirt sleeve, and set
to work.

Following their crafts as they floated down-stream, the
four children came alongside one another.

Presently Charlie, tiring of this sport, had a bright idea.
"Say, Myrtle, look at that thar bank. Les' play slippery
slicks." In a flash they were carrying water in old tins or broken bottles they found nearby, to wet the slope's sides. Then,
solemnly they stood at the top of the bank, and quickly slid
to the water's edge. Giggling, they started back up. Fascinated, Billy and Sam followed suit. This was a new game to
them. Then Myrtle hit upon the idea that one must *earn* a

slide down, by crawling up the slippery slope on hands and knees. There were many slips, tumbles and laughs before the top was reached. But now the slide down seemed twice as sweet.

This was the beginning of the friendship between Charlie and Myrtle, and Billy and Sam. Everyday, while their elders were at work in the mill, unknown to them, two tow heads and two kinky ones would spend happy hours along the creek's bank, floating boats on its muddied waters or sliding down its inviting slopes. For children, like nature, know no color line. Humans are humans to them. Of race and caste they know nothing and care less, until their elders, out of their worldly wisdom, take them in hand.

BILLY AND SAM WERE SITTING, very uncomfortable on the stiff-backed bench in the Baptist Sunday School of the village church, owned and operated by the company for its white mill hands. The teacher, a poor third-cousin-once removed of Mr. Haines, who made her living by teaching in the village grammar school week-days and all-year round in Sunday School (looking upon it as missionary work), was now holding forth on the Fatherhood of God and the Brotherhood of Man. Her text was "Little Children, Love One Another." She had explained how the mill owners and workers were really one big family, of elder and younger brothers.

"Miss Houghton, is black and white folks brothers, too?" Billy interrupted to ask.

Miss Houghton gave him a suspicious glance over her spectacles. It was clear, however, that the child was not trying to trap her, but was in earnest.

"Of course not. That is, in the sight of God, but not ... Billy, what makes you ask such a question?"

"Wal," Billy squirmed, suddenly self-conscious. "I dunno. I jes'—"

Sam tried to help him out. "You see, Charlie 'n Myrtle's colored, 'n I guess—"

"Who," demanded Miss Houghton, scenting trouble, "are Myrtle and Charlie?"

"They lives over to Back Row, 'n their Ma 'n Pa works at the mill. 'N we-uns plays slide togetha."

"What! You play with *little niggers!*" Her scorn withered the two boys. All eyes were on them. Some one sniggered. Miss Houghton, very red in the face, said a good deal more, about Anglo-Saxon purity and white supremacy and a lot of words that Billy and Sam couldn't understand. But one thing she did make clear. They were in disgrace. They had done a shameful thing by playing slide with Charlie and Myrtle.

Miss Houghton lost no time in making a trip to the Crenshaws, and informing Sal of what had happened. Sal, in tears, gave them a good talking to, and had Uncle Mat administer a good thrashing. For weeks Billy and Sam never went near the creek.

Myrtle and Charlie, puzzled at first by the absence of their friends, worried if they had fallen sick. The yearly epidemic of typhoid fever was raging on the hill. Maybe Billy and Sam were sick, dying, maybe dead? So George and Myrtle took their courage in their hands, and ventured into the forbidden land of Row Hill. Going around to the back door of the Crenshaws, they knocked timidly on the door. Sal came to the screen.

"Please ma'am, is Billy 'n Sam sick or dyin'?" they queried.

"No," she shouted, raising a broom at them, "'n if you lil' niggers come 'round hyar agin I'll skin you alive." There was a sputter of dust from four flying heels.

Once out of sight of Sal's wrath, Charlie and Myrtle slackened their pace.

"The ole hag," Myrtle gasped. Tears of anger and shame coursed over her brown cheeks. "Goddam her soul to hell,"

Charlie uttered his first curse—the worst he knew, associated in his mind with pounding fists, bloody mouths and quick-stroking razors.

Charlie and Myrtle, like Billy and Sam, had been taught their first lesson in race prejudice. Never again was the shaded lane of over-hanging trees to be a care-free place in which to play. Part of the glow of the creek was gone forever. Something ugly and mean, dimly comprehended but deeply emotional, entered their souls and tainted their breath.

"What's troublin' ma babies?" Pa Morgan put an arm around each tiny body as Charlie and Myrtle crouched, one against each knee. Little by little the story came out, between muffled sobs. Pa Morgan's face grew stern, while his pipe, forgotton, smouldered and died.

The story ended, he patted their shoulders gently.

"Thar—thar—doan you care. Plenty of good friends to play with in Back Row. Best not to git mixed up with white folks 'n their chillen. Stay on your own side the fence."

"But why, Pappy. What we done?"

Pa Morgan sighed. "It's hard tellin' why, sonny. De debil's done sown seeds of hate in the white folks' hearts. They hates us 'cause we black."

"But what we done to 'em?"

"Nuthin' chile, nuthin'. It's they what done us wrong. Stealin' 'n makin' us slaves, 'n robbin' us of our rights. Seems lak folks allays hates the ones they wronged, worser than tother way round. White folks is scairt, I guess. Jes' plain scairt." He drew a little unsteadily at his dead pipe, then rummaged his pockets for a match.

"I'se sorry this come to you lak this. But you's black, 'n you's got to learn, sooner or later. Black is black, 'n white is white, 'n this here 'n is a white man's world. He gives us a lil' piece 'n say, 'Stay thar.' So long as we stays 'n says 'Yas-sir' to what he tells us, 'n works hard fer him, it's all right. But move a foot, 'n he'll clove you on the head."

A mist rose from the creek and crept slowly over the fields, toward the shacks. Myrtle shivered. Pa, shaking himself, asked, "How 'bout I tell you some stories tonight?" The children's sad faces lit up. "Oh, Pappy, Uncle Remus' stories."

"All right. Which one?"

"'Bout the Tar Baby."

"Yes, tell about how the little brown rabbit outwitted the white farmer who wanted to kill him for poaching from fields. 'Don't throw me to the briar patch, mister. Don't throw me to the briar patch. . . . I was born 'n bred in the briar patch!"

MARGE AND MA MORGAN worked in the same room at the mill. Often, as she swept the lint and thread along the aisles, Ma would hum a spiritual in full undertones, and Marge, tending her spindles, grew to listen for the music of the woman who cleaned the floor—music which broke the monotony of her thoughts and hours before the frames.

One song moved Marge deeply. *Go Down Moses. Let My People Go.*

It was many months now, since Tom had gone. Each day dragged by like the last. Last year, she tended spindles for five dollars a week. This year, she was getting six. In three more years, she could reach nine, then she'd be to the maximum. After that, what was there to look forward to? But sounding behind her, as the Negro woman moved down the aisle, came notes and words of beauty—"Let My People Go."

"Let My People Go"—Ma, Granny, all Row Hill, away from the mills to some better life. Was there no way?

Once it occurred to Marge, "Does that colored woman singing, feel thataway too? Do her people hate it 'n want to git away?"

The day came when Ma Morgan's footsteps dragged down the aisle, and then a morning when she was not there.

Martha came timidly toward the boss spinner. "Please, sar, ma Ma sent me to say she's down with the fever 'n can't come in."

Turning at the sound of voices, Marge's gaze fell full upon Martha, standing in a green slip, in the dim light of the spinning room. Her golden-brown skin was flushed, her hands twisting on one another, her dark brown eyes were full of sparkling depths.

It was the first time that Marge had ever beheld a colored person. True, she had seen them around since early babyhood. But she had never encountered one before—human to human. Now, for an instant, Marge and Martha looked one another full in the eye.

This colored girl must be near her own age; did she have thoughts and feelings like hers? Why, Marge suddenly realized, "her lot's worser'n mine."

For a moment, the distance which lay between them was bridged and Marge caught a glimpse across the miles.

Such moments come, when one sees for an instant into the depths of life—beyond that daily routine which circumstance and custom hedges about. Yet, looking, all too often the looker draws back—fearful of the new world of emotions and ideas welling up to engulf him and break him loose from his old moorings.

Marge had reason to remember this incident, later on.

VI.

Fred and Tom

THE OAKS AND MAPLES beyond Row Hill were already on fire with crimson and gold, and the smell of fall was in the air when word first came from Tom.

It was a picture post-card, directed to Granny. On it was blazoned the Woolworth building in New York City—a startlingly white tower surrounded by pigmy structures painted pink, orange, or red, and shooting far up into a bright blue sky.

The entire family and three boarders assembled around the oil cloth table after the evening meal, listened attentively while Marge read Tom's words scrawled on the other side. "Some town. Hope all are well. Same here. Tom. P.S. Got a job on the docks." The card was passed around and each carefully examined it, and made comment.

"That thar's the tallest buildin' I ever did see," Harry remarked, "Doan see how they evah clum up that far in the sky to build. 'N why doan it tumble ovah?"

"No props or nuthin' that you kin see," Uncle Mat's knotty forefinger moved slowly over its surface.

"Shorely the good Lawd nevah meant men to live in no sech place as that," Sal exclaimed.

"Howevah do they git up them stairs to the top?"

"If you piled all the mill houses in the village on top tother, it'd jes' 'bout reach the top o' that building.'"

"What's that writ under the pitcher, Marge?" Granny inquired.

"Woolworth Building," Marge spelled out. "Why, that's the same as the five 'n tin in Greenville. I do declare."

"Gee, think o' all Tom's doin' 'n seein'," Gertie sighed.

"'N all he's larnin'," Marge thought. "Wisht I could go. How'd he manage it? Guess it's easier fer boys."

Of what had happened to Tom in the year since he had left, and of how he had worked and bummed his way to the great city, there was not one word. He and his pal, Scott, had hitch-hiked as far as Raleigh, North Carolina, in five days' time, sleeping out in the fields at night, and during the day, getting lifts from farmers carrying their load of vegetables into the next town. The boys swiped apples, peaches, or watermelons as they came to them, or did a morning's work for a feed. They were determined not to spend any of their few dollars until they had made their way as far north as possible. They were out to see the world, and New York was their destination.

By the end of their first week, Tom and Scott, being mill boys and unused to outdoor life, found their feet blistered, their limbs aching from so much walking, and their faces and bare arms scarlet from constant exposure to the southern sun. But doggedly they trudged on.

Then, in Virginia they went dead broke, and had to get work. For days they hung around Norfolk employment agencies, growing dizzy with hunger. There were no cotton mills along the Virginia sea-coast, they found, although in the state's Piedmont section, they heard, there was the biggest one in the world.

Lucky for them, the season was still on in the oyster and fish canning business, so Tom and his pal went to work shucking oysters, in order to appease their hunger. They felt ashamed to be at the plant, which they discovered was manned largely by women and children. The floor was covered with water and slime, smells of dead and rotting fish assaulted their nostrils, and the salt bit into the open sores in their hands, cut and bleeding from the sharp edges of the shells. By night, they were too exhausted to "do the town," but flung themselves on their pallets and slept without turning, until called at five the next morning.

Tom, disgusted with the job and noticing the raw hands and pinched bodies of the boys and girls working alongside of them, remarked to his companion, "Guess it's the same fer Po' Whites all ovah. This hyar is worsen'n the cotton mill, ain't it?"

"It shore is. Stinkingest place I evah was in. But we got five a piece saved up now, enough to shove us on our way. Say, Tom, how 'bout blowin' ourselves this last night to a pitcher show, 'n mebbe pick us up two gals?"

But a deep misgiving had seized Tom. Where was the adventurous new life they were seeking? "Was New York gona be no different?" He pushed the thought from him.

Other days of back-breaking work and wondering where the next meal was coming from followed, but Tom and Scott pressed on. In Baltimore they picked up with a hobo who expounded to them at length on the evils of working, and the most successful methods of avoiding this disaster. "Not all hoboes is like me," he explained. "Many a one'll break his back fer the capitalists. But me—it's a principle with me not to do no lick o' work under this present rotten system of government. The capitalists doan woik, why should I?" His philosophy and way of living caught the two boys' fancy for a while, until they discovered how hard their hobo friend had to work to keep from working. Anyway, he showed them how to board their first freight, and the next day they were in the big city itself.

Tom's first shock came when he and Scott found their few dollars gone, lifted off them their first night in a second-avenue flop house. Their southern drawl and home-made shirts and overalls had made them conspicuous and easy targets.

"'N to think," Tom raged, "that all them days shuckin' oysters was fer nuthin'." Disconsolately they wandered up and down the streets, dazed by the multitude of noises, jostled by crowds rushing past them (where could all be going?), and fascinated by the towering buildings which loomed so high they had to lean far back in order to see the top.

"Worse luck," Scott muttered, "we gotta find work, right off. I'm hungry as a calf, ain't you?" Tom nodded. "No chanct to see the city furst, or nuthin'."

A crowd of workmen gathered round a speaker who was shaking his fist in the air, drew their attention and they wandered over. A few phrases of the soap-boxer sailed over the heads of the crowd at them. "The master class of this country keeps us all—native born, foreigners and whites, under its iron heel. . . . We're their slaves . . . made all their money for 'em. . . . Gotta organize 'n fight for our rights. . . . Solidarity. . . . Solidarity."

Tom drew closer. "Say, Scott, les' move ovah." This was something different! A workman standing near them turned at the sound of Tom's soft voice.

"Southerners, by gosh! . . . You new to the city, boys?" Tom, turning, saw a short, thick-set youth, his shirt turned in at the neck, and his freckled face topped by an unruly mat of bright red hair.

"We got in—" Scott began. Tom nudged his companion. "Naw, not exactly. What's this meetin' hyar about?"

"It's what we call our agitation meetin' o' the I.W.W., a union meetin'," and he began an enthusiastic explanation. When the meeting broke up, he asked, "Come in 'n have a coffee-and with me?" Tom's and Scott's stomachs gave a bound at the thought. Scott was ready to accept at once, but Tom hung back. This guy seemed friendly-lak, but they had to be keerful o' strangers.

Their new acquaintance caught their hesitation. "My name's Martin—Jake Martin. 'N I'm from Virginny maself. Been up north now goin' on ten year, so I've lost some of the sound of it."

"Oh," said Tom to himself, "that's diff'rent." Aloud, he said, "Thank-ye kindly. Guess we will."

Over the "coffee-and," their story was soon told. "There's all kinds in the city," remarked Jake, "plenty who'll gyp you, 'n plenty who'll give you a hand. Seems like the city brings out the worse in some, 'n at the same time, makes other workers see they got to stick togetha. . . . I jined the wobblies last year. A fine gang of boys."

"Seemed all right, though that's new talk to me," Tom answered. "You doan know mebbe whar we kin git a job?"

"Wal, now that's an idee. I work down on the docks, myself."

"You 'spose," Scott broke in eagerly, "you could git us took on thar?"

Jake looked them over. "It's worth trying. You ain't full-size yet, 'n doan look too husky. But—"

"You'd be serprised. If they'll give us a try!"

"You're on, boys. Say, have you got a place to stay yet?" Jake recalled his first days in the city, and his heart warmed toward them. It was soon settled that they rent a room directly under his.

Jake had them up at day-break. Dashing in with a pair of socks in one hand, and pulling at his trousers with the other, he yelled into their reluctant ears, "Step on it," and rushed off again, warbling in an uncertain tenor, "Oh, what do you want to break your back for the boss for, when it doan mean life to you?"

"Boys, we're in luck," Jake hurried them along the pier. "It happens there's one mo' boat they expected, 'n they're a lil' short of hands. So the boss'll give you a try. Now do your stuff!"

Scott lasted only a few hours. Already he had mashed a finger, and his back was getting lame. When he was told to work with a crew that included four Negroes, he quit cold. "Not on your life," he exclaimed, "I'm a white man 'n doan evah work alongside no nigger!"

He looked around for Tom to back him up, but Tom, puffing over a crate of pine-apples which he and another longshoreman were manoeuvering onto the truck, did not even turn around. He liked the thing little better than Scott. But a job was a job, and he caught Jake's eye on him. Guess he'd stick.

Later that night, Scott swaggered in and announced, "Wal, I'm shippin' out. Signed up this aftanoon." He laughed at Tom's blank expression.

"See the World with Uncle Sam," Jake chanted sarcastically. "You will, lak hell! But you got it coming to you."

"You're some southerna," Scott retorted hotly, "standin' up fer niggers!"

Jake's face turned the color of his hair. "You big Henry Dubb!" he thundered. "A worker's a worker, no matter what's the color of his skin. Shore, I got over your ailment years ago. Southerner! Bosh! What difference does it make, what part of the country you come from. What'd Dixie ever do for you, to make you so patriotic? Lotta hard work 'n ignorance, that's all."

"Tom," Scott stormed, "you see the kinda fella we took up with. I'm warnin' ya."

"Oh, hold your tongue, Scott, 'n les' talk reasonable."

"There's anotha thing," Jake went on, "doan you evah say 'nigger' round me again, or there'll be trouble. N-e-g-r-o," he spelled out the letters, "Negro. Negro worker is as good as you or me, anyday, 'n don't you be fergetting it."

The two glared at each other. Scott took a half-step forward, then whirled about, slamming the door behind him. Jake blew a deep breath between his teeth and shook his heavy shoulders. "My temper's got the upper hand again. I should have reasoned quiet-like with him. . . . Say, Tom, go after him if you like."

Tom shuffled his feet. "Mebbe I better." As he went down the hall he heard Jake rumbling, "Long-haired preachers come out every night. . . ."

TOM FOUND LIFE ON THE DOCKS and in the city totally unlike the mill life he had known. For several weeks he had to put all his efforts into getting the swing of the new job, his lame back and outraged muscles driven on by the fear of being turned off, and of Jake's ridicule. Once he had mastered the work and even had a little energy to spare, he looked about to enjoy himself.

One Saturday night, in company with two other longshoremen he deserted Jake and the wobbly meeting and started on the rounds of the wharf saloons. In the early hours, when he came to, Tom found himself in bed alongside a dock woman. Where, he wondered, did I pick her up? Head splitting and stomach rebelling, he crawled out carefully so as not to arouse her and made for his own room.

Jake, eyeing him up and down, burst out, "Look here, Tom, you'll tell me it's none of my gol-dern business, 'n maybe it ain't. But as a friend 'n fellow-worker I'm telling you to lay offa that stuff."

"Aw cut it Jake. I ain't gonna repeat it." Tom reached for the pan under his bed.

"That ain't so certain. I ain't no momma's boy, you know that. But there's only a few hours we can call our own, when we ain't slaving fer the ship magnates. Why waste 'em? The capitalists make beasts of burden of us all day, then feed us drink 'n wimen 'n make beasts of us all the time, so we can't think. . . . Cut it Tom, 'n use your head. Wanta stay an ignoramus all your life?"

"Aw, dry up, can't-cha!" He heaved a shoe in Jake's direction but the red head ducked in time for that battered member to clatter against the wall and roll disconsolately across the floor.

Gradually Tom took to hanging out more at wobbly headquarters and reading the pamphlets and books which Jake left conveniently about. And there were many arguments. One constant topic was that of race. Step by step Jake won ground and Tom was forced to give in, gradually at first but as the new world of ideas opened up, he found himself following Jake's lead with some eagerness. As Jake had told him, "Once a southern worker, white or black, gets it straight, he'll go the limit—once he sees how it's held us back."

Events themselves gave point to Jake's philosophy. Working day after day alongside colored men on the docks, eating in the same joints, joining in the same union, and together rushing the cops who tried to break up street meetings, all had their effect.

Over at Jergens one evening, Fred Morgan, a Negro, joined their gathering, and Tom listened in amazement for the first time to one of the Negro race discuss working class questions. Somehow, he had never before realized that Negroes also have brains.

Fred Morgan was a raw-boned, agile type, with hair close-cropped over his high forehead, and sombre, deep-set eyes which lit up when he was making one of his frequent sallies.

"So we two are from the same part of the country?" Fred replied to Jake's introduction, "funny, ain't it, we should meet up here lak this?"

"Yah, I reckon it is," Tom answered. Seeing his discomfort, Fred moved on to others in the gathering, leaving Tom wondering if he or Jake had noticed that he hadn't been able to shake hands with his colored man who severed so much at home here among these white radicals.

Dr. Brandt, a near-sighted, thin-voiced little man, whom Jake said "ran all to brain," slipped his arm under Tom's and drew him toward the table. "Come have a glass of tea?" Over the teeming glasses, Brandt expounded his ideas to the group. "Science is a revolutionary force that will remake the world. Instead of the present crazy quilt, society will then be run according to a rational plan. You workmen at the bench understand the relentless operation of the law of cause and effect. You will be the means of bringing this about." Discussion waxed so hot, and voices rose to such a climax that Tom was relieved to find, at the close of the evening, that all parted seemingly the best of friends.

Truly, a new world was opening up for Tom in New York, although not in the way he had anticipated.

When he first felt the old world of ideas and ways of living crashing about his ears, a thrill of terror went over him, and he fought blindly to right it. Now, gradually, through his reading, arguments with Jake and other wobblies, and his fresh experiences, a new world began to emerge before Tom's eyes—a world of labor, of solidarity, of a cause which he could swing to, and he discovered a new purpose in living. Before, he had been merely a Poor White, mill hand, ashamed and rebellious, desiring only some way of escape from it all. Now—

It was as absorbing and as fearful a process, this through which he was passing, as falling in love. Only in this it was easier to keep one's head!

Tom, as he loaded cargo into the ship's hole, remembered Lucy, and smiled bitterly to himself. Lucy, that dark-haired, grey-eyed sprite whose alternate jeers and wild affection had tortured him and sent him from Row Hill. Did she care for him? What made her act the way she did—almost crazy at times? And what was happening to her now? Maybe some day he'd go back down there to see.... No, better to forget her altogether.

Intent on his thoughts, Tom heard the warning cry too late. The swinging crane knocked him flat and cuffed him off the dock into the dirty current below.

"Man overboard!" the cry went up.

"Quick, the tide's running fast."

In a flash, a longshoreman had his shoes off and was over-board, catching Tom's body as it came to the surface. A line was thrown them, and soon they were on the dock. Tom, dripping and still dazed, was looking with mingled gratitude and chagrin into the face of his benefactor. For the man who had saved him was Fred Morgan, the Negro.

Tom went about his work for the next week, torn by conflicting emotions and ideas. Gratitude to Fred Morgan for risking his life to save his, vied with resentment that he owed his life to a nig—one of them. The old emotional antagonism, prejudice, not entirely up-rooted, struggled against his newer convictions.

Jake, guessing his friend's struggle, left Tom to himself. As for Fred, there was a hurried, friendly nod, and "Howdy, Tom," as he passed him on the dock, and that was all.

Finally Tom's mind was made up. Now he must muster courage to carry through his decision.

At the close of work on Friday, Tom went over to Fred and, his face white and eyes fastened on a spot near Fred's feet, said in a strained voice, "Fred Morgan, I got somethin' I been wantin' to say to you. Kin I go home with you?"

"Shore, Tom Crenshaw. I'd be glad to have you."

Once in Fred's room—a neat, bare place with the minimum of furniture and a small shelf of books—Tom plunged in. "I doan know jes' how to put it. You see—"

"Wal, doan bother 'bout puttin' it. Jes' say it out. Can't hurt ma feelin's."

"All right. I'll jes' speak out," Tom began desperately. "Evah since you pulled me outta th' river, I been thinkin' hard. 'N befo' that, too."

"I know Jake took you in hand, 'n he's been puttin' you through th' traces, I'll warrant, like he did me." Fred chuckled, trying to put Tom more at his ease. "Tole you you's a blasted ignorant Dixie mill hand, I bet?" Tom nodded.

"You should-a seen him clippin' his heels in th' air," Fred continued, "when he found I was a Republican. But he soon ended that!"

Tom relaxed a little. "Wal, yes, Jake jolted me furst. 'N I guess I needed it all right.... You see, evah since I was lil'—you know all the things we're taught down south, 'bout white 'n colored folks not mixin', 'n all.... I guess," his voice dropped. "I swallowed it all, line, hook 'n sinker. So when you pulled me outta the river, I felt almost sorry. I'd almost sooner die than be beholdin' to a nig—I mean, colored man.... I knew, if it'd been you that'd been knocked in, I'd not gone afta you. 'N I wondered, why you did it?... But, Fred," the worst over, Tom hurried on, "you 'n Jake has shown me diff'rent. We gotta stick togetha."

"Yah," Fred replied, "that's right. It's the only way."

"I wanna ask a favor. Do you think mebbe you 'n me could be friends? I mean, shore-nuf friends? You've got a lotta friends, I know. But me, I nevah had a colored friend. 'N I'd like to." Tom looked squarely into the sombre, black depths. Fred searched the blue eyes and freckled face. The kid did put it badly. But back of his words, he sensed a vast earnestness.

He held out his hand. "Put' er thar, Tom. It's a go." Tom met Fred's smile a little unsteadily.

"But, I ain't quite through. Try, Fred, not to mind, if I'm slow, sometimes, 'n mebbe hurt your feelin's, not meanin' to? It takes a long time, seems-lak, to unlearn nigh twenty year o' mean-ness."

"Doan worry, buddy," Fred rejoined, "We colored folks 've learned not to wear out feelin's on our coat sleeves. 'N th' main thing is to know a man's heart is right. Th' res' doan matter. We're fellow-workers 'n friends, Tom, shoving' freight 'n organizin' th' working class, side by side."

As Tom came to know Fred better he found beneath his good-natured, easy-going exterior a rugged determination, a relentless purpose which drove him into denying himself food, in order to get books through which he plowed as laboriously and steadily as his forefathers had plowed the fields. Fred's plan was some day to go back south and organize his people into a great uprising against their white oppressors. This it was that drove him on. He must learn—learn.

"Say, maybe Tom, you'll go back with me, to that hole 'n we'll organize 'em together?"

"Gee, Fred. . . . Well, mebbe."

Once a month Fred spared the time from his books for a brief letter home, to Ma and Pa Morgan, Marthy 'n th' young'uns; and less frequently he had a note in reply, spoken out by the family and written down by Marthy, about happenings at Back Row. He told Tom some of these letters, and Tom, in turn, read him the few notes he had from Marge. In this way and through their many talks they were able to travel back and forth across the color line, studying and comparing the workers lives on each side. Gradually, for Tom, as for Fred, the line became an indistinct, shadowy thing, robbed of its former reality and terror.

This is what lay back of Tom's few words on the postcard, "Some town . . . Got a job, loadin' ships."

VII.

Ole Marge Goes over the Hill

SAL SAT, WITH HER HANDS over her eyes, her mind going round and round the same circle. There was no denying it any longer. Her sight was going on her fast. Little lights and lines danced before her eyes, and the eye-balls felt raw and inflamed.

She'd drawn-in for more than twenty years now, setting the same crude patterns. Even now, when she could no longer see distinctly, her nimble fingers ran in and out among the bobbins and needles, depending on long years of habit, for accuracy. Desperately she tried to keep her plight secret from the boss-man.

But, today she had made another mistake, and five yards of cloth had been ruined before it was caught, and she, who had prided herself on her errorless record, had had to re-set the pattern. There had been a warning note in what the foreman had said. Another blunder like that, and she'd be given her time. And if she lost out here, Sal knew she would never get into a mill again. She was into the forties now, and there were plenty of younger hands and eyes eager and waiting to take her place.

Weeks ago she had gone with Gertie into Greenville—her first trip into the city in a decade. At the five and ten cent store, she had tried on one pair of glasses after another, until she had found the ones that seemed best. But it looked-lak, Sal worried herself, that the things made her eyes worse. The children said she ought to see a real eye doctor. But however was she goin' to git to pay him?

Sal sighed. God's ways were shore hard to understand, sometimes. It tried one's faith.

That night a family council was held, and it was decided that Gertie was to find out a doctor, and on the coming Saturday, Ma was to go in to town again, and have him fix her up with glasses (they needed her earnings). They'd pay him five dollars down, and so much a week.

But the glasses were never obtained, for on Friday Sal was told she had made another mistake, and the next day she got her time. Where, Sal questioned in her anguish, where was God's hand in this? Parson Brown said he sent such things to test you. But hadn't she had more than her share?

Sal's figure slumped more than ever. She was done for. The mill had thrown her on the trash heap. She had given them all her days since early childhood, her eyes had gone into their cloth. Now she was done for. She'd spend the rest of her days like Granny, cooking, sweeping, mending, and taking in more boarders and waiting for her turn to die.

Marge, watching her, felt burning anger and despair. This was what it all came to, then. "Lucky, she's got chillen to care for her," Granny consoled.

"But, Granny, it means Ruth'll have to quit school 'n go to spinnin', too. We'll have to git her a special permit. 'N I'd set sech store by her goin' on." Yes, Marge had planned, Ruth should finish grammar school and maybe even go on, and get a teacher's job in the country, where eight years of training was all they asked of you. "If this ain't Crenshaw luck," Marge wailed.

"Not Crenshaw, chile—mill hand luck," Granny retorted, "doan it go on, ovah 'n ovah? But somewhars, thar's gotta be an end."

MARGE WAS ROUSED out of her despondency by the arrival of a package from Tom. "Oh, Granny, it's a book!" *The Jungle*, she read, by Upton Sinclair. Along with it, there was a scrawled note.

"Dear Sis, you always like to read. This here's a fine story. Tom."

The next few days Marge walked around like one in a dream. She dared not carry the book into the mill, but kept the light burning so late that Ruth and Granny complained that they could not sleep; and she was up before the others, in order to snatch a few pages before leaving for the mill. The work-a-day world around her grew indistinct, unreal, for she was far away, living and laboring with the stockyard workers in Chicago, and, finally taking part in their great revolt.

She read the book over again, aloud to Granny and Ruth, and the three lived it through together.

"Now, that thar Jurgis, he had the fightin' spirit," Ole Marge shook her head, sideways, then let out a long, subdued sigh.

Marge felt a change in her Granny. These past weeks she had become diff'rent somehow, silent, brooding. Going over to her, she slipped her head into her lap. "What's it, Granny. What's troublin' you?"

"Nuthin', chile, nuthin'."

"But thar is. I can feel it."

"It's jest an ole-oman's way, honey, to sigh sometimes." As Sal called her, Granny rose and started toward the kitchen.

She wavered, missed a step, and Marge caught her just in time to prevent her falling. Ole Marge smiled into the startled young face. "That warn't nuthin', chile. Jes' a speck o' dizziness. It's all gone now. Reckon I ain't so spry as I used to be."

The truth was, now that Sal had been turned out of the mill, Ole Marge felt in the way. It was high time she was off their hands. A family could hardly afford two 'round the house, now could they?

Marge, watching the disappearing figure, was sickened by a sudden doubt. Why, was Granny, her Granny, losing some of her strength?

SUMMER WAS HERE AGAIN.

Sal, Marge, Ruth, Billy and Sam were off on one of their Saturday gatherings of huckleberries. Uncle Mat had gone into town and would probably come home, with his pay half gone, and slightly tipsy. Granny couldn't stand the long walking.

"Billy, quit swingin' the pail so. It'll come off the handle." Sal felt glum and impatient. Billy grunted and gave it an extra heavy jerk. "I doan know what makes boys so aggravatin'!"

"Watch out, Sam!" Ruth screamed, but it was too late. Swinging around a curve in the road, a car swerved on them, knocking Sam flat. Without halting its pace, the car rushed on, leaving a cloud of dust in the walkers' throats and eyes.

"Ma Lawd-a-Mighty, Sam, you all-right?" Ma gasped. "Marge, run fer water." As they bathed his face and hands, Sam opened his eyes, and sat up. "I'm all right." They felt him all over. No bones broken, but plenty of bruises. "Jes' knocked the breath outta me, I reckon. Come on, les' go."

"No, Ruthie'll have to go with you back to the house," Ma declared. Sam was led away tearfully protesting.

"But fer all they cared, he could be daid!" Sal was indignant. "That's th' way with them city folks. Us on th' hill's no better 'n dirt under their feet."

As they trudged on, Billy asked, "Who-all was in that car? Did anybody see?"

"Looked-lak that Haines boy in his Pa's car, to me," Marge answered.

"Yah," Sal added, "'n that thar Lucy Martin what Tom used to run around with, was with him in the front seat, 'n he done have his arm 'round her. That's why he drove so wild. I allays did say she was a bad char-ac-ter, 'n 'd come to no good end."

"Oh, Ma, that ain't nuthin'. Lots of gals take rides, but they doan mean no harm."

"Wal, it doan smell right to me. Jes' lemme catch a gal of mine ridin' with them city boys! I tell you, a mill owner's son doan mess 'round with a mill gal fer no good."

As they hunted the luscious, purple berries, briars caught at their fingers and clothes, and the sun beat down on their heads.

Marge, absorbed in her own thoughts, did not think to watch Ma, on the chance of getting another glimpse of the lost girl peeping out of the old sunbonnet. It was as well, for Ma was completely engrossed in getting all the five pails filled in time for an early supper. The birds twittered and called. Sal, a habitual pucker between her straight brows, did not halt to listen. There was the week's ironing to finish, after the evening meal.

"MARGIE, THE MERRY-GO-ROUND'S HERE agin. Give us three cents so we can ride. Please, please!" Billy and Sam danced around her, impatiently, and then were off to the field their fares clutched tightly in their fists. The merry-go-round, a tin affair painted a bright red, bearing twelve ferocious horses, some with saddles and some pulling carriages, was paying its annual visit to Greenville mill villages. Billy and Sam climbed aboard and scrambled wildly for their chosen steeds. A crowd of white mill hands and nearby country folk clustered around the lemonade and popcorn stand, watched the whirling figures, and waved in answer to the youthful riders' salutations, while the pipes alternated between their two wheezy tunes, "Hot Time in the Old Town Tonight," and "Let Me Call You Sweetheart."

Some distance to one side stood a small gathering of Negro children and a few adults. They knew that after the merry-go-round man had exhausted all the possibilities of white customers, he would give them a chance to buy rides. Pa Morgan had brought Myrtle and Charlie, and his neighbor had come along with George. When Myrtle spied Billy and Sam riding, she tugged at her father's hand. "Come on, les' go home." "Why, Myrtle, you've been so crazy fer a ride. What's ailin' you?" But she begged so hard, and her distress was so real that Pa Morgan finally consented to return to Back Row with her, leaving Pa Johnson to wait with the two boys. Charlie threw back his shoulders. "They shan't spile it fer me," he resolved to himself, "guess ma three cents is as good as theirs, any day." But as he waited, and the half-hours dragged by, Charlie squeezed his pennies into his moist palm and wished himself anywhere but here.

ANOTHER VISITOR MADE his bi-annual visit to the mill hills. This time it was the medicine man, with his black silk hat, white vest, and sleight of hand tricks. After entertaining the assembled gathering with his magic, he launched into an eloquent speech. "You folks hyar at Greenville know I'm your friend. Yas-sir, I'm the poor people's friend, 'cause I know they needs 'em. Their way is hard 'n fraught with sorrow, 'n sufferin'. Knowin' this, I beseeched the good Lawd, 'n racked ma brains, how to serve you 'n Him better. 'N the Lawd answered my prayer." Dramatically he produced a bottle of liquid from under his black coat-tails, and held it up to the sunlight. "You see this, friends? This hyar's guaranteed, *positively* guaranteed to cure lung ailments, rheumatism, coughs 'n colds, 'n pleurisy, back ache, piles, 'n in fact it's a general all-round medicine. You may take ma word for it, swore on the Good Book. Now, knowin' mill folks 'n country people ain't got much money, this here's priced at the very minimum—yas-sir, the very minimum. Many men would try 'n sell this at a high price, to fill their pockets with gold. But me, I'm a God-fearin', church-belongin' man. So I give it to you—that's it, almost give it to you—fer one dollar a bottle." Rapidly he and his helper passed among the crowd, offering the cure-all.

As buyers proved not too many, he returned to his stand, placing on it a large container into which he poured another liquid. "Gather 'round, friends, 'n observe this other great discovery. You see hyar, a recent great discovery 'n invention of the leadin' scientists 'n doctors of medicine of the United States. In fact, to speak open with you, of the world. Now what you're axing yourself, can this be? I tell you, when I first heard of it, I drapped on ma knees, 'n with tears in ma eyes, 'n face lifted up, I gave thanks 'n shouted hallelujah to Jehovah, who lead the chillen of Israel out of Egypt, 'n was now gonna lead the mill 'n common people outta their misery.

"For—hyar is the way to tell if you or your loved ones got lung trouble, 'n sotch it quick, fore it's too late. 'N hyar, in this wonderful medicine I jes' tole you 'bout, is the shore 'n sartain cure.

"Now, I want to show you how it works. First I'll blow into this water, 'n if—*if* ma lungs is sound, the liquid'll remain as it is, clear 'n pure. But *if* I should be having germs in ma lungs, the germs'll clutter the liquid, 'n it'll go white 'n murky." All leaned close as the medicine man, Professor Simmons, blew down a tube into the vessel. Nothing happened, the water remained clear. "You see, ma lungs is hale 'n whole."

He poured out the liquid, and refilled the vessel. "Each time, to make sure," he explained, "it's got to be filled fresh. Now, who wants to be next? Come, doan hang back, but step right out." A woman shifted her child to her husband, and, while all held their breath, blew down the tube. The water clouded! "Oh, Lawd have mercy on ma po' chillen," she moaned, while her husband hurriedly purchased a bottle, "I knew the pain in ma chest meant trouble."

Many others followed, and with each test a fresh supply of liquid was poured into the container. Uncle Mat, learning the worse, hastened home for a dollar he had hidden away. Some found, to their relief, that the dread consumption, scourge of mill hills, had not yet touched them; but many more discovered to their terror, that the liquid clouded, from germs exhaled from their lungs.

Professor Simmons nearly depleted his stock. Not only did the afflicted buy, but a fever of buying passed through the crowd. Ole Miz Rhoads purchased a bottle for her daughter, drooping from heat in the weaving room; and Marge took a bottle for Granny's weakness and nagging cough.

The sales at Back Row were equally high. Aunt Polly was among the purchasers, for, as she remarked, "Neither me or George or Pa is ailin' now, but you can't tell what instant one o'us may be struck down, 'n it's allays bes' to be prepared."

"Ain't you got nuthin' fer the pellagry?" one inquired, "that's what mill hands need, a cure fer it."

"Sartainly, most sartainly, ain't I tole you this hyar medicine's the cure-all!" Professor went on his way, unmolested by mill sheriffs or town police, peddling his wares and giving thanks to the Lord. The liquid into which Professor Simmons and the spectators breathed who found themselves unafflicted was pure water; while that which clouded and grew murky was lime water, which ironically enough, clouds *only* when those with moderately healthy lungs breath into it. For breath exhaled from weak lungs lacks sufficient oxygen to interact with the lime water to produce the desired white effect. The famous medicine was also merely water, "seasoned 'n sweetened to taste."

BY DECEMBER, OLE MARGE'S COUGH shook her entire frame, and her eyes were bright with fever. Sal whined at the way she spilled things—everything was so dear in winter, there wasn't a drop to spare. But Ole Marge would not give in. "I'd bes' die in ma tracks," she thought, "ole horses cling to their traces."

Young Marge did all she could to spare her, running and fetching for her as much as possible in the hours when she was not at the mill. Wakened in the night by Granny's muffled coughing, she would get up to wrap the covering around her more securely, and run for the medicine.

"Granny, look what I've bought you." Marge held out a rose-colored shawl, and tucked it around her shoulders. There were tears in Granny's eyes as she thanked her. "But, honey chile, you shouldn't a-done it," she protested.

"Naw," Sal cut in sharply, "you shouldn't. You know every cent counts now."

"Ma!" Marge flared, and no more was said.

By February, Granny could not speak above a whisper, and do what she could, was no longer able to leave her bed. Marge watched over her every minute she was away from the machine. At night, when the coughing was worse, she would hold the now slight frame against her young chest, and croon to Granny as a mother does to a sick child, while tears splashed down on the tight little knot of grey hair.

Oh, the world would be a desperate place indeed, with no Granny in it.

The doctor who had come at Marge's insistence, after examining Granny, shook his head. "There's little can be done. Rest, sleep, plenty of the right food, and no worry might pull her round. But it's doubtful. I've seen others like her, who've simply lost the will to live."

After he left, Granny called Marge over, and reached out for her hand. "Doan take on so, baby. Ma time's come. I've had a long life, mo' years than most. Cotton mills took res' o' ma generation sometime back."

"Oh, Granny, Granny!"

"Doan, chile, doan. Thar, thar."

Gradually Ole Marge became more and more like a child, "cat-nappin'," as she called it, a good bit of the time, eating less and less, and her memory going back to her younger days, in the hills and first years at the mill. She would lie contentedly against Marge's shoulder while the girl hummed one of their favorite tunes. Sometimes she would whisper stories of times long past. Her hate of the mills grew on her, waxing in strength as her body waned.

There came the early morning when Marge was roused by Granny's feeble coughing and struggling for breath. "Better call your Ma," she gasped, "Ma time's come." Silently the household gathered round the bed.

"Uncle Mat, run fer the doctor."

"Naw," Granny's weak voice protested, "tain't no use."

"No doctor'd come this hour, noways, to a mill hill." Harry fumbled the bed post.

"Ma," Sal whispered, "kin you see me?"

"Naw, my sight's failin', failin'." Her breathing grew easier, weaker.

"Ma, what you see? Gona be peaceful ovah thar?"

"Doan see nuthin'. Marge, whar are you? Gimme your hand."

"Here, Granny, close by you."

"That's right, stay by me. . . . Hinry, that you? Young," she marveled, "like when we fust walked ovah the hill together." The last embers of departing life flared in her face and eyes. "Sal, my lil' gal, 'n Jackie . . . Red-bird. Never should-a been caged in the cotton mill. Sal . . ."

"Here I am, Ma." But Granny was not listening. "The mills took all, give nuthin'. The stinkin' mills . . ." She made an effort to rise. "I hates 'em."

"Oh, Ma," Sal was aghast, "doan die with hate on you."

This time Granny heard her. "Lawd help me, I'll hate 'em in the grave. Take all . . ." Her voice trailed off. "Lil' Marge?" "Here, Granny." "Doan moan fer me. I ain't feared to go. Never feart nuthin' in this world, or in next. Doan . . . I'm tired. . . . I wanna rest." Leaning over, Marge looked down into the dimming eyes for the last time. "Marge," Granny breathed, "remember," she made a last effort, "you promised."

VIII.

Young Marge and Bob

THE WEARY WINTER TOOK its yearly toll from Row Hill and Back Row, then gave way to a rainy spring. But it was still winter in Marge's heart. With Granny gone, and Tom far away, what was there in life for her but spinning, spinning, and moving on with the family in a vain search for a better break on the next hill, while winter turned into spring, year upon year, just to have summer come and be swallowed up by fall? And all the while, old age would be creeping up on her, with nothing between her and the poor house at the end of the road. For there would be no children to give her food and shelter in her old age. She would never marry, she vowed to herself. She'd not be like Ma and the other women. Never! Better be ridiculed as an old maid, than that. Life was bad enough without a string of lil'uns coming along as regular as the seasons, weighing you down and sucking your spirit.

Sex? Marge shuddered. What knowledge she possessed had been picked up from the kids in the street, or gleaned from observing her elders. The crowded household allowed of little privacy in such matters. Marge, as a child, had slept in the same room with her parents. One night she was wakened by the sounds of struggle and Ma crying, "Doan, Pa, doan, I'm a-scairt," and a muffled answer. Ma had gotten out of bed and run into the far corner, and Pa had followed. After awhile they had gone back to bed, and Marge, listening, cringed beneath her covers. Then she hadn't fully understood, but now she did. Sex—a forbidden, evil thing, that got you in the corner, and cursed you with extra mouths to feed.

She was going to keep clear. She knew about the carryins-on in the field beyond the mill in spring and summer nights, the scandals of babies without fathers, of city boys taking mill girls for rides. Marge held aloof. Being pretty and desirable as a "girl," this made her conscious. But disgust and fear made her cold, crushed back the strange feelings that welled up in her at the spring of the year. While others walked arm in arm across the fields or spooned beneath the moonlight, Marge pored over a book, or struck out across the fields, alone. Some called her hoity-toity, though they had to admit she was pleasant enough to talk with, at the mill or after church meetings. Because she was gay and glum by turns, Sal whined over her, and even hinted that she was "worrit if your mind is gittin' touched."

"Aw, Ma, fer Pete's sake, leave me be."

Everything went round and round, like the seasons. A monotonous tread mill, with her, Marge, and the other mill hands tromping out cloth. Where was any meaning in it all? Wearily she turned the matter over in her mind. Fight, Granny had said. But how? Everybody was so poor, so ignorant, and down-trodden. Could they ever learn to stick together? Marge struggled against a feeling of helplessness and despair that threatened to engulf her.

In school the teacher had told them about love of country, dignity of labor, and everyone having an equal opportunity to get ahead. Now these seemed just words. The America of

which the books and Miss Sanderson had told was quite unlike the one she knew, on the hill.

On Saturday afternoons, she'd tramp into Greenville and
brave the entrance to the austere-looking library, in search
for books which would throw some light on her problem. The
librarian gave her sentimental love stories of rich girls and
boys, or stories about college and the Wild West, an Elsie
book, "Three Little Women," Thomas Nelson Page, and "Bar-
riers Burned Away." What did all of this have to do with a
cotton mill girl?

Finally Marge took her copy of "The Jungle" with her, and
timidly offered it to the librarian. "Ain't you got any books like
this hyar one?" she inquired. The librarian voiced her horror
in a fifteen minute monologue, then pressed "When Patty
Went to Boarding School" into Marge's reluctant hands. After
this, Marge went less often to the city's centre of learning.

"Dear Tom," she wrote, "please send me another book like
the other one. How much it cost? I'll save up an pay you back.
When you comin to see us, like you said. No news here. Your
lovin sis, Marge."

But there was no reply. What could have happened?

Desperately, Marge turned to religion for peace and understanding. Ma found solace in it, why not she? With summer came the revivals. Every night for a week, meetings were
held in the company church and all turned out to hear the visiting preacher, who exhorted old and young to turn away from
sin and the ways of this world, and fix their eyes and thoughts
on the next. After the singing of many hymns, prayers and
collections, he launched into tearful stories of wayward sons,
daughters plunged in sin, sorrowing mothers and death-bed
repentances, while the audience moaned and wept with him.
Then, in contrast he waxed eloquent over the joys of "the land
whar all is res' 'n peace" and the dire fate of those whom Saint
Peter sent hurtling through space to the lower depths. He

pictured Jesus, arms open, waiting to rescue them. His audience was swayed, lifted up to the heights and plunged to the depths, swept completely off their feet. Forgotten for a few hours was the mill drudgery and their devastating poverty and ignorance, as the revivalist's voice rose and fell, sounding on their ears like poetry or a rushing waterfall. By the time he had reached the climax, moaning and cries of "Praise the Lawd," "Oh, Jesus, save this sinner!" accompanied by shuddering and jerking movements had spread throughout the church. Men and women were clasping each other by the hand or leaned, sobbing, against their neighbor's shoulder.

In a voice vibrating with passion, the pastor gave the invitation to come forward, "as we stand 'n sing, 'Why do you wait, dear brother?'" First bent figures left their seats and went up the aisle, followed by two young boys, paled by their conviction of sin. Girls, sniffling into their handkerchiefs or sobbing openly and unashamed, struggled to the front, while "Sisters" and "Brothers" moved in and out among the benches, joining the preacher in pleading with the sinners to "cast all your burdens on Him." One woman, holding her baby high over her head, half-stumbled down the aisles, shouting "Hallelujah, Hallelujah."

"Let us sing," the revivalist shouted above the tumult, "Are you weak'n heavy-laden, burdened with a load o' care?" Marge was caught up in the emotional fervor that was sweeping through the hall. Feeling strange, powerful emotions welling up in her, she struggled blindly against them. This must be the consciousness of sin? With a shuddering thrill, she felt herself give way, as the pious ones urged, "Doan hold out. It's th' devil promptin' you." Now she was swaying and chanting with the rest "Oh, Come to the Lawd Today," and surging forward, to the Sinners' Bench. At last she was saved, saved!

In through the church windows poured the rhythmic growls of the mill, where the night shift was at work, spinning and weaving cotton cloth for Mr. Haines. "Hallelujah, Hallelujah," shouted the revival meeting, as some threw themselves on the floor, twitching and sobbing with joy. "Growl, growl," rumbled the mill, as other repentant sinners reached high into the air, or threw their arms indiscriminately around one another.

The revivalist, approaching Marge, put his arms around her. "Dear Sister, receive the Savin' Grace of our Lawd Jesus." Involuntarily Marge drew back. The next night he again sought her out, and the next. Startled, she noticed he made a practice of bringing comfort to the young girls. A married man, with grown children, too, why did he do it? Frightened at her half-formed thought, Marge kept away from the remaining services, and Ma could not scold her into going or giving a sensible reason for staying away. "It's as I a-feart," Sal muttered to herself, "ever since Granny ceasted, Marge's gittin' quare. Thar's no two ways about that."

"It's been a wonderful week, a record o'soul-savin'," Sal and her neighbor agreed, "ain't so many gone forward at a Row Hill revival in these nine year." "Uh, huh, 'n that collection we took up of eighty-nine dollars 'n fifty cints, fer the visitin' parson, that was an outpourin' of the spirit, lak he said. He said he'll put this to the sum he's savin' up from meetin's like this 'un, to buy him 'n his wife a house 'n lot." When Sal repeated this at the supper table, Marge shifted restlessly in her chair. She couldn't really have been saved, to have such evil thoughts. Yet, why should mill folks, who had so little, deny their little ones to make presents to that huggin' pastor? He and his family were lots better off than anybody on Row Hill ever would be.

"It ain't two month," Sal complained later on, to her neighbor, "since the revival meetin's, 'n you could never tell we had one, from the carryin's on. Ole man Prescott is mistreatin' his ole 'oman agin, 'n sharp tongues 'n back-bitin' is flyin' all over the hill. The Devil 'n His Forces of Darkness is shore powerful, 'n hard to rout. Sech drinkin' 'n gamblin' over to the lodge too, whar the men's hangs out, a-Sadday night—it's a caution."

Tales of this evangelist drifted back to the village. Down in Georgia, so the story ran, he had gotten into trouble with a young girl and had left in a hurry, not even waiting for the baptizing of the converted! Sal was sure these stories were works of the Devil, but Marge wondered if there was not some fire in all this smoke.

IT WAS HOLY-NESS MEETIN' TIME, too, for those in Back Row. The company had not thought it advisable to build a church and hire a pastor for its colored families, so they traveled out to one in the country, where twice a month they attended preaching, along with Negro share croppers. The services and scene were similar to that at Row Hill, except the singing was more their own, and far more beautiful. At the close of the revivals, baptizing would take place on a Saturday afternoon, in a stream up the county.

At the Wednesday evening service, some rich white folks from Greenville came, with two out-of-town visitors, and sat in the balcony. They told the parson they had come to hear the singing and preaching, but then why did they exchange glances and hide their smiles behind their fans? Martha was not the only one who resented these white folks' curiosity and intrusion. "What they think we is, a circus?" But their resentment the Negroes hid behind a polite servility. For one visitor was young Elbert Haines, the mill owner's son, and another was a daughter of the banker, Mister Alexander, who owned the land which more than one share cropper tilled.

Martha caught Elbert Haines' eye on her, and trembled. For nigh a year now she'd kept out of his way, and the incident in the pantry she hoped he had forgotten. But lately she'd noticed his eyes again wandering in her direction. Martha slumped low in her seat, putting Mammy between her and young Haines' vision.

UNCLE MAT, HURRYING HOME at noon, noted a crowd around the Kendricks' door. Going over, he saw Miz Kendricks leaning against the door sill, and explaining rapidly in angry, helpless tones. "That thar loan shark come this mornin' while we-uns was at the mill 'n took all the furnishin's, 'cause we coulden pay him the dollar last week. Yes-sur, he dumped my baby 'n my sick husband on the bare boards, 'n even went off with the bed. What're we gona do?"

"The dirty, nasty thing."

"Them loan sharks is 'bout the ornerest men what ever lived, I reckon!"

"What're we gona do?" Miz Kendricks wailed, twisting her hands.

"Doan you mind. We'll fix it." While Uncle Mat passed around the hat, mill hands dug down into their jeans, overalls, and apron pockets, and as word traveled along the street, enough dimes and quarters were collected to equal the five dollars necessary, as the first payment on another lot of furniture. Beaming, Miz Kendricks rushed off to use the store phone, and by four o'clock another loan shark had "furnished the house complete," with bed, chest of drawers, table and chairs, on the five-dollar-down-one-dollar-a-week plan.

"I doan know how the poor'd ever manage without they helpen each other," Marge remembered Granny had remarked, when, during her illness the "Home Comfort" had been loaned the Crenshaws by the mill workers' Aid Society. The Comfort included a pair of sheets, bed-pan, and a small chest of medicine and bandages, and was passed from family to family, as the need arose.

During the summer months, like now, hill folks shared with one another the beans, corn, and "taters" which they grew in the little garden patches behind their houses or at the edge of the village. Together with berry-hunting and fishing on Saturday afternoons, living was easier in the summer, though the heat in the close rooms at the mills was harder to bear. The bosses had orders not to let the windows open, because a warm, damp atmosphere, although hard on human lungs, was good for the thread.

In ways like these, hill folks had learned, like the poor all over the world, to share and aid one another. It was a necessity, in order to be able to survive at all. Thus petty mean-ness, drunken-ness, selfish pinching and narrow-mindedness—products of a bare, sickly soil—are blended with kindlier traits. So poverty and common toil weaves its bonds and leavens the loaf which in good time rises.

At the very time Row Hill and Back Row were in the ecstactic throes of their annual revivals, some thousands of miles away, the furies of hell were being turned loose on mankind. For this was August, 1914, when the Wall Streets of Europe launched their death struggle for supremacy.

Although the papers blazoned the news, it meant little to Marge and the others. It all seemed vague, far-away, and rather senseless. Just because an arch duke got shot, Uncle Mat asked, did they have to start a war over that? When lurid stories of defenceless Belgium began to appear, arguments among the mill hands, gathered round the store in the evenings after work, sometimes waxed hot. But it was like arguing over the nature of the sun, or salvation, or some other remote question. While thousands in Europe were being rushed to the front, and slaughtering one another, the daily routine in the village went on as usual. By spring, however, the war had touched even Row Hill. Orders poured in, all mills went on double shifts or worked overtime, new cotton and munition plants sprang up over night. For when food and clothing are being destroyed, along with men, on a colossal scale, they have to be replaced. And it takes a whole industry to supply armies with death-dealing weapons.

"It's an ill wind blows nobody good," Uncle Mat reflected, "from what I hears from Slim Williams, who's back from Virginny, this here Mr. Dupont must be making a pile of money outta his gun factories."

"He says thar's bread lines 'n lotta men outta work in Baltimore," Harry put in.

"Is that so? Wal, we can't kick 'bout that. We got more work'n we kin handle, here at the mills. But a lil' mo' silver'd come in handy."

"You said it, Uncle Mat. But try'n get it!"

"Yah, I'spose." The old man spit neatly between the rails.

MARGE'S PRIDE IN HER independence was destined for a mighty fall. For the weekly shufflings of families in and out brought in the Gregory household, one of whom was a lad of nineteen, Bob. Coming home from work one Friday afternoon, Marge was startled from her hazy musings by a gay voice directing her, "Lassie, hand me that thar knife, will you, I drapped on the ground." Glancing over her shoulder, she spied a bronze-headed, merry-eyed lad grinning down at her. Bob was sitting astride all the Gregory's wordly belongings, which were stacked in rakish fashion in one of the moving carts which mill hands hire for such purposes.

"I'm needin' it," he explained, "to cut this here rope." Silently Marge reached over and handed him the knife. "Whew, what a day for movin'! But the sight of you makes me think this time it'll be worth it." Marge blushing in spite of herself, tossed her head.

"With that tongue, mebbe you're Irish?"

"Yes 'n no. Scotch-Irish. Got all the failin's of both. Say, is all we hear 'bout this hill true? They're needin' extry hands, ain't that?"

It was a second before Marge answered. "Yah, I reckon they is. That is, I hear they're wantin' them. We're workin' overtime." (What'm I standing here for, talkin' with a stranger?) Marge started off.

"Heh, wait a minute. Where do you live, me pretty one?"

Not answering, Marge quickened her steps.

"Oh doan think you'll be rid of me so easy-lak," Bob's voice trailed after her, "if I warn't a-top this furniture, you'd be payin' fer leavin' me so."

"That ain't so easy as you might think," Marge retorted angrily. The anger stayed by her, but she wasn't sure if she was not more provoked at herself than him. Resolutely she determined to put that impudent fellow out of her mind. But on Sunday morning in church she caught herself looking around for the sight of him. He was not to be seen. Those rovin', care-free kind never were. Maybe he'd only be in town a few weeks and then gone. She hoped, Marge told herself, that he would be.

Monday night, at the close of work, Marge felt a hand on her elbow and a gay voice demanding, "Kin I walk up the street your way?" "Naw," Marge answered shortly, "'n I'll thank-ya to drap my arm." The boy's low whistle followed her up the dirt street. Before the week was out, he had arranged with his new friend, Allen, who boarded at the Crenshaw's, to bring him around to the house. "Meet my friend, Bob Gregory," Allen announced, introducing him to each in turn. As he shook Marge's hand Bob grinned, putting a special emphasis on the words, "Pleased to meet-cha." The girl found herself laughing back, "The same to you." But the troubled look had not left her eyes nor did it in the days that followed, except for rare moments when she reached out eagerly, thought-free, toward the bright unknown which beckoned her on.

Such a moment was the hay-ride, when twenty young folks from the hill and Farmer Jones' place nearby had packed into the Jones' wagon and gone jogging down the roads behind his two work mules, frolicking in the straw and warbling sentimental songs at the harvest moon which rested low in the sky, like a monstrous orange waiting to be plucked. Bob was pressed close to Marge's side, one arm along the board behind her shoulders, his warm breath fanning her cheek as he joined ardently in the old favorite, "Let Me Call You Sweetheart, I'm in Love With You." With one hand he was teasing her neck and ear with strands he had pulled from their soft couch. Marge sat quietly, drinking in the smells of the new-mown hay and of the grey-blue fields and black woods which slipped past in magic succession, and marveling at the delicious, terrifying sensations of his nearness.

But the routine of the mill and house broke the spell which the night had woven, and Marge, panicky, took to flight, abruptly refusing all the boy's endeavors at further friendliness. Puzzled and chagrined, Bob stopped his visits to the house, transferring his attentions to Becky Smithers who lived up the street. Often in the evenings he would stroll past the Crenshaws', pulling at his companion's arm while she laughed loudly at the sallies he whispered into her ready ear. Marge gave no outward signs of minding this sudden desertion, even when the girls at the mill tried teasing her about "Easy Come 'n Easy Go," and "that thar Bob Gregory shore has a takin' way with the ladies."

Once more she took to her lone walks along the country roads, and worried Sal with her brooding.

At last there was word from Tom. "Been sick, so coulden write before. Hope to see you soon, will bring some books.

How's all at home, I'm alrite now, Tom." As a matter of fact, Tom had been with Fred in the workhouse for three months, on the charge of resisting an officer. At a street meeting he had gone to Fred's aid when two of the blue coats had decided to "learn this nigger some love fer his country."

"Well, boys," Jake greeted them on their release, "get ready. It ain't gonna be long now, till this land of the free is in the fracas too."

Tom coming home! The dull cloud oppressing Marge's spirits lifted, she felt happier, stronger than at any time since Granny had left her. Tom, her old playmate, coming home with books and news. This Bob Gregory could just take his walking papers and clear out—Tom was coming home!

Bob, however, had no intention of leaving Row Hill, or Marge either—except temporarily—"to larn her a lesson." This reserved, flaxen-haired girl with her shadowed eyes drew him strangely. At a Young People's candy pull which occurred late in the fall, he maneuvered to become her partner. As they pulled the sticky molasses their fingers touched and their eyes gripped, and Bob, his own knees trembling, exulted at the unwilling flush that swept over Marge's face and neck and the unsteadiness of her voice and hands. She couldn't hide it, she was glad to have him back!

Once again the hill observed them walking home from work together, bronze head bending close to flaxen one; and Bob hanging around the Crenshaw house in the evenings, making even Sal smile with his gay nonsense. For a few weeks Marge lived each day as it came, happily and to the full; then, startled afresh into a realization of what was happening to her, drew back and took to flight. Bob, perplexed and deeply hurt, this time kept stubbornly on the trail. Now the old game of hunted and hunter was reenacted, although, as the youth sensed, it was not mere coquetry but genuine dread which sped the girl's footsteps.

"What's it Marge?" he asked her once. They were walking across the now barren, hardened fields of early winter. "What makes you act so diff'rent from other girls?" His voice lowered. "You know I'm crazy bout you, 'n," now he spoke banteringly, "thar's no use you denyin' you likes me, for I kin see it in your eye."

"You flatter yourself, Bob Gregory," she jerked her arm free, "You think any girl you want'd eat outta your hand. You're that conceited!" Suddenly he threw his arms around her, pressed his body hard against hers, kissing her desperately, hungrily. For a moment she responded, then gasping, struggled away. "Oh . . . You . . . You!" One hand across her eyes she started blindly across the fields, then, tripping, she slid to her knees and sat crouched, motionless, on the hard earth.

Disconcerted, Bob kicked with one foot against a clod of stubble and waited for her to rise. "Aw, Marge. Say . . . doan take it thisaway." When still she didn't respond, he dropped to the ground beside her, gently touching her shoulder. "Marge," he called softly, "Marge . . . honey . . . I'm sorry. Honest. Woan you speak to me?" There was no answer. "Marge, I'll not do it again, that is" (even now his sense of humor broke through irresistably), "that is, unless you want me to."

At this she sat up, eyes and cheeks ablaze. "I thought that'd get you," he teased, but his bantering tone fell away when he saw the misery looking out of her face. "Listen, honey," his voice now was gentle, awed, "I'd not want to hurt you fer anything. I've run around some, but . . . but I never meant it like this before." He slipped over the turf nearer to where she sat, huddled up like an old woman. "Because, you see," he hesitated, then whispered huskily, "because lil' Marge, I love you."

She could feel his breath on her cheek, like that night on the hay ride; although now it came in quick, breathless irregularity like a child's. Why, he was frightened, too. For some reason, this gave her courage.

Lil' Marge. No one had called her that since Granny had died.

"You like me some . . . doan you Marge?" Her face turned from him, she nodded. Searching, he found her hand. "Mebbe more'n a little?" Again she nodded. "Woan you say it?" he pleaded. There was no answer. Gladness, desire struggled against tormenting fear. Oh, how could she ever make him understand?

"What is it, Marge?" Girls were sure queer. "Was I too rough or sudden-like? Seemed lak a feeling went through me." Her palm felt moist, hot against his. "I woan again like that."

Marge turned toward him. "Please Bob. I can't say why. But just-doan."

"All right," he agreed. Yet, as they walked silently back toward the village, both knew in their hearts it was a futile promise. For the yearning that was in them, growing with each month that passed, was not to be denied.

Very soon all of Row Hill took it that Marge Crenshaw and Bob Gregory were as good as engaged. Sal, disgruntled, tried questioning her daughter, but all the information she was able to obtain was that Marge had no intention of marrying anybody. "Leastways, not fer another year," Sal counseled, "till you're eighteen." "Not next year, nuther," the girl retorted, "Bob knows I ain't aimin' to git married. We're just good friends." Sal slammed the lid down on the kettle, "Wal, of all fool notions, this hyar's the beatin'est yet," but her daughter had already fled beyond earshot.

IX.

Lynch Terror

THE MONTHS HAD PASSED over Back Row with the same monotonous tread with which they bore down on the rest of the village. There were a few more toddlers around the doors—part of the yearly spring crop which sprang up like dandelions only to be struck down by the grim reaper almost as ruthlessly as the gale tosses the bloom of wild flowers across the fields. Some new faces and families in the shacks had come to take the place of those vacated by one moving on to another village or back to share-cropping, or to that dark country from which there is no return. There were a few more leaks in the patched roofs, and an annual increase in the race of flies and other of nature's small creatures which pester human habitations of the poor. And Edna Jergen and her brood had been deserted by her man who, tired out with the battle against want and too many mouths to feed, had shoved out in the night and left her behind to struggle it out alone.

As Aunt Polly Johnson put it, "Jes' workin', bornin', courtin', marryin', dyin', 'n more workin'," that was life at Back Row, varied sometimes by singing in the dusk and dancing to Uncle Ben's banjo. And always there glowered over all the fearful shadow of caste; the white man's hatred and the black man's bitterness, intermingled with dread.

LIFE IN THE MORGAN HOUSEHOLD moved on as usual. Pa was still pushing cotton bins and Ma now back at the mill, sweeping lint and thread along its worn mill floors. Martha was cleaning and waiting on the women folks up at the Haines, while Charlie and Myrtle were now big enough to hire out in the fields in summer, in the winter months trudging three miles to the one colored school in the country. Here sixty-five youths ranging in years from seven to fourteen were crowded into one room, sitting on benches or grocery boxes, while Miss Jane Grey, the perfumed, sleekhaired teacher from Richmond endeavored to instruct six different grades in the mysteries of the three R's and American history.

Miss Grey sighed as she faced her solemn-eyed, eager pupils. There were no desks, only a handful of books, and she had had only seven years of schooling herself. She could get no help from the county superintendent, a white man, and as for the state superintendent, he had publicly stated more than once that it wasn't necessary to have any laws requiring colored parents to send their children to school, they seemed only too ready, as it was. As soon as work in the fields started, school must close, for her sixty-five pupils would be busy in the cotton rows, from sun to sun. Then she would seek work in the mill or as a maid, until the next five and a half months of school came around.

MISS GREY HAD STARTED OUT with high ideas of helping her people, but the grind and narrow environment had reduced her vision to one ambition: to get a normal school license and go into a city school and away from this sodden routine.

The Johnson family were still living next door to the Morgan's and Pa's ready laugh and humorous stories were well matched by Ma Johnson's dreary predictions and her detailed narratives of all the murder and crime cases which the local press supplied. She was always on the track of the one or two papers which reached Back Row and sending George scurrying for cast-off sheets in town. It was a familiar sight to see Aunt Polly of an evening puffing at her home-made pipe while one of the younger ones spelled out the day's happenings. Her memory was nothing short of remarkable, for although she had never taken any of the correspondence courses so widely advertised "to improve your memory in one evening," she could relate almost word for word all the evidence produced in a divorce suit or murder trial, giving names and dates with careful accuracy. In this way she won a morbid pleasure out of what otherwise seemed to her a dull existence.

She had also amassed many choice tales of white folks' doings, most of which she had gathered in her years of work as menial in their households, and a few of which were myths that blended awful truth with weird fancy of the evils practiced against the colored people by their white masters. Such were the stories she told of medical students kidnapping Negroes by night, hanging them by their hands and letting them die by inches as blood dripped from wounds in their feet. Then, Aunt Polly said, the dead man or woman was used as a "stiff," for them to cut open and go exploring about their insides. For days after she told this story Myrtle, George and Charlie would be afraid to venture beyond sight of the cabins. Also there were accounts of lynchings. The cruelty and horror of these, even Aunt Polly found it impossible to exaggerate.

This afternoon Aunt Polly, on her way home after returning the white folks' washing, stopped to pick up a crumpled newspaper which she smoothed out carefully and slipped under her apron. When again on Back Row she took it out to look at the pictures and speculate on the choice bits of news it might contain. Here, at the top of the page was a picture of a woman in ear-rings and low-cut dress. "Um," Aunt Polly ruminated, "that's a society lady or chorus gal. That'll be a divorce or breach of promise suit, or mebbe a charity ball. 'N this here fat man, with his watch chain 'n puffs under his eyes, likely he's some mill owner what's ceasted. Or, mebbe he's gittin' brought into court fer bigamy or crooked dealin's. Or mebbe it ain't nuthin', jest he's give money to the church, or buyed hisself another work-house." Next she turned to the funnies, chuckling over the cartoons and imagined sayings.

Before the next picture she stopped short. It was a dull photograph, taken at night by means of a flash, revealing a dark form, hanging limp from a tree, at which flames licked greedily while white-hooded figures crowded around, feeding the fire and posing for the photographer.

"Lawd-a-Mercy," she moaned, "Po' fella . . . Gawd rest his soul in peace." Slowly she folded the paper and lay it aside for Marge to read to her that evening after work.

When the news spread that there had been another lynching, nearly all of Back Row crowded around Aunt Polly's door stoop to hear the details. Angry terror once more held sway. The Negro lynched, so Martha read them, had been accused of killing a white farmer in a quarrel over the wages due him. "Fer once they couldn't say none of their lyin' tales bout rape," Ma Morgan muttered. Aunt Polly declared that the man had no business holding out for his wages, better be cheated than strung up. A number agreed with her, though Uncle Ben remarked that it's hard sayin' what any man or woman 'll do till the time comes.

THE LANDSCAPE WAS BLURRING in the first half-hour of dusk as Martha hastened across the town and along the road which leads to Row Hill. She must give notice the end of this week and leave the Haines' household for good'n all. Even if it meant Mammy 'n Pappy'd have to leave Back Row, she dared not go on.

She had promised Miz Haines to stay on three more weeks, right up to the time that she 'n Jim was gettin' married. But now she daren't, not with that young massa tryin' to git fresh again. Why wouldn't he leave her alone?

Martha hesitated before the short cut through the woods which she sometimes took, though never after dark. Tonight, something prompted her to go the longer, safer way.

Yah, she'd have to tell Jim 'n the others 'n they'd be put-out that she hadn't told 'em sooner.

Hearing a car tearing down the road behind her and two voices high on the air, Martha stepped to one side to let it pass. Then, with a sickening pounding at her temples and stomach, she recognized young Haines and his chum. Quickly she jumped back into the bushes—but not quickly enough for Haines had also recognized her. There was a sound of grinding brakes, as the car lurched and came to a standstill.

What should she do,—run or stay still. Which was worse? Mebbe they mean no harm.

"Hello, you pretty nigger!" Haines called, coming toward her where she hung back among the dusty bushes.

"Please, now, Mister Elbert, I ain't troublin' you. Please leave me be." Seeing the drunken leer in his eyes, curving his mouth, the girl turned and struck blindly into the woods.

"Not so easy, you bitch," Haines snarled, and the two men started after her, cursing at the briars and underbrush which tore at their hands and clothes. Hearing the crash in the bushes behind her, panic seized her. "Help! Help!" she called, then clamped her hand over her mouth. Fool, to give them her direction. "Coming! Coming!" her pursuers taunted, while the crashing grew, louder, nearer. Oh my gawd, Pappy, Jim where are you now? Lawd Jesus, help 'em hear my cries.

If only she threw them off her trail . . . get through the woods and to the other side.

The moon looked down through the treetops from a darkening sky. The birds, roused by the tumult of breaking branches and rushing bodies chattered excitedly to one another. Squirrels raced to the tree-tops, and a hoot-owl blinking slowly sent out his warning cry into the gathering night.

Martha, tripping over a root, fell flat, then was up in a flash and on. But she had lost her direction, the woods she knew so well had suddenly become a strange land. The running behind her grew closer and closer. Oh, Lawd Jesus, have mercy, Jim—Jim.—

Now they were up with her. Terror gave way to rage as Martha turned to meet her pursuers. Grabbing a heavy stick, eyes staring, her back against a pine trunk, she gasped, "Come a step nearer 'n I'll crack your skulls plum open!"

"You will, huh?" young Haines' face was an ugly sight, scratched and convulsed with passion and hate. As he sprung directly at her, Gross, his companion, creeping upon the girl from behind wrenched the stick from her upright arm. Struggling and screaming she was thrown flat, Haines astride her, tearing at her clothing while Gross silenced her cries.

Finally, they choked her, making sure that she would never be able to spread any ugly rumors. Wiping the blood from their hands and brushing off their clothes, they started back through the woods to the car.

"Say Gross, you suppose anybody saw the car standing there?" Gradually what they had done broke through their inflamed brains.

"Naw. The dirty wench, to try 'n slam your bean. I choked her proper fer that!"

"Dam that hoot owl. Come on, can't you hurry faster?" Young Haines stumbled ahead.

Gross snickered nervously. "Say, El, did-ya ever see prettier breasts?" His companion shook him violently. "You dam fool, keep your mouth shut . . . You doan know nothin', see?" Glumly they hurried on. Seated in the car once more, young Haines exclaimed. "By gosh. We forgot all about the dance at the Country Club tonight, and our dates . . . Listen, Gross, that's our alibi. We're been at the club all evening!" The motor purred, the car speeded back toward town.

Rapidly they changed into fresh dress suits. "What're we gona do with these bloody things?" Gross whispered, "Is there a reliable tailor in town?"

"No jack ass, we'll burn 'em, tomorrow. Come on, we're late enough as it is. The girls'll raise a row for keepin' 'em waitin'.'"

While the car glided over the sandy roads, Martha's unseeing eyes stared up out of a swollen, blotched face at the stars which shone quietly down through the tall southern pines. The birds settled themselves once more for the night, unmindful of the broken body which rested on its soft bed of pine needles.

MA MORGAN WALKED NERVOUSLY up and down near the shack, peering into the dusk for the sight of Martha's swinging figure. "Pa, what you reckons's keeping Marthy?"

"Nuthin, honey, 'cept you know they had a big dinner party up to Haines' fer supper. Doan worry, she'll be along soon. I'll jest walk over to meet her 'n we'll be back directly."

Beyond Ma's sight, Uncle Ben quickened his pace, keeping a sharp eye out for his daughter. There was no sign of her. Mebbe he should have gone for her tonight—no colored gal was safe in the white well-to-do section after dark. No law would come to her aid. Martha's smiling gentle face rose before him—the apple of his eye, Ma teased him.

By the time he had reached the Haines' estate, Uncle Ben was almost running. The big white house was all alight, from within came sounds of laughter and singing. He made his way around the back, to the servants' quarters.

At his query for Martha, cook's eyes grew big. "Lawsy, Mister Morgan, she left here pretty nigh two hour ago. Jest about dusk. She must've stop fer visitin' somewhar?" Throwing a shawl over her shoulders she added, "I'll jest come with-ya."

As they hurried along, she tried to down their growing fear. If Marthy hadn't gone visitin', then mebbe Jim had got off unexpected 'n the two of 'em was strollin' home, or—"You sho' a got a fine gal, Mister Johnson, I set a heap by her. Sweet tempered 'n willin'."

"That's right. Mis' Lancey, they doan come no finer'n my lil gal." Mebbe he'd missed Marthy on the road, mebbe he'd find her home when they got there.

As they neared the shacks, Ma ran out to meet them. "Whar's Marthy?"

"Ain't she here?"

"Lawd in heaven, what coulda happened?" Ma wrung her hands distractedly.

"Thar, thar, Ma we'll find her in no time." Uncle Ben tried to steady the arm he put around her.

In short order a searching party was organized: Uncle Ben, Earl Perkins, who'd lost his wife and baby sometime ago, and the two Hughes boys (Uncle Joe was down with the fever). Young Phil Hepburn was sent after Jim, to the farm three miles away.

With lanterns and heavy sticks they set grimly out. None thought of asking help from the law. That was for white men.

While Charlie and Myrtle clung to her ample sides, Ma Morgan sat rocking back and forth, staring ahead at some fearful spectre. Miss Lancey, Aunt Polly and the Hughes women crouched nearby. The oil lamp sputtered and flared, casting weird shadows on the wall. Ma Morgan loomed like some grotesque giant, making mysterious passes in the air.

Once in awhile some one broke the heavy silence to advance another reason why Martha might be late—any reason but the one at which Ma Morgan stared so hopelessly.

One by one the reasons were exhausted. The muffled sobs of the children grew louder, songs of weeping and praying broke loose in the shack.

Uncle Ben and Earl Perkins were the ones who several hours later stumbled over Martha's body. One swing of their lanterns over the swollen face and mutilated form, and Uncle Ben dropped beside his dead girl. His body writhed, his hands clutched and tore at the mossy earth. The others, roused by Earl's hoarse cry, came running.

Jim, for a moment not realising that Martha was dead, gathered her in his arms, pleading, "Marthy—sweetheart— here's your Jim, come to take you home. . . . Marthy, can't you hear me?" The men turned away, muffling their sobs. Roused, Jim reached for one of the lanterns propped against a tree trunk. As he raised it in the air, the shadows about him lifted. Throwing it from him in horror he lurched to his feet, his rigid arms holding the girl's body high above their heads.

"Whar's the white beasts that done this? Whar is they?"

"The bastards—the cowards—whar is they?"

Uncle Ben crawled to his knees. "Jim . . . Jim . . . what they done to our lil gal." His voice broke, he slipped back toward the earth, but Earl grabbed at one of his hands, wrenching loose an object which glistened among the earth which he had torn from the sod. "Look," he gasped, "they musta drapped this." By the dim light of the lanterns he made out the lettering on the gold handle of the pen knife:

To Elbert Haines, From Mother, Xmas, 1915.

With an oath Jim forced the body into the kneeling man's arms and started running toward the road. The Hughes boys raced after him, calling, "Jim . . . Wait . . . Wait . . . Doan do nuthin' rash . . . Jim . . ." By the time they reached the road, his powerful figure was a mere speck on the white stretch before them.

"We'll never catch up with him, now."

"Naw ... By gorry, he's right. I'd do the same in his place."

"Yah, I reckon. Even though he'll get strung fer it."

Silently they rejoined the others and the group started toward Back Row, bearing their burden. As they neared the shacks, Uncle Ben halted. "Ma ... this'll ..." "Yah, Uncle Ben, you go ahead. ... We'll come later." Slowly the stricken man dragged himself on. The sky was growing yellow in the east. Was it only last week he had played for the young folks, and they had frolicked beneath the moon? Now ...

Ma Morgan, at the first faint sounds of his heavy footsteps, bounded from her chair and rushed forward to meet him.

THE DANCE AT THE COUNTRY CLUB was at its height when Jim crept along the shrubbery, across the dim lawn and into a clump of bridal wreath bushes which stood against the building between an open window and the wide veranda with its high, colonial pillars. Completely surrounded by their white blossoms, he crouched on all fours and struggled to quiet his hurried breathing. His brain was on fire, yet cold and hard as the steel plow which he drove up the furrow.

Through the open windows and into the sultry night drifted the tones of a wailing saxaphone, "You Made Me What I Am Today, I Hope You're Satisfied."

Jim reached in his overall pocket, then drew his rifle across his knees. His aim at the foxes who came foraging among the farmer's chickens had never failed him. Surely it wouldn't fail him tonight.

Cautiously he drew back the bushes and looked through the window into the ballroom. Where, among the whirling couples, was his man? Girls with dazzling white arms and necks, be-jeweled women in their satin evening gowns swung past, their marcelled heads pressed against the white bosom fronts of their swallow-tailed partners. Along the walls stood stiff palms and three equally stiff and dowdy chaperones. At both ends of the hall were tables containing large bowls of heavily-spiked punch and trays of wine glasses. Obviously more than one couple had imbibed too freely, for many lurched slightly as they shufled around the floor, collided with other dancers, and clutched one another in ever more amorous embraces, half-leaning on their partner or any who came within reach. This was the cream of Greenville society.

A branch across his chest and covering his face, with only his eyes glittering through, Jim peered about for his man. Gawd, what if he weren't here!

The violins and saxaphone died away, the dance had ended. Drawing back in the bushes as a couple came near the window, he heard a male voice drawling, "Shay, I heard another good nigger joke today . . ."

Nigger joke! Nigger joke! Marthy's broken body . . . Nigger joke . . . His brain reeled, snapped back into place.

With a crash of cymbals the music re-commenced—this time a jazz one-step, "Everybody's Doing IT—Doing What? Turkey Trot!"

One woman with brilliantly-painted cheeks glancing coyly over her companion's shoulder, stiffled a surprised out-cry. She had seen two black eyes glaring through that open window! Her companion laughed at her. "Too much hootch, that's what's wrong with you." Nevertheless he and another man searched the bushes, but there was no one there.

Jim, lying face-down under the veranda steps held his breath, inwardly cursing his carelessness. He must get his man.

Again the dance ended, and couples wandered across the porch and out onto the lawn.

"Oh El Haines," a soft voice giggled, "you're such a kidder."

Jim sprung from his hiding place. In the full light which streamed from the dance hall stood a girl and alongside, his man. Bringing his rifle level with his shoulder and taking deliberate aim, Jim pulled the trigger. "You rape-er 'n murderer!"

At the first shot young Haines slumped to his knees. The last two were fired into his prostrate body. Panic and confusion broke loose among the revellers.

Slipping back into the bushes Jim made his way rapidly from the club and back to the country road.

Nigger joke . . . Why hadn't he kicked him in the face, choked his white throat? . . . *Nigger joke* . . .

The pounding at his temples blurred his vision. His mind dulled, clung tenaciously to one thought. He must warn Back Row, then make for the woods.

On the dance veranda, Gross, between drunken sobs, poured out the story. "That nigger's kinsfolks did this to Haines."

In the greying light the shacks stood silent, deserted. All except one. Their occupants had taken hasty council, thrown a few belongings into a sheet or head shawl and fled in the wagons which the Hughes boys had quietly seized from two neighboring farmers. With a few hours' start, they could make the next town and hide among friends till the terror died down. Miss Laucey had gone to friends in Greenville.

What could thirty adults and five shot guns do against a wrecking mob of several hundred whites, reinforced by the law? One or two hot-heads were for fighting it out, "But thar'd be no fair fight, jest a massacre," the others retorted angrily.

The wagons were full, all except the Morgans were aboard. "Hurry up, git in 'n let's be off," the driver urged. Ma Morgan drew herself up and scanned the black horizon. "Me 'n Pa is stayin' behind," she answered, "till Jim comes." In vain the others argued, pleaded. Uncle Joe propped on a pallet, wept with his helplessness, begging to remain behind also. Uncle Ben reached over the wagon's side to grip his hand. "Good-bye, Joey." The reins tightened, and the mules were off.

Myrtle and Charlie slipped from around the out-houses. "Chillen!" Ma's eyes started in horror, "how'd you git out of that wagon? Ain't we told you—" They threw themselves on her. "Ma, Pappy, we had to stay by you."

Silently, swiftly they set about their grim work. It would be an hour or longer before Jim could reach here. Pa Morgan went into the fields and began digging while Ma collected provisions and wrapped them securely in a grey blanket. This done, she joined her husband and the two dug frantically, the tears and sweat dripping from their faces over their hands and into the open grave. This task done, they carried Martha's shrouded form from the shack and lowered it into the earth. Gently, hurriedly, the grave was re-filled. "Lawd . . . Gawd," Ma sobbed, but the prayer died on her lips. They placed their shovels aside. Pa hesitated. "We gotta tromple it 'n bring that chicken coop, so's *they* can't find it."

Now there was nothing to do but wait for Jim. "Ma," Uncle Ben urged, "go ahead with the chillen." Slowly she shook her head. Somewhere a cock crew, it must be near dawn.

With a dull thud Jim threw himself against the door-sill.

"JIM, YOU GOT HIM?" He nodded, gasping for breath. The woman pressed the blanket into his hands. "Here, provisions. Be off." His eyes cast wildly around the cabin. "Whar's— whar's?" Pa Morgan shoved him through the doorway. "Safely buried. . . . Run, man, soon they'll have the bloodhounds. Make fer the haystacks till nightfall. We'll blur the trail."

As his foot-steps grew fainter, disappeared, the children and their elders smeared salt pork over the door-stoop and up the path in the direction he had gone.

"Now, Ellie, we'll make off." But it was too late. The sound of motor cars and barking dogs drew rapidly closer.

"Charlie, Myrtle—you all we got. If you love your Mammy, hide thar till I tells you to come out."

Uncle Ben placed his shot gun on the kitchen table. As the mob surged around the shacks, Ma Morgan stepped out upon her door-stoop. "What you-all want?" she demanded. Her face was yellow, drawn, but her figure stood erect, defiant. *"Mebbe you come to see what that Haines bastard did to my gal?"* Pa Morgan stepped close beside her.

The crowd snarled, surged forward. Only a few wore masks. All of the business section of Greenville had been mobilized, as well as the mill and county sheriffs.

"We come fer that nigger. Whar is he?" Two men in dress suits jumped on the door-stoop. "He ain't here, 'n he ain't been here," she told them.

"That's a lie. You god dam nigger, we'll make you talk!" Pa Morgan raised his shot gun, but it was smashed from his hands, and twelve men bore him to the ground, kicking at his ribs, head, and sexual organs. As his wife bit desperately at the wrists of his assailants, a white man with a curse brought the butt end of his gun down against her skull. Screaming, Myrtle and Charlie rushed from the cabin. Grabbing his father's banjo, the boy swung it to right and left. It jangled faintly as its battered sides were grabbed and tossed aside.

Whipping out his revolver, one sleek-haired youth fired rapidly into the four prostrate bodies. A half-dozen grabbed at his arm. "Wait, you fool. They shouldn't die so easy." Uncle Ben bound but not gagged was tied to the rear of a Packard. As the car tore over the road his body dragged, then jolted in the air. Curses and drunken yells broke upon the sleeping country-side.

"Hell, the woman's done fer, 'n the brats too. . . . Now fer the nigger." Those remaining behind ransacked the other cabins and swore at the dogs which found it hard to pick up the scent. A shack was fired, but the sheriffs soon smothered the blaze. "You blasted idjits. Doan you know this here is mill property?!"

The motor party, finally tiring of their game, bore Uncle Ben's dying body to the woods—the very woods in which seven hours earlier he had stumbled on Martha's body. Should they hang him or burn him, they argued among themselves. Finally a rope was tossed over a limb and around his neck. "Now pray, you gol dam nigger. Pray." Propped against the trunk, his eyes closed, Uncle Ben pressed his lips together. "Then dance, you black-faced devil." They drew their guns. When he did not move they fired at his legs, breaking his shins. With a moan, he tipped forward. "Here, quick, or we'll be too late." The body was tossed aloft, and Uncle Ben Morgan—banjo picker, mill hand, and story-teller—kicked feebly, then hung limp while bullets rained into his face and sides.

Jim, however, robbed the mob of their prey. When the dogs had once more picked up his trail, and he found fifty armed, frenzied men closing in on him, and his gun emptied of all but one shot, he turned the last on himself. "You'll never hang this nigger," he yelled, "my turn at a nigger joke."

X.

After-Math

WHEN NEWS OF THE PREVIOUS NIGHT'S happenings reached the white section of Row Hill, talk was rife and opinions sharply divided. Little groups of mill hands would gather after work on the porches or around their supper tables and discuss in hushed, agitated voices. They knew better than to even whisper about it at the mill.

Two of the mill hands, who had been hanging around a pool room in Greenville that eventful night, had joined the lynchers. To their stark account as eye-witnesses there was soon added the story of Martha's death at the hands of the murdered mill owner's son.

"What did you two mix up in it for?" Bob demanded of the village participants. "Twarn't none of our business." Many shared this opinion, but some felt otherwise. "Say, we got to keep these niggers in their place, ain't we?" Billy and Sam listened in silence, occasionally shivering as with the cold. Their former playmates kicked in the face ... murdered!

"That Haines boy got what was comin' to him," young Allen declared. "Now he won't be able to do no more devilment. I don't blame that darky. I'd done the same in his case." The argument became heated. No one defended Haines. "Everybody knows he was a rotter," but a few felt that, "No matter what had happened, no nigger got the right to shoot a white man."

Old Mrs. Turpen hitched herself forward. "This here lynching business, I'm agin it. It ain't no civilized way to act."

Uncle Mat bit off a chew of tobacco and slowly scratched his head. "The whole thing's bad business. I knew Uncle Ben Morgan, seen him round the mill. He was a good, quiet-kind of nigger, 'n a handy one with the banjo. Now that mob had no mind to lynch him and his 'n what'd they done?" He looked around, a puzzled frown on his bewiskered countenance. "They must go crazy-like, to do a thing like that—crazy for blood."

An oppressive silence fell on the group. Before Marge's eyes there rose a picture of dark-eyed Martha as she had looked that morning in the door-way of the spinning room, her golden skin gleaming softly against the green slip she was wearing. In her ears sounded Ma Morgan's singing "Go Down Moses—"

"Wal, it's a terrible thing all round, 'n wrong on both sides." Turpen rose to take his leave, pulling at his wife's arm. "But when all's said 'n done, it comes back to this—we white folks got to stand together 'n keep the niggers in their place. We Po' Whites is bad enough off as it is, without the niggers getting uppity."

Marge jumped to her feet. Her voice choked her, coming in horse, broken gasps. "That ain't so. The wrong's nigh all one way. . . . What's more, we white folks ain't together. There's the mill owners 'n there's us." She halted, overcome by emotions which she did not understand and suddenly confused by the circle of faces that stared at her so intently.

"Marge," Sal implored, "for mercy sakes keep quiet."

"Wal for my part I'm glad that nigger Jim did what he done," Allen repeated.

"He sure had courage," Bob added, "you have to give him that."

THE MILL INTERESTS KEPT the whole affair out of the papers, except for a brief announcement of young Haines' death and the "justice meted out to his murderer." Feeling ran high over the entire state. The colored population kept more to themselves than ever, many left for other parts, while the night rides of hooded Klansmen grew more frequent. One night the empty shacks at Back Row were razed to the ground. Since the local police could get no information from Greenville's Negro section, they arrested three of their strongest inhabitants and sent them to the chain gang for ten years each.

"I never saw the likes," the judge fumed, "the way these niggers stand together. They're a close-mouthed lot."

The day of young Haines' funeral, extra police were stationed in the city and around the mill village, but it was an unnecessary precaution, as there were no disturbances. Everyone, however, breathed easier when the day of the burial had passed.

Work at the mill went badly. The shacks at Back Row were rapidly rebuilt and colored families from Georgia and Alabama were brought in, but when they learned the history of recent events, they quickly moved on again. It was several months before the company could hold together a competent working force, and even to this day, Row Mill has a bad reputation among mill hands, although the events which gave rise to this reputation have become obscured with time.

AS MONTHS WENT BY, Fred Morgan grew worried at not hearing from his people in Back Row. Letters from there were always few and far between, each one representing, he knew, a painful effort, on the part of Martha and the rest of the household. Perhaps there was sickness, and they were waiting until the ill one was well toward recovery before writing, "so as not to worry you with it." Fred scratched off a note, asking for news. After two weeks, still not hearing, he wrote to the Johnsons and was waiting impatiently for their answer, when Tom told him of his plan to make a visit home.

Fred had missed the small item which had appeared in the New York papers several months previously of another lynching below the Mason and Dixon line.

"Well, boy, I wish you could go along." Tom grinned across at his friend. "Pass me that shirt, will you? This gettin' ready is the only bad part." Fred joined in the packing and tried to down the longing for the sight of his people's faces.

He had been away four years now. Ma would laugh and weep at having him back, and stuff him full of applesauce and cornbread, and they'd all sit together in the dusk and hum to the tune of Pa's banjo.

"It'd sure be nice, Tom," he said aloud, "but I ain't got the dough. In a couple of year from now. But once in Dixie, it'd be white folks for you 'n black folks for me, I reckon."

Tom, pulling at his suitcase strap, straightened up to put a hand on Fred's shoulder. "Naw, Fred. We're friends—real friends. I ain't leavin' no friend of mine, whatever they say. Besides, you 'n me know that southern laborin' people got to wake up to their real interests 'n get out of their old ways."

"That's right. But it'll take time, 'n plenty of guts."

"Well, you sure get your share of 'em, Fred, 'n that's a fact." He dropped on the cot beside his friend.

"You ain't short-handed yourself," Fred retorted. His face sobered. "Say, Tom, do me a favor while you're thar, if you can?"

"Sure thing. What is it?"

"Well, I ain't heard from my folks for over three months now. Doan guess anything's wrong. But maybe you could in-quire around casual-like 'n get some news of 'em?"

Tom flushed. Why hadn't he thought to offer! "Why, of course. I'll go over 'n see 'em 'n tell how you're making out. Any messages or presents you want to send? I'll be glad to deliver 'em."

Fred's face lit up. "That'd be swell. But it'd cause talk down thar, wouldn't it? 'N have you room, that suitcase is bulgin' already!"

"Doan worry, we'll squash 'em in. I guess if I want to go vistin' in Back Row that's my business. This here's a free country aint' it?" At this the two wobblies laughed. Fred bounded to his feet, pulling at his dollar Ingersoll. "There's an hour yet before you go? I'll run over to a store near here 'n be back before then." Soon he had returned, his pockets bulging and his hands full.

"You know, Tom, they'll be that surprise 'n pleased. In here's some dress goods for Mammy, a new pipe for Pa," he began emptying his pockets, "'n a top 'n real doll for Myrtle; 'n for Marthy, some dress goods, too. You reckon you can manage all?" He looked doubtfully at the overflowing suitcase, for Tom also had bought his share of gifts for the great trip home. He had been saving for over two years for this visit, and had even purchased a new suit for the occasion.

"Look him over," Jake teased turning the traveler about for Fred's inspection, "ain't he diked out? Gonna show his home town, he is!" Tom squirmed, grinning sheepishly. "Well, you know how it is. . . . Anyways, I got my overalls in the bag."

At the gang-way (Tom was going by boat as far as Charleston), Fred gripped him by the hand. "Tell my folks about the union. Tell 'em thar's a great day ahead, 'n in a few years I'll be down to help 'em organize."

THE WHOLE VILLAGE DROPPED IN on the Crenshaws to see Tom and hear news of the north. Here was a mill boy who had escaped, who lived a different life than theirs. For the first time Sal felt pride in her eldest son, now bronzed and tattooed, and with a bit of swagger, that she noticed caught more than one girl's fancy. It was a good thing that Lucy Fields had left the village, and there was nothing to worry over on that score.

Sal passed around the presents for all admiring visitors to examine and make comment on. For her there was dress goods and a green pillow top on which was painted in bold red letters, "Greetings from New York," for Gertie a rhinestone bracelet and silk handkerchief on which was emblazoned a battleship, for Uncle Nat, a pair of silk suspenders and for the boys brightly colored ties and picture albums of the world's largest metropolis. About Marge's gifts she felt a little uncertain. The silk handkerchief like Gertie's was all right, but the books over which the girl seemed so tickled she decided it best not to pass around. There was one called "Looking Backward" and a smaller one entitled "Wage-Labor and Capital." "This ain't so easy readin', Marge," she heard Tom explaining, "but it's worth studyin' over." No doubt full of badness, Sal concluded, and the less noticed, the better.

Marge was struck by the changes in her brother. It was not only his appearance, though his once slight figure had filled out and hardened almost beyond recognition. There was something deeper. As they talked she discovered what it was, this union business had made a man of him. When she tried to convey her impressions to Tom, he nodded.

"I can't explain it exactly, sis. But I feel different, like new. I got something' to live by, now."

Marge sighed. "Wisht I had."

Tom looked down at her. They were walking across the open fields, the sky was brilliant with the blue, purple, and rose colors of a southern sunset.

"You're changing too, Marge," he hesitated. "You look worn-lookin'. They're workin' you too hard at the mill."

"I reckon. You know, this war in Europe's givin' the mills lots of orders 'n we've been doin' overtime all summer."

"This war!" he exploded, "it's a hellish slaughter. 'N first thing we know, we'll be in it, mark my word. Wall Street bankers have loaned England some millions of dollars—'n the flag follows the dollar. What's more there's markets Germany's got, like in South America, that the capitalists here are hankerin' for."

"Aw, we'll not get in it. Didn't we jest elect Wilson for keepin' us out of war? The people ain't wantin' no war."

"Rattlesnakes! Do you think the people makes a war? Listen, thar's two classes in America, Marge, the capitalists 'n the workers 'n—" Tom expounded carefully, while the girl listened in troubled silence.

As they started slowly toward the village Tom, making an effort to sound casual, asked, "By the way, sis, what ever happened to that Lucy Fields? You know, that gal I ran around with some. Is she still about these parts?"

His voice didn't deceive her, but she also tried to speak casually. "Well, after you left things seemed to go bad for her. That Haines boy chased after her," she stole a look at her brother's half-turned face, "and—well, I guess he got her in trouble, 'n the boss made the family leave the hill. They went to Selby's I heard, then moved on from thar, too."

Tom swung angrily at the bushes on either side. "'N now she's down 'n out. Maybe bummin'." His voice hardened. "It was her loves of clothes 'n good times that done it."

"If she'd been a rich gal, Tom, that'd been no harm. But for a mill gal to want a good time—thar's only one way to get it. Anyways, it was that boss son's fault, temptin' 'n leadin' her on." The brilliant colors were fading, now blending into soft-toned lavenders and greys.

After a while he asked, "So no one knows whar she is now?"

"No, not as I know of." She took her brother's arm and the two started homeward, here and there a light glimmered like fireflies in the early dusk. The frogs had begun their hoarse serenade, the smell of wild honeysuckle and primroses was heavy on the air. Their foot-steps sounded dull against the soft dirt. Her arm pressed against his side, she felt a quiver run through him. But when next he spoke, his voice was calm and even, as before.

"Thar was somethin' else I wanted to ask you, sis. Would you happen to know a colored family by the name of Morgans, who works at the mill 'n lives at Back Row? Why, what's the matter?" Marge had stopped short, jerking her arm free.

"Ain't you heard yet—about the lynchings?"

SAL, UNCLE MAT, AND BOB, sitting on the small porch, wrestled with the mosquitoes and wondered what could be keeping Marge and Tom so long. As it neared village bedtime the youth, finally responding to Sal's hints, took his leave and started disconsolately up the street. In the next block he met Marge. She was alone, walking with head down. "What kept you?" The night sky was clear and lit with stars, so that he could see the traces of tears on her cheeks, the distracted look in her eyes. "What's wrong, honey? You 'n Tom been quarrelin'?"

"No, not that. . . . Tomorrow I'll tell you." She broke away and ran toward the shack.

Tom did not return all night. Sal voiced her suspicions in no uncertain terms but it did her small good, for her son acted as though he had not even heard her, and talked to no one but in whispers to Marge. It was plain they were wrought up over something. "It's this radical talk of his 'n," she muttered, "What if it gets to the boss-man's ears? I mighta known he'd bring trouble." She tried quizzing and scolding Marge, but that failed her also. "Gawd forgive me, I'll not rest easy till he's offa the hill."

FOR THREE OR FOUR DAYS he made mysterious trips into Greenville and nearby hills, in both colored and white

sections. He must, he told Marge, get all the details for Fred
and make sure if there was anything which could be done to
those murderers in that mob. At last he located Miss Lancey,
who had been at Back Row that fateful night. She and her
friends, like the Negroes in Greenville, cautioned him against
"stirrin' up sleepin' dogs. Nuthin' 'd come of it but more misery for the colored folks." Tom had written a scathing letter
which he proposed taking to the *Greenville Times* in person, demanding that the leaders of the mob be arrested and
brought to trial. "You know that editor-man'd never print it.
It's a millman's paper." Slowly he tore it up. "Yah, I reckon
you-all's right. The company's got a strangle-hold on everythin'! It'll take an uprisin' to break it." "'N," Miss Lancey spoke
querulously, "we ain't aimin' on no uprisin' in these parts."

"By gorry, thar's gotta be some way to stop such things!" a
slightly-built Negro with deep-set eyes threw out his arms.
Then Tom thought of Fred's message to his people. "Listen,
thar is a way, 'n thar's one comin' to help you, *'n by the Lawd,
I'm comin' with him.*"

When Sal caught Billy and Sam snickering over the words
to "Long-haired preachers come out every night, Try to tell
you what's wrong 'n what's right," she snatched the song-
book from them, stuffed it into the kitchen stove and waited,
with arms folded, for Tom's return. After a heated quarrel, in
which she called him "No-Count" and "Devil's Pardner," and
he replied with pointed remarks about "mill slaves, in body
'n mind," Tom began throwing his clothes into the suitcase.

"Oh, Tom, you ain't goin'?" Marge plead.

"Yah, high time I did." He halted, lifted out the package
which Fred had entrusted him to deliver. "Here, sis, do somethin' with these."

"What? Tom, doan leave 'em with me, what'll I do with
'em?"

"Anything.... Yah, it's time I was goin' north."

She walked up the road with him, clinging to his arm, dragging him back. "Gosh, sis, wish I could take you along, out of this." She shook her head. Now that Gertie had run away with the boarder Harry, how would Ma manage with her gone, too?

Besides, he added, "Maybe you're marryin' that Bob Gregory soon?" He spoke grudgingly, as brothers often do. Again she shook her head.

With a promise to write often and send books, an awkward peck on her cheek, and he was gone. Once more she was alone on the hill. Now there was no one. Only Bob, and he . . . Why bother so over things, he told her, it didn't help none. Life on the hill was the way it was. Why not come on 'n get married like everybody else did 'n get what they could out of livin'?

How would things work out, she wondered, the company so powerful 'n the mill hands so ignorant. Could they ever learn to stick together? Pulling open the battered screen door, she went down the dim hall to help her mother fix the evening meal.

TOM CLIMBED SLOWLY up the stairs to Fred's room. From within came singing, "When Moses was in Egypt-land." Overcoming his desire to make off, he knocked, and at his friend's call entered.

"Why, Tom Crenshaw!" Fred came toward him, hands outstretched, eyes and teeth gleaming. "When'd you get back? 'N what's the news?" His face working, Tom slumped into a chair. "What's the matter, you sick? Then what . . ." Fred dropped on the edge of the bed. "*Tom, my people. What's happened?*"

"Fred . . . I . . . Fred, we're friends, real friends. We're together, understand in everything." All the careful plans he had made on the way back, how to break it, where had they gone? "We believe in organized action, ain't that right?"

Fred seized him by the wrists.

"Yah, Tom, but for Gawd's sake, speak out. What is it?"

THE NEXT DAY FRED was not at work. That evening, Tom and Jake found his room empty, and the landlady said he had gone off that morning and told her not to hold his room, as he'd not be back for sometime.

What had happened? Fred had promised Tom not to do anything desperate, but . . . They searched union headquarters, and even the dock saloons. No one had seen him. Returning to their quarters they found a note scrawled on the back of an old leaflet.

"Boys, I'm shipping out. Back in two months. Know you're standing by. Fred."

"I guess, Jake, he did the wise thing."

"I reckon. Didn't trust hisself ashore now. Say, you're shaking like with a chill!"

"Aw, it's nothin'. Listen, I never knew anybody with as much guts as Fred, Jake, not even exceptin' present company."

XI.

War!

TOM EDGED HIS WAY through the milling crowd which jammed the entrance and into the close hall which was already packed and humming with people. At the docks he had been handed a leaflet,

COME AND HEAR
DEBS EXPOSE THE WAR

Jake had objected, "Those socialists are a dam bunch of fakers, keep away from 'em," but Tom's curiosity to see and hear the man who had won both the masses' devotion and the bitter hatred of the press lead him to disregard his friend's advice for once, and come anyway.

As he strode down the aisle hunting for a seat, a small, black-haired girl thrust more papers into his hand, "Here, comrade, take one." Tom looked over the audience. All Eastside must be here. He'd never seen anything like it before, every type and age. Mostly Jewish and immigrant workers he judged, from their appearance and conversation. They chatted with one another in excited undertones, while children clambered over their laps and knees, wriggling in and out of the waiting throng. Others sat quietly, an expectant look on the worn faces which they turned toward the platform, now empty except for the American and Red flags which draped its sides. Tom felt strange and yet also at home, among his own kind.

A stir rippled through the sea of humans. Necks craned. A thunder of applause and the audience was on its feet, singing in a score of tongues, "Arise, ye prisoners of starvation." The speakers and reception committee walked slowly on to the platform.

An uneasy, disagreeable feeling went through Tom as he looked them over. What a contrast between those on the platform and the poorly-clad, toil-marked humans seated around him! Only three of the committee seemed common folk like themselves. The others were handsomely dressed, with sleek hair and a soft, comfortable look about their bodies that smacked of too much lounging in cushioned chairs. The chairman he instantly disliked. In answer to a query his neighbor told him, "That's Allquitt, a big lawyer and a member of the national executive committee." A lawyer! He looked it, too. Maybe Jake was right. What had a swell lawyer to do with working people, calling them comrades? Where could such as he lead them—to Wall Street? Imagine a fellow like him over at the wobblies' hall! They'd boot him out fast enough.

When the speaker rose and came forward, Tom noted with relief that he was one of the three with a good, plain look about him. As he listened to the railway man's simple, direct eloquence, the distrust which the chairman had roused was forgotten. The enthusiasm and elementary faith of the hundreds around him who had come from their tenements to hear Debs' denunciation of imperialist war communicated itself to him, warming his blood and firing his imagination.

Against the war! Against the war! Keep America out! Let the masses force peace.

As the audience ebbed slowly from the hall and others crowded forward around the platform, Tom, undecided, hung back, then made his way toward the literature table in the rear. The black-haired girl stood giving out the last of her leaflets and calling, "Comrades, please take one." When all but a few stragglers had passed out the girl came over to him.

"Comrade, what can I do for you?"

"Please, ma'am, could you tell me more about your organization? I'm an I.W.W. myself." Immediately a half-dozen gathered around the sandy-haired youth and proceeded jointly to enlighten him on the shortcomings of the wobblies and the superiority of socialism to syndicalism. Long after midnight Tom took his leave, his head buzzing with new and conflicting ideas. Dog-gone, just when he'd gotten the world straightened out, sewed up in a bag, along comes this to upset him, and start the thing all over again! Somehow, inter-mingled with his thoughts was a picture of glowing brown eyes in a rounded face, topped by black curly hair and a small sturdy figure with quiet moving gestures that gave an impression of compact, intense energy and a decision of character that he'd never before seen in a woman. "Tom Crenshaw, you old fool! Just because you ain't seen a girl in months, to have her go to your head." They called her Bessie. "You old fool."

Nevertheless, Tuesday night he was on hand for their meeting, as he had promised. Afterwards he and Bessie walked from Fourteenth street across the Brooklyn Bridge and back to her flat, arguing their philosophies and exchanging experiences. Bess, he learned, had come to this country when scarcely eleven years old with her parents who had fled from Russia following the defeat of the uprising of 1905. Revolutionary socialism she had sucked in with her mother's

milk, as a child she had wept over Gorky's *Mother* and resolved to give her life to the cause like her parents and uncle
had done before her. America she had learned on New York's
and Chicago's East-sides, and in their sweat shops and garment strikes. She had been among the sixteen girls initiating
the great walk-out of forty thousand clothing workers in the
windy city in 1910, and had served as shop chairlady in one
of Koppenheimer's plants after the settlement. Later, the
union had sent her to St. Louis to do some organizing work,
but she had quarreled with the officials over policy and had
been fired. For the last three seasons she had been in New
York, back at her trade and carrying on agitation among the
rank and file.

The steel arches of the bridge curved about them, below
the water flowed swiftly in currents of black ink. On either
side, darkened sky-scrapers, climbing like rugged cliffs into
the blue night, pressed close to the river's edge. Lights flashed,
the muffled hum of the city drifted from the shores, while
ferry boats and tugs plied their trade endlessly back and forth
along the Hudson. Tom drew a deep breath and threw a quick
look at the girl striding beside him. "Gee, it's funny, ain't it?"

"What?"

"How alike but diff'rent things can be. Now take you 'n me.
We're nigh the same age, 'n both worked since we're little.
But you ... Well, you're like it, here, 'n me, I'm like Row Hill."

She laughed, threw out her hands in a characteristic gesture. "Sure, we're not the same. But we're more alike than
diff'rent. I'll tell you something," she stopped short, "we'll
never have a real movement in this country, one worth talking
about till the New Yorks and Row Hills get together. How do
you like that?"

"By golly, you're right. But that's a long way off."

"Not so long as you might think.... Say, kid, it's time to hike
for Second Avenue."

As they pushed their way through the crowds massed around push-carts piled high with fruits, vegetables, suspenders, and table cloths, he inquired cautiously, "Thar's somethin' I been mindin' to ask you since the meetin' when Debs spoke. You got two kinds of folk in your organization, ain't you?"

The girl plunged into a heated explanation of the struggle within the party and her group's determination "to drive that Allquitt crowd out. And in every country there's opposition inside the ranks to a ruling clique that's for the war. You wobblies are dumb in many ways, Tom, like your not believing in political action, but we have to give you credit on one score: you're solid against the war."

Every night when he was not busy with union affairs and she had a free evening Tom would go over to Bessie's place which she shared with another girl, and they would drink tea and argue. Later he would try the arguments out on Jake, to see if he could produce a convincing answer. His wobbly friend gave voice to his suspicions in loud, unmistakable terms.

"Listen, youse, what you doing playing round with a socialist jane? Ain't I warned you they're betrayers of the working class? Look at what they done in Germany and France and all over Europe—broke their pledge of solidarity and told the masses to fight for their fatherlands. Fatherlands me eye! And they'll do no diff'rent here. Just because you go and get soft on a skirt ain't no reason to forget your principles!"

Tom flushed angrily. "Now lookahere Jake, get it straight, once 'n for all. My likin' her or not likin' her ain't the point. What's more you can't say I ain't with the union through thick 'n thin."

"That's so, but ..."

"What's more, I don't believe they're all fakers. The leaders, maybe, but the members ain't so diff'rent from the fellow-workers over at the hall."

"They're poisoning your mind, with their talk about political action. Then sending petitions to Wilson!" Jake spat contemptuously into the bucket under the table.

"That's dumb, I admit. And I ain't falling so quick. But it ain't no harm to get new ideas is it? It was you, Jake, that first showed me how to wake up my mind. I ain't lullin' it back to sleep for *nobody*. You get that?"

"All right, I warned you. If the boys have you up on charges, it'll be yourself to blame." Swearing gruffly, Jake made off. Tom roamed the streets that evening alone. Up on charges— that cut deep. Fred was due to be slippin' into port any day, now, 'n a good thing, too.... This was no time for quarrelin' in the ranks, with war clouds gatherin' so fast.

THE MORNING PAPERS BLAZONED the news: "Russian Revolution Overthrows the Czar." Tom scrambled for a sheet, tossed two coppers to a hoarse newsboy. "Gee, Bess'll be wild." After work he found her over at socialist headquarters, striding up and down the floor, declaiming excitedly to an equally agitated group of listeners. "They've won their freedom—the freedom they bled for in 1905. This is the first break in capitalism's chain. *And it won't stop here.*"

Everywhere in the city working people were celebrating. The first break in the chain.

Wall Street and Washington received the news with apprehension. Its press, however, carried glowing headlines, since this helped to prepare a generally reluctant people for America's coming entrance into the war. The ruthless Czar of All the Russias (awkward to explain as an ally in a War for Democracy!) was overthrown; Kerensky, his successor, could be relied upon to take his directives from the banking and industrial classes. However, the statesmen asked among themselves, Would the revolution stop here? Could this Kerensky keep the hungry, war-sick Russian people in hand?

It was April, 1917. Wilson, who had been re-elected on the slogan "A Vote for Wilson is a Vote for Peace," Wilson with his talk of neutrality and "Too Proud to Fight" went before Congress and passionately demanded a "War to Make the World Safe for Democracy.... History demands of us that we save civilization...." Eighty-six men in Congress, claiming to speak in the name of "the people," promptly voted one hundred and ten million into the conflict that had been tearing Europe asunder for more than three years.

Over-night the scene changed. Word had gone out from Wall Street to the White House, and from the White House War, glorified and ecstatic, swept into the schools, press and churches of the country. Headlines screamed "Huns Attack Defenceless and Aged," "Children's Hands Cut Off at Wrists by Germans," "Women Branded on the Breast With Iron Cross," "Huns Plan Attack on America by Way of Mexico." The British and American intelligence offices worked overtime, concocting ingenious atrocity stories. One, internationally famous, about which an English lord boasted his authorship some years after the war was over, pictured dead allied soldiers being carted behind the German lines to be manufactured into soap! Movies reeled off pictures of "Our Boys in Khaki." Gay posters suddenly appeared everywhere. *Liberty*, a beautiful woman, was shown harassed by the terrible Hun. A soldier pointing directly at the spectator accused, "Your Country Needs You." Red-cheeked young men in natty uniforms stood before army tents on street corners, flirted in a guarded way with admiring girls, and enticed young men in to join up.

Soldiers, with flags flying and bands playing, marched through the streets while crowds lined the curbs, hurrahed and came to attention as the "Star Spangled Banner" boomed forth from brass trumpets. School programs were practically set aside for patriotic services, where white-haired men and maiden school teachers exhorted the children in trembling accents to do their bit in the great cause.

Middle-class women deserted their bridge tables and afternoon teas two afternoons a week to cut bandages. Gossip gave way to horrible tales of what was happening to defenceless peoples on the other side, and to tearful boasting about their sons who had donned the uniform and were fighting the war behind desks in Washington, dancing late with pretty girls at Fort Monroe or one of the other army posts.

Liberty Loans, Red Cross drives followed fast upon one another's heels. No one was safe who did not have a button or window card to prove he'd "given till it hurts" and "done his bit for Uncle Sam."

Preachers thundered from the pulpits, making of the war another holy crusade to wipe out the iniquitous heathen. Just as the Hebrews and ancient peoples had offered sacrifices and made promises to their national gods if they were granted victory against their enemies, so the modern high priests burned candles, draped their altars in flags, chanted hymns of hate, took up collections, and wept and pleaded to their national god to lead their armies into battle against the forces of darkness that "Democracy may reign supreme throughout the world." Dark threats were made against "the secret enemies in our midst." Community songs were organized in every hamlet, and the entire nation chanted "Keep the Home Fires Burning Till the Boys Come Home."

Men were drafted from field, office and factory, and women poured in to take their places. Bankers and manufacturers left their offices to go to Washington as dollar-a-year men, organizing the economic phase of the war machine and simultaneously becoming millionaires in a few months' time.

War, which long ago had penetrated the factories, now redoubled its hold there. There were noon hour talks by local patriots, flags were raised over the buildings, posters were placed in work rooms and toilets, pointing out the role of good workmanship and speed of output in winning the war. The manager, with instructions from the central office, would call in foremen who, armed with subscription lists would go from one machine to the next, putting the factory "over the top" for the Red Cross or Liberty Loan.

Samuel Gompers, president of the American Federation of Labor, from his comfortable headquarters in Washington, uttered his solemn proclamation, "This is labor's war," became a member of the Council of National Defense, and gave Wilson his aid in ending strikes. Meanwhile Bill Haywood and the wobblies organized strikes and opposed the draft. Certain official spokesmen of the Socialist Party stated publicly "We will certainly not embarrass our government in this hour of crisis." Many, however, in the ranks of the membership joined Gene Debs in protesting "this ruthless slaughter of millions for the profits of a few" and were immediately branded as German spies and clamped into jail, along with the wobblies and a handful of pacifists.

UNDER THE ESPIONAGE ACT, Bess was among the first jailed and later held for deportation as an "undesirable" alien. Tom made frantic but unsuccessful efforts to get her out, or at least to see her once before she left. Then, together with Fred who had returned from sea to take part in anti-war activities, he was also seized and put behind the bars.

At the meeting at which they were later arrested Fred's voice boomed across the sea of faces. "They say that we should fight to honor the flag. What is the flag? An emblem for business men. It's got the dollar sign all over it. Wall Street's made millions out of this war, shippin' munitions and supplies across, 'n now they're steppin' in to grab all they can. And who's to be the cannon fodder for 'em? Their sons? No sir, but common workin' stiffs like you 'n me. What we got to fight for, tell me that?"

Murmurs from the crowd.

"That's right." "What about the Belgian children?" "You're a blasted Hun!"

"We say," Fred drawned their voices, "*stop this war*. Let the workers of Europe, England and America refuse to fight—put an end to the war by a general strike!"

"Hurrah! Hurrah!"

"You slackers. . . . You dam traitors!" Policemen's billies descended with dull thuds on the listeners' heads as blue uniforms hewed a path through to the speaker's stand. The crowd, recovering from the suddenness of the attack, hurled itself on the police. A few slunk off down side streets. Fists shot out, bodies went down, and were trampled underfoot. Over head the L roared by on its serpentine course. More bluecoats rushed to the scene, revolvers drawn. Tom, one eye closed, wrestling madly with a monster in uniform, felt his knees give way as another sprung on him from behind. "You dirty coward." His last vision was of Fred, teeth bared and blood running over his face from a gash on his forehead, dealing blows to right and left as a circle of police closed in on him. Handcuffed and still shouting "Down with war," "Keep up the fight," they were hauled into the waiting Black Maria.

At the station, Tom and Fred were charged with sedition and resisting the draft.

"Cowards, that's what!" the desk sergeant sneered.

"Coward!" Fred lunged at him. "Take these handcuffs offa me 'n I'll show you. Coward not to fight for, but against a system that raped my sister 'n murdered my old parents!" The guards shoved him back against the wall.

"Do your worst," he muttered under his breath, "if you send me into the army I'll know where to point my gun!"

During the night guards and plainclothes men entered the cells where Fred and Tom had been herded, and in a business-like manner proceeded to beat the two handcuffed men to the floor, kicking the unconscious bodies, hurling curses at the devils who dared defy this great government of law and order.

Jake, who on the outbreak of the war had gone west to do agitational work, was likewise rounded up and placed where his fiery words would find their echo only from three narrow walls and a steel-barred door.

"Free speech, hell!" the burly officer growled, as he jabbed his prisoner in the back with the point of his gun. "This is war. Anybody who talks about free speech rights now is a blooming fool or a blasted traitor."

XII.

The First Time
in History

THE ONWARD SWIRL of the war current reached Row Hill, engulfing Marge and her neighbors in its flow. At first the general feeling was one of indifference, mixed with suspicion. "'Tain't our war," a few mumbled, and others, "A bunch of foreigners fightin' in Europe, why we got to mix up in it?" But the drive widened, carrying all before it. Even Sal, roused by events, remarked, "It's like it was in the Spanish-American War—like a circus, somethin' doin' all the time."

Her words caused Marge to pause. What had Granny told her about that war? A hoax, she'd called it. And Tom had said ... Disturbed, yet feeling herself powerless in the great flood, fearful of being called a slacker, Marge was swept on with the rest.

Bob, however, threw himself into the on-rushing torrent with boisterous enthusiasm. Its throb and glamor fired his blood. He and Marge were standing on a corner in Greenville, where they had walked to see a movie. The beat of drums and thumping of marching feet to martial airs was more than the youth could stand out against. "Marge," he cried, "I'm gonna sign up!"

Fear and anger engulfed her. "Come on Bob, we'll be late to the show," and she pulled him along the crowded sidewalk.

Over the entrance an electric sign glared in monstrous letters, "Passion's Flower." Marge stole a look at the bill board pictures, her heart thumping. They sure looked sinful, just like the parson had said.

"How much is it, ma'am?" Bob inquired of the girl behind the ticket window. Marge gazed at her in awe; her tightly curled hair, brilliantly painted cheeks and her jaws which opened and closed with a persistent regularity as they bore down on her piece of gum. Maybe she was an actress, herself?

"Tin cints each," the movie queen announced. Bob fished around in his trousers for the dimes and they went inside, feeling their way in the dark for empty seats. A news reel was on. French soldiers and English tommies marched across the screen. "Our Allies in the Fight for Democracy." Clapping and hurrahs. Then flashes of the scarred fields of France and Belgium. "What the Huns are Doing." Next, a mother with child in arms, bearing the caption, "My Daddy Is Doing His Bit—Fighting for Mamma and Me—Is Yours?" Finally, "Uncle Sam's Boys." Wild applause, and the audience clammering to its feet as the pianist played "Oh Say Can You See?" Bob and Marge joined in the singing. When they sat down, she could feel trembling in the arm that Bob placed around her.

Now the main picture was beginning, "Passion's Flower." A triangle story, in which a man made violent love to another's wife. Marge gasped at the luxurious clothes and surroundings passing before her eyes. When the inevitable bedroom scene was reached, she felt her face growing hot, and the arm around her tightening like a vise. She was glad it was dark. Maybe the parson was right, after all, maybe it was a sin to see and think such things.

Slowly she and Bob started on the two mile walk back to the village. Once clear of the town, the road stretched before them, shimmering white in the moonlight. On each side the oak and maple trees made towering black shadows. In the afternoon there had been a brief rain, now the air was fragrant with the clean smells of early summer. Bob led Marge into the shadows, and leaning against a pine trunk drew her to him, laughing in quick breaths. "Sweetheart . . . sweet as honey." Their bodies clung, trembled. "Marge, woan you marry me? I can't go on this way no longer." His hands grew frantic, one slipped within her blouse. Moaning, she broke away from him. "Doan . . . Doan." Sex—an evil thing—only marriage and children could justify it.

His hands dropped to his sides. "What's the matter? Doan you . . . You're scairt."

"Yes . . . I . . . Oh, let's go home."

Sobered, sullen, they started on, one on either side of the road. When they reached Marge's house, he said gruffly, "Well, it's up to you. Either we get married or quit, that's all."

Marge lay alongside Ruth, staring up into the dark. Occasionally her shuddering shook the bed so that Ruth tossed and fretted in her sleep. What was she to do? She couldn't give Bob up, he was the one spot of light in the dark grind of hill life. She couldn't see him pick up with that Becky Smithers again. But what if she married him and got tied down with a string of lil'uns? Why wasn't thar a way for poor folks not to have so many children? The rich didn't have them. Near dawn she dropped off to sleep, only to wake sobbing and clutching at Ruth who shook her off angrily and turned over for a last slumber.

All day at the machine Marge puzzled and got snarls in her cotton. At noon Bob was nowhere to be seen. Fear of a new kind gripped her. When the day shift left the hills Bob was waiting for Marge by the entrance. His face told her even before his words, "Marge, I've signed up."

Later, when he begged, "Woan you, afore I go across?" she gave way. So they were married that Saturday afternoon, in the company church, with all the family and neighbors present. Sal sniffed quietly through the service, Billy and Sam stared with wide eyes. Marge, her fingers clutched tightly between Bob's, torn between fear and joy, listened to Parson Brown's voice as it droned from a great distance, "Dearly Beloved, We Are Gathered Together in the Sight of God and Man ..." Why did Bob have to go? Would he ever come back? Would she be lucky, or would she get caught right off and have a kid? Was it wrong or right, what they were going through with? An insane desire possessed her to call out, "Stop, parson, I ain't sure." But when he directed his question at her, "Marge Crenshaw, do you take this man?" she colored and murmured "I do," and it was over.

Monday Bob left for Camp Lee at Petersburg, Virginia, and Marge went back to her machine. She heard whisperings and caught eyes sympathetic, envious, looking in her direction. Bob had been acknowledged the catch of the village, and now he was one of Uncle Sam's heroes, too. While her fingers flew from spindle to spindle, she lived over the past two days and tried not to look at the uncertainties that lay ahead.

As more and more men were drafted or voluntarily signed up, more mothers and young girls crowded into the mills, and when news of the first dead reached Greenville, the feeling against "slackers" waxed higher. Those Huns had killed some of their people, the war had come to their own door-steps.

All of Bob's letters were stamped, "Passed by the Censor." What right, Marge asked, had the government to do that? What she and Bob had to say to each other was their own affair! Once or twice there were sentences blacked out. What could that mean? Not until long afterwards did she find out.

Bob had written, "A terrible thing happened here at camp." Quite a number of boys from the Blue Ridge mountains of Virginia and North Carolina had been drafted and brought to Camp Lee. In general they had come unwillingly. The mountain people had felt, "Tain't our war." Here for generations they had battled with Federal agents over moonshinin', why should they fight for 'em they'd allays fought against? Why go across the seas to fight furriners they'd no grudge against?

Now if it had just been a war against the agents, an army could have been mustered in a few hours' time!

Much persuasion and a few shots had been exchanged before the recruits had been rounded up. Among those brought to camp from Deep Hollow was Will Hendricks, a raw youth who had never seen a train or electric light, and though versed in the ways of the out-of-doors and quick on a trigger, had never opened a book in his life. He shared the Hollow's contempt and dread of the outside world whose few intrusions into the valley had created a suspicious dread of the stranger.

Lined up for inspection one morning, the snappy second lieutenant ordered Will to step out. "Why's your collar open?"

"Can't stand the dam thing," Will stuttered. The men snickered. The second lieutenant, not long out of the classroom and very conscious of his spurs, took this as an affront to the dignity and authority of his position. Glaring at the awkward figure whose wrists dangled from sleeves that were far too short, he said curtly, "That is no way to answer an officer. Your manners are as bad as your dress. Three days K.P. for you."

This was the beginning of a feud between Will and his commanding officer. It was not long before the mountaineer was charged with insubordination and thrown into the guard house. Here he brooded sullenly and grew homesick for his Mammy and the mountains. As soon as he was released, he struck out for Deep Hollow. Later, when caught by a detachment of soldiers sent after him and brought back in disgrace as a deserter, Will was more defiant and confused than ever.

The major who came to cross-examine him in the guard house was frankly puzzled. "You know," he had confided to others on the staff, "we've got to learn to handle these mountaineers right. It can't be they're yellow, you know their traditions, yet this isn't the only camp that's having trouble with them. They're excellent marksmen, but dam hard to discipline."

All threats and persuasion had been equally ineffective in drawing out the prisoner. He only jerked at his neckband and waved his arms about to show his disgust. Once he shouted, "Gimme a gun, 'n let's start warrin'. This ... this ..."

"Then it's not that you're afraid to fight for your country?" the lieutenant inquired. Will swung around on him and the officer beat a hasty retreat.

After two weeks solitary confinement and many lectures on his duty, Will was replaced with his company. Some of the men avoided him but Bob, seeing how distraught he was, and knowing enough of mountain life from his grandpa's side to sense Will's feelings, went out of his way to make friends. He showed him Marge's picture and talked to him of Row Hill, and the hill boy, once his suspicions were allayed, responded as eagerly as a child with stories of the hills. All this drillin,' dressin' up, and doin' woman's work, peelin' taters! If this was a sure-nough war, why didn't they fight! "Anyways," he confided, "it taint our war. ... I'm hone-ing fer the hills, 'n to see the last of this place." In spite of Bob's entreaties, he again disappeared.

This time he reached the valley before they caught him and brought him back to the guard house. After a good thrashing and no food or water for twenty-four hours, he was visited by the colonel.

"You know the way we treat deserters in the army?" his superior warned him, "we shoot them. You try this again, 'n that's what you'll get."

Will, cowed and sullen, was finally returned to his company. For several days he went about his duties in a wooden manner, refusing to talk even with Bob. When the mill youth, fearful of his friend's restlessness tried to break through, Will snarled "leave-me be."

For the last time Will left for the mountains. The soldiers sent after him ran him down near the railroad tracks at Staunton. Before they could lay hands on him he jumped in front of a passing freight. There was not enough of his mangled body left to bring back for burial.

The story crept around the barracks. Bob, oppressed, longed to be out of it and back with Marge and the simple life on the hill. This camp part was sure different than he'd imagined. Somethin' was plum wrong somewhars, and he'd be full glad when they shipped 'em over. Could Marge's brother be right? Did Will know more than he seemed when he said dully, "it ain't our war"?

Before the month was out, Bob's detachment had entrained for Hampton Roads. The order had come suddenly, there had been no chance to send word to Marge or his people. Now they were massed aboard a steamer whose sides were painted in black, green, and orange zig-zag lines—"to disguise it from the enemy submarines" a corporal told him—and heading for France. He stood by the rail, straining his eyes for a last glimpse of the dim shore-line, and nibbling at the chocolate which some tearful young ladies had slipped into each soldier's hand as the officers counted and hustled them on board.

THE WAR HAD ALSO come to High Point, North Carolina, where the Johnson family had gone to live when they left Back Row. Aunt Polly, broken by the lynchings which had robbed the Johnsons of their friends, had come down with heart trouble and crossed over the river a few months afterwards. There were only Uncle Joey and George left.

The passion to serve his race which Uncle Ben Morgan's stories had kindled in young George had been blended, since that fearful night, with a burning hatred and determination to right the wrongs of his people. Just how this was to be done, he did not know. Shyly the boy tried talking it over with Pa, but the old man only grew troubled, cautioning him to mind his own affairs.

"No good'll come of it, my boy. Polly was right, thar's but one way to git along with white folks 'n that's to let 'em have their way. They allays have ruled this country, 'n allays will. You're nigh sixteen, 'n maybe feelin' your oats. But mark my words 'n leave things be."

George snatched his cap and made for the street. Poor old Pappy, he was done for. Since those days at Back Row, his once barrel-shaped body had shrunk, like an apple left to dry in the sun, his ready laugh had shriveled too, and in his eyes had crept a brooding, humbled look that curled his son's lips and brought tears to his eyes. Poor Old Pappy—he, George, would have to find help somewhars else.

He thought over the young fellows and girls his age. Most of 'em, when work was over, were too taken up with jazz 'n craps to pay other things much mind. "Oh, go way with you, long face," they jibed at him, "doan come round here with your moon's eyes." Yet George located three others who were willing to ruminate over what could be done. On Sunday afternoons they'd ramble into the country, sing work-songs or spirituals and try to figure it out.

When the war spread its flood over High Point the Negro section of town underwent a great transformation. For silver-tongued orators set forth a doctrine from pulpit and press which fell like sweet music on the ears of Negro people. "In this great War for Democracy, the colored people, like the white Americans, have their part to play and much to gain. They have shared in the country's benefits, and they must share in its hour of trial.

"Unfortunately at times the colored race has not shared equally with the white, and has even been mis-treated in some respects. But if they will just forget past mistakes and do their part in this emergency, this country will live up to its obligations in the full sense of the word and undertake to see that the Negro gets full justice." Wilson's talk about the rights of minorities and the self-determination of peoples was interpreted by national and local patriots agitating among the colored population as a virtual pledge to these twelve millions that "Full economic and political equality is at last to be the heritage of the colored people—if they do their bit."

Many, Uncle Joey among them, shrugged their shoulders and others openly muttered to their own kind, "Their words sound sweet, but when white men talk soft, they's after somethin'." Nevertheless, when those looked upon as outstanding Negro leaders added their voices, when an editorial appeared in the *Crisis* "Close ranks. Stop Agitating. Fight the Common Enemy," many doubters joined in the swelling tide of fervor. At last their race was to be free!

In far-away India and Africa, Great Britain statesmen were using similar eloquency, backed by machine guns, to persuade some three hundred million dark peoples to place their youth and resources at the disposal of the allies who were fighting to establish Democracy throughout the world. George and his friends saw in the war their great opportunity. America needed, called on them, offering a chance to win freedom for their people. With shining eyes and high hopes George signed up. Although far below minimum recruiting age, he was a husky, over-grown lad and the officer, following instructions, did not question too closely but wrote down as George had given it—"Age, eighteen years."

In the midst of the war, the November Revolution in Russia broke like an earthquake, rocking old foundations as it thundered around the world. The allied press which a few months previously had welcomed the overthrow of the Czar in screaming headlines now grew silent altogether or wrote in constrained tones of hostility, tempered at first, however, by military considerations. For was not Russia an ally strategically placed for holding the eastern front?

Nevertheless behind the public scene Wall Street bankers and industrialists conferred with Washington and European statesmen. Aghast, they read the handwriting on the wall. Beneath their feet the earth trembled, shaken by the impact of millions of hungry, war-sick and on the march. Today Russia. Tomorrow Germany, Austria, and the whole of Europe? How to throttle this rabble upstart—that was the question!

Some of the most far-seeing among the world's financiers had anticipated a day of rising. Judge Gary, head of the Steel Trust had said at a public dinner in 1910: "Another French Revolution is coming. . . . Once more the people will rise against their oppressors. . . . But this time it will be our class, the business class, attacked by the laboring class. . . . Against that day we must prepare."

Now it was upon them. The Russian people had committed the unpardonable crime of not stopping with the Czar but had kept on until they had cleared out all those who, as Tolstoi once vividly described it, had ridden on their backs. The workers in the city, together with the toiling masses of the countryside, crying "Peace, Land, Liberty and Bread," had seized all power and were proceeding to rule the country with a firm hand. They had abolished the sacred institution of private property in the means of life—that holy of holies, the corner stone of western, capitalistic civilization!

Simple, toil-stained men and women had come from the fields and factories, soldiers had left the trenches to attend the first Congress of Soviets which their leader—Lenin—opened with the words, "Comrades, we will now proceed to construct the socialist society."

Tom in his cell seized on the news with quivering hands. At last it had happened, what Bess said. Maybe she was there, taking part in it! Now the war would end, the Russian people would make peace. Oh, to be out of this place . . . Feverishly he scrawled off a note to Marge, ending "Hurrah for the Russians. . . . Us American workers will learn to follow suit!" The guard caught him trying to smuggle it out and Tom got solitary for his pains. The hours in the mouldy blackness were lit by the radiance of a hope fresh-born. "The First Time in History . . . The first, but not the last."

Only faint echoes of the struggle taking place in the ranks of labor in the industrial centers of the north and west reached Row Hill. Marge, heavy with child and drugged with labor barely noted that somewhere, in far-off Russia, so the papers said, an unknown people had murdered their rulers and chaos and immorality were running riot throughout the land (How could she know that behind this lying smoke-screen rattled the guns of Wall Street, London, and Paris? That, Bess and her comrades manning Petrograd's barricades had resolved "Better death than defeat to the first Workers' Republic.") . . . When would this war be over, and Bob safe home? How much longer could she hold out at the machine?

George Johnson was driving army mules along the Mexican border and cursing himself for the fool he was, to fall for the white politicians' talk about a war for democracy. Here he was, who'd planned on winning everlasting glory for his people, driving mules in Texas! Being called "nigger," treated like one. A low-down trick the government'd pulled off. They were afraid to give the Negroes guns, afraid to train them how to fight. All they wanted of us was to drive mules. Disgusted, he thought of making off, but the quick fate meted out to one boy in the company who tried it led him to abandon the idea. No sir, he'd not be shot down in the back. He was going to live to get even.

Then, almost before he knew what had happened, he was bounding along in a cattle car and herded with his mules aboard a ship headed for France. Here, alongside black, brown, and yellow coolies who spoke in many strange tongues, he labored endless hours in the mud and rain, and was cursed and ordered at the point of a gun, until a fog settled on his brain, blotting out everything but one dogged thought: Wait till this is over. Sullenly he heaved logs, dug ditches, hitting back wherever he dared. Just wait till this was over, and he was back in the old U.S.A.!

XIII.

Marge Questions

THE MACHINE BELT HAD BROKEN, and the women spinners, glad of a moment's respite, sat on window sills, leaned against the frames or gathered in the toilet "to pass the time of day," while Art, the handy-man-about-the-mill worked at his repairing.

"The cost of vittels 'n coal's gone plum out of sight." Little Miz Jones ran her hands down her apron. "But our pay envelopes ain't swelled any."

"'N look what goods cost now," Marge threw in, "it's scandlous."

"I wonder how soon this here war for democracy is gonna quit? If it don't halt soon 'n our men-folks come back, we'll sure have to do somethin' bout more wages." Haggard discontent, puckered brows, loosened rasping tongues. The women drew closer, looking around to make sure the boss-spinner wasn't in hearing distance.

"All these here drives they wants us to give to, I tell you, it's never endin'." Bertha, who reminded Marge of a young elm, twisted a piece of cotton thread between her thumb and forefingers.

"Yah, but look what happened when Fan MacGray didn't sign up. They found somebody for her place." Miz Jones hit her palms together and chewed her under lip.

"It sure is hard times. I tell you the truth, honey," a Negro woman sweeper who had been standing nearby, listening in, broke in on the conversation, "this here's my last rag, 'n when it goes I ain't seen whar another's comin' from. Winter is here 'n my young'uns ain't shoes or coats to cover 'em." She sighed and leaned on her broom. Some of the white women deliberately ignored her, but Marge, always friendly, and remembering Ma Morgan and her talks with Tom, answered her, "Yah, Annie, it's hard-goin's now."

As the belt swung into place and the power was thrown on, the hum of the machines drowned their talk. The women's spare bodies in their straight calico slips moved down the aisles, back to their places at the frames.

Marge's feet dragged. The whirling spools danced and swam before her eyes. Gee, she mustn't get took sick now, it was two and a half months yet before her baby'd come. She must hold out. The few dollars the government sent her would not pay the doctor's bill, let alone take care of her other wants.

As she felt the child's kick against her side, a fierce resentment of this added burden went through her. In the weeks after Bob left, worry for him was soon drowned in frantic dread, when she didn't come round. For days she hoped and waited and applied all the old-fashioned, useless methods known to Poor White women folks: sitting in a washtub of hot mustard bath, dosing with salts and oil, meanwhile praying desperately "God, doan let it happen . . . doan let it happen." Nevertheless, the weeks passed and she didn't come round.

When morning nausea commenced, Marge gave up hoping against the inevitable. Gertie, observing her vomiting spells, remarked, "You're caught, ain't you?"

Detecting an ill-concealed satisfaction in her voice, Marge turned on her angrily. "Mind your own business."

One child pulling at her breast and another swinging to her skirt, Gertie lumbered out of the room. Tired of her whining and Row Hill dreariness, Harry had deserted her to take up hoboing again, but not before he had left these two legacies to the Crenshaw household. Gertie, like her Ma before her, had accepted them with dull resignation, as part of God's will. According to custom, each baby had been insured for one hundred dollars soon after its first squawking appearance on the hill. The ten cents a week payment proved a shrewd ghastly foresight, for the death rate kept pace with the high birth rate among mill operatives and their sandy-haired offspring.

Marge hardly knew where to turn for aid. She had heard whispering among the women of how Miz Briggs had got rid of hers with a long carrot, shaved down at one end to a sharp point. But she'd come nigh to dying that time and had never got her strength back, since. Then Sara Hendricks, who'd used a hairpin straightened out to full length—they'd took her to the hospital and she'd died there of blood poisoning.

The older women shook their heads, telling the younger ones, "that's what you get for tryin' to interfere with God's laws."

Everybody knew how the rich city women kept from having kids. And if it came to the worst, there were doctors who'd operate, if you were influential and had money. But for those on the hill, there was nobody.

Locking herself in the smell-laden toilet, Marge tried to bring on an abortion, like Miz Briggs had done, but her only results were loss of blood and a fever that reddened her pale cheeks and brightened her eyes until the girls at the mill told her, "You look more like yourself than you've done in two years. Maybe thar's good news from Bob?" Marge jerked her head sideways.

Was there no way out of this nightmare? Would Bob ever come back? There'd been no word from him for six weeks. For her part she had never mentioned the coming child in her letters to him, nor let Gertie or Ma talk to her regarding it. Secretly she prepared a few clothes, and let out her waist bands. Not mentioning the matter made it seem less real.

The typhoid that summer gathered up Sal in its gaunt harvest, and Marge, sitting dry-eyed among the mourners in the parlor thought bleakly of Ma's life, now ended, and the unwelcome life yet to begin. Round and round, over and over, mill hands' living was always the same. What did it all come to? Years of slaving and a pine coffin at the end.

GRIMLY MARGE HELD to her place at the machine. There were but three weeks more to go. When the dancing before her eyes got too bad, she clutched with both hands at the frame or leaned against the window sill. She mustn't let the boss-spinner see her faint or slowing down, or she'd lose her place.

Another ten days she held out, wordless, unyielding. The other girls avoided her, she acted so queerly toward them.

The boss-man came down the aisle. "We're needin' five extra hands on the night shift, tonight." Among those he called off was Marge Gregory. Bertha, the girl who worked alongside, stepped out. "Say, you know Marge ain't in no condition to put in any more hours today. I'll take her place." The man growled something under his breath. Marge, pushing her friend aside, cut in, "Oh, no, I want to work tonight, 'n I'm all right. I need the work. . . . I . . ."

Toward midnight she found the dancing before her eyes growing brighter, the singing in her ears louder, more insistent. The mill lights blurred, blackened; she slipped quietly to the floor. Two mill hands carried her on a piece of canvas to the company dwelling where the Crenshaw clan lived as so many rabbits in a burrow, and laid her on a cot. The bed in which Ruth and Gertie slept and the pallet for her two children were removed into the dining room for the night. The next afternoon, Marge's little girl was born. By nightfall, the bed was moved back into its former quarters and the pallet spread on the floor. Marge drifted in a haze, too tired to mind the baby's weak crying or Gertie's whining that she couldn't sleep.

She woke to find the company welfare worker, Miss Gipson, bending over her, the infant in her arms. "Here is your little daughter, all bathed and ready for a meal. You're fortunate she's alive," she added reproachfully, "you should never have worked as long as you did at the mill."

Sharp words caught in Marge's throat. Many a time she'd passed Miss Gipson on the street in the past weeks, only now was the first time the lady'd spoken to her. Well, maybe she knew it'd do no good.

"Yes'm," she answered softly, "I reckon you're right." At the feel of the tiny mouth pulling at her breast, tears slipped over her pale cheeks and ran down her neck.

"Why are you cryin'?" the older woman inquired, "aren't you pleased to have the baby?"

"Yes'm . . . that is . . . I reckon so . . . I doan know why."

The peace of exhaustion glued her to the bed. The last of her strength was flowing into the child.

The week that Marge lay in bed the life of the household surged around her. Petty bickering, continual worrying and night and day shifts forever coming and going to the mill. Gradually as strength returned there developed an unexpected tenderness for the tiny form that lay beside her, stretching out its fists and eager mouth for Marge's sagging breast. With its tilted nose, reddish hair, and one-sided smile, "You're the spitting image of your Pa," she murmured.

"Ruth," she asked her sister that evening, "write me a note to Bob. Tell him about Roberta." However, by the time her letter reached Bob he was unable to read it. Gassed and delirious from a hip wound, he was keeping two orderlies busy with his attempts to leave his cot, meanwhile raving of horrors he had seen and something a German soldier had said to him.

Marge puzzled over her feeling toward the nurse. She was grateful to her for her daily visits that first week, her care of the baby and herself and the instructions she gave. But for Miss Gipson she could not have managed, every one else was at the mill. Yet, in spite of the nurse's official kindness, Marge resented her—her condescending tone, and the gingerly way in which she approached the bed and handled their things. "She doan act like one of us," the mill woman reasoned, "she belongs to the comp'ny, that's what." She knew how the mill used the nurse to spy out those who stayed away sick, who should—so the company said—have been at the mill, working.

The entire household was relieved when Miss Gipson's visits came to an end.

In two weeks' time Marge was back at the machine, and hurrying home at noon and evening to nurse and tend her child. The baby stayed weakly. Marge's milk was scanty, and little Roberta missed many feedings while her anxious Ma was in the spinning room. But it couldn't be helped. Miss Gipson, happening by one late afternoon, told Marge that she needed to drink more milk, eat fresh eggs and oranges. Marge looked up defiantly. "Yes'm, if the mill paid more I could." Startled, Miss Gipson, muttering to herself, made off. During the morning the mill super called Margie aside.

"You know, the mill held your place 'n you ought to appreciate it. You're a good hand 'n all that, but if you ain't satisfied, we can find plenty of others."

Afterwards Marge accused herself. "How can I hold myself above the others? Ain't we all cowed! Here I run to cover at the first crack of their whip."

As the summer heat beat down on the village's shallow roofs, young Roberta's whimper grew fainter and her eyes took on an empty stare. "Lawdy," Marge moaned to her sister, my baby's wastin' away."

"It sure is gettin' thin 'n peaked-lookin'." Gertie bent over the younger woman's shoulder to gaze at the tiny form lying on her knees.

"What can I do?"

"Call Miss Gipson."

"All she says is my milk's poor. Doan I know that! ... Lawdy, I'm starvin' my baby." She rocked back and forth in her misery and waved away the flies.

"You're washin' it away," Gertie retorted. "I never heered of sech doin's. Washin' it all over every day! It's a wonder the poor child doan catch its death. A lil' dirt's healthy. That's what Ma allays said." This was a sore point between them.

"Naw, it ain't that," Marge replied listlessly.

"I reckon I ought to know," her sister, starting into the kitchen, couldn't resist a final shot, "ain't I borned two already? So I ought to know."

When Roberta grew worse, "Will," Marge asked the boss-spinner, "Can't I change to night time? My baby is awful sick 'n I need to watch over it day time, when nobody is there. In case it has a spell, it might strangle by itself."

"SORRY, MARGE, BUT YOU KNOW how it is now. Us rushed with orders, 'n nobody to change off with you."

Instead, she paid forty cents a week to a twelve-year-old girl to watch by the baby. "'N remember to lift her head if she's chokin'-like. If she gets too bad, you come for me."

"To the mill?"

"Yah. I doan care. If it gets as bad as that, I'm a-comin' home."

The baby fretted most of the night. Gertie wanted to give it warmed tobacco juice, a time-honored remedy, but Marge, remembering that Miss Gipson had cautioned her it was hard on a weak stomach, held out against it.

Red-eyed from lack of sleep Marge hastened toward the mill. She noted mechanically the numerous moving vans piled high with shabby furniture, and new families scurrying in and out of the frame dwellings. "Looks like us people is ever movin' 'n rovin'. Allays lookin' for somethin' better on another hill. 'N the war's made it worse. Mills sproutin' up all over 'n families crowdin' in offa the land."

She, Gertie, and the rest of the household had moved to Brandon, and then on to Judson, in hopes of higher wages. But nothing had come of their trouble.

At noon she hurried, half-running, toward the house. Roberta lay in the crib, blue in the face and choking for breath. Gently Marge picked her up and sent the twelve-year-old girl on the run for a doctor. Placing the baby against her shoulder she struggled with it for air, murmuring "Thar now honey, be better soon honey." Inwardly she prayed, "Gawd Jesus, doan let it die. . . . May be I sinned, not wantin' it. . . . But now it's here. . . . I done all I know how. . . . Doan let it die." Not faith but habit deeply imbedded since childhood years—prompted her words.

The doctor, turning away from the stricken look in the young mother's eyes, returned the stiffened body to its crib.

FALL HAD NEVER BEEN more gorgeous than this year. The woods were riotous with golden reds and browns. Yet mill people were too harassed and hurried by the war, life itself was too barren, too meaningless, to take notice of the natural beauty around them.

Marge, standing over the tiny grave in the cemetery looked
at the scene with sightless eyes. "Bob'll never see our baby.
All that sufferin' 'n denyin' . . . Now she's gone." The wind
ruffled her fading hair and blew crisp, yellowed leaves across
the green mounds. Pulling her shawl more closely around her,
she retraced her steps among the tombstones, and along the
winding, dirt road.

XIV.

The Loaf Leavens

"IT DOES LOOK LIKE there oughta be a way to get more of our deserts." Ben Tilson, his chair tilted against the side of the house, his long legs twined about its spokes, chewed reflectively. A Sunday afternoon gathering on the Tilson's porch were enjoying a few hours of autumn sun and a bit of neighborly conversation. Naturally, the talk had soon drifted to the subject of local conditions. "The mill's makin' money hand over fist. All of them puttin' up these here community buildin's to save theirselfs war taxes. Why doan they give us that money in wages?"

"That's right. But how we gonna make 'em?"

"What with overtime 'n all, it sure wears a body down." Miz Jones released a whistling, patient sigh.

"What we need," Ben went on, "is leaders. Somebody to organize us. Then if we all holden out, the comp'ny gotta come through."

"Now you said truth." Marge spoke rapidly. "My brother Tom told me about a union, when he was down. All stick together, 'n just walk out 'n stay out till the boss-mens give in."

"Wal," young Bert Peters drawled cautiously. "Wal, when I was over to Woodside tother day, lookin' for a better place, I heerd somethin'." He looked around impressively. "I heerd tell thar was an organizer thar come down from the north."

"How's that?" Everybody strained forward. Bert felt his importance.

"They's been holdin' secret meetin's, 'n goin' from house to house."

"Ah, Lawdy," Gertie moaned, "now thar'll be trouble brewin'."

"Oh, do hold your tongue, sis," Marge nudged her, "so we can hear all Bert knows. You say they's at Woodside?"

"Uh-huh, and," he paused dramatically, "thar's two of 'em, a man 'n an 'oman!"

Ben Tilson slapped his knees. "I'll be gol-darned!"

"Ben, mind your words, it's a Sunday," his wife reminded him.

"Can't help it, Becky, the words slipped out. What the women gettin' to, these days. Organizin'. No 'oman can organize me!"

"I'd like to know why not!" Miz Jones was indignant.

Bert was labored with questions. Everyone unconsciously lowered his voice; the comp'ny allays had plenty of ears on mill hills!

"They tells us how," Bert explained, "they's all signin' up in the new organization. It's called the I.W.W. . . . . 'N soon," the last words came in a whisper, "thar's to be a walk-out fer higher wages 'n no over-time."

"The I.W.W.!" Marge exulted, "that's Tom's union. We gotta get 'em over here." Gertie's dissent was lost in the general approval. It was arranged that Bert make another trip to the neighboring village, to talk things over with the organizers and bring them here on Friday night. "We'll keep this to ourselves." "Except we oughta have Tillie 'n Herb Gray." "Yah, 'n old man Roberts. He knows everybody 'n ain't scared of nuthin'."

After nightfall on Friday, Bert brought the two organizers to the small group crowded into Tilson's kitchen. Shades were drawn, a look-out was stationed near the front door. "Friends, this here," young Bert gestured awkwardly from the visitors to the mill hands who had risen and stood waiting, tense behind their quiet watchfulness, "this here is— Fellow-worker Joe Mattheson 'n this here is . . ." "Fellow-worker Edith Grady," a small, Irish type of young woman stepped forward and finished the sentence for him.

"I'm right glad to make your acquaintance." Ben extended his ample hand. After that they shook hands all round, then fumbled quietly for their seats. Expectantly they looked toward Ben. An awe rested upon the little gathering, something significant was happening in their lives.

Ben cleared his throat. "Us mill hands here heard tell how you was organizing over to Judson 'n Brandon, 'n we calculate we wanta organize too."

"Good, good, that's fine." Joe Mattheson rubbed his palms together in vigorous fashion, so that all brightened at once. He was a heavy-set, middle-aged man whose dress, bearing, and manner of speaking marked him as springing from the hardy stock of western lumberjacks and farm hands.

Standing at the end of the kitchen table he spoke in husky, ponderous tones, occasionally pounding its smooth surface to emphasize a point until Becky Tilson and one or two timid ones glanced around nervously for fear they'd be heard outside. Seeing their concern, he tried to speak more quietly. The stranger said a lot of things, only part of which his listeners followed, about capitalist exploitation and it being the historic mission of the workers to overthrow present society and establish a socialist one through the weapon of the general strike. When, however, he spoke of their terrible conditions all wondered how they'd been able to put up with them so long. "You know what the bosses say about you up north?" he shamed them, "you're cheap and contented labor!"

"That's slander!" Ben exploded, "plain slander!"

"That's for you to prove," Mattheson retorted. When he touched on the power of organization, the swift victory from striking the job, a new confidence flooded their faces, tightened their calloused hands.

"Now to get down to business. This is how we go about organizing...." He and his companion were kept busy answering questions and planning out the details of the campaign until toward midnight when the organizers were smuggled out of the village and the mill hands left stealthily one by one, by way of the backyard.

Marge threw herself into the organizing work, making the rounds after supper from house to house, persuading them to sign up. "We been sheep long enough." At the next meeting night, the Tilson's kitchen and dining room were jammed to the doors, spirits ran high. Seemed like everybody was for joinin' up. At the organizers' suggestion, they selected a committee of Ben, Bert and Ole Man Roberts to put their demands to the super, the following Monday. No one thought of including a woman—this was a man's job. Small stickers to be pasted on posts and walls of the building were handed out.

"We gotta line up the rest of the hill afore Monday," Ben reminded them, "that means a bigger committee. Now it's me, Bert, Marge Gregory 'n Ole Man Roberts to do all the visitin' 'n cajolin'." Two or three were nominated, but made excuses. "Scared cats," Miz Jones threw in their faces, "I'll go on." John Nelson, a Georgia farmer who had lost his five acres last year and been forced into the mills, agreed to serve.

"I'll be right glad to go on the committee," Lewis White, a good-looking youth who'd been in town only a few weeks, volunteered.

"What about it?" the organizers demanded, "is it all right?"

"Wal, I reckon so. Anybody object?" Ben looked around. Marge felt uneasy, but there was nobody else handy. It was getting late, and besides, what did they have against him?

"What about the Negroes? They should join in too," Edith Grady proposed. Immediately a heated controversy arose.

"This here's a white man's or-gan-*iza*-tion, ain't it?" White thundered. "I, for one, ain't gona mix up in no niggers' union! Bring 'em in 'n we walks out. What about it?" he called on the others.

John Nelson rose to his full six feet three inches. "'N so does I. I done lost my land, but a lotta no-count niggers still got theirs. Lewis here is right, the two doan mix."

"But they're workers too," Mattheson and Grady argued. "What do we lose by it?" Marge asked timidly. "Give 'em a chance to better theirselfs too."

Lewis White pounded the table and thundered like Parson Brown when he was painting the terrors of the Day of Judgment. "You Mattheson 'n Miss Grady come down here from the north, 'n maybe you doan know our ways here. But we whites is Anglosaxons 'n holden ourselfs above the blacks. If we let 'em in the same union, the next thing they'll be workin' at the machines 'n takin' our jobs, 'n runnin' for public office, 'n . . ." He looked mysteriously from Marge to Ben and on around the circle of agitated faces, "'N they'll be wantin' next to marry our sisters 'n daughters, too!"

Mattheson and Edith Grady conferred hastily, then agreed to drop the matter. Marge felt uneasy. What would Tom and his friend Fred think about it?

The next morning Ben Tilson and young Bert were told outright their services weren't needed any longer. Old man Roberts was called into the office to be questioned about the rumors going round about labor troubles stirred up by two German spies. "The company's allays liked you Roberts, you've been a faithful worker here for close to twenty years. If you'll do the fair thing by us, the mill will continue to do the fair thing by you."

"Yes-sir, but I doan know nuthin'." The weaver held his hands behind him, "I guess somebody's carryin' false tales."

"You know well enough, my good man! That's all." The superintendent whirled contemptuously in his chair back toward his desk. Roberts stood a moment, then walked out. A hurried meeting was held that night in Tilson's kitchen. "Thar's a leak somewhar, somebody's a-tatlin' to the boss, Ben accused.

"I seen old man Roberts goin' to the office today," Lewis White suggested.

"You shut your mouth, you young snapper," the old man shook a fist under his nose. "Say that again, 'n I'll sprawl you out. The mill folks here know me, they know I ain't no tatler. Maybe they doan know as much 'bout you!"

Lewis gave him a shove across the room. "You shut up, or for all your gray hairs, I'll pummel you proper."

"Order, order," Ben thumped the table, "this thing's gotta be gone at in proper fashion. Now who wants the floor?"

"I do," Lewis spoke with assurance. "I want to say that this strike plan oughta be called off, afore more lose their jobs. Somebody's tatlin', that's sure, 'n what's worse, the mill hands ain't gona stick by one another. We're licked afore we start. So let's act sensible. Nobody wants to be turned offa the hill, like Ben and Bert's gona be, do they? With tales followin' 'em from hill to hill?"

"That's crooked talk!" Ben lunged toward him, there was a confused uproar. "Order, order." Ben strode back to his place as chairman. "Lewis is a good boy, 'n faithful at vis-itin'. I reckon he doan mean no harm. But this ain't no time for gettin' down-hearted. The organizers got a big meetin' tonight to Woodside, so they'll be a bit late gettin' here. But they sent word, what we gotta do is go right ahead, present our demands next Monday, *'n add to 'em that me 'n Bert be taken back*."

"That's the talk!" "Right-o!" Dismayed confusion gave way to lust for the fight.

"'N," Roberts glared at Lewis, "we gotta take steps at once to spy out the tatler."

"Yah, 'n wash his mouth with soap!" Miz Jones exclaimed. "'N we won't stop thar, nuther," Bert added, "he or she'll get all's comin' to him!"

Crudely lettered posters stuck in the toilets of the mill announced an outdoor meeting right after work in the baseball clearing. All sorts of rumors were circulating in the plant: the mill would close down, Mattheson had been caught with papers on him that proved he was paid by the Kaiser and lodged in the state penitentiary. The strike was called off. The strike would start that night, with a vote at the mass meeting.

By six o'clock the field was dense with mill hands, the drooping sun sending its last slanting rays across their sallow faces and slight bodies. To their backs loomed the mill and the gray rows of company houses. An uproar went up as Ben and Edith Grady clammered on the improvised stand. "Fellow-workers," Ben drawled, "you're called here to hear the truth 'n take action. . . . A lot of lies been spread today. They call us slackers to want more bread for our chillen. Is that right?"

"No! no!" thundered his listeners, pressing in closer.

"Is it traitorous to wanta work no mo'n eleven hours a day?" "No. . . . Boy, you tell 'em!"

"They've done put one of our organizers in jail, 'n spread lies on him too, but the other one is here with us 'n is gona speak to you now." As Edith Grady stepped forward a shower of rotten eggs and old cabbage descended upon the stand, breaking against her face and sides, splattering Ben, and rolling into the infuriated crowd.

"You dam rowdies!" Bert, Ben and a dozen more rushed toward the throwers, among whom stood Lewis White, whiter than his name. "Thar's the dam skunk! Let the dirty dog have it!"

In the turmoil Edith Grady was dragged off by three company men, shoved in to a waiting car. In Greenville they put her under armed guard on a train going north.

"You slacker," they told her, "labor agitator! If you weren't a lady, 'n us southern gentlemen, we'd treat you proper! Show your face in the state of South Car'liny again, 'n we doan answer for the consequences. Comin' down here 'n stirrin' up our contented help!" At Richmond they handed her over to Federal police, who lodged the charge against her of espionage for the enemy.

There was no sleep on Row Hill that night. When the whistle blew for work, the mill hands formed in glum rows on the opposite side of the narrow street. The spinner and weaver bosses rushed over. "Why ain't you comin' to work?" "Not till the comp'ny meets our demands—no overtime, a ten-percent increase in wages, 'n me and Bert tooken back at our jobs." Ben acted as spokesman.

"To hell with you, ain't you got no patriotism? Doan you know your country's fightin' a war for democracy, 'n you ain't right to strike now?"

"All we know is," Miz Jones quavered, "we plum wore out with so much overtime."

"Yah, 'n skrimpin' our vittles," John Nelson threw out his hands, "we're patriotic, but that doan mean we gotta starve our young'uns, do it?"

Finally the super came out and made an eloquent speech, flaying spies and traitors, and trouble-makers, reminding them of the company's love and many services for them, calling some by name, threatening them with dire things if they held out in their absurd demands. The mill hands stood silently listening until he had ended. Respect for the great man weighed them down (hadn't they minded the word of him 'n his kind since childhood?). But a common need held them back, kept their ranks firm.

"Mister Murphyboro, we heard you to the end. But we stand by our rights. I guess, folks," Ben gestured to those around him, "it's time we was headin' home. This here's the first vacation you ever got, so enjoy it, 'n remember the meetin' tonight in the old lot behind the tracks." As the operatives shambled slowly down the street, Ben turned toward the superintendent. "Tell Mr. Haines for us that his hands ain't workin' till we get a better deal. Any time you want to talk business, we got a committee ready."

For an entire week the looms stood idle. The company made frantic efforts to man the machines, for orders were pouring in, but the labor shortage and the alertness of Row Hill's pickets soon buried this hope. The Negro help, although ignored by the white mill hands, stayed away from the mills of their own accord. Saturday afternoon the superintendent sent for the committee.

"Now thar's one final thing." Ben cleared his throat. "We doan mean no disrespect, but the mill folks wanta have this here agreement 'bout no overtime in writin'. Just in case, you know. In future years it might come in handy."

XV.

"Rich Man's War— Poor Man's Fight"

"PEACE! PEACE!" MARGE AND RUTH were jerked out of their sleep as a shrill voice broke in on the night's stillness. "The war's ended! Peace! Peace!" Snatching a wrapper Marge ran to the door. "Boy, here, here!" she held out her coppers for the paper.

Quaking with the chill, she sat on the edge of the bed to read the news while Ruth and Gertie, huddled up, the bedclothes pulled around their shoulders, listened with strained faces. The children on the pallet whimpered, blinking at the lights.

"Thank the Lawd it's over," Gertie murmured and dropped back on her pillow.

"Come on Ruth, let's dress 'n go outside," Marge laughed hysterically. "I'm too restless to sleep."

Lights shone dimly from the grey shacks that lined the street, doors banged as mill hands joined the rapidly gathering crowd, pulling on jackets and shawls as they ran.

"Hurrah, the war's over!"

"The slaughterin' 'll stop 'n our boys come home."

"We'll have a real Christmas this year!"

Villagers pounded one another's backs, shook hands all round each time a new-comer joined them, threw caps into the air, and paraded the narrow, dirt street singing and hurrahing until the stars paled in the greying sky and it was time for a bite to eat before going to the mill.

The super and foremen raced from one department to another, scowling angrily. "You all gone crazy? Sure the war's ended. But these here orders got to go out!"

After the super left, Miz Jones slipped over to Marge to whisper, "what you know, thar's some that ain't glad this war's over! They been makin' a pile of money, the mill has. 'N it warn't *their* sons across!" She spit viciously into a rusty pail standing nearby.

Marge caught a glimpse of Bertha's sad face as she wove in and out among the frames. Poor Bertha! Thar'd be no home comin' for her; her man lay over thar, blown to smitherins.

"We're sailing the end of this week," Bob wrote in shaky, zig-zag lines, "and should be home by March." Marge sung at her machine. She had Bertha over to supper and made her a chemise for Christmas. When Bertha wept on her shoulders, "why did the Almighty let it happen?" Marge felt guilty in her own happiness.

The mills, banks and business firms closed for half a day to greet the returning Greenville boys. Once again flags flew, khaki figures tramped, bands played martial music, flaming speeches were made. These boys (sons of farmers, mill workers, doctors and small business men) had won the War for Democracy! They were heroes, let them ask the best that America had to offer, nothing was too good for them!

"Bob!" Marge's vision of his thin, limping figure, his crooked smile, blurred. "You've come home."

"Lil' Marge . . . Yah, I've come home."

"SO UNCLE MAT BROKE DOWN 'n went to spend his last days at his son's farm in Georgy? That's too bad." Bob, his second day back, was still catching up on the news. "'N what's happened to Tom?"

Immediately the entire table ceased eating, staring at him in a strange way. The two boarders, excusing themselves hastily, went outside.

"You see, Tom opposed the war," Marge began.

"Tom brung disgrace on us all, that's what," Gertie blurted out. "Ma allays said he would. But," her voice broke, "I never expected to have a jail bird in the family." Billy and Sam reddened, looked down at their hands.

"Doan you dare say that 'bout Tom!" Marge retorted, "he ain't no ordinary criminal."

"Marge, for goodnes' sakes, keep your voice down!" Ruth gasped.

"Wal, I ain't ashamed of Tom, if the rest of you is. He done what he thought was right. He's got convictions 'n the govern-ment put him in jail for it."

"Convictions or no convictions, he's in jail, ain't he?" Gertie demanded. "If they find it out at the mill, they'll turn us offa the hill."

"Let 'em," Marge answered. "Jest let 'em. I'll give 'em a piece of my mind."

"Lotta good that'll do us," Ruth grumbled. "Marge, this time's Gertie's right."

Bob shook his head. "Wal, I ain't so sure." Later he asked Marge, "Just what is it Tom believes?" They talked far into the night.

"Now the war's over, why doan they let him out?" Marge questioned anxiously, "If he was a rich man's son they'd not keep him locked up like that."

"If he was a rich man's son, he'd never got took up in the first place."

Bob was restless to be at work. "But wait a while," Marge begged, "till you get rested up a mite; 'n I can feed you up on grits 'n gravy, 'n take that peaked look off'n you. Your lungs 'n side ain't right yet, the doctor says."

"But honey, I can't be a-livin' offa you. You look like a rest would set you up right smart, yourself."

"I'm all right, now you're back." Her voice dropped. "Lil' Roberty's goin' went hard with me."

He put his arms around her. "Doan you grieve, honey. Soon as I'm well again, 'n workin' steady, we'll have another to take Roberty's place." Marge didn't answer. The old doubt assailed her, altho challenged now by a longing for motherhood which Roberta had awakened in her.

"Soon I'll be back at weavin' 'n we can start out fresh, in four rooms of our own. . . . Gee, Marge, it's good to be back; those fifteen months were the longest I ever spent." Only fifteen months! They looked at each other. Where were the carefree youth, the starry-eyed girl of a brief year and a half ago?

"Marge!" Gertie's whining voice sallied forth from the kitchen, "time to be a-fixin' supper."

It was evident, even to Bob, that he couldn't do a day's work at the mill. As Ruth remarked, even odd jobs around the house tired him out. What troubled Marge more than anything else was that he didn't seem to improve very fast. Then he was changed. The old Bob, with his ready laugh and boisterous confidence, was gone, and in his place was this quiet, brooding creature who wandered about the house as though looking for something he couldn't find.

She'd come upon him sitting with his hands hanging down between his knees, eyes staring ahead. "The war's done somethin' to him . . . somethin'." Coming up close behind him, she slipped her arms across his chest and pressed his head against her breast. "What's it Bob, what you a-lookin' at?" she whispered. Turning, he wormed his head against her body like a small boy. "The things I seen over thar . . . Looks like I can't forget 'em."

Sometimes he would break down and sob, clinging to her, gasping out his horror. One time he'd plunged his bayonet through a fair-haired lad. "His eyes haunt me, his cry rings in my ears." He told her of Will, the mountain boy at Camp Lee who had been driven to suicide because he was hone-in' for the hills 'n didn't hanker to fight in a conflict that 'tain't our war. Of bomb raids, gas attacks, of birds of prey stalking the fields.

"Honey," his grip tightened until she held her breath from the pain, "If I could just be sure it was for somethin'. But it 'pears like I lost all my belief over thar in what we were fightin' for. I'd have come away, if I could. But thar warn't no way, 'n you had to keep killin' or get killed."

Marge, as shaken as he, tried to comfort him. "You did the best you knew how. Now it's all over 'n behind you. You're back. We *got* each other, 'n we gotta helpen our people here."

"Yah, us mill folks gotta fight for our rights. If I can jest get my strength back. Seems like they done for me."

"Doan say that. It takes time, but you're perkin' up a lil' every day. When you spose we'll hear 'bout that govern-ment compensation you been writin' about?"

"Aw, the govern-ment doan care 'bout us no more, now the fightin's over!"

"But at the parade they said . . ."

"They said! Then what for they put so much in the way between me 'n Burke'n the others what got hurt over thar 'n the pay that's due us?"

"I dunno. Reckon it takes time, or somethin'."

"Somethin' is right, somethin' we mill hands ain't got. Pull."

BILLY AND SAM WERE persistent in their questioning of Bob and his two buddies, Burke and Walter. "Ah, go on, tell us more about what it was like, fightin' in France. Was it sure-nough like the movies shows it?" The family was still grouped around the cleared supper table, various neighbors had dropped in.

Bob's fingers drummed restlessly on the red cloth. "Thar ain't nuthin' worth tellin'."

"Ah, Brother Bob," Sam wheedled, "doan act tightmouthed. What about the night of the gas attack when you 'n Burke . . ."

"Do leave 'em alone," Marge urged, "can't you see they doan wanta talk?"

Walter pulled irritably at his empty right sleeve. "If you wanta be filled up to the guzzle with war stories, go in town to the American Legion. Thar's plenty boys thar who lap up this hero stuff. Us here ain't the stomach for 'em."

"They sure is modest ones," Ben Tilson's wife spoke in an admiring stage whisper.

"Naw, that ain't it, Miz Tilson," Burke gave an embarrassed cough. "Beggin' you pardon, ladies, but—" suddenly he exploded, "me 'n my pals here is plum shet to hell of the war 'n war talk."

"Let's change the subject." Marge looked around uneasily.

"Tell you what," Billy, unheeding, addressed his young brother, "what you say in a coupla years we join the army? Oughta be more to it than jest workin' at the mill."

Abruptly Bob lifted his head. "All right, Bill, Sam 'n all of you, we'll tell what war's really like." He spoke sternly. "Maybe you young folks can larn some sense in time. Though I doubts it."

Toward the end Burke described the unrest and near-mutiny in his battalion because of bug-infested rations, the brutality of the officers, and the senseless wasting of lives.

"More'n one struttin' Napoleon near got shot down—by mistake you understand. 'N soldiers wisecracked between theirselfs 'I loved this country, but let me get outta this war'n I'll never love another.'" And Bob related his experience with a German soldier. "I was in a detail carryin' prisoners of war to the rear. On the way we got a lil' friendly, though it was contrary to orders. One fella, about Ben's age 'n size offered me a smoke. He could speak a bit of English, too.

"'Why you fight?' he asked me. 'You workman, me workman, why fight?' He told me he was a textile weaver from a place called Saxony. Jest think, a mill hand like us!" Bob marveled. They talked this over for awhile.

"By gorry!" Ben exploded, "you mean?"

"Yah," Bob nodded wearily, "It was all lies, 'bout them bloody man-eatin' Huns. I seen a lotta other prisoners, 'n once you got to study 'em, close-like, they turned out to be just common folk like us. . . . Now this one I was tellin' you of, he showed me a picture from round his neck of his wife 'n lil' boy." Bob gulped. "'N he said, 'I'm glad I'm a prisoner, no more fightin'. 'N he asked me again, 'Why workmen fight each other? For their rich men! Workmen should stand together.' Then an officer come up, 'n we didn't get to talk any more. I never saw him again."

His listeners talked this over.

"When you come to think of it, what we got out of the war?" Ben ruminated. "Us here on the hill is bad off as ever, with talk of wage-cuts flyin' round."

"I tell you what we got," Walter spoke bitterly. "Bob'n Burke got bad lungs 'n me, I got an arm missin' outta the war, 'n thar's a new crop of millionaires outta the war. That's what we got."

"The mill owners sure musta made money. Look at the new places they bought down in Floridy. You seen the pitchers in the papers? 'N all the new mills what went up."

"That thar war for democracy," Walter continued, "it was one rich man's war 'n poor man's fight." This saying was taken up and spread from hill to hill throughout the Carolinas, Georgia, and Alabama. "Yas-sir, it was a rich man's war 'n a poor man's fight."

"The next time they wanta war," Bob frowned intently at Billy's perplexed face, "they can go fight it theirselfs."

"Democracy me shirt-tail," Burke bumped his chair against the wall, "they sure can count me out."

"John Nelson was a-tellin' me," Ben spoke cautiously, "that thar's a rich man over to Atlanta what says thar's only one more war a-comin' 'n that's between the poor 'n the rich. A new civil war."

"Wal," Walter also made to leave, "when it comes, I guess me 'n Burke 'n Bob'll know on what side to fight."

"Doan speak thata way!" Gertie rasped.

Walter stared at her. "Wal, I reckon," he spoke slowly, "when it comes we boys'll be ready."

THE FOLLOWING SATURDAY, MARGE was given her time, and Gertie also.

"Drat the bossmen's excuses, they ain't foolin' me none!" Marge pulled nervously at her sister's arm. "Jest 'cause Bob ain't strong enough to work reg'lar, they want a family in this here mill house what can supply more hands."

"That ain't all," Gertie mopped her eyes angrily. "They ain't overlooked Bob's bitter talk 'n your part in that thar walk-out last year. Now you see what trouble you all brung on us."

Marge turned away impatiently. "If our union'd lasted, they'd not be able to do this so easy!"

"That union! A fly-by-night it was, like a black crow. . . . Now we're turned offa the hill, whar'll we go? Whar'll we go?" The older woman looked around helplessly.

"Aw, Gertie, leave off. I for one am plum glad to be shet of this hill."

After a family consultation it was decided to move out of the state entirely. Billy had heard that wages were pretty fair at Charlotte, so on Monday the household began the trek northward.

The Winstons who lived next door to their new home in Borders Village proved to be very friendly. The first evening the entire family of eight came over for a visit, and the small dining room buzzed with mutual questioning and relating of experiences on various hills.

Suddenly Ted Winston clammered to his feet. "By gorry, I plum forgot the meetin' down at the union hall."

"Union?" Marge queried.

"Yah. Ain't you heerd about it? We got some or-gani-*za*-tion, with headquarters right here in Charlotte."

"Is that so?!" Bob and Marge exchanged glances.

"Sure as Mike. It's some strong, too. I reckon as how forty thousand in these here two states belong. It's called the United Textile Workers of America."

"You doan tell!"

Ted Wilson hitched up his trousers preparatory to taking his leave. "When we got more time I'll tell you all about it— how we organized, 'n the union come 'n said to jine up with 'em 'n we did. This here ain't no fly-by-night, it's a real union."

"Uh, huh." Each syllable came out with characteristic emphasis, as only a southerner can draw it. "I reckon," Bob and Marge agreed, "this Sadday, after work, we all'll go down to the union hall 'n sign up."

XVI.

Closing Ranks

GEORGE STOOD BY THE RAIL of the liner which was bringing him back to America. Bracing himself against the wind, his black eyes followed the gigantic, multifold rhythm of the purplish green waters. The sea fascinated him. "Like our Blue Ridge mountains was rollin' 'n rumblin' back 'n forth, with spray like lil' clouds aridin' on the top . . . I wisht I could stay on this boat 'n not have to get off."

The war was over; in three days this ship, loaded with men who'd "done their bit Over There," would pass under the stature of Liberty and land in New York. George knocked his clenched fists against the rail. What sort of a country was he coming back to—where men and youths like himself were not considered men, but just "niggers?"

The wind heightened its speed, whistling around the forecastle and along the decks, tossing the few soldiers who had not gone below about like crazed tops, wrenching George loose from his slackened hold at the rail. Shuddering, the ship lifted, then sank with a groaning thud as a whale-backed wave slid from under her. Gleaming sheets of water broke over her bow, men scrambled on all fours for the hatchways. George fought his way once more to his stand at the rail, lashing himself with an iron grip to its dripping sides. The ship alternately pitched and rallied. Her engines throbbing, her crew working with redoubled efforts, she plowed stubbornly on.

Drenched to the skin, exerting all his strength to prevent being swept overboard, George found a grim, unexplained satisfaction in the storm.

He knew he was going back to fight for his people. But he was tired, tired to death. Besides, he didn't yet have a workable plan. And he was still under twenty. The power, the rage of the storm gave him courage. He'd not be alone. There were other men on board, men of his own race, who felt as bitter and determined as he.

By the time the ship had docked at New York he had made up his mind not to return south, but go west with Sol, a new pal of his who was going back to Chicago. Now that Pappy had crossed over the river, six months ago, there was nothing to take him back to that hell-hole. "And you'll like it in Chicago," Sol promised him, "it ain't nigh as bad as the south. You can live with me 'n my folks 'n we-uns'll get us jobs in the stockyards."

So George stood all day, his hands dripping with animal blood, his apron and face spattered, a small stream of red fluid gushing over his straddled feet. His job was to slash the throats of hogs as they swung by him, suspended head downward, their feet tied to a moving chain. For ten hours he plunged his knife until his head reeled from the stench of stale blood and the sight of that never-ending line of squealing, lurching animals moving toward him.

Sol had a job in the section where they slaughtered cattle—where if a man slipped on the bloody floor, and bungled his jab at the cow's throat he was liable to be gored by the crazed animal.

"All I got outta fightin' for democracy," George thought ruefully, "was—slittin' pigs' gullets." Rapidly he drew his sleeve across his face. That dam hog had squirted blood right into his eye! This was like the war, with animals instead of men movin' up, line on line, just to be hewn down. But thar was more sense to a slaughter house: hog's meat made good food.

Sol was right, the old Hog City was sure diff'rent from the south. The girls were diff'rent, too. Thar was Susie, a yellow-skinned, laughin' gal he'd met over to Sol's friends, the Thompson's. She was a game lil' thing—fallen for him right off 'n met his courtin' more'n half-way. She was cash girl at a neighborhood movie in Chicago's Black Belt. After work George would shoot pool or, when too tired, just hang around until the movie's last showing, 'n they'd go over to her place'n he'd forget everythin' else, lovin' her up. About the time she began to hint broadly about how low-down the stockyards were, and his getting a better job elsewhere, George took to staying away evenings, to go with Sol to union meetings. Susie, he found, cared for little except her own good time and frankly told him his ideas were wild ones.

"You see, honey," he tried to explain, holding her pert little face away from him, so as to see her better, and make her serious for awhile, "We-uns gotta fight for our rights. Ain't that so?"

Her face clouded. "What you mean—fight for our rights? That's bad talk, it'll bring trouble. Ever since you took to going to those secret meetings, you ain't been the same. All this talk and scheming'll come to no good end!"

"But can't you see? You know the way they treats us at the yards, worser'n the hogs we're killin'. It can't go on that-taway, we gona call a halt. 'N in this here union of ours—the Stockyard Labor Council—they done lined up both white 'n colored!"

"Union!" she scoffed, "union is for white men. Don't I know? My brother what's a waiter got turned off his job by a white man's union! Right here in Chicago, too. He'll tell you about unions!"

George taken back, dropped the subject; but the next time he came over to Susie's he resumed the argument where they had left it. "You say white folks'll never stand by colored, 'n most times they doan. But this time," his young face was set, "this time it's gona be diff'rent."

"Oh, yeah?"

"Yeah. I used to think it was all whites against all blacks, but our leaders showed us diff'rent. How we gona win more wages if we butchers doan all stick together? Oh boy, thar's some fight brewin'! 'N it won't be no wash-out like the last I messed in."

Susie tightened her hold on his arm. "George, I'm scared. Awful things are going to happen. Won't you drop this—for me? You know what's going on. They're breaking windows of colored folks' houses 'n making threats in open daylight. Out at the lake t'other night, a white crowd tried to stone a black man what swam over on their side."

He jerked himself free. "Sure I know. The papers are to blame, all the lies they're spreadin'. Hate-breeders. 'N the union says the packers are back of a lot of it. Tryin' to divide us."

"There's fighting, race against race, in many cities—what if it breaks out here?" She crouched beside him, covering her face with her hands. He put his arms around her.

"Don't give way, Susie child. If it comes to a battle, we ain't a-scared of battlin'. But the fight we're aimin' at is for more pay at the yards. 'N we got more'n 30,000 of both races lined up in our union. Think of that—a good-sized city of folks of both color, standin' fast." His face shone. "This Friday night thar's gona be a big mass meetin', you wanta come along?"

She shrugged her shoulders. "Can't, honey boy. Gotta shuf-fle the tickets." George's countenance hardened, his arms loosened. He knew she wouldn't come, anyway. Hadn't he seen her wriggle up her nose at the stockyard people, hadn't he caught her lying to her friends about his line of work?

"LAWD WHAT A STINK! The wind is from the yards tonight." Sol blew violently into his red bandana handkerchief. He and George were on their way to an open air meeting. "What's gripin' you, buddy? You look kinda down."

"Nuthin' much. Just my gal 'n her high-fallutin' notions."

"That all? I thought it was somethin' serious. Like this here democracy we won over thar."

"Oh, that!" George scowled, then brightened. "Did I tell you what a fella over to the union hall was tellin' me? He's travelled around a lot, I reckon, 'n reads some laborman's paper. He says the whole colored world's a-movin'—India, Africy, 'n all over. Great Britain told 'em just like they told us here, if they'd fight the war, they'd get self-government when it was over. But Great Britain tricked 'em the same as us. So they made up their mind to take it. Thar's a war for indepen-dence headin' up in India."

"You don't tell! That's what we gotta do here—*take* it. The white man ain't givin' us blacks *nuthin'*. Look at Haiti, what the government grabbed a few years back, 'n Porto Rico. Right while we was over thar, killin' 'n riskin' our skins for democracy!"

A shower of rocks pelted the two men on their shoulders and about their heads. "Niggers! Niggers!" A street gang of taunting Irish-Americans, dashed down alleyways and up tenement stairs, George and Sol in hot pursuit. On the sec-ond landing, hearing doors slammed behind racing feet, they halted. Slowly they retraced their steps. Sol rubbed the knot on his skull. "Drat their hides! It's a good thing I didn't get my hands on 'em."

"Gosh—it's close to meetin' time. Let's step on it." Glumly they quickened their speed.

"George," Sol burst out, "maybe we're fools, taken' in by this union game. Maybe they'll trick us, like in the war."

"Gowan, buddy, don't let a kid's rock rattle your brains! The union's stickin' by us, ain't it?"

"That's what they say. If they stand by us, we'll stand by 'em. But," Sol whirled around, "you know as well as I that hell's gona be poppin' in this burg in no time. Like in Washington, Atlanta, 'n St. Louis. White men's bustin' up colored folks homes, drivin' 'em offa their jobs—'n down south lynchin's! He swung his palms together in a thundering stroke. I tell you, thar's gotta be fewer lynchin's 'n more riots in this here country. Riots is whar colored folks fight back."

George's shoulders twitched, desperately he fought against the dark suspicions which assailed them. "But riots ain't the right way, Sol. Remember what the union says—that's what the packers are after to get us fightin' between ourselves. If they get us divided, we'll never win our rights. I tell you, the union's gona stick by us."

"I ain't so sure," Sol rejoined.

"Us butchers're together so far," George insisted, "and our Council's got most of the men at the yard lined up. 'N we got one of our own color as vice-president, 'n seven paid organizers, ain't we?"

"Yeah, but look at the steamfitters. They won't even let a colored man in their organization. 'N they ain't the only ones, nuther."

"But the Council's bigger 'n got more say'n the steamfitters. It's tryin' to make those high-hats let down the bars. 'N any Negro what they won't take in, the Council takes 'em direct."

"All right, but it ain't the same." Sol fingered a slip of paper in his pocket. "You know Harvey Nelson, he says thar's talk among the white fellas, since the Packers done brung so many colored folks up from the south to work at the yards, that the union's gona back down on us Negroes, so the whites can have our jobs."

George pulled his friend about, searching his face. "That's a lie, Sol, a Packers' lie. The Council 'n Johnston ain't sellin us out. If the Packers try turnin' us Negroes outta the yard, the Union'll strike. That Harvey Nelson may be a Y.M.C.A. secretary 'n a smart man, but what for he's peddlin' bosses' talk?"

Sol kicked at the pavement. "Would you trust a white man afore a colored? Nelson's one of us, ain't he, 'n Johnstone he ain't."

"I don't care if Nelson is black, I don't trust *him*, carryin' such tales. We been warned against stools, ain't we, 'n troublemakers? I ain't sayin' Nelson is," he added hurriedly, "but that talk is Packers' talk, 'n you can tell him I said so."

Sol didn't reply. His fingers twisted the paper in his back pocket, a paper which Nelson had passed him, and on which was written:

"Get a Square Deal With Your Own Race!

   "Time has come for Negroes to do now or never. Get together and stick together is the call of the Negro. Like all other races, make your own way, other races have made their unions for themselves. They are not going to give it to you because you join his union. . . .

   "This union does not believe in strikes. We believe all differences between capital and labor can be arbitrated. Strikes is our last motive if any at all.

   "Get in line for a good job.

   (Signed) *"American Unity Packers Union of the Stockyards."*

How could Sol know that the Packers were backing this move to split the strikers' ranks?

"By Jiminy, look at that!" George's face cleared, he and his companion broke into a run. The blocks ahead were dense with workers, thunderous shouts echoed along the narrow streets.

They edged in toward one of the speakers' stands. The night was sultry, sweat poured from the closely packed bodies of Polaks, Russians, Yankees, Negroes. "Must be close to 2,000 at this one meetin', 'n thar's more'n dozen more such," George whispered to his friend. "You see?"

A low growl, beginning at the edge of the crowd, spread rapidly through its ranks. "The cops!" The Packers' cops, come to bust up the meeting! Billies swung, fists flew, heads cracked. A mounted police lunged at George but his club hung in mid-air as two white workers, cursing angrily, yanked at his blue coat from the other side and a dozen others, including Sol, dragged him down from his horse.

Further up the block the crowd was vigorously protecting two speakers whom the law sought to arrest. Women and children, watching from tenement windows, yelled their encouragement, and more than one mounted officer received a well-aimed cabbage or a pail of dirty water dumped from a second-story balcony over his head.

On the way home George demanded of his friend, "You see? When that dam cop went to brain me, you see how the white fellas helpen me out?"

"Yeah," Sol felt his left eye tenderly, "this here's the first black eye I ever relished."

STREET FIGHTING BETWEEN NEGROES and whites grew more common, bitterness mounted. Susie and her family fled to relatives who lived on an Illinois farm. The *Chicago Tribune, Herald-Examiner* and the Negro paper, the *Defender* (all backed by packing and financial interests), seized on these incidents and headlined them in such cleverly distorted news that both white and colored populations were incited to fresh and more far-reaching acts. White men, with faces blacked, burned down the homes of Polish stockyard workers. Although the union proved that the men had been hired by the Packers to commit this outrage, the white press ran top-page streamers: "Black Terror Destroys Whites' Homes." The following night two houses in the Negro section were set afire.

Meanwhile the Stockyard Labor Council redoubled its efforts, its membership now had reached forty thousand. It was decided on July 6 to stage a parade of solidarity of white and Negro workers through the main industrial and business sections of the city. The police forbid the joint parade; both Chicago Federation of Labor officials and Negro politicians pleaded with the Council to "show some sense. There'll be bloodshed if you hold that checkerboard parade."

George listened in silence to the news that there would be two separate marches which would merge later at Beutner Park for an open-air meeting. The Union backin' down! Maybe the leaders knew best, but—"What'd I tell you?" Sol muttered, "the whites're weakin', already. Us colored butchers better pull out 'n make our own union." He felt for the paper still resting in his pocket.

"Don't give up so quick," George retorted, angry at his own doubts as well, "you ought to know as well as me that blackman's union is a Packers' fake. Beside, we're holdin' our joint meetin' anyway, ain't we?"

He looked in vain for Sol at the parade.

George had brought Sol along to the mass meeting. "We gona vote to strike, buddy, you can't miss that! After all we been workin' for these weeks, 'n all—you can't quit now." The great hall, packed to the roof rocked with applause when

Johnson, secretary of the Stockyard Council, declared, "the Negro has the same privileges in organized labor as you have. It is up to you white workers to protect him. The non-union Negro is being brought into the yards by the Packers, he must be brought into the Union. There is no color line in this Union, and any man that attempts to draw one violates the Union code and has no right to protection."

George nudged Sol. "You hear that?" He looked around and below him at the sea of light and dark faces. His last doubts disappeared. This was the right way, the only way.

As thousands of men streamed out of the yards the next morning, their aprons and boots spattered with blood and manure, they brushed past troops standing glumly at their posts, awaiting orders. George heard a man near him demanding, "You no shoot on fellow-worker?" The trooper kept his gaze on the ground. Pressed on from behind, the strikers jammed the streets, overflowing up back alleyways. George, his breath coming fast, looked about for his buddy. During the picketing, and later on, at the mass meeting, he could catch no sight of him. But surely Sol was here! No doubt searching for him. In so many thousands, it was easy to miss.

Late that night George hurried over to his friend's place, his nostrils quivering with the smell of battle. The Meat Trust was powerful, but man, what a might the men had on their side. 'N what a spirit!

He found Sol, a scowl on his dark face, busy cleaning his army pistol. "These white devils!" he glared up at George, "Rapin' our gals, bombin' our homes, spreadin' terror. Ain't tens of our race been stretched out? It's time we fought back, blow for blow."

"Sol . . . buddy . . . you ain't quittin' the strike!"

"I ain't scabbin, if that's what you mean. But I tell you, our fight's for the black men against the whites. You hear what happened today? The white bastards tried to fire the

Thompson's, 'n when we drove 'em off, they swore they'd be back to shoot it out afore sun-up. Well," jamming his weapon in a hip pocket, he prepared to leave, "we'll be waitin' for 'em."

George threw his weight against the door. "For Gawd's sake, listen to sense. Ain't I as much reason as you to hate white folks? Ain't I? Doan I know what's goin' on? Doan it make my blood boil, my hands itch, too?" He caught his breath, lowered his voice. "But the union's showed us our real enemy, Sol. The Packers. 'N it's showed us that white'n black at the plants can stick together for their rights. Ain't that so? It's not the white workers raisin' the cain. It's the Packers 'n their troops stirrin' up this riot hell, 'n you know why as well as me. If we lick the Packers, that's the quickest way to end this riotin' 'n win our rights, ain't it?"

Sol strode toward the door. "Step aside, it's time I was on my way." George held his ground. "You're my buddy. I ain't forgettin' what you did in France for me, that time. But I ain't in no mood for argument, nuther. Step aside. I tell you, the time's come for us black men to fight back."

"But can't you see, Sol, we gotta choose the best way to fight? We can't fight both ways to once. The union . . ."

"As for the Union . . ." Sol gave the other a warning shove, "I'm through. I've joined up with a blackman's organization."

Their eyes clashed. "That's a comp'ny union. You . . . you . . ." George's face worked.

"Go on, say it!" Sol threatened.

George's hands opened and shut spasmodically. "No buddy. We ain't gona quarrel. We both got other work to do. In a few hours I gotta go on the picket line . . . and you . . . We see it diff'rent, that's all. . . . Only, promise me one thing, Sol?"

"What?"

"I'll go with you now to Thompson's, till time to go to the plants. Then tomorrow . . . after . . . promise you'll give me another chance to reason it out with you. On the quiet."

Sol held out his hand, his lips quivering. "I promise. S'long. Till tomorrow."

On the morrow Sol was beyond the reach of human voice. Noting the grim set to his mouth, George knew that his friend had died secure in the thought that at last he was fightin' for the freedom of his people.

THE STRIKE REACHED its third week, with ranks firm. Finally the Packers withdrew the armed forces from the yards and surrounding sections. Immediately the rioting lessened. The men, their demands won, returned to the yards.

What followed was for George a terrific, confused nightmare of falsehoods and treachery. The *Tribune*, *Herald-Examiner*, and *Defender*, and other papers launched a fresh campaign against the Stockyard Labor Council, this time accusing it of having organized the pogrom against the Negroes! The Packers followed by discharging four hundred white workers, Union shop stewards who had led their departments on strike. The Government, through its Food Commissioner Alschuler, condemned the Council for striking in support of the Negroes. Mayor Thompson, who had disappeared from the city during the strike, likewise censored the Union. "The Packers must run pretty nigh everything," George told himself. "I allays knew this here was a whiteman's govern-*ment*, but I didn't calculate before it was a rich man's govern-*ment* as well."

The National President of the Butcher Workmen's Union, Dennis Lane, denounced the Council's leaders as Bolsheviks and expelled the Council, with its thirty thousand members from the National Union, and the Council was also dis-affiliated from the Chicago Federation of Labor. Council leaders, unprepared for developments, spent themselves in angry counter-charges and heated discussions among themselves as to the best policy to pursue.

"Why doan we go on strike again, 'n make the Packers take back our shop stewards?" George asked of a fellow member. "They lost their jobs because of us, didn't they? Then why doan we fight for 'em?"

"Well, you see, the Packers've bought off all but our Council leaders. 'N, well, it's tough, all right. I don't know." Walking away, he left George standing alone in a corner of the hall, wishing a bullet had taken him off along with his friend.

They'd been let down, though not in the way Sol had feared. The Union had stuck by the Negroes all right, and they had their jobs back at the yards. But, now four hundred white stewards were fired, and the Union let it happen! And all this wild talk in the papers about Bolsheviks—what were they anyhow?

There was something about it all he couldn't understand. And there was no-one else who seemed able to explain it to him. Disgusted, not even waiting to bid Susie goodbye, he jumped a freight and headed east.

He'd read in the press about half a million miners going out and the big steel strike around Gary and Pittsburg. He'd have a look at these. He'd see if the papers weren't lying about forty thousand black men brought up from the south to take the strikers' jobs. If that was so—by golly!—The track's rail hummed under him, overhead there stretched the brightness of a night in early fall.

George thought over his years since Back Row. There were signs now of his people stirring, even in the Black Belt. Maybe he'd go down there some day? Maybe. He rested his tired body against the side of the jogging train.

XVII.

Betrayal

"I GUESS I'LL GET ME another job, Marge." With his left foot Bob carefully traced the pattern of squares and triangles in the faded carpet. "Come this Monday, the super says he'll give me some easy work around outside, till I get more on my feet, 'n can keep at weavin' steady."

"That's good, honey. Now that spring's comin' on, the fresh air'll do your cough good." Marge's voice was deliberately cheerful. Both knew that outside work was an old man's job, the leavin's for those too broken for work inside. The pay was a scant seven dollars, the same as hers. "We'll make out," she added, "since thar's only the two of us."

"It's jest for awhile, till I get on my feet." Bob repeated. "Once I get back to the loom steady, we'll be sittin' pretty."

"Sure, honey, by fall we'll be sittin' pretty." Already she was busy figuring out how they could cut down further on expenses. Bob must have fresh eggs and milk, the doctor had warned her, else his lungs'd never be right. Maybe she could find some mendin' or sewin' to do somewhar, in the evenin's. She'd allays been handy with the needle.

Altho both the doctor here and in Greenville had declared Bob disqualified by his war injuries for steady, indoor work and his lungs seriously impaired, and had sent the requested statements to Washington to that effect, the only results had been more forms to fill in and other doctors to see—one of whom affirmed that Bob had probably contracted tuberculosis in the mills since his return.

"It's jest a game that the govern-ment's playin', 'n a nasty one at that. Must think we-uns here are big fools not to see the point by this time." Bob tore the official letter into fragments.

As they neared the mill on Monday, Marge sniffed the biting freshness still in the air. "Look Bob, the trees are buddin' out!"

"Sure 'nough, 'n old man sun is gettin' up earlier." Its pale globe barely skimmed the mill's low roof. "Soon it'll be summer."

"In a few weeks the apple 'n peach blossoms'll be out. Then, on a Sunday afternoon, we'll go for a walk in the country. Shall we?"

"Uh-huh."

As they entered the mill the sight of angry, gesticulating mill hands gathered around the bulletin board drew them like a magnet. The last color left Bob's face. Marge's knees threatened to give way, her hands went damp.

"My gawd, another cut!"

Pushing their way in they read the notice:

In view of the present business depression and deflation following the war, the management regrets to announce that in order to keep the plants running and curtail expenses, it will be necessary to reduce wages by ten per cent, this change to take effect April 4, 1921.

(Signed) Phillips Manufacturing Company, Inc. Clarence R. Phillips, President.

A gray-haired woman ran the back of her hands across her forehead. "How'd they expect us to live? We barely keep soul'n body together, as 'tis."

"Is Mr. Phillips 'n his'n curtailin' 'spenses, I ask you?" Jem Simmons, a raw-boned man in his early thirties peered from side to side. "Tell me that, is Mr. Phillips 'n his'n curtailin' 'spenses?"

"Naw, by golly, that's right. Let'im sell some of his horses, if times are pinchin' him, 'n his extry automobile. My chillen need shoes for school." A pregnant woman clasped her hands across her protruding stomach.

"Shoes! Now it's gettin' toward spring, mill hands' kids doan need no shoes!"

"They do too. Amanthy's cotched the hookworm last year from . . ." Her voice trailed off in the general murmur.

"Jem's right. Why doan the comp'ny cut down 'spenses. Why's it allays got to come outta our pockets? 'Course time's hard 'n all that, but . . ."

"I tell you what," Jem lowered his voice, "It's high time the Union took a stand."

"Yeah, the Union's gotta do somethin' beside collect dues!"

After work Marge and Bob went along with the entire shop to union headquarters. Silently they climbed the stairs and massed around the glass door on which was painted in black letters: *United Textile Workers of America, Affiliated to the American Federation of Labor.* Jem opened the door and the crowd surged in. Clem Parker, the business agent, a bald-headed, full-cheeked man, rose to his feet and stood behind his brightly polished desk. "What's up?"

"Another ten per cent offa our wages, that's what!"

"What's the union gona do about it?" All eyes centered on him expectantly.

Clem Parker fingered his gold watch-chain. "Uh-er. Well, that's bad, bad, very bad. Uh-er. The union will of course take up the matter immediately with the proper authorities. Enter into negotiations, you understand."

"But you did that last time, 'n what come of it?" Jem demanded. Restless shuffling of feet.

"What if the mill comp'ny won't change its mind?" Bob cleared his throat. "What then?"

The organizer threw out his hands and rocked back and forth on the soles of his feet. "Difficult—very difficult. You understand how times are now. But surely Mr. Phillips is open to reason. If, as you say, you can't live on such wages—and I'm sure you can't then ..."

"If they go through with this here cut, we'll walk out, that's what. We'll walk out." Old man Jones broke in. "You tell the comp'ny that—we'll walk out."

"No, no," Clem Parker interrupted, "this is no time for hasty action. Why, there are seven million men walking the streets, looking for work, and you speak of strike. Negotiate, that's the way. Besides, you can't go on strike without the sanction of the National Office."

"Wal, office or no office, we ain't gona see our chillen robbed without we take some action." Angry voices broke in from all sides.

Exasperated, Clem Parker banged the desk for silence. "You mill people got the wrong way of going at it. You got to act in an organized, sensible fashion. Now you look at the company as though it was your enemy. That's a mistake. It's your best friend. Doesn't it give you work? The right way is what the Union tells you, management and workers cooperate for common interests. Leave it to me and the executive committee, and it'll come out best."

Bewildered, uneasy, the workers started home to their belated supper.

By the following nightfall, the news had traveled throughout Charlotte mill districts. There had been a general wage

cut of ten per cent announced; the sentiment for strike was widespread. Spontaneous mass meetings were held, but the villagers stayed by the machines, waiting for the Union's report on its negotiations with the owners.

The night came when Clem Parker was ready to report. The hall was tense, overflowing. Mill hands stood along the aisles, sat in window sills and jammed the entrances. His speech was a long, impassioned one, full of flowery metaphors and closing in an appeal for "Trust in the Union and the Newer Methods of Co-operation in Industry between Labor and Capital."

When he had ended, a lank man sprang to his feet, shoving his hat backward over his ears. "Mr. Organizer," he drawled, "from all the high falutin' talk you've said I gather one thing. The mills woan take back the cut!"

Clem Parker stepped forward on the platform. "Well, you see, at the present time they are losing money, and to keep the mills open at all, this readjustment is necessary. But as soon as times pick up, the managements promise to ..." An angry roar drowned his words.

Jem Simmons ran toward the platform and swung himself up. He held out his long arms for quiet. "Brothers 'n sisters. Thar's only one thing for us to do—walk out."

When the shouting and hand-clapping lessened, the organizer was heard yelling angrily, You're crazy. It's suicide. . . . The National Office'll not back you up!"

Firmly, gently, Jem pushed the organizer back with one arm and continued, "he says it's suicide for us to walk out. Ain't this now, suicide?"

"Yeah, yeah." "You're dam right."

"Mill hill life is slow death, 'n not so slow, nuther," Jem went on. "'N what kinda of a Union'd it be that'd see its members starving' off 'n not lift a hand?"

"Vote, vote!" Voices from the crowd broke in. Jem stepped forward solemnly. "All right. I move we take a show of hands. All in favor of walkin' out against the cut, raise your hands." A forest of arms shot into the air. A few looked about, fearful, uncertain. Their neighbors nudged them encouragingly.

Jem looked down at the mass of grim faces turned toward the platform. "If the National Union'll helpen us, good. We paid our dues reg'lar, 'n done the best we know how for our organization." He paused, adding slowly, "if it doan back us up, *we strike single-handed!*"

When it was again quiet, Jem announced, "now we'll proceed to elect a committee."

On the way home, Marge heard an anxious voice behind her. Thar ain't much in the larder. Supposin' our credit's cut off at the comp'ny store?"

Another couple pushed past them. "Doan you think," the woman was asking, "that the Union'll helpen us?"

"Aw, no tellin'," her companion answered, "what's that Clem Parker good for, noways? Livin' swell in a hotel in Charlotte, 'n mixin' round with rich city folks. What's he care?"

In the strikes that broke through the Carolinas against the wage cuts, the national union refused its endorsement and financial support to all of them.

Want stalked the mill hills, but for several weeks the bulk of the strikers held firm. As hunger's pinch at their empty stomachs grew more insistent, many families went to friends or relatives on nearby farms, others sought work in different sections of the state. The companies began evictions of striking families for non-payment of rent, and replacing them with new recruits from the hills.

The confused dissension caused by the national union's pressure to call off the strike was further increased by local pastors who went from house to house counseling the villagers. "Remember the words of our Lawd Jesus. Let both sides forgive 'n forget." "My poor people, your feelin's mislead you. You've struck the hand that feeds you. Go back, while thar is still time."

The local press denounced the strikers in biting editorials. The company evicted more strikers, brought in more families from the hills to take their place.

Jem and his small committee of helpers, all of them inexperienced, held on grimly.

Gradually the mill recruited enough to start the plant. A few who had struck went back to work. The pickets jeered at them all, pleaded and threatened. Jem drew Bob to one side. "They've licked us, dam 'em." His eyes were moist with anger and bitter defeat. "Our folks can't hold on any longer. You see, they've begun to break ranks."

"Yah, Jem, I guess we're licked. The hands can't stand their kids cryin' for vittles any more, 'n seeing their places took at the plant."

"By golly, son," Jem burst out, "I've been a church-goin' man all my life. But after what Parsons Brown 'n Antell done to break this strike, I doan believe I'll ever set my foot inside a mill church again. They've been stools, that's what, jest ornery low-down stools."

Jem's prediction proved correct. At first a little stream trickled shamefacedly back to the mills. The Negro hands also went back. The strike had promised them little, anyway, the white hands had not raised a single demand in their interest or made any effort to get their co-operation. All the white hands had cared about, the Negroes felt, was that they stay out of the plant till the strike was over. Well, they had stayed out mainly because up till now there had been no work for them. Now the boss had sent word to come back, and they were going—disgusted, glum, they returned in a body.

The dam broken, all except a few of the most stubborn rushed to the mills, begging the company to give them work.

Jem, Marge and Bob were among those who refused to return. "It'd do us no good, nohow. We're on the comp'ny black list. Why belittle ourselves for nothing?"

Everybody on the hill felt discouraged, and as the expression went, "outdone."

"All those weeks of stayin' out, 'n to have to go back like licked dogs!"

"Mill hands just woan stick together enough. It's no use."

"What we lacked was leaders."

"Thar warn't no plan to this," Bob mused. "We just walked out 'n waited for the comp'ny to give in. It got busy, 'n we stood by, watchin' ourselves get outwitted! Thar's no sense to that."

Mutterings against the union and Clem Parker ran like weeds over the hills. "We're shet of Parker 'n the United Textiles for good. What good's a union, nohow? All it does is to take up dues."

"But a *good union*," Marge protested desperately, "a *good* union'd be diff'rent. We gotta keep on." She pointed toward a group of mill children sitting around the pump. Their one-piece garments hung limp against thin, warped frames, their large eyes staring up at their elders out of solemn, pinched faces. "Look at 'em. Enough to break your heart. We *gotta* keep on. Somehow."

Marge and Bob and the others prepared to move on. "We better go separate ways," Jem advised, "we'll not be so easy to trace thataway."

"Gee, Jem, we sure hate to see you go." They grasped his long fingers. Suddenly his eyes glistened. "Good-byes ain't easy. Maybe our paths'll cross again. The mill hill world ain't so big but what we should. Marge, you 'n Bob here, swing on. These times now try the spirit. But cling on."

"We will, Jem. You can count on us." That night Jem, a small bundle over his shoulder, left for Spartanburg, and in the morning Marge, Bob, and their household set out for Millton, in western North Carolina.

XVIII.

"The Mills Take All"

"WHAT HE NEEDS," THE DOCTOR told Marge, "is a complete rest for six months. He's had a narrow call with this grippe. Rest, and plenty of eggs, milk, fresh fruit and sunshine. With his lungs, he should get away from the mills for good. Otherwise..."

Marge twisted her hands. "But how'll we manage that?"

When Bob was up once more she begged him, "take off a few weeks, honey. For my sake." He shook his head. "Go up to my cousin Allie's, nigh Asheville. See, I wrote him, 'n he says they'll be right proud to have your comp'ny. Get yourself good 'n well. I'll make out. Ruthie'll help, 'n we can pay her back, later.... Oh, doan, doan..." Great, coughing sobs wracked his body. Dropping to her knees, pushing aside his hands she lay her wet face against his. "Doan... Doan..."

"Marge, I'm done for. A no-count. Drag on you."

"Never Bob. You're all I got." Her voice broke. "Can't you see? *You gotta go.* Doctor says it's your one chance to get your old strength back. I," her words came halting, whispered, "Bob, I couldn't stand for nothin' to happen to you."

After a while he took her face between his hands and looked down at her. She was barely twenty-eight, yet worry and long hours of close labor were already doing their work. With one finger he gently traced the fine lines etched around her eyes and mouth. Her eyes were not as deep blue as they were a few years back.

"Lil' Marge," he said softly, "I love you more'n ever before."

"Me too, Bob. No matter how hard work 'n livin' is, we got each other. 'N you'll go, woan you?"

"Without you?"

She sat up, startled. "Well, you see, it'd be hard for me to get away, now." *Her* leave off at the mills when able to work. Mill hands never did such things! In the whole fifteen years she'd never missed a day, except when too ill to stand up on her feet.

Bob's mood shifted. "Money . . . money! Allays poor folks can't do things account of money. 'N them in town jest rollin' in it."

"But woan you go Bob—anyway?"

"Naw I ain't goin' off to loaf, while you sweat in the mill this hot weather. I reckon if you can stand it, I can too."

Once again back at the mill, his cough grew worse. Marge was desperate.

When word came from Tom that he and his friends were out of jail, Marge sat down to send him the news from home for which he had asked. Gertie was the same, allays frettin' 'n her kids ailin'. Ruthie was a grown girl now. The last they'd heard from Billy and Sam, they were workin' in Tennessee. Times were hard. Wages had been cut three times. Over in Charlotte there'd been a walk-out, but it had come to a bad end. Bob had lung trouble, but wouldn't go away without her. She was at her wit's ends to know what to do.

There was a quick reply. As Marge took the letter from its envelope, three five-dollar bills dropped out.

"Dear Sis," Tom wrote, *"the thing to do is for both of you go up to Cousin Allie's. You stay a couple of weeks, and make Bob stay on longer. Get a spare hand to hold your job. You need a rest almost as much as him.*

"These bills are to pay your fare. Will send some more as soon as I can, in a week or ten days.

"Don't get down-hearted because you lost the strike, and over that union sucker. Labor fakers wil sell you out every time, if you let 'em. Right now is a hard time for labor. Things are at low ebb. But the tide's bound to rise again. So swing on (Just what Jem had said). We're fighting to get Fred outta jail. They got a special grudge on him, because of his color.

"Now take my advice and go up to Cousin Allie's. You'll al-lays be glad you did. Your brother, Tom."

So it was arranged. Marge had a sparehand take her place in the spinning room for a week and Bob agreed to go and if he liked it, stay on after she came back.

Ruth and her latest fellow saw them off. An old straw satchel that their neighbors, the Cornfelds, had loaned them was placed securely under their seat. In her lap Marge held a parcel of food for lunch on the way. This was her first trip on a railroad.

As the train began to climb and wind among the mountains, Marge pressed her face against the window pane, her hand in Bob's, her eyes drinking in the constantly changing views. How green the close hills were, shading off in the distance, to a hazy blue. Granny should be here! Her vision blurred.

Cousin Allie was waiting for them at the Asheville station. Marge spied his sandy colored head looming above the crowd as it surged past his motionless figure. Waving her handkerchief at him, she caught his eye.

"Wal, wal, Maggie, I'm that glad to see you. Been nigh ten year since last I set eyes on you. 'N this is Bob, eh? Son, you're right welcome to these parts."

"Where's Aunt Ellen?"

"Waitin' for us, to-home. We calculated it'd be more comfortable with only three on the front seat. Gimme your car-
ry-all." He lead the way to where his mule was hitched to a
lamp post.

As they jogged along in the cart, Cousin Allie let the reins
go slack as he fired a line of questions at Marge for news of
folks he knew who'd gone down to the valley. While answering questions, she and Bob gazed around them.

"Lookathar, Bob, way up the cliff. Those pink blossoms."

"What we call mountain laurel," Cousin Allie explained.
"A right purty flower. This time of year the mountains'll be
full of it."

The sun dropped behind the hills. They took deep breaths
of the cool fragrance and peace about them. "How quick daylight fades," Bob said.

Cousin Allie tightened the reins. "Ellie'll be expectin' us.
Git up thar, Peter, stir your lazy shins." It was nearly dark by
the time they drew up before the shed where they kept the
mule. Cousin Ellie came out to greet them, wiping her hands
on her apron as she ran.

Marge was always to remember this week. Cousin Ellen
wouldn't let her help much around the house. "Now you jest
get right outta here, honey. You two are vacatin', you didn't
come up here to spend time 'round the kitchen. Get outta
doors. Bob'll hang round if you do." They worked a while in
the garden. Allie protested, "Doan feel you got to work for
your keep. Go on off, enjoy yourselves."

Later they would go for a walk in the woods. Sprawled on
sun-warmed rocks, they would watch the clouds drift and
bank over the mountains. "Gosh, Bob, it feels queer to be jest
lazin'." "Yeah, doan it?" The soft, myriad sounds of outdoor
life at high noon hummed around them.

"You know, I hope it storms once, jest once, afore I go."

"Why?" Bob was chewing contentendly on a long blade of grass.

"Oh, I doan know. Granny told me about how the thunder 'n lightnin' goes rumblin' 'n rollickin' down the mountains. Houses shiver 'n trees are pulled out by the roots."

"That's a funny idea of yourn, to wanta see that. Which way's Milltown, Marge, from here?"

"Must be over thataway." Her face grew thoughtful. "Think of all the mill hands down in the valley, 'n we-uns up here. Mill hand life is a sorry one, ain't it? When you come to think of it. Whar's the sense to it all?"

Catching her hands, Bob pulled her to her feet. "Doan spile it honey. We only got a few days. Doan start us worryin'. Come on, it's time for dinner. 'N I'm hungry as a new-hatched chick."

Drowsy after a hearty meal, they lay in a field close by the house, arms outstretched, eyes closed, the smells of new-mown hay and wild flowers blowing over them. Each day some of the weariness slipped from them, they could feel new life flowing from the earth into their bodies.

With new strength the ardor of their first love returned. At the mills they were toil-worn and worry-laden—sunk in the routine of hill existence. But here . . . Bob gazed at Marge who had raced ahead and now stood on a ledge jutting out above the valley. Her sun-tanned neck and arms gleamed softly in the after-glow, a gathering wind lashed her clothes against her body, outlining its still young curves. She stood like a bird, alert, ready to take wing.

"Marge," he called, climbing up beside her, "Lil' Marge, you've come back." Eyes shining, she laughed up at him. "Dear heart . . ." she lifted an eager mouth. Quietly the shadows lengthened and the stars came out.

"FROM WHAT YOU TELL," Cousin Allie reached for the corn-pone, "mill life doan bring any betterment to poor folks. They'd better stay by the land."

"Naw, that ain't exactly it. What I mean is, either place, it's a struggle to make ends meet." Marge studied the grotesque shadows thrown by the lamplight, flickering on the walls.

"Wal, I allays figgered like Hinry—your Grandpa. It's best to live up here, close to the earth. The good Lawd put us in the Garden, 'n that's the way he intended us."

Bob lay down his knife. "But you jest told us how the farmers round about are losin' their land. What they gona do but go to the mills?"

"Ever since the war, it's been gettin' worser. Doan pay nothin' for crops. But dress goods 'n seed 'n things still cost the same. I doan understand it." Frowning, Cousin Ellen dished out the applesauce. "Everybody round about is sunk deep in debt. Them what ain't already give up or been closed out."

"Those skinflints!" Cousin Allie swallowed rapidly. "Those skinflints that run the banks 'n hold the mortgages, they'd take the flesh right offa your bones without blinkin' an eyelash!"

They finished their meal in silence.

Outside the crickets hummed dreamily. "Tomorrow'll be a hot day," Cousin Ellen observed, "by the sound of them."

Later seated in the dusk around the stoop, Marge added, "it's sure nice up here 'n a lot healthier, like you said, than hangin' over looms, but ouside of that, it makes small diff'rence which place poor folks are."

"One thing," Bob felt for his words, "up here you're so spread out 'n cut off, 'n it's each man for himself, like. But down at the mills, we're close together. We all work for the same boss. So we can learn quickern you farmers to stick together, 'n work to better things."

"From what you tell, mill hands ain't learned much, yet," Cousin Allie uncrossed his knees and took a generous bite at his plug of tobacco.

"That's so. But we gonna." Marge spoke with renewed confidence.

"Wal, I ain't so sure."

"We are. Me 'n Bob gonna helpen 'em, ain't we?"

He nodded. "That we are, honey, the best we know how."

When the week was up, Bob and Cousin Allie drove Marge down to the Asheville Station. Bob had given in to the other three's urging, and agreed to stay on for two weeks longer, anyway. "We ain't lettin' you leave us so soon," Cousin Ellen whisked her apron to her eyes, "We lost our own boy 'n . . ." Cousin Allie cleared his throat. "Besides, son, you can give us a hand around the place, enough to earn your keep, 'n make you feel satisfied. Maggie wants you to stay on, doan you? So it's settled."

As the wagon jolted along the narrow, winding road Marge, squeezed in between the two men, gazed about her in all directions. These pictures would stand her in good stead when she was back at the frames.

The train wound through the mountains, over to Milltown. The woman it was returning to her old world sat with clear eyes, hands folded quietly in her lap. Tom, good, kind Brother Tom was right. She's always be glad they'd gone.

Painstaking notes from Bob were frequent. The refrain of all was the same: "Feelin' fine . . . lonesome . . . hadn't I better come on home?"

"Stay on. We're all right here." Marge wrote back. "Get sure enuf well."

At the end of the third week Bob followed her back to the village. In spite of doctor's orders and Marge's pleading, he went back to his old job at the looms. "I'm feelin' fit as a fiddle now, what you worryin' over?"

By December, Marge was again heavy with child. "Doan know whether I'm more glad than sorry," she told him. "Looks like mill hands can't have nothin' but what it means worriment." Secretly she was concerned over the soundness of the child's lungs.

"This time it'll not have to be like it was before," Bob told her, "now I'm here to watch out for you." He wanted her to stop work at the seventh month, but finally she agreed to leave off three weeks in advance of the event. Bob's cough grew rapidly worse. "You're losing all you gained up at Blowing Rock," she fretted. He shrugged his shoulders. "What's a workin' man gona do?"

Their boy was born in April. "Look at that cow lick 'n one-sided smile. It's the spittin' image of you. Might as well name him for you too," Marge insisted.

By the time the child was three weeks' old, she was back in the spinning room. Then Bob came down with the flu. "I knew the heat 'n noise in the weave room'd be too much, 'n bring back your trouble."

Marge never knew how she got through those weeks. Bob, burning with fever and coughing blood, Gertie grumbling over the extra work of nursing him while Marge was at the mill, the baby sick and fretting because it was so long between feedings and she herself barely able to stand at the frames and anxious to be home, doing for them.

At last Bob was up and around the house again, though too weak to go out. He would sit for hours, with his little son in his lap, "fondlin' the child," Gertie remarked, "like an old 'oman." To Marge he confided his plans. Their boy was not to grow up to be just a mill hand, not if he could help it. They'd see he learned a good trade—carpentry or machinist.

"Your husband really should go to a sanitarium," the doctor called by the company nurse, told Marge. "It would be better for you and the child. Also, it's his one chance."

"You mean—?"

"Just that," he answered her quietly. "His case of consumptive lungs is pretty well advanced."

She felt for a chair. The dread white plague! "Oh, I can't lose him, I can't"

"With proper care he may live for years." He avoided her eyes. Although he had been called in to diagnose hundreds of cases of mill tuberculosis, he had never grown sufficiently hardened to this moment. He always felt uncomfortable, in a way, guilty. Though certainly it was not his fault if the companies let conditions remain the way they were!

Picking up his hat, he prepared to leave.

"Another thing, Mrs. Gregory, one characteristic of your husband's disease is extreme cheerfulness and a refusal to realize the dangers of his condition. It'll require constant watching on your part, both of him, and to protect yourself, the child, and the rest of the household against the disease. In the meantime, I will have the nurse inquire if there is a free bed open at the sanitarium."

There was no bed open at the hospital, and a long waiting list ahead of Bob. Gertie soon made it clear that Marge and Bob would soon have to move out else she would lose all her boarders. Also, she had the children's health to consider. Like the rest of the village, there was nothing which she had learned to fear more than tuberculosis.

"I'll go along with you, sis," Ruth, indignant at Gertie's behavior, told Marge. "You'll be needin' help."

Marge's lips quivered. "No, Ruthie, you'd better stay here."

"Say what you like, I'm coming along. That's that." The younger sister began packing her things.

So the four of them moved into a two-room shack over near the edge of the village, Tom's brief letters and the small sums of money which he sent regularly helped carry them through. He was employed now in Passaic, in a sheet mill. These Italian and Portugese in the plants were real guys. Some Reds had come to town, and they all were making ready

for a strike soon. Something was going wrong with the wobblies. He himself wasn't sure about things. Fred had joined up
with the communists and had left to go to school in the Soviet
Union. When he came back, they were coming south together,
to start organizing down there.

As Bob's condition grew constantly more serious, Marge
wondered desperately if she could manage to take him back
to Cousin Allie's. Then word came that her cousins had lost
their small farm—the bank had foreclosed the mortgage. The
two old people were living for the time being with kind neighbors and looking everywhere for some work to supply them
shelter and board in their last years.

Reading this, Marge broke down and wept. "To think of
'em who slaved hard all these years 'n stinted themselves so
as to have a place in their old age—those who never did harm
to any one—ending up in the poor house. 'N me not able to
stop it."

Another letter came from Tom. "This is some strike. The
best I've seen yet. More later."

Day after day, in spite of all she could do, Marge saw Bob
growing thinner and weaker. She stinted herself in every way
she knew, wore shoes and patched dresses that a few years
back she would have felt ashamed to be seen in—so as to get
the fresh eggs and milk that he required.

Still he grew weaker.

Occasionally Gertie sent over soup and food by her oldest
girl or came with them herself. "She's so figgety when she
comes," Margy confided to Ruth, "Like she was goin' to get
the plague by puttin' her foot across the door-sill. I'd as soon
she'd stay away."

"She's an ornery one, all right," Ruth agreed.

"Doan be too hard on her. She means right."

"Maybe. Say, Sis, listen to this." Ruth spread out the
paper on the kitchen table. "Old man Duke's died 'n left nigh

a hundred million to his thirteen-year old gal, Doris. What d'you think of that! You know, the tobacco man. It says she owns a house in New York that's worth two million dollars. What'd so much money look like? 'N she owns all the tobacco farms 'n plants now, 'n gets richer ev'ry year. They say she's a train car all her own with her name printed on the side in gold letters. Things must be a lot diff'rent for a gal like that, eh?"

"Yah." Marge shuffled the pans angrily. "Doan read me any more of that society news. It just makes me mad. Now that thar ball in Charlotte last week, what that Mr. Manville give for his gal—why the flowers alone'd cost enough to put Bob in a good hospital for three months. It sure ain't fair 'n right, the way things are."

Bob's violent coughing in the next room sent her running to his aid. After the spell had passed she smoothed his bed and propped his pillows. It was a ghastly game they played for each other, trying to pretend that at last he was taking a turn for the better, when to her at least it was clear that his spells were becoming more frequent and his breathing more labored.

After his first hemorrhage he lay weak, with eyes closed, his breath coming in fluttering gasps. Slipping to her knees, Marge buried her head in the covers. Bob slid his hand until it rested against her wet cheek. In silence they admitted to one another at last the fatal truth.

It was not necessary for the doctor to tell her that it was a matter of a few months now until Bob would be gone. Marge grudged every minute she had to be away from him. Mrs. Lancey, an old woman who somehow reminded her of Granny, came in mornings "to keep an eye on the sick one 'n tend the baby's needs."

Tom, still on strike, had no funds to send and the account at the company store mounted to nearly forty dollars. "Doan worry, they know we're good for it," Ruth assured her sister.

"Yes," the older woman thought bitterly, "they know soon all I have'll be gone 'n I'll be able to cut expenses 'n pay off the bill."

Wakened in the night by his coughing and choking, Marge turned over to find his pillow dark with blood. Later he lay on her thin chest, as Granny had once lain, eyes closed, his faint wheezing barely lifting the sheet.

Seeing his lips move, she bent over. "Lil' Marge," he whispered, "sing to me." She knew what he wanted. The songs they'd sung together as young lovers. "Aunt Diana's Quilting Party," "Darlin' Nellie Gray." Halting to steady her voice, she felt him relax, a faint smile lighted his wan face. She mustn't give way now, she mustn't. He was reliving those days, the bright, early days before youth and hope had gone. His eyelids quivered. He was waiting for his favorite. Summoning all her courage she began crooning, "Sing me to sleep, the shadows fall..."

Breaking off, she leaned over to place her lips on his. Un-noticed tears slipped off her cheeks and ran over his still features. For Bob was already gone.

THE LITTLE PROCESSION WOUND over the hill to the grave-yard, following the pine box. Marge had had to borrow from everywhere she could to pay for the simple funeral. Even dying and burying cost money. And the parson expected his return for coming.

As he lifted up his eyes and hands, intoning at the open grave, "The Lord giveth and the Lord taketh away. Blessed be the name of the Lord," Marge looked across the browning fields and wondered dully, "what's God got to do with it? 'Twas the war 'n the mill what took Bob." The voice droned on. Fearful thoughts pushed up through despair. "Is there a God, noways? Is there..."

XIX.

The Stretch-Out

"BETTER MOVE BACK UP to our place, Marge." Gertie looked with knitted brows around the shack, poking her fingers into holes and crevices in the walls. "This place's got so many leaks you two'll nigh freeze here, this winter."

Leaks were here when Bob was alive, Marge thought resentfully. "It'll be too crowded up your place, won't it?"

"Well, may be a mite crowded. But this here ain't no place for a woman to live by herself. Best get away, 'n quit your mopin'. We'll set your bed in my room next to Nance's cot.

"You can't stay on here. It doan look right, now that Ruthie's gone—married to that good fer nuthin'." Gertie sniffed. "Doan know what made her act so like a fool. Run off that way, with a triflin' no-count."

"Just what . . ." Marge caught herself.

"Just what I done, eh?" Her sister flushed. "Well, I paid time over for it."

"No—only, doan be hard on Ruthie. I guess she'll be all right."

Little Ruthie's pinched face with its deep hazel eyes were before Marge's vision. She missed her powerfully now that Bob was gone.

"When old Joey comes round tomorrow, he'll give you a hand with your things. He's a good darky, 'n right glad to earn an extry quarter. I'll send him down with the Thompson's wheel-barrow."

Marge fumbled with the baby, debating in her mind.

"All right, Gertie. I'll make ready to move over tomorrow night, after work."

UNCLE JOEY SURVEYED the pile of boxes and bundle of clothes packed into the barrow. "I guess this here is all the wheel barrow'll tote this load. 'Bout one more load's worth. Yah, that cot 'n two chairs I'll just tote myself."

Marge looked at his bent shoulders and white kinky hair. "Doan you think," she inquired anxiously, "that's right much for you to carry?"

"Naw'm. Why at the mill I used to tote *real* weights, till my back give out. Yes'm," he chuckled softly, "for twenty-five year I shoved cotton bins 'n rustled cotton bales just like they were no more'n marbles."

"'N now you used yourself up for 'em," she drew in her breath, "they turn you off without so much as thank-ye. You'n your ole 'oman can shuffle as best you can."

His face clouded. "That's sure God's truth. Use us up 'n throw us out. White or colored hands, it's all the same." Shaking his head Uncle Joe started down the dirt path toward the better part of the hill, where Gertie ran her boarding house.

Marge, carrying Bobby, followed on behind. Resting to catch his breath, the old man saw her halting, gazing back over her shoulder. "Poor lil' 'oman, she's sure stricken with grievin'." Turning around to move on, Marge caught his eyes full on her. "Why, he understands better'n Gertie." Hastening toward him she exclaimed, "Uncle Joey, I hate the mills! It takes all we got." He put a hand on her arm. "Thar now, missy. You still got him." He pointed to little Bobby. "'N he's a right cute lil' fellow."

"Yah, I got him. All that's left. But can I raise him? He's a puny child. . . . Well, let's get on. It'll soon be dark, 'n Gertie frettin'."

"EV'RY SPRING THE BUGS 'n ants nigh drive you crazy in these mill houses. Chillen all so bit up they look like they got the measles or prickly with the heat. All of 'em cryin' with the itchin', too." Gertie swung her broom in angry flourishes, as though vanquishing an invisible enemy. Every few strokes she stopped to loop a bothersome strain of hair behind one ear, only to have it escape again and straggle across her vision.

"Miz Newsome's baby is real ailin' from the bites." Marge was filling the tin cups in which the bed posts stood with kerosene. "Even this kerosene doan keep 'em away."

Gertie halted her broom in mid-air. "A lotta good that'll do! Already I've lost two boarders on account of these ants. It all comes from not repairin' the houses like they oughta. But doan say a word, Marge, now mind you."

"Well, Sis, if they woan fix it, we can move offa this buggy hill."

"Maybe you can, but I can't. Now you looka here, Marge Gregory." Each word was emphasized with a vigorous shake of the broom-handle. "I took you in 'n gave you a home, 'n I doan want no trouble with the sheriff. Like you 'n Tom done down in Greenville. You 'n Tom allays had too much mouth."

The younger woman straightened up. "If thar was more like us on mill hills these ants 'n bugs 'd be gone long ago, 'n a lot more things, besides. As for takin' me in—I've paid like any other boarder 'n helped you with housework, too. I guess I ain't beholden to you or nobody that you can order me about."

Gertie's face grew livid. "What you carryin' on so over the ants for? It ain't ant's bites that's wrong with Bobby. He ain't growin' right. From the looks of him, his bowlegs 'n head too big for his body, he's gona get the pellargy if you ain't careful."

Marge stared at her, wordless.

"I ain't meanin' to scare you," Gertie rushed on, "but you've no cause to stir up a fuss 'bout the ants."

The next day Marge told her sister, "Ruthie's wantin' me to come over to Riverton, 'n I'm agoin'. I guess I know where I'm wanted 'n where I ain't."

RUTH AND HAL WERE WORKING in Corey mill and boarding with Mrs. Hollis. It was arranged that Marge was to share a room with the two Hollis girls. A cot she had brought along was placed in one corner and it was on this she and Bobby slept.

"It's just temporary," Ruth explained, "later you 'n us can take a four-room house 'n maybe rent out a room."

"This is all right, Ruthie. 'Course a place to ourselves'll be better. But Mrs. Hollis is real kind-like. It's good here for Bobby, 'n that's all I care about. Mis Hollis or her grandchild Mable can keep an eye on him while I'm at the mill."

"I've spoken for you at the plant, Marge, like I said I would. The boss-man says bring you in this Friday." Ruth walked around restlessly. "Miz Hollis figgers six-fifty a week for you 'n Bobby, 'n that's right reasonable. That'll leave you two'n a half for other things."

"We'll make out, somehow. What you wanderin' around so for? Come sit by me. It's four month since you left. How things goin' for you?" She pulled the girl down beside her. Ruth smiled a little wearily. "Oh, all right I guess."

Her sister studied her. Maybe she was old-fashioned, but she didn't like all that red on her cheeks and lips. It gave her baby sister a queer, hard look. There were dark circles under her eyes. Marge's arm about her tightened. "I've missed you a mighty lot, Ruthie, since you left."

Suddenly Ruth crumpled up, burying her head on the other's shoulder. Marge's face whitened. "If that thar Hal ain't good to you I'll take his hide off."

"Naw ... naw. He's all right. That is ... A mill gal's got no sense to get married, has she?"

"I see. You're worried, maybe?" Marge stuttered, blushed. Sex was a taboo subject. "You ... you ... ain't caught so soon?"

"I dunno. I doan think so." They looked at one another with drawn faces. "Marge, how ... that is ... do you know how ... ?"

"Naw, I doan. I wisht I did. It'd saved me'n Bob a lotta sufferin'."

"Hal," Ruth's voice dropped, "he's bad thataway. Woan leave me be."

"There's one thing you can do. Put salt-peper in his food. It'll cool him off. Bob told me they done that to men in the army. But him, I daren't after he was so sickly."

"Gosh, but how can I at a boardin' house? Besides, Hal's an awful temper. I'd be scared for him to find out."

Marge gripped her hands in her lap. To think that Ruthie should have to go through what she had. That was a bad law, that let the rich folks know but kept the poor from knowin' what to do.

Marge soon discovered that Hal was all that Mrs. Hollis charged—"a triflin' soul. Layin' off all the time, complainin' of his back, 'n livin' offa Ruth's earnin's. In six months she'll see the last of him, 'n good riddance too." Marge nodded. But what if he should leave Ruth with a child to support?

Late one night she wakened to find Ruth leaning over her. She was in her night gown. "Let me in." Lifting Bobby on her chest Marge slid over and her sister slipped under the covers. The bed shook with her trembling. "What is it?" "Hal—" her voice caught. "Hush—doan wake the others. What is it?"

"He's drunk and—I'm scairt of him when he's thataway. He doan know what he's doin'."

Ruth slipped back across the hall before the others were up. Hal, head thrown back, mouth open, was snoring loudly. She looked at him with new eyes. Was this the creature she'd tormented herself over! When she left for the mill he was still sleeping.

At the supper table Hal began a loud argument. Marge saw her sister wince. "Please doan, Hal, not here." His voice grew louder. Ruth jumped up, Marge beside her. Mrs. Hollis came running from the kitchen, her flour-spattered face red with more than heat from the stove. "You get out, Hal Jenkins," she thundered. "Yes, get out. I keep a respectable house. I woan have the likes of you here another night. The only reason I let you stay so long is on account of your wife. But the way you act—drinkin' 'n flirtin'! You're a no-count. As fer Ruthie, she's welcome to stay, 'n she knows it."

The girl turned yellow under her paint. "Thank-ye, Miz Hollis. I'll stay. As for you," she turned on Hal, "I say, too, get out!"

He made a lunge forward. Old man Hollis grabbed him by the collar. With the help of two of the boarders he pushed him into the street and bolted the door. Through the window he called, "we still got our shot-gun hangin' over the door. You mess around here or bother Ruthie 'n we'll fill you full of lead."

TOM WAS WRITING to Marge:

Dear Sis,

    I'm sorry to hear the sad news with you. It sure is tough.

    That's the way it is for workers in this country. We've sure got to make a change.

Well, since we won our strike a lot has happened. There's a fellow I got acquainted with over at our Party headquarters, who's from Back Row. His name is George Johnson, and he knew Fred's people.

Well, Sis, your brother has joined up with the Reds. The wobblies have gone shot but the Reds are the real thing. Doan believe what the papers say against us. It ain't so, that's all. I'm gona send you some papers and things to read. Oh, boy, wait till we start organizing the south! Then you'll have something to live for, like I said.

Say I got a letter from Fred, from Russia, and he says that's some country. No fat mill owners and millionaires to live offa working people, no bosses to drive 'em. Labor owns and runs factories, government, and everythin'. Things are like the way he never realized, till he saw it with his own eyes. He wants me to come over and see for myself.

Once he got sick, so they sent him to a rest home with all expenses paid and wages beside. Everybody else there was fixed up like him. All because they were workers. And what a place it was! It used to be a palace of some noble before the revolution; and Fred says the white marble pillows and red carpets'd dazzle your eyes. All over the country it's like that—fancy houses what used to belong to the rich now used for laborers. Wouldn't be so bad if we took over the white houses of Mr. Haines and the others for sick mill hands?

Another thing Fred told about, how everybody can go to school. He says he thought he was a book worm but that these people put him in the shade, they're like famished to learn. You'd like that, woulden you?

Over there there ain't anybody to look down their nose at anybody else. All they ask is if you live by your

*labor. Fred says one white fellow from the States tried
to get uppity with him once, and the Russians told him
where to get off in no time! There's no color line allowed.
Fred says it's the first time he ever felt he could breathe
deep and free. The best of all, he thinks, is the spirit of the
people.*

*Well, I've writ a lot, but thot you'd like to hear this. It
means for us workers more than anything that's happened since you and I was born. So when you read the
lies about the Soviet Union in the papers, just say we
know why they say that. They're scared the common
people here might get a notion to try it themselves. And
they will too, before we kick in.*

Another thing—

(Tom's eyes shone, his pencil hesitated, then raced across
the sheet.)

*Fred met up with a girl I used to know there, named
Bessie. She used to work in a dress shop here but got sent
away, during the war. What do you think—she's a delegate from her shop to the workers' city government (they
call it soviet). Yes-sir, she's helping to make laws for two
million people in Red Moscow. Could such a thing happen in this country? Bessie is a fine girl, the nicest next
to you I ever knew. I got a letter from her too. But I can't
write all she had to tell in this letter. It is past twelve, and
I got to be at the mill at seven sharp.*

*Doan get down-hearted, sis. As soon as Fred gets
back, we'll be down your way, or maybe sooner. Keep
ahoeing.*

Yours, Tom.

"THIS HERE'S SURE a big mill. How many frames you say in
here?" Marge asked her neighbor.

"More'n two hundred spinners in here. All told, there're two thousand in the plant."

"Uh-huh! As many as four mills together whar I come from."

"They say as how it's owned by a comp'ny from up north—the Jenkins comp'ny." Dolly Grady deftly fastened a broken thread. She was an olive-skinned woman with high cheek bones and glistening black hair pulled tight over her ears. There was Indian blood in her veins. She was one of the descendants of the Cherokee tribe whose land had been cheated and stolen from them by the early white settlers. "The Jenkins got another mill in Rhode Island," she continued, "'n some more down this way, in Georgy 'n Alabamy."

"Is that so! I notice thar's a lotta Yankees startin' up mills down here. They likes 'em big, too."

"I reckon." Dolly rested her hands for a brief moment on her hips, surveying her line of whirling frames. "They must make a lot of money. Onct, so they tell, Mr. Jenkins was down this way, with his wife 'n two gals. They were some diked out, in silk 'n furs 'n diamond rings. Looked fit for the movies, the hands 'lowed. He's *got* a big house in Floridy, whar they go for the winter, 'n in summer he takes the missus 'n chillen for a trip across the water."

"Ain't that somethin'! You know whar they get all that money?" Marge demanded.

Dolly wrinkled her brow. "Wal, I calculate it comes from his mills. Whar else? Or maybe he owns buildings 'n things up north. How should I know?"

"I tell you. It's outta such as you 'n me, what spins 'n weaves his cotton. My brother Tom says . . ."

"Hush," Dolly warned, "thar comes the boss-man."

Later the two met in the toilet. "What you think of this here hill?" Dolly inquired.

"Oh, like most other hills—no better'n, no worse. Not so many bugs here as whar I was last. I tell you what, honey, life for mill hands is the same all over—comp'ny store, comp'ny houses, comp'ny everythin'—'n us just hands to feed the frames."

Dolly drew in her breath. "You're a funny one, talkin' like you do."

"Ain't it God's truth?"

"I reckon. But the way you say it 'n all . . . It's good to get offa our feet a few minutes, ain't it?" The half-Indian woman shuffled her worn shoes.

Mary, another spinner appeared in the entrance.

"Bill says it's time to come outta here, you two."

Dolly was furious. "Of all the nerve! Can't do nuthin' in this mill but rush. They stretchen us out till our bones crack. 'N now it's come to the place whar we can't even go to the toilet!"

"All over it's the same," Mary replied. "My man works at the weave room 'n he says it's gettin' so they woan let you take time to spit." The women filed out.

"What's a chawin' man gona do, when he can't spit?"

Later on Dolly asked, "I hear that brother-in-law of yours is back at the Hollis?"

Marge snapped the toothpick she was holding. "Yah. He 'n Ruthie made up. He's promised to behave. So Miz Hollis give him another chanct."

"That's the way with women, when they get sot on a man."

"I reckon." She returned to her spinning.

The two spinners became fast friends, Marge's heart went out to the three brown tots at Dolly's house, as well as the patient woman laboring to feed them and Joe, her invalid husband, on seven-fifty a week. Joe had been lame ever since an accident in the mill several years ago, but the company had not paid even the doctor's bill. "Even my religion doan console me the way it should," Dolly told her friend, "but I'm on my knees asking for more Grace, every night 'n mornin'."

GOING HOME ONE NIGHT Marge heard rapid steps behind her and her name called "Marge . . . Marge Crenshaw. What on earth you doin' here?"

She turned. "Why Jem Brown." He worked her hand up and down. "I'm right glad to see you." "The same to you. When you'd get in?"

"Last week. I got a job as machine tender up at Jenkins mill. You?"

"I'm spinnin' thar. Been thar four month now."

"Wal, it's right good to lay eyes on you again." His voice dropped. Startled by her drawn mouth and darkened eyes, he inquired, "How it's been with you 'n yourn?"

Marge turned her head. "I've lost both."

"You mean . . ."

"Bob died six months past. 'N lil' Bobby—" she waited until her voice steadied. "He's gone now, too."

"Lawd above us—how'd it happen? My poor gal." Choking he readied out his hands.

"Pellagry took my baby. It got so bad that—you know what it does . . ." Yes, Jem did know. He had seen many hundreds of mill children in the past two decades taken off, crippled for life, or made hopeless idiots by the dread pellagra. Starvation's child—the scourge of mill hills, that was pellagra. As fearful as its twin brother—the white plague.

In heavy silence they walked on for another block. "Gee, Marge, I can't tell you how I feel." Jem pulled one ear awkwardly. "Anything I can do, you know you can count on me."

She found comfort in his kind, tired-looking eyes. "Thank you, Jem."

"Ain't thar somethin'?" he asked anxiously.

"Naw, nothin' I think of, right now."

Before they parted she remembered to tell him, "Ruthie, me 'n her man live up at Hollis' on Main Street. Come over any evenin' to see us, 'n get acquainted."

"Thank-ye kindly. I'll drop in an evenin' soon. 'N let me know if thar's anything I can do."

JEM HAD COME VISITING. He felt cramped and self-conscious in his stiff white collar. What'd he changed from his overalls for, Marge wondered. All the boarders and family were assembled in the Hollis parlor, discussing the stretch-out at the plant.

"You take Sat Wilson now. Listen to his tale of woe." At this invitation Sat hitched his chair closer into the circle. "They got me oilin' the twister room 'n the spoolin' room, keepin' bands of spoolers, takin' down spools 'n rollin' 'em down the elevator, bringin' up pieces, helpin' on creelin', huntin' bobbins for doft-twisters, takin' out 'n separatin' waste ..."

As he caught his breath, Hollis asked him, "How you crowd all that into sixty hours? What you say they pay you?"

"Fourteen-forty. 'Course I know it's more'n most get, but it's little enough, for five brats'n a hungry 'oman. 'N believe me, I sweat for it."

"This stretch-out is sure bad. Used to be a mill-hand was good for fifteen or twenty years at his place, but now they drop most of us off around thirty-five years' old." Phil Murphy thumped his knees.

"Take me, now." Ted Burnham snapped his suspender strap. "I used to run twenty-five cards, now got to do forty for the same ten dollars. 'N ev'ry third man of us been lopped off."

Hollis and another weaver told how in the weave shop where there used to be twelve looms to the alley, three weavers, three inspectors and one loom fixer, they increased the looms and reduced the force until now there were eighteen looms for every two weavers, one inspector and one loom-fixer. At the same time, pay had been reduced from twenty-eight cents a thousand picks to eighty-seven cents for one hundred thousand picks. "We ought to be on roller-skates, so as to keep up."

"It's the same all over," Jem observed. "Some mills is worse'n here. The thing is—what we mill hands gona do? Ten years it's been since the war, 'n thar's been nothin' but wage-cuttin' 'n stretch-out ever since."

"What can we do?" Hal demanded. "Mill-hands doan never stick together!"

Marge felt her face grow warm. "What you mean we can't? We can, too!"

"Naw we can't. Hal's right. Mill hands ain't the stickin' kind. Look what happened over to Charlotte. A wash-out, that was."

"The union idea is all right, I reckon," Hollis spoke cautiously, "but the way it's run it's worse'n nothin'."

"It's clear somethin's gotta be done. They're gettin' us lower 'n lower ev'ry month." Miz Hollis threw up her head. "I know mill hills gotta a lot of pryin' ears, but I said what I said, 'n I ain't scared to stand by it."

Before he left Jem called Marge to one side. "Say," he whispered, "you know that brother up north what's in a good union."

"Yah? What about him? Your hands are shakin' like a leaf."

"Can't you see things are so hot here, a spark might start a fire any day? We gotta lay our plans careful this time. If you're *sure* your brother's in a gen-u-ine union, then couldn't he get 'em to send somebody down here?"

"Why, maybe they would."

"Doan mention it to nobody, but you write him a letter. In the meantime we'll lay low."

GEORGE HAD COME OVER to his friend's room to spend the evening.

"Look-a-here, what my sis in Carolina writes." Tom passed him the letter.

"Gee wilikins! Maybe the time's come. Shall we take it up with the Party this very night?"

Tom laughed. "You big goose. Look at the clock. But tomorrow after work, the first thing."

George executed a light-footed clog. "Oh, boy. At last we'll organize the South!" Tom joined in. Angry voices, a threatening pounding on the floor from below stilled their feet. "That Miz O'Hannessy with her broom. I bet we woke her up."

They dropped to the side of the bed. "You know, George, this means a long, tough fight. When the mill barons feel their pockets pinched, thar'll be hell a-poppin'."

"Thar sure will. Maybe, lynchin's."

"No, by gorry!" Tom grasped the Negro's hand. "Not this time. We'll see to that."

Their faces grew thoughtful. "Lucky we got the new union. Even though it's so weak yet."

"Yah, 'n the Party to lead us 'n organize support on a big scale. We'll be needin' plenty of both, afore we're through."

"Well, see you tomorrow." George slipped on his jacket. Tom grinned at him. "Only one thing I'll worry about—mail comin' reg'lar."

His friend snorted. "You sure got it bad. 'N for a gal halfway across the world. Sure crazy, if you ask me."

"All right. Just wait till you fall."

"Not me. No time for such doin's—till after the revolution."

"Aw, that's big talk. Just you wait."

XX.

New Times—New Songs

"THE WARM CLIMATE'LL FEEL mighty good these nippy March days." George turned up his collar, hunching closer into his seat.

"Yah, we're goin' back to the land of sunshine 'n flowers, buddy." Tom's sarcasm lacked edge, for he felt in high spirits. The train's lurching made his voice quaver ludicrously over the words:

> Oh Dixie land, whar I was born in
> Early on one frosty mornin', Look-a-way, look-
> a-way, look-a-way,
> Look-a-way, look-a-way, look-a-way, Dixie land.
> Oh, Dixie land, the land of cotton,
> Old times thar is not forgotten—

Old times thar is not forgotten. George looked around with a scowl. "Ah, can it Tom, can't-ya!" The song ended abruptly. The younger man stretched his long arms over his head and rose to his feet. "Gosh, I'm cramped from sleepin' on that seat all night, ain't you? It must be all of seven o'clock. I'll have a turn through the cars 'n stretch my legs a bit."

Tom stared after him. "Gol-dern, what a low-down trash I am. Old times—huh." Old times. Those days at Back Row, that had been branded with a white hot iron on his friend's memory.

When George returned to his seat, he dropped a hand on his friend's knee. "Sorry, buddy. But this—" he gestured toward the flying country-side, "this brings it all back. Not even a poor white can know what the south means for us *niggers.*" He spat the word out contemptuously. His friend knew enough to keep silent. "It's creepin' back on me now, like pizen in the blood." He paused. "But now I know how to fight it."

Breaking off, he turned toward the window. "Look at the dawn over those cornfields." Crimson streaks shot through the purple shadows which momentarily grew lighter, blending with the dusty yellow of the arch above.

A white hand slipped over the black one resting on Tom's knee. "It's a good omen, George. A new day's dawnin' down here."

"I dunno. I hope you're right. Looks to me like a long sleddin' ahead."

"Fred writes the sun's already rize across the waters."

"I'd sure like to see that country. Seems too good to be true, somehow." George laughed ruefully. "I was took in so easy a few years back, guess I'm from Missouri now.... Sure want to meet that Fred Morgan, too. If he's anything like his Pa ... You know, I told you how Uncle Ben used to take me between his knees 'n tell me stories, 'n play the banjo. I most worshiped that man. Then come the dark days ..." George's face dropped in his hands. "I never forgive myself for not stayin' behind."

"But you were no more'n a kid, George. Besides, what could you've done? As it is, now it's so we can do somethin' to help free your people, 'n mine too. Now we got an organization to back us."

"That's so. But it rankles all the same—that I run away. It rankles."

The train lumbered on into broad daylight. "How shabby everythin' looks," Tom remarked, "'n the further south we go, the shabbier'n slower it'll get."

"You noticed that too? It's like a movin' picture runnin' down. Everythin'—folks, animals—move slower."

"Maybe slower. But look at the hours."

A country store flashed by. "Look at those fellas just settin' thar. If they ain't the lazy ones, 'n natural as life!"

"Country-life allays slower'n the city. You know, whar thar's factories 'n traffic a-hummin'. Just wait till the south gets her industries more built up. Then the movie reel'll wound up 'n things go speedier. In more ways than one."

"From what Sis writes they've sure wound up the cotton mills. It's gona cost the mill barons a-plenty afore it's done, too."

A conductor with a face like an eagle's threw open the carriage door and called in ponderous tones, "Alloffor bally-mo."

"With his voice 'n face," Tom observed, "his talents are wasted. He ought to join a circus."

"Baltimore, is it?" George inquired. "Say, soon beak-nose'll come through 'n make me go to the Jim Crow car. Soon we'll be across the line 'n in White Man's Country. So we better put in a good hour now, finishin' up our plans."

"You doan think," the other demanded indignantly, "I'm gona stand for that sour-face drivin' you out!"

"What you want—to have us both locked up in Alexandry jail?" the Negro retorted cooly. "Lotta work we'd do thar! We gotta act sensible. When we got a whole town 'n county full standin' together, than we can say to hell with 'em."

Tom's jaw was set. "Then I'll go to the Jim Crow car with you."

"They'll not allow that either."

"What the hell—" Suddenly his eyes twinkled. "What you say we take a private car. Like those swells we saw boardin' the Pullman. Between Washington 'n Alexandry, we'll shift to a baggage car."

"You're on."

They settled themselves cross-leg fashion on the floor of an empty car.

"Got a light? Thanks. You know, George, this is some big job we've signed for."

"'N how! Some of the northern fellows mayn't know it. But you 'n me warn't born on mill hills for nothin'! The comp'ny got a strangle hold on everythin'. It owns the roof over the mill hands's heads, it owns the food for their stomachs."

"'N it owns the food for their minds, too. That's pretty nigh the worse of all. Blessed are the poor! Turn the other cheek; Servant, love your master; and all the rest."

"Boloney!" George agreed. "What's more, mill hands know next to nothin' about organization. 'N the two races are suspicious as hell of one another. Doan forget that.

Tom whistled between his teeth. "I ain't forgettin' it. Geminy crickets, but I wish Fred was back! Seeing George's expression he added hastily, "it's just he must've learned a heap these four years across. We need all the light we can get. This here's the toughest job the movement tackled in many a day."

"Doan I know it! But from what your Sis says, thar's a ferment brewin' that'll bust through anything."

"That's the thing. Well, let's get down to brass tacks. Now our plan is—"

While the train lumbered through villages and countryside, they talked in low tones, meanwhile keeping an eye out for a trainman who might happen on their private car.

Tom and George reached Riverton by separate ways. The white organizer went straight to Mrs. Hollis, rented a cot in a room with two other men borders, and in a few days had a job in the mill. Only Marge and Jem knew why he had come. To others who inquired he answered, "Things are gettin' slow in textiles up north. Lotta the companies are movin' south. So where the mills go, mill hands follow." He began to hum:

> "Where the mills lead, I will follow—
> Where He leads me I will follow—"

Marge, smiling, shook a warning finger at him. "Miz Hollin's'll think you're blasphemin'."

Not even Ruth was told the real reason for his return, until several days later. "Only you, Jem 'n me know Tom's principles," Marge cautioned her, "'n it's up to us to lay low. That is, for a while."

"You know you can trust me," the younger woman reproached her.

"Not even to tell Hal?"

"Oh, all right. I know you doan trust him. Though you've no cause to suspicion him, he's got his faults, but he ain't a turn-coat."

When Tom reported for work, the boss-weaver eyed him up and down. "You didn't join no union up north?"

Tom looked indignant.

"You know no good Americans take to labor organizations!"

The boss-weaver looked relieved. "That's so. But the super said to make sure. You know our help down here is contented, 'n we ain't lookin' for no rumpus."

GEORGE FOUND IT HARD to get even a place to stay. Up and down the dirt paths which straggled in front of the two dozen shacks which made up the Negro section of Riverton hill he tramped and made inquiries. Back of the Hollow, as the tiny settlement was called, the fields were rippling with daisies and buttercups. George stopped to watch them.

An old woman, with red bandana knotted about her head, took her corn-cob pipe out of her mouth, and squinted up at him. "Boy, what you want round here, noways?"

"I want me a bed 'n a job over to the mill."

"Uh-huh. Wal, hard tellin' what luck you'll have.... Your speech doan sound right. You ain't from these parts, be you?"

George laughed. "Pretty shrewd, ain't you? Wal, mammy, I was born in South Caroliny, but I been away ten year now."

She knocked the ashes out of her pipe, wiping her hands on her full-gathered black calico skirt. "You know we have to be mighty careful. The comp'ny keeps out a sharp eye, 'n if anything they doan like, it's 'Niggers, git out.'"

He grinned down at her persuasively. "Mammy, I'm tellin' you—I ain't no nigger-in-a-woodpile."

Leaning back, balancing herself by her arms akimbo, she cackled joyously. "Lawsy boy, nobody could help but give in to you. The folks next door to us have an extry cot in the kitchen. Come on, I'll step over with you." She hobbled off, leading the way.

"How're things around here now, Mammy?"

"Tolable, tolable," she answered sourly. The canny old creature, George thought, she's still being careful of me.

Mammy Branson knocked at the open door. "Howdy, Matilda, howdy, Sonny. This here's George Johnson, come for a job to the mill 'n he's wantin' a bed. Can you 'commodate him?"

After this was settled, George went to the mill. Cap in hand he approached the foreman. "Please sir, you needin' a hand for the dye room or to shuffle bins?"

The foreman eyed him sharply. "We ain't after hirin' no Yankee niggers."

"But I was born 'n raised in South Carlyny."

"That so—whar 'bout?"

For a fraction of a second George hesitated. The foreman noticed this.

"Greenville."

"Why'd you leave the south to go north?"

"I went in the army durin' the war. Afterwards, I just stayed north."

"How'd you like it up thar?" the white overseer demanded.

"Not so good" (but a sight better'n here, George added under his breath).

"Why'd you come south now?"

"Get me a steady job. Be among my own people."

The foreman swung on his heels. "I guess we ain't needin' no extry hands now." He spit in George's direction.

The Negro's hands clenched. He'd like to swing him one! Instead, he walked rapidly in the opposite direction. On the way he decided he'd have to practice up on the talk. It ought to come back, quick-like.

"Nothin' doin' for a few days I reckon," he answered Matilda's look of inquiry, "guess I'll have a look roundabouts, tother mills, too." He had to find something, and soon, for there was less than a quarter jinklin' in his pocket.

After supper the Hollow families gathered around Matilda's stoop to question the newcomer and hear news of distant parts. Women in brightly colored blouses and slips sat with childern resting on their arms or playing hide-and-seek behind their skirts. The pipes of the older folks gleamed in the dusk, a few of the younger men lit what Mammy Branson scornfully referred to as "those weeds of Satan." That new-fangled way of smokin' was sure an abomination. She'd been told that Mr. Corey's gal and all the other millmen's daughters what ran with the society folks in Riverton were smokin' these here what-you-call-'ems—lil' see-gars. 'Couse she hadn't seen with her own eyes, but those who had swore it was the Lawd's truth. That just went to prove what she already know,—they were a triflin', sinful lot. Their drinkin' 'n lazy ways were bad enough. But to smoke those what-you-call-'ems—couldn't tell her any real lady'd do that! Mammy Branson puffed furiously on her homemade pipe. White quality'd sure stepped down in her eyes.

"First thing you know, Granny, your own grand-child'll be smokin' lil' see-gars too," Wren teased.

"Go way with you!" the old woman made a pass at the light-colored youth whose small stature and darting movements had won him a nickname which he secretly despised. "You're no bigger'n a hopper. If you sass me, I'll turn you cross my lap." The crowd laughed heartily at Wren's discomfort. "Go ahead, Mammy, let's see you." "Whippen him one." "That's it, lift him up 'n paddle him good."

Matilda held her shaking sides. Gradually her face sobered, she turned once more toward George. "You been up north many a year now. Tell me is this so—Did my cousin speak true, that black men can sit anywhar in a street-car he's a mind to? 'N go to the same churches 'n scholls as white folks?"

"Yes, that's so. 'Course, thar's no place in this country a black man's got a full equal chance. Up north, like here, the bosses give us the worst jobs 'n pay him the lowest. Thar's places bars us from goin; in like the swellest hotels 'n parts of town whar the rich live. But it's not like the south, not by a long shot."

There was much discussion. Young men left off joshing their girls to take their turn at questioning. "Why, over in Charlotte last week, a nigger nigh was lynched for sittin' in the whitefolks' part of the street-car! He claim he was from Chicago. I guess he'd been drinkin' some, 'n was new to these parts, 'cause he gave the conductor an argument. He said he'd a fought for this country, 'n he'd a right to sit anywhar he pleased to. Yes-sir, they rode him outta town. He was lucky to get away as easy as he did."

"Speakin' of the War, you said you was over, didn't you?" Nannie's dark eyes shone. "What was it like?"

George wrenched his gaze away from her eager face. "It was a mess."

"Nannie's allays moonin' bout the war!" Uncle Alex Brown thumped his foot impatiently. "What I want to know of the stranger," he shot a swift glance upward, "is why he ever come back south, to this hell on earth?"

George answered cautiously. He wasn't ready yet, to reveal his plans. He must pick his men, one by one.

"Uncle John, my Simbo's beggin' for some of your music," Matilda drawled softly.

"Yeh, that's it, it's time for music." As Uncle John brought forth his banjo and began strumming the strings, tuning in, the crowd settled back with a sigh. The newcomer's eyes filled. He had come home, back to his own people. But for the want of familiar faces, this might be Back Row, or High Point. The same old songs. The same bonds of outcast and down-trodden holdin', bindin' 'em all.

What was this Uncle John singin'?

> Went to Atlanta
> Never been thar afo'
> White folks eat th'apple
> Nigger wait for the core
>
> Went to Charleston
> Never been thar afo'
> White folks sleep on feather bed
> Nigger on the floor
>
> Went to Raleigh
> Never been thar afo'
> Whitefolks wear the fancy suit
> Nigger his over-all

> Went to Heaven
> Never been thar afo'
> Whitefolks sit in the Lawd's place
> Chase nigger down below

"Whar'd you learn that'un, Uncle John?" George inquired. "It's new to me."

"Oh, I picked up a lotta ones, one place 'n tother. 'N some just come into my head, like. You know, rumminatin' over things, I got to hummin' what I was studyin' over. Now here's one that come like that." The old man thrust his head on one side, closing his eye-lids, his lips barely moving.

> Nigger go to white man
> Ask him for work
> White man say to nigger
> Get out o' your shirt

> Nigger threw off his coat
> Went to work pickin' cotton
> When time come to git pay
> White folks give him nothin'

> Lil' bees suck the blossoms
> Big bees eat the honey
> Nigger raise the cotton 'n corn
> White folks get the money

> Here sit the woodpecker
> Learnin' how to figger
> All for the white man
> Nothin' for the nigger

> Slavery 'n freedom
> They's most the same
> No difference hardly
> 'Cept in the name

Wren stirred restlessly. "What for you sing such mournful songs? Let's have somethin' lively."

"Hush that talk," Matilda broke in, "we like Uncle John's songs! Later on, you young'uns can have your dancin'. George, if you like new songs, get Jerry that to give you some." She gestured toward a massively-built man with skin of polished ebony.

"Jerry," Uncle John called, "sing that one you learned on the chain-gang." The old man turned toward George. "Maybe you doan know how they do it here. When they wants men to work their roads, the white folks just go out 'n arrest the strongest-lookin' black ones they can find. 'Come on, you're charged with vagrancy.' Or sometimes they say it's for stealin' chickens or a no-count wheelbarrow, or whatever crosses their mind. They clop the hand-cuffs on 'n that's that. With pick'n shovel, ball'n chain, you break their rock 'n lay their roads. Jerry here knows."

The big fellow shrugged. "You gol darn right. I've helped to lay more'n one road in North Carlyny—with no red cent for pay but a whip cross may back."

"This one I'm singin' first," he explained, "we sung 'n timed our picks to. The fellow what first learned me it, got shot through his lungs for sassin' the white boss-man. Wal, here goes:

> Clothes all tore
> Toes on the ground
> Got no job
> None to be found
>
> I'm hungry 'n cold
> Got nowhar to go
> In my face
> Folks slam the door

Poor man sure
Is hard enough
Pour man 'n nigger
Lawd—that's tough!

Mammy been taken
Friend's gone too
Lawd, I'm lonely
Doan know what to do

Hear me Lawd
Let me be gone
How soon oh Lawd
Oh Lawd, how long.

George ran his hands rapidly over his close-cropped head. These new songs—they had a different note. Maybe the war and years since had roused his people from their slumber, maybe . . . Straddling his legs, throwing up his head, the heavy-set youth broke into a resounding chant:

Stand boys stand
No use arunnin'
Look up yonder hill
White men acomin'

He got rope in one hand
Pistol in 'tother
Stand boy stand
Brother stand by brother
Stand by brother

As the last phrase was hurled into the night, George jumping up, seized the singer by the shoulder. "You know what that song mean?" he demanded, "You know what it means?"

Jerry looked him full in the eye. "I reckon I oughta. Ain't it plain? It means what it says—black man, brother, stand by brother."

"Yah . . . but thar's more'n that in it. More'n . . ." George broke off. "Jerry, boy, you'n me gona be pals. We gotta lot to talk over."

XXI.

Strike!

THE FIRST SATURDAY AFTERNOON, the two organizers met, as agreed, at the crossroads in the woods a mile beyond the village. Tom introduced his friend to Jem, who had come along to take part in the laying of further plans. "Glad to know you." George put out his hand. The white man flushed, shifting his feet. The hand he extended was cold with sweat.

This was the first time he had ever been called on to shake hands with a member of the colored race. Tom had won him over. But, Jem realized, it was much easier to talk than to do diff'rent. The way he'd been trained to believe all these years, he was goin' against. Fear, prejudice, paralyzed his movements. Then, as he felt the other's firm grasp, a sense of relief went through him, of being freed from something that had held him captive, unawares.

The three moved off into the woods. "Marge planned to come. She's anxious to meet you," Tom continued, "but they kept her department workin' over-time today, so we had to come on without her. How'd you find things over in the Hollow?"

"Things are as bad as I've ever seen on a mill hill—'n that's sayin' a mouthful. The folks are fearful 'n suspicious too, of what they figger are white folks' plannin'."

"They've sure a cause to be, judged by the past," his friend replied. "More'n one strike has left them standin' out in the cold. We've gotta show 'em that this time it's all millhands together, against the comp'ny."

"That's it. Thar's a couple I've talked open with—a fella named Jerry, who works in the dye room, 'n a sweeper, called Uncle John. They're with us."

"That's good. Bring 'em to our next meetin'." Tom answered.

"We gotta work fast, it looks to me. Things are apt to pop before we're fully ready. You know, it takes a lot to rouse mill people, but once they get started, they're hot-headed 'n quick on a trigger. Besides our committees in each department, we oughta get committees organized in all the mills throughout Gaston County, so as to spread the strike as far as possible. We could too, if we had the forces. As it is, we'll have to work fast."

"Right-o. Now this is how I size it up—"

As they talked, George became aware of Jem's intent gaze which usually shifted as soon as he looked in the white man's direction. It nettled him. What was the white man thinking anyhow? Tom, troubled, wished for Fred. After all, George was still pretty much of a youngster.

Just before they separated Jem said to George, "You'll come to all our meetin's woan you? I want all our committee to get acquainted with you. You know how it is down here—" he faltered, looking to Tom for help—"Go on, Jem," his companion told him, "doan mind George, he understands." All at once Jem and George felt more at home with each other, "You know our ways, in the south 'n how slow folks are to change. This black 'n white comin' together feels a lil' strange at first. But it's the only way. I'm sky-blue certain of what. We want you in our union. Tell the Hollow folks that. We'll stand by 'em, 'n we want 'em to stand by us."

"It's a beginning, George," Tom added, "step by step they'll learn."

"That's so. . . . Wal, so long, comrades." They shook hands once more. "Till next Wednesday evenin'."

DIM SHADOWS GLIDED SILENTLY among the dark firs and assembled in the clearing near Pine Grove. Here they were beyond company ground and the long reach of company cars.

The moon was not yet up, it was hard to distinguish faces. "That you Dolly?" a gray figure whispered.

"Uh-huh. Come on, Marge, let's sit on these here stumps." They peered about them. "Looks like a goodly number here already, doan it."

"Gona be twenty, all told," Tom said. "All the departments got a member."

"And some black folks from the Hollow?" Dolly asked doubtfully.

"Sure, that's only fair, ain't it. The dye house 'n all the hands gotta go out together, else how we gona win?"

"I guess it's sensible. Only—"

"Only what?" her companion demanded. "I thought we all thrashed this out, once for all."

"It's all right with me, like I told you. Only, thar's some white hands ain't gona join any org-an-i-za-tion that takes in niggers."

"Dolly! Wipe that word offa your tongue. Tom says that's a rich folks' word for colored folks 'n no millhand should use it."

"Shucks, it just slipped out. You know, Marge, if my old man knew I'd come to a meetin' after dark with ni—colored men at it, he'd crawl outta his sick bed on his hands 'n knees to drag me home."

"Then it's time you learned him some sense! Hush, I think it's gona start."

An angular shadow walked to the center of the circle and motioned for silence with its long arms. "Brethern 'n sistern," Jem began, "we're gathered together tonight to lay more plans for building our Union 'n winning our rights. Thar're some new folks with us tonight, both from Riverton, Mesmer City,—'n the Hollow." Stirring among the seated figures. "First I ask you all to take the pledge of secrecy about this here meetin'. We ain't ready yet for the comp'ny to know our plans. All raise their right hands 'n say after me—" The oath was taken. "Now you all know," Jem went on, "how bad things are at the mill. They're gettin' us lower 'n lower." A low mumur of assent. "Stretchin' us out nigh fit to snap our ligaments, 'n pullin' the screws tighter ev'ry week. It's plain what we gotta do—plain as daylight. We gotta stick together for our rights, 'n put a stop to such doin's. Else whar'll it end? Now I'll call on Tom Crenshaw to say a few words, 'n explain us more about makin' the union."

Tom ended his talk. "Your brother's a movin' tongue," Dolly whispered. Marge nodded. To think that this man was once the tow-headed boy she'd played prisoner's base with, the youth who'd tired of Ma's naggin' 'n the mill grind, 'n set out to leave the mills forever 'n make his own way in the world. Now he'd come back south to lead his people, 'n they trusted him. She gripped her hands. The way ahead looked long 'n hard. Would the hill folks stick? Even Dolly here was weak-kneed 'n doubtin'. Marge swung by what Tom had told her, when she put this question to him. What about you, will you stick, he had asked her. You know I will, Tom. Thar's nothing else to do. That's the answer, he told her, the working people will stick, for thar's no other way. Some may drop off by the way, 'n thar'll be side-steppin' 'n mistakes 'n many hardships. But the lessons will drive home. The mill people will learn to stick. They've nothing to lose by it, but all to gain. Thar's no other way outta their misery.

George spoke next. "Wal, I swarn," Hal muttered, "I never aimed to listen to no nigger telling me 'bout my business."

"For Pete's sake, he'll hear you." Ruth clapped her hand over his mouth. He jerked it off, but remained silent, scowling at those around him.

The moon, now up, threw high lights on the speaker's eager face and those of his listeners, some dubious, all curious to hear what those in the Hollow had to say.

"Friends and fellow-workers," George called them. "My people are starvin' in the Hollow 'n on other hills. That's why I know we can count on their support in this comin' strike. That is, provided they can be sure of gettin' a square deal. You must know that in the past the Negro mill hands have been left standin' out in the cold. So they're grown suspicious, like you white folks are, for your part. The old way doan get either race anywhar. The boss-men use the Negroes to keep the white millhands down, 'n scared they'll have their job took away from 'em—"

"Now you said it—" a listener interrupted.

"And"—George looked directly at the man—"the white hands have been used to keep the black down." An uneasy movement, like the rustling of leaves, among the listeners.

"Haven't the mill owners poisoned your minds'n hearts against us?" he demanded. "You know it's so. 'N colored people know whenever they strive to better things for themselves,—get schools for their children, set out to vote, demand more wages—the Poor Whites are allays ready to help the rich men push the Negroes back 'in their place.' Wal, as comrade Tom told you, so long as you white workers act this way, so long as the colored race is kept down in slavery, just so long your wages 'n livin' conditions will be what they are, or worse.

"Now your joinin' up with our union, 'n meetin' here with us from the Hollow shows you're wakin' up. We—Jerry, Uncle John, 'n myself—can say for our people 'You stick by us, 'n we'll stick by you.' Tom 'n I know it can be done. We've seen it done, time over, up north. It'll not be easy for the two races to stand together in the South. Thar'll be everybody against us—the millmen, the newspaper, the preachers 'n school marms,—all to tell us we're headed plum to hell. But the only thing that counts, is to stick together, 'n make the comp'ny give in to our rights."

Jem stretched out his hand. Turning to the committee he said hoarsely, "I just want to say that I've been with Tom over to the Hollow, 'n talked more'n once with George, Jerry 'n Uncle John here. Ev'ry word George spoke was true. It's high time we got together 'n offa our knees to the boss-men, George, here's my hand 'n word that the white hands'll stick by the colored ones."

The meeting ended, the villagers slipped away by twos and threes. "That was a right sensible speech that colored fella made," Marge overheard Phil Murray tell his wife as they started off for the road. The members of the Hollis household began the trip back together. At the edge of the wood, they would separate and return by different ways.

"Funny doin's. That George callin' a white man by his first name," Hal repeated. "Did you hear him call Tom, Tom?"

Marge whirled. "Wal, that's his name ain't it?"

"Why all this fuss over the niggers anyway?" Hal retorted. "There ain't but about two hundred in the whole plant! We ain't depenin' on 'em for winnin'."

"Hal, you must be dumb. Ain't you understand all was said tonight?" His sister in-law was exasperated. "It's the only practical way. Besides, it's a principle."

"Principle, what's that?" he wanted to know. Marge was aghast. "Principle, why—a principle's a principle. Somethin' to live by. Anybody ought to know what's a principle."

"I guess it's all right to let the colored hands in the union," Ruth offered quickly, "let 'em do their part 'n we'll do ours. But they should keep to their own side, 'n us to ourn."

"That's not how Tom 'n George plan it," Marge thought, but not sure of what to say, she kept still.

"How'd you get that thar tear in the seat of your overalls, Jem?"

As he placed his long-fingered hands hastily behind him, feeling about rapidly for the supposed tear, the three mill hands walking behind him burst into peals of laughter. "April Fool! April Fool!" "Gee, you were easy." Jem laughed too, rather ruefully. He was glad Marge hadn't been there to see. "Here things are way they are," he reproached the boys, "'n you still got mind for April Foolin'."

For the first hour in the mill many of the younger ones found time, while tending their machines, to have their sallies and jokes about "All Fool's Day." It was an old custom brought over from England centuries earlier, and still observed, like Hallow'en and May Day for the simple pleasure that was in them. Buttercups soaked in amonia were passed around to the unsuspecting as well as green violets, and pieces of peppered candy.

But the fun was short-lived this year. There were more important things to consider. At ten o'clock Tom and Jem were called into the office. The workers looked at one another. What did this mean? Had the company got word? When a half-hour passed and the men didn't return, word went round, "Tom 'n Jem're fired for makin' a union." Phil edged over to the window. After one look he beckoned the other weavers. "Come here, boys, see what's up." Men and women crowded around the sill. Down below Tom, Jem, Marge, Jerry, and Red were standing outside, and about a dozen others around them. They were grouped close together, talking earnestly, every now and then glancing toward the plant.

"Wal, I be dog-gone, they fired the whole bloomin' committee!" Phil exclaimed.

"Somebody snitched—the dirty skunk!"

"Who could it've been?"

"What do we do now?"

"Shall we go down too?"

Uncertainly they clung around the sill. Phil pushed up the window and leaned out. "Hey!" The crowd below looked up. Jem signalled, "Come on out!" and young Red made a dash for the entrance.

"Red's comin' for us!"

"The whole bunch's headed toward the mill."

The boss-weaver came running over, his face dripping.

"What the hell's up? Get back to work!"

Phil shoved him aside. "No more work today, boss. It's our turn now for a lil' April Fool on the comp'ny." The weavers started down the stairs. They met Marge and Red coming up. "Wait a minute," they panted, "first let's get all the others." Marge ran toward the spinning room, Red and Phil headed for the spooling and sorting departments. "All hands out. Against the stretch-out!" In the room above Marge threw off the power. "Come on, women, we're walkin' out for more food for our chillen." The foremen ran about frantically, waving their arms, getting in the way. Jerry and Tom strode to the dye house. "Outside, ev'rybody. The strike's on."

In a few minutes time the whole force was outside, overflowing the entire block in front of the giant brick structure, milling about in the side alleys, talking, questioning in agitated, angry, jubilant undertones. Marge, herself flushed with excitement, noticed the happy defiance of the youths and girls. The silent troubled faces of many older men and women, struggling with their misgivings. The grim set to Tom's jaw. The Negro hands had grouped in one alley. They hung back, doubtful, on guard.

Tom worked his way toward them. "George'll sure hate missin' this, woan he?" Jerry greeted him. "Too bad he has to work way over to Vesner. Wait till he hears the news!" "That's right. Jerry, you or Uncle John'll have to speak for us. We're gona start a meetin' right off, then march through the village. But first let's have a few words with your fellow-workers here." "We'll coax 'em not to hold off, but mix in. This is their strike, as much as anybody's." He and Uncle John started for the entrance, where others of the committee had gathered.

"All right, comrades, let's begin." Red was pushed toward an upturned soap-box which someone had brought from a field. As the closely packed throng saw his shock of red hair glowing in the sun a shout went up. "Folks," he began. "Louder! Louder!" they called impatiently from the crowd's edge. Red made a cup of his hands. "Folks," he began once more, his young voice rasping with the effort. He'd weak lungs, Marge remembered. "At last we've struck for our rights."

"Hurrah! Hurrah!" Caps and sunbonnets shot into the air. Red took courage.

"We been the comp'ny's April Fool long enough," he shouted. Laughter. Hand-claps. "This mornin' they pulled their last joke on us. They fired our committee that was makin' our union. Now we all walked out, 'n we'll stay out till we win!" He made a wide gesture, lost his balance as the box toppled to one side. Jumping down he made way for Jem who deliberately placed the box firmly on the ground before mounting it. His eyes that surveyed the hundreds of upturned faces were calm, exultant; his voice carried its customary Alabama drawl. Only the dark blotches on his neck revealed his inner ferment.

"Fellow-workers," he began, "I reckon we've stood about all we can from this here comp'ny. It's high time we took action. I've worked on many hills but the stretchin'-out 'n pay-cuttin' we've been visited with these past months has been the worst ever. Now I ain't gona make a long speech for this ain't the time for a lot of speech-makin', but for *doin'*. I just want to say this: this ain't the first strike we've had on cotton mill hills, but it's gona be the best one!" The shouts bounded against the buildings like waves thundering on the shore. "The comp'ny'll do its durnest, like allays, to bust up 'n starve us back. But remember this—nothin' can stop us, if we all stick together, through thick 'n thin."

Tom motioned to Uncle John to take the stand. The old man's knees trembled under him, but his low, ringing voice could be heard by the farthest off. "Folks, I've been fifty-nine year on this earth, 'n this here's the happiest day I've had yet. I feel like drappin' down on my knees 'n thankin' the good Lawd for at last wakin' my people up. He sent Moses to lead His people from the land of bondage, 'n I believe He sent George 'n Mister Tom here to deliver us from bondage."

"No, Uncle John. It was the Union who sent us," Tom corrected.

The old man looked down at him. "Maybe, son, that's what you think. But I feels the Lawd's hand in it, somewhars. For I never dreamed to see white 'n colored hands standin' side by side. But I can see it's right. It's the only way." He spread out his arms. "If you want to feed your hungry chillen, if you want a decent dress instead of tatters on your wife's back, if you want to put a few more years to your stay on this earth, then stand by the union! If you wanta quit livin' like hogs 'n beasts of burden, 'n get to live like human bein's, then stand together! No matter what! Stand firm like the Rock of Ages!" His black eyes flashed about among the aroused throng. "My old eyes'll never live to see it, but thar's a Great Day comin' bye 'n bye, a day of deliverance from mill slavery, when all will live like freed men. If you only stand firm!" He dropped back into the solidifying mass.

"Marge," Tom nudged his sister, "woan you say a word? We ought to hear from the women." She stepped forward, then back. "Oh, I can't." "Sure you can," Jem urged. "Go on. Tell 'em what it'll mean to get the hours cut 'n more pay." She let herself be lifted to the platform. A cry broke from the strikers at the sight of a woman on the stand.

A thousand things rushed to her lips, choking her. The sea of white, strained faces pressed in. Everything went black before her eyes. Somewhere far off she heard a thin whisper—"Mill hands, white 'n colored, we've slaved long enough for Mr. Jenkins. Women-folks gotta do their full share to helpen win." The whisper died out, in a panic she slipped from the platform. "Oh, Tom I can't. I know I oughta, but I just can't." He put his arm around, her. "That's all right, Sis. You made a start. Next time it'll be easier."

"Tom! Tom! Let's hear Tom," the waiting hundreds called impatiently. Steadying from Jerry's shoulder he climbed up. Marge, still quivering, listened in awed wonder. How plain he made it all. How easy it seemed to come for him. Straight from his heart to her 'n the others. Reasonin', quiet—now fiery, defiant. Full of confidence in his people and the justice of their cause.

It's like he didn't know it was himself standin' thar, speakin' out to all those mill hands. He's that sot on what's he's sayin', she thought. Uncle John was the same—his mind all on his thoughts. Maybe that's the way to do it. Forget that its me, Marge Gregory, darin' to speak out before two thousand people, 'n think hard, about one thing only: "This is what we gotta do. This is what we gotta do." She wished she could try it again. There was so much she had to tell. Even Tom couldn't say it. The thing would torment her until she got it out—something her people had to know.

Tom's words, now sharp, bitter, drew her whole attention. "You know what the mill owners down here say about us up

north? You know what the Chambers of Commerce write in
their bulletins about us? They say: 'Wall Street bankers 'n
textile barons, invest your money in Carolina mills, for we've
a *plentiful supply of cheap and contented labor.*' Those are the
very words. *Cheap and contented labor!!* Look at yourselves—
your worn wives 'n stunted children. You're cheap 'n contented labor! Cheap—at five, nine, and twelve dollars a week!
Contented—to slave eleven hours a day! Contented—to be
stretched out 'n speeded up till hands drop from exhaustion
at their machines!" Angry muttering ran through the crowd.
"We're throwin' that lie in their teeth. We'll show the mill
kings that southern mill workers can fight as well as their
northern brothers for shorter hours 'n higher pay. We'll
make 'em take back the stretch-out 'n recognize our Union!"
The strikers broke into an exultant uproar. "This day," Tom
declared, "will go down in history. The day that southern
mill hands started their Declaration of Independence from
mill slavery. This strike must spread through all of Gaston
County, the biggest textile center in the world. It must start
walk-outs throughout the entire southern region! 'N we'll
get support from all over this country, 'n from all parts of the
world. You'll see. Now we're gona march through the village
and back. We'll line up eight abreast. After the march, we'll
all go home for lunch. This afternoon thar's a mass meetin' at
four o'clock, in the lot back of the school house. Everybody be
on hand, for thar's a lot of plans to be made, 'n plenty of work
to be done. The committee must be at the lot by two o'clock.

"Now before we line up, thar's a song I want to learn you—
to sing as we march. You know the tune already, 'n the words'll
come quick. It's a song the textile workers of Passaic made up
when they were on strike. It's our Union Song."

As the dirt streets sounded with the thud of marching feet
Marge felt a new life rising in herself, in those around her,
uniting them in one tremendous mass. Over-head the white

clouds raced madly in a brilliant blue sky. Throwing back her head she joined in the song. Her voice was husky, for it was the first time in many months that she had sung.

> Solidarity forever—
> Solidarity forever—
> Solidarity forever—
> For the Union makes us strong.

Back and forth between the rows of shabby houses the long line of men, women and children trudged, finally verging on the mill which rose like a brooding giant in the center of the village. Shouting, holding arms they surrounded it, forming a length-wise circle. "Some day it'll be ours," Tom told Marge. She looked at the structure and those around her with new eyes. Its walls echoed—

> Solidarity forever—
> For the Union makes us strong.

XXII.

Solidarity Forever

EARLY THE NEXT MORNING the picket line assembled and started for the mill. Many carried banners which they had made by crude lettering with stove polish on strips of old sheets and pieces of cardboard. On the one which Marge and Ruth held between them were the words: "We've slaved long enuf for you, Mister Jenkins." Dolly, her two oldest clutching at her skirts, bore a sign which she had made from the top of an ancient hat-box: "Milk for our Babies." Phil and Red headed the march, proudly carrying a banner which they had worked over, far into the night: "All mill-hands join the National Textile Workers Union." Underneath in smaller lettering was written: "No more stretch-out." "Shorter hours, higher pay."

Tom, seeing the small group of Negroes keeping to themselves near the rear of the line signalled to Jem and the two dropped back to join them. Jerry and his wife Nancy had brought a sign that they had made according to Uncle John's directions: "In Union there is strength." George also had his, stating, "There's no race lines in this Union." He grinned at his friends. "Pretty good turn-out, eh? Boy, did we have a time, presuading the Hollow that the whites really wanted 'em to come. Jerry'n I've been roundin' 'em up since four this mornin'."

"Yah, it's a good turn-out, 'n spirits are runnin' high." Tom, however, was worried. He drew George to one side. "It ain't right, the way the two races are keepin' separate. We gotta get 'em more united."

"Sure we have," George retorted, "but you know what the first move's gotta come from—from the whites. 'N look at 'em!"

"Gol dern, doan I know it. All 'cept a few holdin' off. Dam their fool notions."

"Say," Jerry called testily, "it's time we got started."

"All right," Tom answered. "Say, Jerry, you 'n Jem step over here a minute. You see how it is—blacks 'n whites walkin' separate. We gotta mix 'em."

Jerry shrugged his shoulders. "Can't do it. Not so quick. You know the way the white folks are, 'n George here knows what a time we had, gettin' the Hollow willin' to come at all. Sure as you start a rumpus, they'll make off."

"Even goin' in the same march is somethin'," Jem argued. "Things doan happen so quick, Tom. This here'll take a lotta ejication. We gotta be practical. If we ain't to the mill soon, it'll be past startin' time."

"Those of us what ain't scared or backward about marchin' together," Jerry proposed. "The rest, you gotta let 'em go the way they are. They woan go no tother way."

"Come on, let's start."

Marge, spying Tom's worried face, and guessing the reason, handed her side of the banner to the next in line. Her face crimson, but step firm, she dropped back until she stood next to Nancy. Everyone stared. A white woman marching with ... what'd happen next!

The line started toward the mill. "You work at Corey's too?" Marge asked her companion. "Yes'm. Cleanin'." "What'd they pay you?" "Four dollars." Four dollars! Why, seven was hard enough—four dollars! "You're Tom's sister, ain't you?" Nancy inquired. "All the Hollow likes Tom. He's 'bout the first white man to—you know, act like we was *folks*. If all hands were like him—'n you—it'd be all right. But they ain't. They're pesky to us. Look down their noses our way, the most of 'em. As if they warn't as common as us colored hands, any day!"

Marge writhed. She felt guilty for her kind. "Yah, we're all in the same boat, only not many see it thataway yet. But this here strike'll learn us somethin'."

Nancy surveyed her companion. A change went over her. "I reckon it oughta." The line started forward. "I reckon it oughta."

As the marchers neared the brick structure there was an angry rush forward. The company had stretched ropes across the streets, blocking off the passageways. The cords snapped like so many pieces of string. Unhindered, the marchers circled the silent mill while boss-men and superintendent scowled at them from its gaping windows.

The following day all the mill boss-men were sworn in as special deputy sheriffs and the National Guard arrived, sent by the Governor at the mill company's request.

"What they want here, a war?" Red demanded. "They better watch out, or they'll get what they're aimin' at."

"You reckon they gona try 'n send us back to the frames at the pint of a gun?" Mix Hoppin was indignant. "What for the govern-ment gotta mix up in this here for, noways. This here's betwixt us 'n the comp'ny."

Old Mister Holly slapped his long thigh. "Wal, for our part, we ain't aimin' for any trouble, but if they bring it on theirselves—let 'em watch out." Marge remembered the shot gun that he'd brought down from the hills several decades earlier and kept hung over his doorway. Over at Dolly's too there was a gun, and plenty more scattered about the hill.

"No hot tempers, boys." Jem spoke quietly. "What the comp'ny's aimin' at, is to get us wrought up so they can slap us all in jail. Then who'd keep the scabs outta the mill? Remember, all gotta mind what the strike commitee 'n leaders say. Thar's time 'n place for everything, but this ain't it. Our job's to hold out the mill."

Miz Crane hobbled over. She'd spent forty years spooling, "'n dryin' up 'n crinklin' like an autumn leaf," her neighbors commented, "till you can see her shrivelin' away right afore your eyes."

"Jem," she asked, "you reckon they're aimin' to bring in folks to work at the mill?"

"Sure they're aimin' on it. Truckloads from Tennessee 'n Alabamy."

"The low downs—to take our jobs!"

Jem made a clucking sound under his breath. "But we ain't aimin' on them truckloads gettin' in. Every mornin' our pickets gona guard each highway 'n meet 'em comin' in. We'll explain 'em to go back whar they come from. 'N if they ain't open to reasonin', we'll change their minds for 'em. Wal, come'n Red, it's time we were down to the hall."

The two old cronies gazed after them. "You know," Ma Hoppin sighed, "these last five days've sure been upsettin'. First time I ain't worked in thirty year, except when I lay off to birth a child. Now I ain't good for nothin' but to tend to meetin's 'n walk in line afore the mill."

"Strange ways for us in our old days, ain't it?" her companion mused. "The whole hill's upset, same as we. I bet thar ain't five wimmen got their washin' done, 'n here's come to the middle of the week."

"Have a pinch of snuff?" Miz Hoppin offered. "Listen, honey, did you hear tell how that thar Hal Dennis was the onery skunk what snitched to the boss-men?"

"Sure I did—the low-down worm. His Ma ought to turn in her grave, poor 'oman. I feel right sorry for Ruthie. The rest of 'em such good union folks, it's hard explainin' Hal tatlin', ain't it?"

"Does look quare, but I guess thar ain't any mistake. They cornered Hal with it, 'n caught him red-handed. Ruthie told him she never want to lay eyes on him again. Said as how this time she was shet of him for good. 'N ole man Hollis got down his gun at him, but 'lowed as how it'd be a pity to waste the shot on trash like him."

"I guess we seen the last of him round these parts. If he knows what's good for his skin."

"Lawsy," Miz Crane looked startled, "here I'm forgettin' that it's time to go to the union hall. Be you on the relief committee, Miz Hoppin, too?"

"Naw'm. I ain't chosen for it, 'n it's just as well, I'm busier 'n hornet as 'tis. But that's good work. Plenty of families are gettin' plum out of vittels, 'n the comp'ny store ain't 'lowin' no striker to get even a bag of beans."

"Yah, we gotta get food from somewhars. Else how we gonna hold out? Wal, good-day to you." Straightening her sunbonnet, Miz Crane started off.

The union hall was located in a one-story wooden building which stood over the tracks just beyond the reach of company land. Mister Yancey, the small store-keeper, who owned the place, had so far withstood the deadly enmity of the company, continuing to sell his potatoes, beans, and hard back at one-fourth lower prices than those which the mill hands were forced to pay at the mill store. The strikers had made shelves and benches out of old boxes which Yancey gave them and from wood which friendly farmers nearby had let them take from their land. A few chairs and a table had been garnered from the village.

"I can spare a chair, I reckon," Miz Hoppin volunteered. "Since my ole man died, I doan really need but one. I says to myself, says I, 'Ma Hoppin, what you doin' so stingy-like with two chairs, 'n down at the meetin' hall folks ain't got place to set theirselfs.'"

THE STRIKE COMMITTEE had issued instructions; "Fraternize with the troops. Win them over to our side, away from the boss-men." "Most of those boys in the National Guard," Tom explained, are sons of farmers or mill hands in different parts of the state. They'll naturally be with us, once they get to understand what it's all about. It's our job to tell 'em. Especially you girls 'n women."

So the strikers in small groups of two or three strolled past the guardsmen stopping here and there to engage them in conversation or friendly argument.

"Boys, why you come here?" Miz Hoppin demanded. "You're born from our own folks. You ain't against us, be-ya? Then why you come here with these baynits 'n guns? Wal, if the governor sent you, you can just tell him it's time you went home. We're peaceful, law-mindin' folks, just askin' for what's due us. That's all. We ain't needin' no soldiers paradin' round this town. . . . Howdy Elsie, Howdy 'Manthy," she nodded to a brown-haired girl and her laughing companion who walked past, swinging to the arms of two embarrassed guardsmen. "That's right, girls, shame 'em. Tell 'em some sense." She glanced at the fresh-faced khakai figures standing around her. "Boys, I'm gona tell you why we walked out."

Phil and Jem, crossing down the street stopped before a small group of guardsmen. "Have a chaw?" they offered.

The soldiers hesitated, looked around. There was no officer in sight. "Wal, thanks. Doan care if we do."

Jaws worked in unison. "You fellows know what this here's all about?" Jem inquired. "Then we-uns gona tell you."

Before he and Phil had ended the men listening wore troubled expressions. Things were sure bad. "Reckon you had to walk out. Couldn't do different."

"You'd done the same in our place. But," Phil persisted, "you know what the mill had you brung here for, doan you? To helpen get the scabs in the mill. Now just what you plan to do about that?"

The guardsmen shifted their feet. "'Course now, we get our orders 'n we have to—"

"Listen, fellows," Jem looked calmly around the crowd, "some of you fought in the last war, maybe? Wal, so did Phil 'n me." He held up a twisted forearm down which ran a ragged scar. "That's what I got, fightin' for democracy. Wal, us on the mill hills ain't seen one sliver of that thar democracy we heerd so much about a few years back. No more'n what your folks has. This strike is aimin' at gettin' some of what we was promised, back thar in '17. 'N I doan calculate you fellows gona stand in our way."

His gaze traveled from face to face. "Come on, Phil. It's time we got to the hall. So long, boys. Remember, it's workers, stand by workers."

MIZ HOPPIN HAD JOINED Marge, Dolly, and Miz Crane who were talking with men stationed on the south side of the mill. "Now I got four chillen 'n a sick man to care for outta eight dollar. Can I do that?" Dolly was demanding.

"Naw'm, I reckon you can't." The lad in mufti twisted his gun.

"Then why doan you go home, 'n leave us to tend our own business," Miz Crane broke in. "You think you boys actin' right, totin' guns 'n baynits against women 'n chillen. What we done to you?"

"You guardsmen ain't aimin' to run one of them baynits in an old 'oman on the picket line?" Marge's tongue stung the color to their cheeks.

"Naw'm. I tell you we ain't got any harm against you." Why couldn't these women leave them be?

"You better mind out," Miz Hoppin warned them, "or some of these nights one of these here guns you're totin' 'll go off 'n thar'll be trouble afore we know it."

The youths grinned uncomfortably. "Doan worry, granny. Us boys ain't startin' nothin' so long as you doan start no more riotin'—"

"Who start riotin' we want know!" Marge challenged. "Oh, I know what the papers said. Most of it was plain lies. We have a peaceful parade downtown with our banners 'n all to show people what we're strikin' for, 'n along come the laws to start a rumpus. Shovin' 'n cursin' 'n pullin' at our banners. Naturally some of ours begun woofin' 'n shovin' back. But our leaders call 'Keep marchin' 'n we did. Then the papers say we rioted!"

"I'd think that that fella what writes up the news'd sleep uneasy, the lies he tells on us in his paper!" Miz Crane shook with anger. "It's a sin 'n a shame, 'n so I declares it!"

"That 'Gazzy Gazette' puts down what the mill-men says put down," Marge rejoined.

"'N what it doan say!" Throwing up her hands, Miz Hollis rolled her eyes sky-ward. "Callin' us—" she stopped short, choking over the words. "The Lawd'll sure punish the mill men for their wickedness, else my right hand's my left. Doan you believe 'em, boys, but go on back to whar you belong. Leave us be to win our rights."

As the women left, a soldier beckoned to his comrades. "I doan like this business, 'n that's a fact. Now my sis is married to a millhand down at Greenville."

"I got an uncle myself workin' over to Selby."

"Hell, what can we do? It ain't our fault is it? We go where the Big Cheese says, that's all."

Two days later the Governor of North Carolina receiving reports that the National Guard had "become disaffected," recalled the Guard and replaced it with state troops. The section about the mill became an armed camp, with tents pitched and machine guns mounted.

"No jokin' or sassin' these guys," Red observed, "they're hard boiled as they make 'em."

"The comp'ny's rounded up all the extra riff-raff 'n drunks it could find in town, too, 'n sworn 'em in as deputies. I doan like the looks of it." Jerry lifted his heavy shoulders. "Some of 'em already makin' loose talk about 'stringin' up the black brats that doan know their place.'"

"The low-down cusses!" Red exclaimed. "We'll shut their mouths!"

"Guess it's just talk, so far. Anyway, over at the Hollow we're postin' watch every day. Just in case, you know—"

"Listen, Jerry," his companion grabbed him by the arm, "you know you can count on us. The first sign it's gettin' beyond the talkin' stage, you understand, you're to let me know."

AS THE NEWS OF RIVERTON STRIKE reached other hills, spontaneous walk-outs took place in half a dozen other mills in Gaston and neighboring counties.

Like fire leaps over fields of parched, hungry, underbrush, so the strike spread from hill to hill—"against the stretch-out."

The local union office was swamped with calls for help. Over-alled figures, dusty with tramping, came from mill hills as far away as Georgia demanding information and organizers.

Many, however, when they learned that Negroes were taken into the new union on an equal basis, sorrowfully went their way. Others decided "we'll chance it." A few agreed, "You're right. It's the only way." One middle-aged man plead with tears in his eyes, "Can't you give this up? You know white folks ain't ever gona mix with niggers. But we sure need a union bad."

"Listen, brother," Tom leaned across the counter at him, "we white hands'd cut off our noses to spite our faces if we did

that. The mill owners are a powerful lot. This is the only way
to lick 'em. Our union is only too glad to help you. But it woan
leave the colored hands out. Solidarity and united effort of
all labor, regardless of color or sex, is the corner-stone of our
organization. We'll never go back on that."

"Wal," the man replied slowly, "I reckon that's that."
Reaching for his ten-gallon hat the Georgian started off.
An hour later he came back. "I figger I'll see what my folks
back home say. So maybe you'll hear from us." But they
never did.

"You know, Jem," Tom turned to his companion, "this race
prejudice stands in the way of southern workers more than
anything else. Makes it an up-hill job every foot of the way."

"Yah. It's sure no picnic. But we're makin' headway.
George 'n Rose, now, send back good reports from Highton 'n
Charlotte." Each had been sent to one of these towns to help
organize others.

"That's so. Only it's so dam slow." Tom felt tired, depressed.
The strain and long hours were telling on him.

"It'd be a lot easier," Jem reflected, "if the colored folks had
a bigger part in the industry. A lot easier, you understand, to
make the white hands see it."

Tom looked up. "I've been thinkin' the same thing my self.
Take Birmingham 'n Chatanooga, for instance. In the steel
mills 'n mines the Negroes play a big role. But here in the cotton mills . . . Oh, the bosses are a clever crew, Jem, you gotta
give 'em that! They know their unions. Up north they play
native against foreign-born, 'n here, white against black."

"'N how we poor fools fall for it." Jem laughed ruefully.

Swinging to his feet Tom clapped his friend across the
shoulders. "Never mind, old boy. You woke up, 'n thar're
plenty others like you. I tell you, the trend of the times are
with us."

"You're right, Tom. Strugglin' for bread will unite us 'n
mould us into one."

AT LAST THE RELIEF STORE was opened.

Each morning the strikers lined up with their baskets and relief cards, waiting patiently while the supplies were measured out, according to the number in each family. Carrie Hapman, who had come down from the north to take charge, rustled about with a harrassed look on her heavy-lined face. It was no simple matter to feed two thousand families day after day, and get the necessary medicine for children suffering from pellagra and all other diseases which torment the off-spring of the poor.

Carrie was surprised to find how far the women and men on the relief committee could make the supplies go. "Lawsy, Miss Carrie," Miz Crane told her, "were used to doin' without 'n stretchin' the last penny."

"Just think whar this comes from, too." Marge patted a flour sack and gestured toward the neat shelves of canned goods. "To think the mill hands up north collected the money for this carload of eatin's! Beans doan taste like just beans, when you know that."

"Sure, the workers all over the country are rallying behind this strike. Only—" Carrie ran a nervous hand across her mouth, "the relief's gotta come in faster. Look how quick those two carloads from New York were used up. By Thursday these shelves'll be cleaned out. The next shipments from the west can't possibly reach here before Monday. The National Office will wire us whatever funds come in. But the main thing right now is for us to get our local committees out among the farmers again, and to the city workers and small store-keepers.

"We should send all we can spare, to tell why we're strikin' 'n need their help," Marge agreed. "We can carry the union message to a lot of hills thataway, 'n help spread the strike. That's what we're aimin' at, ain't it?" she inquired of Herb Sampson, who had come into the store while she was speaking. "Sure," he agreed. Along with Carrie, Rose Morris and Max Stone, Herb had been sent south by the union to help lead the strike. The local papers had grown hysterical over "these foreigner agitators and outsiders in our midst who are trying to raise Hades in our peaceful villages." "Their sole aim," an editorial declared, "which is inspired directly from Moscow, is to incite the help to ill-considered acts against their employers, and spread the bol-wevils of radicalism throughout the cotton region. All right-minded citizens must demand immediate action against this new pest that threatens Southern Civilization."

The strikers, for their part, accepted the newcomers readily, although not without curiosity. Red summed up the general attitude: "If Tom 'n the Union says they're o.k., that's jake with us. I guess we're needin' all the help we can get." Nevertheless the new organizers' Jewish features and mannerisms, their "high-fallutin'" language with its East-side accent, and their habit of "wearin' Sunday-go-to meetin' clothes every day in the week" made them a strange sight on the hill. Used to overalls and coarse cotton garments, the older women especially eyed the girls' silk stockings and whispered behind their hands about their scant, flimsy nightgowns. "It's sure the beatin'-est yet," Dolly remarked when Marge explained that all workin' girls, so Carrie had told her, wore things like that in New York City. "Anyway," Dolly added, "you can see Carrie's just folks, silk dress or no. As common 'n friendly-like as an old shoe." Today, Marge noted, Carrie and Rose had on cotton dresses not unlike her own.

"That Herb, now—he's a might diff'rent."

"How you mean?" Marge countered, though she felt the same herself.

"Oh, I doan know. I bet he ain't smarter'n Tom 'n Carrie. But he kinda acts like he was." Dolly, sniffling, glanced at her friend. "You know, kinda like he knows it all. When he talks to you, he makes you feel 'bout nothin' a-tall. He's polite 'n all that, but—I 'low he ain't used to our kind of folks, is he?"

"He doan mean it thataway," Marge defended, "it's just his way, I reckon." Uneasy, she determined she would speak to Tom about Herb. Maybe he could set him straight. Dolly wasn't the first one to mention this. A few days back Herb's grand manner had riled ole man Hollis until she was afraid he'd plop him one.

As Dolly moved off Marge's hand slipped into her pocket feeling for her book. There'd be a minute now before relief duty. Miz Crane nudged her elbow. "You're readin' up so I reckon you'll soon've read all the books Tom brung with him, eh? Goin' from morn till night I hardly see how you manage it." The little woman spoke with that awed yearning which all mill hands feel for the education they've been denied.

"I got such a heap to larn. I gotta manage somehow," Marge answered.

"Lawsy, chile, your ignorance doan hold a candle to mine. It's a sin, the way we've been kept in darkness." Miz Crane sighed heavily.

"That's what it is. But now we got a chanct," the younger woman went on eagerly. "Tom 'n Carrie are helpin' me a lot, 'n we're startin' a class tomorrow. Maybe you'd join?"

"Me? Honey," her voice sunk, "I can't even read my own name. But my boy Will, he's a smart 'un, 'n he'd be right proud to join."

"That's good! 'N we'll find some way for you too. Now the Union's come, we all gona have a chance. . . . You know," Marge's eyes grew hazy, "I never thought to see it happen. It's what my ole Granny hankered afta, for me 'n all hers. I only wish—" she gulped—"that Granny 'n Bob coulda lived to see this day."

THE COMPANY AND PRESS CAMPAIGN grew more bitter. Mob spirit of all "Anglo-Saxon self-respecting, law-abiding citizens" was openly appealed to. Rowdies were hired to call after union members "Nigger lovers," "free lovers," and "Bolshies,"—the latter with an ugly variation that had led to more than one fight. Taunting notes were left under striking villagers' doors.

A certain amount of confusion and dissension had followed in the strikers' ranks.

So it was decided to call a meeting to explain and discuss thoroughly just what the Union did and did not stand for. George and Rose had been called in to attend.

On the way to the meeting Tom and Herb had a heated argument.

"I tell you, Tom," the other organizer repeated emphatically, "you're going too fast for these white workers. Now on the red issue, we can't hedge. But on the race question: I tell you, we've got to re-consider and compromise a bit. Otherwise, the bulk of the white strikers'll pull out. Some have already."

Tom fought to keep his temper. "Listen, Herb, You're new to the South. Up North you found it easy enough to talk loud about full equality for the Negroes. Now you're up against it, it's nigh floored you."

"The thing is, to keep our balance," Herb began.

"That's it!" Tom continued. "Keep our balance 'n our principles clear. The Party 'n union know what they're doin'. Suppose we do lose some of the whites. Doan you think I knew we'd lose 'em? But no more'n we can help. That's why we've called this meetin'."

He made a pass at the bushes along the road. "The biggest thing about this strike with all its shortcomin's, is the beginning of solidarity of white 'n Negro in the South. We'll swing onto that, no matter what. It's the one way to build a movement."

As they neared the clearing where the strikers were seated, waiting, Herb explained, "Of course I'll stand by decisions."

Tom nodded, "Of course."

Marge was sitting on the ground near Ella May Wiggins, a brown-skinned, dusky-eyed woman whose slight frame vibrated energy to all around her. Ever since she had heard Ella May sing, "How it hurts the heart of a Mother," and her other ballads about the Union, Marge had felt drawn to this woman. One of those quick, deep-going friendships that natures like theirs sometimes form had sprung up between them. Ella May's four young-uns sprawled around them.

Jem opened the meeting. "As far as all that paper talk about Reds and Bolsheviks go, I'll tell you how I feel about that. I've found out, 'n I guess most of you have, that it's what the boss-men doan like, but it's all right for us. A Red is a mill hand what stands up for his rights. . . . All of us used to be just Po' Whites 'n mill hands. Now we're Union men 'n called Reds—'n proud of it!" Startled laughter. Applause. A few looked uncomfortable.

"No matter what they call'em," Miz Hollis threw in, "we know our leaders, 'n they're all right." This time the clapping was more general.

Herb spoke next: Taking off his glasses he wiped them repeatedly, glancing around at the circle of tense faces with his near-sighted eyes. "What the National Textile Union expects is that white and colored unite for common economic interests. . . ." Tom felt dissatisfied, glad when he was done.

Elliott Brandon, a local lawyer who was active in defending arrested pickets, asked the floor. "As I understand it," he drawled persuasively, "many of you are upset unnecessarily. Now what the National Union wants that you two races organize together, just as you do in your lodges, churches, and other places."

Tom came forward. "It's true we stand for organizing together, but not in the old way, like the church 'n lodge plan." His voice was crisp, stern. "That's a Jim Crow scheme. The A.F. of L. claims to do as much. . . . Our Union stands for the full rights of the Negro in everything. . . ." While he talked the sun dipped behind the trees, shadows stretched like straggling giants on the grass.

THE AFTERNOON PICKET LINE wound down the dusty street toward the mill.

"Wonder how many the mill's got workin' now?" Dolly asked.

"Some say a hunderd, some two hunderd. Doan mean much, whatever it is." Marge lifted the sign she was carrying higher in the air.

"Naw, the mills can't run on that. . . . I hear all the bossmen are workin'. Do 'em good for once—the slave drivers!" Dolly leaned out to scan up and down the line. "Ain't so many as used to come that first week, is thar? Some gettin' lazy; 'n some, I 'spose, scared off by these here laws with their baynits 'n guns."

Jem, walking in the same line, jerked his head sideways in her direction. "A considerable number of 'em have gone to the farms or hills to wait till it's over. They doan know what a strike means. They seem to think we can just set 'n wait for the comp'ny to settle. Humph!"

"Thar's allays a plenty who'll say 'Let Jack do it!'" Red threw in, "but me, I prefer to do my fightin' myself."

"Same all along this line." Jem gazed with satisfaction at those about him. "Wal, as Tom says, that's allays some that takes the lead, 'n the majority follow on behind."

Miz Hoppin, stumbling quickly out of place, plucked Jem by the sleeve. "What about them laws? Think they gona act ugly? Like they done yestiddy?"

"Doan you worry," he placed a quieting hand on her arm.

"Come back here whar you belong, Beccy," Miz Crane told her sharply, "I guess we ain't a-scared of them laws."

Carrie laughed. "That's the spirit. We'll show 'em."

Two blocks away from the mill the marchers found the state militia drawn in solid ranks across the street, four deep. On either side stood company deputies, glowering and swinging their night sticks.

"Don't come a step nearer!" the militia captain warned.

"We got orders not to let you in two blocks of the mill."

"We got a right to the streets!" Tom retorted.

"And to march!" The lines moved a foot closer. "You're aimin' to let the scabs in, that's all!" Overalled and cotton-clothed figures stared across at blue uniforms.

The militia drew their sabres. "Turn about, I tell you!" the captain threatened.

"Come on. Forward!" Tom gave the signal. Tightening her grip on her banner, singing "Solidarity Forever," Marge pushed ahead, the others following.

Immediately militia and deputies went into action. With the flats of their sabres they swung to right and left. "Get the three niggers!" the captain ordered. "The black bastards!" Five troopers sprung at Jerry, bearing him down. Screaming, her black eyes staring wildly, Nancy flung herself upon them. Oaths, a dull crack, and she slid to her knees.

Knocked to the ground, her precious banner torn in shreds, choking with dust, Marge clammered to her feet, yelling shrilly, "Scabs! Scabs!" Down the street Miz Hoppin and many more were running, troopers and deputies at their heels. Children, crying distractedly, were cuffed to the sidewalks by cursing maniacs. Young workers, grabbing clumps of dirt and sticks fought back.

Jem, blood running from a gash on his leg, caught a glimpse of Jerry's prostrate form. "Quick, Tom," he pointed. Two score of men and women, quickly organized, swooped through the milling crowd to where they lay, before the troopers realized what had happened they had carried Jerry and Nancy to safety in the heart of their thickly packed ranks. Slowly the strikers retreated down the street toward the opposite side of the village.

That evening, after the mass meeting of long and indignant protest, the strike committee members made their way singly to Farmer Thompson's place, where they could hold their meeting without fear of company interference or spying. Armed guards were placed near the door, however, and a watcher down the road. A row of shot guns stood ready along the wall, in case of a surprise attack.

Jerry and Nancy lay in cots in a room over-head. It had not been thought wise to take them to the Hollow. Here they would be safely hidden until well again.

Uncle John, scratching his gray wool, ruminated, "I reckon I'll be 'bout the only colored man 'round the Hollow. Every soul's cleared out to sleep in the fields tonight, fearin' the deputies might try to start somethin'. 'N the Jergens 'n around six other families packed up 'n left for good. They say they're for the strike, but what's buck shot against machine guns?

"But I ain't figurin' to budge. No sar. I ain't many more years on this earth, 'n I 'low to hold out to the bitter end. But for my lame hip," he mourned, "I'd been a-marchin' n wrestlin' this afternoon. It oughta cure soon."

"Uncle John," Herb looked at the old man with pride, "it's men like you that build a movement. The unflinching spirit of the proletariat."

"What's that you call me?" he inquired. "That big word, at the end."

Tom yanked his chair alongside. "Doan mind Herb's big words. That particular word now, means workers. Mill hands." Drawing his fellow-organizer aside Tom said impatiently, "Herb, can't you learn to speak plain? You know, I've told you often enough that they doan understand you. Talk of 'inner contradictions,' 'third period,' 'n all the rest of it. After you speak the fellows come over to me 'n say, 'That Herb now, he's a nice guy 'n all that. But what's he tryin' to tell us?'"

"The workers have to learn they're proletariat, haven't they? And what the class struggle means?" Herb demanded.

"Sure. But your way woan learn 'em." Tom spit in disgust. He was sure glad that the National Office was takin' Herb out of the south. "The strike itself is learnin' 'em pretty fast. What we gotta do is explain 'em in words they can understand. You claim to read Lenin a lot. Wal, that's one point he allays made—not to use high fallutin' phrases. Workers ain't fools, but you come close to actin' like they were. Handin' down the gospel from the mountain! ... Say, Herb, I'm sorry I said that. I know you doan mean it thataway. But can't you see?"

Jumping up, Herb went outside. "Gee," Tom thought to himself, "For all his weeks in the Passaic strike 'n down here, he's never got over goin' to Harvard. Glad I was born in overalls."

"Wal comrades," he raised his voice, "time we started, eh? Give Herb a call, will you, Red?"

The discussion was long and bitter. "This is how I see it." Red's brilliant hair glowed in the lamplight. "We gotta take our guns to the picket line. We gotta give blow for blow 'n shot for shot. Tom, you just gotta see it our way."

"That's right," Phil agreed. "It'd shame any able-bodied man havin' the troopers whallopin' folks with swords 'n us havin' to take it. I tell you, it's the only way to keep a strong picket line. Any t'other way—" he shrugged his lean shoulders.

"Who-all's been spreadin' this notion?" Jem's eyes snapped. "Wal, whoever it was, that Jip Lampson 'n his pals or what-not, they ain't real friends of this strike. Oh, I know it's a natural idea. I'd relish plumbin' some of them yellow dogs myself. But it ain't practical, that's all. We gotta fight other ways."

"What's buck shot against machine guns?" Marge argued. "Like Uncle John said, it'd just be a massacre."

"I swarn, I can't figger you-all out." Phil twisted his head from side to side. "I know you ain't quitters. So why—?"

"What's these guns linin' up against the wall? They ain't for looks are they?" Red asked.

"Nobody questions the workers' right to self-defense," Carrie retorted quickly.

"Listen boys," Tom spoke slowly, weighing each word, "let's talk sense. You're right that nobody on the committee is afraid to fight. Marge, Dolly, 'n the other women would step out any minute the committee said so, along with us men. That time will come—when another Civil War will be waged—this time between the rich ownin' class 'n all of us laborin' poor. But that time ain't now. First a lotta things got to happen. We gotta organize millions of working people. Economic conditions will get a lot worse, 'n Wall Street'll begin to totter on its throne. Then we'll swing the soldiers and sailors over to our side.

"That time'll come. I firmly believe in the life-time of all of us. But it ain't now, 'n thar's no use to kid ourselves. You propose armed war-fare, but you can figger out what the final results would be as well as anybody.

"The way to win this strike—'n that's what we're all after—is bigger picket lines 'n redoublin' our efforts at organization. Build the Union! Spread the Strike! are our answer. 'N I'm here to tell you it'll require all the guts 'n fightin' spirit all of us've got."

Finally the vote was taken. Phil counted hands. He and Red were voted down, twenty-five to two. Well, Tom knew that as good Union men they could be depended on to follow orders.

XXIII.

When Hills Rise

THE STRIKE WAS NOW at its height. While Matthew Woll and William Green, President of the American Federation of Labor, stormed against it, warning employers of the dire consequences of "the Communist menace in the South," the international revolutionary movement hailed its red flare with growing enthusiasm. The national center of the Communist Party worked far into the night over knotty problems of leading labor's struggles in the south. At the same time support was organized among the rank and file of northern and western workers who readily dug into their pockets to help feed the revolting ranks.

No longer able to ignore the strike, which had assumed national significance, many large capitalist dailies sent their reporters to the scene of action. Soon after a succession of agitated ladies, of professors who prided themselves on their liberalism, accompanied by a well-known writer descended upon the strife-torn community, interviewing strikers, owners, mill foremen, and whomever they could find.

"Some of 'em mean right well by us I reckon," Miz Crane puzzled aloud, after one harrowing interview. "But of all the outlandish questions they ask! takes all a body's breath, tryin' to explain."

"We showed 'em plenty, I reckon." Phil rocked on his long feet. "One gentleman said he never knew folks in Ameriky had to live the way we do, on the hill. Whar you 'spose he's kept his-self, all these years?"

"One frock-coat asked me why we didn't sit down 'n reason it out, peace-ful like with the mill men." Jem spat vigorously. "He sounded plumb ignorant of what it's all about. I guess he ain't even read the papers or he'd know better'n to ask that!"

"Some of 'em smelt kinda musty to me." Dolly wrinkled her nose. "For smart folks, they sure can act dumb."

Marge snorted her agreement. "One lady with high-top shoes asked me what our leaders mean by all the talk of classes. She was from Boston, she said, 'n wore her specks on a string. 'Lady,' I told her, 'come with us on the picketline 'n I'll show you quick enough.' That's the last I saw of her!"

"They mean right well I reckon," Jem reflected, "Only— they doan know *what* they mean."

Carrie gave one of her rare laughs. "That sums up the darn pinks the best I ever heard!"

THE SILENCE OF MIDNIGHT brooded over the sleeping village. Murph Yancey, snoring in a cot over his store, was jerked to his feet by the crash of shattered glass, the pounding of hammers on splintering wood. The relief store! Thieves—or comp'ny thugs!

With a bound he was down the stairs. The place was jammed with men, some masked, swinging blackjacks, wielding knives in a mania of destruction. Shelves of provisions, intended for hungry strikers, were smashed and their contents strewn on the floor. Men danced gleefully on sacks of flour. "We'll learn 'em to start Unions!" Cans of milk, planned to nourish sick babies had been ripped open. The ground outside was still wet with pools of white liquid.

Yelling with rage Murph sprung on the men nearest him. "Stop your devilment!" Quickly he was over-powered, gagged and bound to a post where he would be in full view of their ghastly acts. The company sheriff scowled at him, "We told you, did'n we, that you were gona get it, if you mixed in this Union game?"

Murph struggled against his bonds. If only Tom or some Union folks'd hear 'n come! Was the relief store too far off the hill for this racket to be heard there?

"What's that?" Two men dropped the flour sacks they were slashing. Peering out, they sighted Phil Murdock and the Jonas boy, who lived on the edge of the village running up the path. "You dirty thieves! Stop your—!"

"Throw up your hands 'n pipe down thar!" a masked figure covered them with his gun.

The last of the supplies, store shelves and counters were destroyed. Suddenly the alarm was given, "Here come the laws!"

"Timed just about right, eh?" a deputy laughed. Rapidly the mob began to disperse. Stocking masks were pulled from over heads. "Look," the Jonas boy called shrilly, "thar's Silas Horton, the boss-weaver."

"Shut up, you—!" The blue-coated officers seized the boy by the shoulder.

"Leave me be. I ain't done nothin'. It's them!" The lad together with Phil pointed out the members of the mob, demanding their arrest. It ended with Phil and the Jonas boy being lodged in jail, charged with resisting an officer. Not one of the participants in the destruction was arrested.

"Hell 'n Maria!" "The dirty dogs!" "Thar's justice for you. Mill justice!" The strikers milled about the wreckage, dimly visible in the early morning light. "Leave us lay our hands to 'em—the comp'ny bums!"

"Marge, looka here!" Dolly, face working, pointed to the Union banner which lay torn and mud-streaked, tangled among the mass of broken chair-legs and sunken counter. "All the pride we took in it. 'N Miz Hollis givin' one of her good sheets to make it!"

"How can anybody be so onery?" Miz Crane demanded. "Pouring milk in the gutter what's meant for ailin' babes!"

"They'd not stop at anything to break the strike," Carrie answered her. This was a dastardly, clever move, especially now when relief supplies were so dangerously low.

Red, burrowing among the ruins, let out a low exclamation. Bringing forth a heavy wrench he passed it around for general inspection. "That belongs to the boss mechanic at the mill. I've seen it more'n once. We'll just keep this for evidence."

"All right. But the big question," Carrie told them, "is to find another hall, and to get fresh supplies as quick as possible."

All that day and the next the union committee sought to locate a hall. Most of the owners interviewed gave evasive answers. "I got another prospect already." "I'm aimin' to sell, so—" Finally, exasperated, Marge asked, "Tell us outright, why you woan." The shop-keeper eyed her sheepishly. "All right, ma'am, I'will. I'd like to oblige you, 'n all that. But if I do, the mill'll have the bank call in the loan I got 'n take the mortgage over my head. You might as well quit lookin' for a place, 'cause thar ain't a store man in Riverton City but what's beholden to the comp'ny, one way or t'other."

"We're gona feed all the people tonight," Carrie said grimly, "even if we have to do it from the curb." In the end supplies were handed out from the side of a truck. A grey rain drenched the waiting line as well as those distributing, but Red kept up their spirits with his nonsense about mermaids and sea-horses, while Jem and Marge mustered the few

umbrellas that the hill possessed. "Right away," Tom promised them, "we'll find land 'n start buildin' a new headquarters
all our own. 'N post our own guards about, to see the mill doan
try any more monkey business."

"IT JUST WARN'T NO USE," Jem explained. He and Red had
just returned from Marmon, where the Union had sent them
to establish connections with the strikers who had recently
walked out there. "We were too late to do 'em any good. We
should've gone right off, the first day they walked out. Me 'n
Red tried to 'splain 'em the difference between the United
Textile 'n our Union, but we got no chanct. The Union officers 'n the mill sicked the police on us nigh as soon we come
to town.

"It's a shame to see such a good bunch of fightin' mill
hands 'n those onery no-counts misleadin' 'em. Some calls
theirselves 'progressives,' too. Progressive my great aunt! You
see, the hands thar was never in any kind of union before,
so when the United come 'n soft-soaped 'em 'n offered their
help, they took it, gladly enough. The United 'n the papers've
poisoned the Marmon workers against the National Union.
I reckon they gotta get sold out once, afore they'll wake up
to some sense. I located one fella that was friendly, though,
'n he's comin' over to talk with our whole strike committee.

"He told me how that United officer—Hogman—I thing
they call him, come to the hill in fine clothes, talkin' sweet
nothin's. He calls himself a progressive. Humph! When he
saw how the mill hands looked at him sideways, he bought
himself a pair of overalls. It was a sight to split your sides.
The overalls shiney new, 'n Hogman fat as his name, bulgin'
out of top 'n bottom! He even forgot to take the tags off, till he
sat down on one 'n rize up pretty quick.

"Wal, the mill over thar has got the laws usin' guns, baynits 'n
whallopin' picket lines, same as here. So, this fella told me,

the workers 'lowed they gona show 'em. Most of 'em over thar ain't so long down from the mountains. So this Hogman, he tells 'em 'Leave your guns at home, men, 'n take Bibles to the picket lines instead.' At that, the crowd boos him. Yas-sir, boos him. This Marmon striker, he tell me, sorrowful-like, 'This here's the civilizest strike I ever seen.'"

"Huh? Sure they're gettin' plum disgusted with the Hogman bunch. But it'll not be so easy to get 'em to switch horses the middle of the stream."

"That United now, is sure one sorry or-gan-i-za-tion, ain't it? A real boss-man's Union. You know Jem," Marge spoke slowly, feeling for her idea. "Unions are like folks, ain't they?"

"How you mean?"

"My granny used to tell me that a person might as soon be dead if they'd lost all their fightin' spirit. Wal, this United is worse'n dead. It's a haunt, the way I see it."

"THEY'RE STARTIN' to turn us out!"

"Takin' the roof right from over our heads—'n for what! 'Cause we want more bread." Dolly, Phil, Red, Miz Hollis and two score others of the most active had received eviction notices. "Doan make no difference to the comp'ny whether thar's sick folks or lil' babies in the house or no," Miz Hollis exclaimed. "Down at Red's place they're expectin' a young'un any day now. But he gets his notice all the same! What they care if the child's born in the open field!"

"This means tents," Tom drew Carrie to one side. "Wire New York for a first shipment of at least three dozen. For this is the start of wholesale evictions."

"What I'm gona do with my sick man?" Dolly asked frantically. "I just ain't gona stand for 'em throwin' us in the street."

"You can move in with me," young Sally Jackson offered. "That is, till we get a notice, too. I doan see how they missed us."

"That's right good of you." Dolly went back to her porch to wait for the sheriff and his men. Down the street she could see the Silas Martins huddled around their belongings which jammed the walk. Their girl Daisy, who had a severe case of small pox lay in a cot, whimpering and blinking at the light. The Board of Health had been notified of the proposed eviction of this family, but had refused to act.

Defiant strains of "Solidarity Forever" floated down the street.

"Good mornin', Dolly greeted sheriff Carson and his men with sarcastic politeness. "I see you've done a good day's job for the comp'ny—turnin' poor folks outta their homes what's got no place to go." Her gun, they noted, lay across the kitchen table. They carried out the chairs, table, and dresser. Dolly stood to one side, arms folded, watching. The children ran in and out, crying, pulling at her skirts and crowding around the cot on which Sol Grady, her sick husband lay. Finally the men took up his cot and started toward the door. Carelessly they jammed it against a wall. Sol's face twisted in pain. "Be careful!" Dolly made a move toward the gun. "You hurt him again like that'n I'll plum you full of lead."

"The comp'ny'll have these things stored for you till you get another house," the sheriff told her.

"Naw thank you. I ain't no better'n the rest. You can let' 'em set whar they be. The comp'ny doan get the guilt offa its hands so easy."

The committee worked frantically to get everyone under shelter before nightfall. "We'll just put this furniture back whar it come from. We got a right to these houses." Toward afternoon it began to drizzle. "Now what's the Lawd lettin' it rain for?" Miz Crane cast distressed eyes at the glowering sky.

"Maybe He's sidin' with the mill," Jem teased her. He was helping her boy get her things on the wagon. "The Lawd might as well be, all else around here is—the town folks, the govern-ment."

"Hush, doan your blaspheme! That's what I doan like about the Com-*mun*-ists—no respect for the Almighty."

"Now Ma," Jem told her, "you know you think us Reds are about it."

"You ain't so bad, she admitted grudgingly, "exceptin' this ... Mercy sakes," as drops slid down the neck of her blouse, "soon it's gona pour. I bet the good Lawd's weepin' to see what's happenin' to His people here on Riverton Hill."

Over each disordered pile of belongings their owners hovered protectingly, spreading sheets and carrying smaller pieces to neighbors for shelter. Ole man Hollis hurried off, his gun and his fiddle clutched close to his chest. His wife made angry, helpless jabs at the dripping furniture. "These drops of water just gona ruin my lamp shade 'n run the roses in the carpet," she mourned, "before we can set 'em anywhars inside. All the years we been savin' up! The lamp ain't paid off yet. Now these draps gona ruin 'em all." She glared around at Ruth, standing alongside. "But if it was all to do over again, we'd do the same. I'd rather be in a tent with some pride on me than sleepin' under a comp'ny roof 'n actin' like a whipped dog."

"HERE'S TWO LETTERS for you Tom, with foreign-lookin' stamps on 'em." Red fished them out of his pocket.

Watching Tom scan them he observed, "Must be good news, from the shine on your face."

"It is, boy, it is." With an excited chuckle Tom stuffed the letters in his blouse. "Wait till George hears, 'n Marge." He went in search of his sister.

"Walk up the road a piece with me, Sis? I got something' to tell you."

What could it be, to make him look so? Had the Charlotte mills come out?

"Watch out whar you goin'," she took him by the arm. "Somethin's sure upset you. Here you leadin' us to knee-deep in grass!"

"I'm a lil' excited, I guess." He ran his hands over his unruly hair. "You see, I just got word across. . . . Fred's on his way home."

"Oh, that's fine! We're needin' his help a-plenty."

"That ain't all. . . ." Tom flushed, pulling at the tall grass. "You remember Bess, that gal I knew in New York, some years back?"

"Sure—that you been writin' to, in Russia."

"Uh-huh—Wal, you see—that is—they figured they could spare her—to work here. You see, she's comin' too."

Puzzled Marge asked. "You mean—?" Then seeing her brother's eyes she threw out her arms. "Oh, Tom—I'm glad—glad—"

Later she added, "If I was Miz Crane, I'say it was like a sign from across, the help they're goin' to give us here."

MARGE HAD KNOWN it would happen. With dread she had tried to fortify herself against the day. To be dragged off the picket line and forced into the waiting black wagon that would jangle its way through the streets to the city jail—how could Tom take it so calmly?

Yet, now that her turn had come, and she was lodged in jail with the rest of the strike committee, for "disturbing the peace," it had been quite different from what she had expected. All the way down they had kept singing and had only quit now to catch their breath. She went over to Miz Hoppin, who sat sniffling into a damp ball of a handkerchief. "What's the matter honey?" she asked. The little woman dabbed at her eyes. "It's the shame of it," she sobbed, "bein' behind the bars." "Is that all!" Marge felt relieved. "Thar ain't no shame in this.

Ain't we actin' for our rights? We can't help it, can we, if the govern-ment's on the wrong side. The Governor of this state bein' a big mill-owner, what else could you expect?"

"But it's like the world's turned upside down. 'N my head's splittin'."

Marge slipped her arm around her. "Never you mind. We'll be bailed out by tomorrow, 'n back on the picket line."

TOM WAS ARRESTED AGAIN—this time on the charge of having kidnapped Ruth! Hal had sworn out the warrant when Ruth had gone north with three other strikers to help there in the collection of relief.

"Of all the yellow brass!" Miz Hollis exploded. "Just let the mill men try to bring this to court! I'll testify. 'N what I'll say'll be two moutfuls. That Hal's livin' offa the fat of the land since he turned stool pigeon."

After the trial Miz Hollis observed with a grimace. "Wal, we sure made a fool out of Hal 'n the comp'ny too. Think of him claimin' Ruth as his main means of support. That was over three months afore this here walk-out started."

"Yah," Jem added, "we made such a fool outta that Hal thar in court, I was nigh feelin' sorry for the weasel."

THE CHAMBER OF COMMERCE of Riverton City was giving a dinner. All the leading business and professional men and their wives of this section of the state had been invited. Local reporters and press representatives from the north, whose papers had sent them south to cover this spectacular strike, were also gathered around the heavily-laden tables.

Mr. Jacobson, rotund president of the Duke tobacco plants, was presiding. On his right sat Mr. Jenkins, the owner of Corey mills. He had come down from Newport especially for the occasion. His lean face, pointed like a wolf's toward his beak, stared about at the perspiring rows of grimacing faces seated on either side. Mopping his brow,

he stole furtive glances at his watch, and made mental cal-
culations as to when he could make a train back for the
north. . . . This strike now, was deucedly inconvenient. Bad
publicity, and hard on profits. The heat was terrific. He'd be
glad to get back to the shore. . . . Why some northern papers
had taken up the strike was beyond him. Must be backed
by competitors. . . . His friend Haines had told him that two
New York reporters had been mistaken for strikers and
given a severe beating by the deputies. Served them right,
but all the same . . .

What was that? His mind returned to the scene around
him.

Mr. Jacobson had risen to speak. Smiling down on those
around him, his short fingers stroked the smooth whiteness
of the bosom shirt he wore. . . . "Ladies 'n gentlemen, we welcome all of you in the name of our fair city 'n state. . . . We
of Riverton 'n Gastonia know that the textile 'n tobacco industries are the backbone of our entire life. When all goes
well with, then there is prosperity 'n harmony for all. When,
however, men with evil intent would bring harm to these, the
community rises as one man 'n declares, 'Back Invader!'" He
thrust an arm forward, nearly upsetting a glass of punch over
Mr. Jenkin's knee. "You gentlemen of the press at least some
of you, have been misled about this strike. . . . Our purpose
is to enlighten you. . . . Until lately there was no more law-
abiding, industrious, peaceful-loving people in the whole
country than to be found on our southern mill hills. Now . . ."
As he thundered on and on, stiff collars melted, bowls of iced
punch disappeared, and the room grew foggy with smoke
from expensive cigars.

"THIS UNION TOWN IS sure one swell scheme." Red, swinging
his hammer down on the stake he was driving, called across
to Jem, busy fastening tent flaps.

"Yep, it's the real thing." The older man surveyed the neat rows of tents with obvious satisfaction. At one side, in the shade, stood several planks propped on grocery boxes and loaded with the plants the strikers had brought with them from the village. "Just shows what mill folks can do, once they get started."

"We got it up in record time. It's not been a week since Farmer Hoskins let us have the land, 'n already seventy-five tents are up, 'n the new hall ready for its roof. I never knew some of the hands had it in 'em to hustle about this-away." Red straightened from his knees.

"I tell you why. You never saw 'em workin' for themselves afore." Jem came alongside. "You know I figger this strike's just gettin' its second wind. This is the eighth week, ain't it? A lot of the weaker ones've moved on by now to other hills or gone back to the land, 'n a few low-downs are scabbin'. Here at the colony we got the pick. If the freight comp'ny'll loosen up on our other tents they're holdin' we can move in the rest of the families in short order. If relief can hold out 'n our picket lines strengthen, we'll have those folks in Corey Mill walkin' out 'n organizin' with us in short order. Then we'll bring the ole moss-back super to terms."

"Reckon you're right. Reports from them we sent inside the plant sound pretty good. 'N lots of the scabs are comin' to our meetin's."

"They ain't real scabs, like," Jem corrected him. "They're just ignorant."

"Gosh!" Red's hands gripped his hammer convulsively, "we just gotta win this strike. We just gotta."

Jem's eyes glittered. "That's how we all feel."

"If we can just hold out—"

"We're holdin', ain't we. Thar's only one thing, that is, two things by rights that're worryin' me."

"What's that?"

"First, the other mills ain't comin' out so fast as we ex-pected." Jem hitched his overall strap. "Then, what's the comp'ny up to next? It's cut off our groceries from its store, turned us outta our homes, clubbed 'n gassed us on the picket line. Thrown us in jail. Busted down our union hall 'n made all kinda threats besides. Still we're holdin', with prospects ahead pretty fair. But the comp'ny'll stop at nuthin', *nuthin'* to break us. So I'm just a-wonderin' what it'll try next. We gotta be prepared."

"Last night," Red dropped his voice, "when me'n Phil were on guard, about two o'clock we heard somebody prowlin' down in the bushes near the creek. We run over, our guns primed, but they hurried away. Now what you reckon?"

Jem stood silent, pondering. "You tell that to Tom?"

"Sure. He said not to spread it. Our folks are wrought up enough as it is. We'll take it up in strike committee meetin' 'n caution the guards to be extra careful from now on."

"Thar goes Tom now." Red cupped his hands. "Hay, Tom, come over here."

"Hello boys, I was just looking for you two. Let's step over thar in the woods whar no-one'll interrupt us. You see, Red, Jem 'n me've been aimin' to have a talk with you for the last two or three days."

The youth looked from one to the other, "What's up?"

"Nothing to worry you," Jem reassured him. "In fact, just the opposite." Then what, Red wondered, made them both look so darn serious?

When they were comfortably stretched out under the trees, Tom began. "This is how it is. You're one of the best fighters we've got, Red, 'n a natural leader. The others trust you. On every issue, you click true. You're the kind, buddy, we want in the Communist Party."

So that was it. Red flushed with embarrassment and some-thing else he couldn't quite explain. "Wal, I doan rate your words." He hesitated. "'Course I've heard you speak of the Party, Tom, more'n once. Still I ain't right clear the diff'rence between belongin' to the Union 'n belongin' also to it?"

"The Union's for all who work in the mill. No matter how backward their ideas may be, so long as they're willin' to stick with the others 'n fight for better conditions, that's all we ask. But those in the Party we ask more of. They're a picked group—the flower you might say, of the working class. . . . Look here, Red, it's a battle, you know that, between the bosses 'n us—a battle to the finish. This strike is just one engagement. Thar'll be many more to follow, till it comes to the Civil War 'n our class seizing all factories and settin' up its own power. Wal, every army has to have its leaders, doan it? Its vanguard who go in front, mark out the way, lay out the plans, as to how best to conquer the enemy. That's what we Communists have to do. Lead the way 'n bear the main brunt of the fight."

"It's some big job." Red turned a broken twig leaf between his fingers.

"That it is, son." Jem's calm eyes rested up on the bronze head. "It puts a big responsibility on each one's shoulders who joins up. But it's a big honor we're payin' you, too. I hope you know that?"

"Sure thing. Only, I doan feel fitten. I ain't had much schoolin'. Just been a mill hand all my life 'n—"

"Stop right thar," Tom broke in. "Didn't I say this was the advance guard of the workin' class? That means mill hands like Jem, you 'n me, 'n coal diggers 'n fellas that run the railroads. Whar else should our class look for leaders except among its own kind? Of course thar's a small number of what's known as intellectuals that can play a big part too. That is, the best of 'em, that get tested out in the fires of the struggle. But get this straight, Red, if the working class is to win its way to freedom—and it will win—it'll do so by the power of its own might. As for bein' ignorant—how much schoolin' do you think me or Jem or Marge had? But you'll be surprised how quick you learn, once you set yourself to it. I noticed how you caught on in our class."

"Gee I dunno—You say Marge's joined up?" Red inquired.

"I reckon she was the first, next to Tom 'n George," Jem answered. "Jerry, Dolly 'n me joined a few days back."

"What about Phil?"

"We didn't ask him," Tom replied, "for the reason that while he makes a good Union man 'n even knows it's a scrap against the government as well, he can't see it eye to eye yet on the race question. He does his best, 'n in time no doubt he'll get over the last of his prejudices. But in the meantime— you see we gotta be able to depend on our vanguard on every issue. They gotta set the example. It'd be wrong to expect it of Phil, yet."

Stroking the green down which stretched before him with toil-blunted fingers, Tom went on, "You remember our talk about what Fred wrote us, in his last letter. Here in the Black Belt, a long, bitter scrap's brewin'. Us Communists, white 'n colored, gotta organize 'n lead it—the fight of ten million Negro peasants against their white masters. The first Civil War didn't free them, but this one will. By Gorry, this stealin' their crops, cheatin' their chillen of schoolin', lynchin', rapin'—the whole rotten business has gotta come to an end!"

Red's eyes flashed back. "You know I'm for that."

"You can do a lot to make it clear to Phil 'n other white workers," his friend told him, "why this is their scrap, too." All through the States, and the same in Europe and Asia, the line-up was growing sharper. On the one side, the owning class, on the other, the wage-slaves, poor farmers, property-less, and oppressed. In the Black Belt the scrap would get hotter and hotter. At last the Negro millions would rise up, arms in hand, "Away with the white landlords! To hell with their government! The land belongs to those who till it." And so it would.

At or around the same time (maybe even a bit before, how could a fellow say, so long ahead?), millhands, miners, and railroad boys would be seizing factories, banks, stations, and power plants. The White House would be emptied. Everywhere Soviets would be forming, laying the basis for the new government of workers and all who toil. In the Black Belt, where Negro toilers form the vast majority, they'd likely establish their own self-government. It was a good chance that Soviet America would include a Negro Toilers' Socialist Republic.

At Tom's words, Red's hands gripped, tore apart, closed again. "By Jiminy! You think that's the way it'll work out?"

"Looks thataway," Tom answered. "Naturally, it'll depend on what the Negro people want, when the time comes. The Party stands for their right to decide for themselves. Look how it's workin' out in the Soviet Union. I've been studyin' this over, particular. All the peoples who used to be outcastes and enslaved to the czar now have got their own socialist republics, united on a common footin' into one. Before the revolution they fought 'n hated each other something' terrible. Turcomans fought with Armenians, Ukrainians with Russians, the poor Jews got it from all sides, while Georgians warred on all. But not any more.

"That's the way it'll be with us—we'll get to live 'n work in harmony. Doan worry, the only ones who'll get it in the neck'll be the white rullin' class. For the same scrap that gives the Negro croppers land will do the same for the Poor White farmers. Yep, it'll be a lot better all around."

Jem, plucking a long weed, carefully gnawed it from end to end. While he and Tom waited, Red's forehead ridged with effort. Up the tent street they could see Miz Crane watering her plants, and the children playing their new game, "Chasin' Scabs."

"Wal, what you say Red?" Jem asked slowly. "Or maybe you'like to think it over for a couple of days?"

"No. I can answer right now." He looked them full in the face. "If you're sure you want me, I'll be right proud to join."

YOUNG BINNIE CAME RACING over to Marge, her thin face aglow. "Look!" she waved a newspaper over her head, "the Daily's printed my letter 'n a lot more besides. Just like Tom said."

"Here, stand still a minute 'n give me a chance to see." Marge laughed at the slight little figure dancing up and down on its toes.

"Read it out loud," Miz Crane begged. "Now which one's Binnie's? Begin with it."

"I am a girl of 14 years of age," Marge read. *"I've been working here in Corey mills since one week before Christmas, and the company hasn't been out 20 dollars for me since I've been working for them.*

"They double up work on me every day of my life. I have worked every day but a half day and never got more than five dollars a week.

"Just to think back, I wil never work any more for any such pay. I worked two weeks in Corey for nothing. Cleanup day was every day and the section man had many pets, some would have to clean up their frames every day and I would too. I ran four sides. They beat me out of two. But I wil gain it back some day. I am your union friend. B. G."

"That's a pretty fine letter, Binnie," Miz Crane nodded her head.

"Now I'm writin' about when I got beat up on the picket line 'n Miz Hoppin got down on her knees to find her glasses 'n those yellow dogs kicked her flat. I bet they'll print that." Binnie pushed her sandy hair behind her long ears.

"Here's one that Elm musta sent in. It gives all about how his pay envelopes were. Listen:

Wages due $6.80

———

Rent 2.00
Lights 50
Coal 2.20
Coupons for groceries 2.00

———

Balance . . . . $ .10

By now a crowd had gathered around. "Say, Phil, here's one you wrote printed here." Marge began to read:

Take the mill owner. He don't want you to have any thing but man, he wants a new car, all right, every six months, and his big, fine horse, and his twenty-five cent cigars and his servants.

I want every worker to study this.

You take this rich man, he don't want you to have anything but work, and he wants you to work in the mills for and he gets up any time he wants and has his own corn likker. But we, every morning we must get up at 4:30 and go to work, only being able to eat one egg and at dinner eat some potatoes and then back to work again.

Let the poor man try to save anything, and the rich man has the government on his side and they will try to put you down like dogs.

I was collecting money for the strikers the other day and the poor people gove 100 dollars and the rich give 25 cents. This is the good truth.

If the cotton mill hands go to do anything the big man is ready to do any thing he can to keep them from it. It don't do any good to go to church.

What the rich man wants is for the hands to work for nothing, though you have a wife and three children to go to the table three times a day, you have to work for twelve dolars a week. Now if Governor Gardner had to do that and if Mayor Rankin and Sheriff Anderson, then everyone of these would strike.

You never heard of a rich man in this country going to jail, though he has got plenty of likker right in his house today. The rich man always has everything but we can't buy books for our children to go to school.

This is the good truth and is written by a mill hand of Riverton Hill.

"My, but that's full of good truth!" Dolly looked at Phil admiringly.

"Yah, that's tellin' 'em boy. That'll make the Governor's skin crawl, plenty!"

"This here's gona be the best of all," Marge announced. "It's called 'The New Twenty-third Psalm' 'n is poetry like. It doan say who wrote it, though, except it's 'By a Riverton Striker.'

> Corey mill is my sheperd and I shall not want
> He maketh me to lie down on park benches,
> He leadeth me beside the free soup houses,
> He restoreth my doubt in the textile industry.
> He leadeth me in the paths of destruction for
>   his company's sake.
> Yea, tho I walk thru the valley of starvation to
>   uphold the union, I do fear evil.
> For they are against me.
> For their policy and their profits do fight me.
> They prepare to reduce my wages in the
>   presence of my enemies.
> They anoint my wages with reductions.

My expenses runneth over my income.
Surely poverty and starvation will follow me all
    the days of my life
And I will dwell in a rented house forever.
P.S.—That is, if I don't stand by the Union and
    fight like hell!

"That's a right smart piece. Who could've written it?" Everybody looked about, questioning.

"It's worth settin' to memory," Miz Crane observed, "that is, all exceptin' the word in that last line. To think this paper'll print all us mill hands'll send in."

"Catch the *Gazzy Gazette* doin' that! All it's got room for is the mill men's side." Dolly reached for the Daily. "Any more of these around?"

"Sure," Jem answered, "we got a whole batch. We gona sell 'n give 'em out at the meetin'."

Binnie and many of the younger children went through the village and into Riverton City with armfuls of papers. Little Bobby Murray carted his along in a small wagon. "Buy the Daily Worker!" they piped, "Read all about us strikin'!" When the laws chased them they ran around the block and came out on the other side. "Buy a paper! All about why we're strikin'."

MARGE, IN A FRESHLY STARCHED slip of blue cotton stood near the entrance way the colony had erected.

ALL WELCOME TO UNION TOWN
STRIKERS OF COREY MILL
LOCAL 39, NATIONAL TEXTILE WORKERS UNION

The Carolina sun danced across her slightly stooped shoulders, waking to life the scant gold still slumbering in her hair. Jem, waiting nearby, observed, "Marge, you've picked up some since the strike started. You ain't so peaked-lookin' as a few weeks back." A slight tan had softened the sharp outlines of her sallow face, lightening the blackness of the sagging hollows under her eyes.

"Bein' outa the mill has done more'n one good," she answered, "marchin' on the picket-lines 'n all. Besides," she looked up at him, "it's—oh you know. We got somethin' to live by now."

They stopped to greet more visitors and direct them to their new hall. "Sure a grand crowd, ain't it?"

"That it is." Shading her eyes with her arm, Marge gazed about. "Must be nigh to four thousand here, already. Never saw such a crowd in these parts. A lotta farmers, you notice 'n mill hands from miles around. This here strike of ours has won a lotta sympathy. In spite of all the lies the comp'ny keeps spreadin'."

"Look how the farmers, poor as they are, been givin' to our relief. They got plenty reason to hate the mills too, I reckon. Wal—" Jem flocked his ear, "thar's a feelin' growin' up—it's the rich against the poor, 'n the poor against the rich."

Ole man Hollis sauntered by, fingering his fiddle nervously. "Howdy, folks. Howdy!"

"Howdy yourself, Uncle Holly. You gona make some music today, eh?" Marge asked.

"I doan know, honey. Seein' such a multitude, I've nigh lost my heart for it."

"Go way with you," Jem hit him lightly across the back. "If Marge 'n me here ain't scared to speak at 'em, you-all can sure tickle the strings."

"What'd you have to remind me of that for?" The woman felt suddenly cold. "Just when we were havin' such a good time." Could she go through with it today? She must. Since that first meetin' before the mill she'd had to say a few words more'n once. As Tom had told her, each time it came a little easier. But before so many thousands . . .

"Come on. It's time for the meetin' to start." Passing down the row of tents they joined Tom, Red, George, Uncle John and a small group of Negroes who had been persuaded to attend. Some of the white visitors looked askance in their direction.

Jerry and Nancy were still too ill to come. Recently, with company terror on the increase, these two, under cover of night, had been moved further up the county to a more remote hiding place. The strike committee felt that it "couldn't take any chances on a lynchin'," and there was a likelihood that Farmer Thompson's place had become known to the mill authorities by now.

"Let's begin. You first Tom, 'n then Ella May, with her ballits. After that thar'd be George, Uncle John, Red, young Binnie, Marge, the fiddlin', 'n Jem to wind up."

Ella May left Marge to mind the youn-uns and mounted the fresh pine platform. A burst of applause, then a vast silence as the crowd pressed closer, straining to catch each word. For the mill hands this tiny woman had come to symbolize the will to win. Flinging back her shoulders Ella May began to sing the songs she had composed about the Union.

> We leave our home in the morning
> We kiss our children good-bye,
> While we slave for the bosses
> Our children scream and cry.
>
> And when we draw our money
> Our grocery bills to pay
> Not a cent to spend for clothing
> Not a cent to lay away.
>
> And on that very evening
> Our little son will say,

"I need some shoes, dear mother,
And so does sister May."

How it grieves the heart of a mother,
Yet everyone must know,
But we can't buy for our children,
Our wages are too low.

Now listen to me, workers,
Both women and men,
We are sure to win our Union
If all will enter in.

I hope this will be a warning,
I hope you will understand,
And help us win our victory,
And lend to us a hand.

It is for our dear children
That seem to us so dear,
But for us nor them, dear workers,
The bosses do not care.

But understand, all workers.
Our Union they do fear,
Let's stand together, workers,
And have a Union here.

"More! More!" her listeners demanded. "Sing us more of
your ballits, Ella May."

"That's all for today," she told them. "But one thing I've
got to say. We mill hands are a rovin' lot. At last we got our
Union, somethin' to stick to, 'n that'll stick by us." Now it was
Marge's turn. For a moment the old dizziness threatened her.
She caught Tom's eye. Her long fingers pressed against her
flat chest, she began to pour out the things she had for long

wanted to tell them. Her people, about Granny and the long years from hill to hill. "What's happened to me is the same as what's happened to us all. . . . The mill takes all, 'n gives nothin'. . . . It took my youth, it took my babies. It took my man. One thing it can't take—that's my fightin' spirit. That's what I gotta tell you. Stand by the Union. Hold onto your fightin' spirit. It's all we mill folks have got. But it'll see us through to victory!"

XXIV.

Class Against Class

MARGE HASTENED ACROSS the railroad tracks which ran between the mill and tent colony, up the short village streets, and out along the dusty highway. It was a three mile trip to the Wiggins' shack, which stood off company land near Vesmer mill.

Ella May had not been around to meetings for several days. Something must be wrong.

Striding across fields studded white and gold with daisies and buttercups, Marge chuckled, "Dog-gone if they ain't noddin' to me." She sniffed eagerly at the strong, earthy smells running in zigzag heat waves up to her knees and throat. How still the pines were. These past weeks she'd nigh forgot the glow on the fields, under the morning sun.

Yah, once the workers took charge, Dixie'd be a pretty fine place to live in.

The shack's leaning door swung on a loose hinge. She knocked, "It's me, Marge."

"Come in, honey," a weak voice called, "'n right welcome."

She found all five huddled together in the one bed. The greenish color about their drawn mouths startled her. "What's happened? What you-all come down with? 'N to think you here alone 'n us not knowin'!"

"Were better now." Ella May elbowed to a sitting position. "The low-downs pizened us!"

"What!" Marge yanked a chair beside the bed.

"That's what they done," Elsie, the oldest girl whispered. "Four nights ago I spied two men a-skulkin' 'bout the place whar we got our water. I called Ma 'n we hollered at 'em 'n they lit out for the bushes."

"So," Ella May went on, "we didn't think much of it. Only that night when we were havin' some warmed-over grits 'n water, Pete says, 'Ma,' he says, 'this water sure stinks,' 'n Ike, he spews out his'n. So that sot me to thinkin'. 'Best not drink more,' I told 'em. We went over to the spring, 'n thar we found these two empty sacks," she pulled the bags from under the pillow. "You see thar's a lil' white stuff in 'em still. That's poison!"

Marge's eyes stare. "Are you sure?" The comp'ny'd stop at nuthin'—nuthin'. Even murder.

"Sure I'm sure. Ain't they promised to get me for makin' up all them songs? Lucky we didn't drink more or we'd all been sretched out, dead as a door nail. You know, I been lyin' here sayin' to myself, what if we-all passed out 'n no way to warn the others. Supposin' they come to the tents the same way? Yesterday I tried to set out for the colony. But I passed clear out 'bout a hundred yards from the house 'n had to come back."

"Likely they have been to the colony. But we cotched 'em first." Marge related how they had caught the men prowling about the stream. "If we'd a-known what they were aimin' at! Just wait till I tell our folks what they tried to do to you!"

Marge busied herself straightening up. "Soon as I get you comfortable I'm gona take a bottle of this here water 'n these bags to Tom, 'n we'll go to a drug store in town 'n have 'em tested. Then, I'll come back 'n stay by you for the night. Spread a pallet on the floor."

"That's right kindly, if you can be spared. Tomorrow I gotta be back on my feet. How," Ella May asked anxiously, "is the strike?"

"Pickin' up a bit. Thar's a lot more evictions, though. We got five new commitees in Gaston County mills 'n . . ." Before leaving Marge stooped over the bed. "This ain't a place for you, Ella May, livin' on here with these skunks about. You gotta move into our colony."

"Naw, honey," the sick woman answered, "I ain't a-scared. We're needin' ev'ry tent we got 'n more besides, to cover the ones ain't got a place to lay their heads. We'll stay right here. If worse comes to worse, I still got it." She pointed to the gun slung over the door.

When the sample of water was tested it proved to be strongly polluted with a poisonous acid. The same as the traces of white powder in the bags.

The following night the home of Phil's brother, who lived and worked off the hill was shattered by a bomb. "Only that we all were to the meetin' saved us from bein' blown to smithereens!" Phil's wife moaned. "'N Walt's place he was buyin' on the installment plan all gone up in smoke!"

Jem looked at Tom. "What's comin next?"

"Down in the city," Red said, "thar's talk all over 'bout this Committee of One Hundred the mill men've organized boastin' how it's gona shoot up our place."

"Let's keep cool," Tom warned. "What they're aimin' at is to start a young riot. 'N Red, call together the strike guard. We'll just talk things over."

In a few minutes twenty-five angular boys and men in shirt sleeves or overalls had lined up in the open space back of the hall.

COREY MILL WAS GOING to be struck again. The hill and lowland people brought in to work were grumbling over conditions in the plant and getting increasingly restless under the stares and calls of the pickets.

Tom and Jem had held secret meetings with a small committee from the plant. "It ain't gona be so easy," one of them explained, "to get the hands out. First they fired some for speakin' over the union. Next they put armed men in every room. Last Tuesday some tried to walk out to join the pickets. 'Whar you goin' ?' the boss-man hollered. 'We're quittin' ' we told him. 'The hell you are,' he said. 'N he locked the door 'n they pointed their guns at us. 'Get back thar to your machines,' they said, like a order. So . . ."

"Gee—'n they call this a free country!" Jem whistled.

"You know what that is?" Tom asked, "the same as slavery. That's the way Mussolini over in Italy put over his gag. Black shirts with guns in every factory. You want it thataway here?"

"Like hell 'n Maria!"

"We'll bust through. They can't hold us all back. We'll give those guys the bum's rush."

"Squirt tobacco juice in their eyes."

The plan, as finally agreed upon, was for the night shift to walk down on Friday night just as the picket-line circled the mill. That would give the day shift courage not to go in the next morning.

"Nine o'clock sharp we'll be expectin' you. See that everybody turns out."

"You bet—men, women 'n chillen."

"Work fast, you on the inside. But watch your step. No leaks. A lot depends on the comp'ny not gettin' wise."

THE SUN WAS SETTLING behind the horizon. The tents took on a grey tinge.

"This here lot's buzzin' like a bee hive," Ole man Hollis observed. "I ain't seen so many to a meetin' in many a week."

"Thar's a big meetin' at Rockdale tonight, too." Red added. "Rose sent word for George to come. We'll kinda miss his speakin' tonight, 'n Uncle John's too. The colored folks's got a handy way of sayin' things. You know, make you laugh one minute, 'n the next bring tears to your eyes."

Tom, fearful for Uncle John's safety, had persuaded the old man that Jerry and Nancy needed his attention for a few days.

"It's a sorta funny time to call a meetin', ain't it?" Miz Hoppin inquired.

Red grinned at her mysteriously. "Naw'm. We've had lots of late meetin's."

"Somethin's up. I feel it in the air." Binnie bobbed up and down, swishing her skinny arms about.

"Do keep still child," Miz Crane begged, "you give me the figgets."

Everybody had the figgets. The air bristled, crackled, pricking at your skin. In some way the strike had sensed that the critical moment of their strike had arrived. On now to victory, or—

Ella May squeezed Marge's arm. "Two more hours," she whispered. "Two more hours."

Tonight, all the weeks of sacrifice and struggle were to bear their fruit.

Tom signalled them forward. As Ella May stepped on the platform a barrage of tomatoes and eggs sailed over the heads of the crowd in her direction, splattering on the side of the building behind her.

A scuffle at the edge of the gathering, cries of "You stool!" "Throw 'em out!"

"Put 'em offa the lot," Tom directed, "'n let's go on with the meetin'." (Did this mean the company had been put wise?)

Ella May began to sing. Bit by bit the light faded. Her listeners pressed around the stand, blended into one throbbing, grey mass. The last rays caught on the woman's face—passionate, commanding—as her voice run out, "My people—let each stand in his place!"

The time had come for Tom to announce the night march on the mill. As he came forward a man at the rear, unobserved, took careful aim.

A woman, a drowsy infant against her shoulder unwittingly moved between him and the platform.

He edged to one side, his pistol hidden. Risky business, this. Worth five times what he was gettin' for it. Again he sighted Tom. Somebody had brought a lamp and set it on the boards. The light threw directly on Tom and on Seth, his body guard, who stood alongside, sombre eyes resting quietly on the dim crowd.

The man signalled his pal.

Phil, hearing a suspicious click behind him, whirled in time to slam the assailant's arm to the ground. The shot missed, tearing at the earth. The gunmen fled, Phil and another strike guard speeding their retreat.

As the picket-line crossed the tracks, armed men in cars swooped down, firing in the air, clubbing, yelling drunken threats. Behind them the deputies massed five deep across the highway. Beyond, the lights of the mill beckoned. Its rumbling growl mingled with the tumult of struggling bodies and infuriated cries.

Again and again the unarmed mill hands pressed forward, were driven back. Routed, at last the line withdrew to the colony. Within her Marge groaned, "They didn't come out. ... They didn't come."

"Tomorrow, fellow-workers," Tom said, "we'll try again. Now, everybody home 'n to bed." He went inside to bathe his blackened eye and write up his daily statement for the press. This, he had found, was the only check he had on being grossly misquoted. Marge and Jem walked a piece of the way with Ella May. On their return they found a crowd milling about the lot, talking in excited, angry undertones. The strike guards were at their posts, faces set. Hurrying on to the hall, pushing past Seth, guarding the door-way, she found Tom crouched over his typewriter, labouriously picking out the letters, one by one. How could he sit there so calm? she wondered. Inside, she knew, he was as disappointed as anyone. "You better come," she told him, "they ain't goin' home. Anything might happen."

Tom made a brief speech and the crowd, somewhat calmed, began to disperse. Some went toward their tents, others headed for their quarters on neighboring hills. Tom, Jem, Marge, and Carrie went inside the hall, to talk things over. "We'll pull the plant tomorrow," Tom repeated, "I feel certain of that."

Overhead the stars glimmered fitfully. Sounds of the mill's machinery drifted down the streets toward the colony.

Carrie jumped up. "What's that?" The quick thud-thud of running foot steps grew more distinct. Down the path the strike guard halted the runners, then sent them on to the hall. The youths dropped over the door-sill.

"It's all right, Seth, I know them." Tom stooped over the boys. "What's up?"

"They're comin'!"

"Who? Where?"

"Committee of One Hundred. We heard in town . . . Nigh two hundred . . . guns . . . ropes . . ." Gasping painfully the youths fled across the fields.

"They'll outnumber us ten to one," Jem calculated, "'n only twelve guns on the place."

Ludlow, Tom remembered. Striking miners, their wives and children massacred in their sleep. Lucky he had sent Uncle John away, and that George was over at Rockdale. Aloud he said, "Keep your heads. Everythin' depends on that."

Already the first cars were bumping across the railroad tracks, parking opposite the colony. Men reeling slightly, flourishing revolvers came toward the hall. In the lead was Chief of Police Anderson; close behind him, his assistant, Maxwell Park. Park, so the talk about town had it, had long been angling to get Anderson's job. A feud had grown up between them.

Seth and Phil blocked the doorway. Over their shoulders Anderson spied Tom, Jem, Marge, and Carrie, standing, unarmed, gazing at him with narrowed eyes.

"What you want?" Phil demanded.

Anderson leered. "Make way for officers of the law. *Them's* what we want."

Tom stepped forward. "Whar's your warrants?"

Park slapped his pistol. "This here's all the—warrant we're needin'.'"

Seth and Phil lifted their guns. "You can't come in here. This is our land 'n our hall."

Anderson's gaze shifted uneasily. Where in hell were the others? How many guns were on the place? "Come on, Park, we'll look around first."

The dogs had begun to howl. The warning whistle of a freight wailed into the night. Its engineer, guiding the empty cars past the village, leaned out to stare at the line of machines packed along the mill side of the tracks, and the mob of swearing men shaking their fists in his direction. "Off on a spree, after some banquet I reckon," he concluded. "I'll just learn 'em to swear at a railroader." He backed his train several times three quarters of its length down the track. The type of spree they'd planned he never realized, nor the fact that quite by accident he had been the means of saving the lives of two score of his brothers whom the majority of the mob never reached.

For in the few minutes of delay caused by the lumbering freight, events transpired at the colony that brought the Committee of One Hundred's plan to an abrupt end.

Out on the lot Anderson and Park had grabbed Binnie's young brother Ross, twisting his arms until he screamed with pain.

"Drap his arms, you!" Phil called. "Leave that boy be."

From behind the parked cars shots whistled through the air toward the Union hall, tearing at its thin partitions. Women and children came running from the tents. Now both sides were firing. "Those that ain't got guns lie flat on the floor," Phil ordered. Out in the lot a man dropped, then another.

Slowly the invaders retreated, the strikers holding their ground.

Deliberately Park took aim—at his ranking officer. With a wail Anderson reeled to one side. "The bastards," Park screamed to his fellows, "they've shot our chief." "They got me in the arm," another moaned. In panic they fled with their wounded to their machines and set out for town.

"Ross, you're hurt!" Red exclaimed.

"Tain't nothin'," he answered, "just a flesh wound."

"Come on, I'll take you to the hospital." Tom urged him forward.

"No, Tom. They'll get you sure!" Miz Crane wrung her hands.

"Nonsense. Get a car somebody. We'll be back. In the meantime, Jem, you Phil 'n Red clear out the women 'n chillen." Several families were already making off. Phil, remembering Ella May, sent two guards to give her warning.

As Tom reached the car, supporting Ross, Seth leaped in behind them.

"Seth, you doan need to come," Tom said, "go on back." The youth did not reply, simply settled his gun between his knees. Cars were already patrolling the streets, armed men peering out. Seth yanked off his cap, puffing it down over Tom's head.

At the hospital, while they were waiting for Ross to be cared for, they glimpsed Park and another deputy bringing in Anderson and a wounded sheriff. "Anderson's dyin'," they heard them say.

Ross jumped up, slipping quickly out of the door. Seth and Tom followed him to the car. "Come on, afore they see us," he whispered, "or thar'll be a lynchin' sure."

"They're chasin' us," Seth observed, "driver, give 'em the dodge."

"We gotta get back to the colony." Tom commanded. Also, he must find a way to phone the New York office.

The car shuddered, wheeling about. "I ain't a-drivin' into that," the driver waved down the street where cars blocked the road-way.

"Hell! Then try the long way about."

The open Ford bumped down the country road. A quarter of a mile from the colony, the driver slammed on his breaks. "What the—" Marge and Red were running up the road, blinking at the lights, waving frantically. "Tom—George..."

Then he remembered. George had planned on coming back after the Rockdale meeting. Some strikers had arranged for a friend to go after him in a car. Even now he was probably walking down the road toward Riverton, looking to be picked up, knowing nothing of all that had happened.

"I heard 'em say 'Whar's the nigger?'" Marge gasped. "Supposin' we're too late!" She and Red climbed in. "The others said, 'You save George, we'll take care of here.'"

Whirling once more, the car headed for Rockdale. Tom and Marge sat with clenched hands. Memories of Back Row, sinister, threatening . . . "What if we are too late?" A pale moon crept above the dark pines.

"Can't you go faster?" Tom shouted.

"Givin' her all the gas she'll take."

Far down the highway to their rear powerful flashlights gleamed. "They got our trail," Red observed.

"Look, thar's another close behind it."

"They're gainin' on us."

"Sure. They got twice the speed of this wagon."

"Just so we're not too late!" The white road slipped beneath them; through the pine tops the wind whistled with a strange, moaning sound. Suppose George had gotten an early start and they missed him on the way? Supposing. Another mile . . . another.

"Keep your eyes out now. Any time we might see George footin' it along here." Tom leaned out. "Reckon you better slow down a mite, so we can see better."

"Stop. Thar is he—thar!" As the car lurched to a standstill Tom bounded over the door. "Here. Get in for Gawd's sake. Lie on the floor."

Red looked over his shoulder. "We got maybe a half-mile lead, still."

"I'll head for Charlotte," the driver stepped on the gas.

"Naw. By this time they're patrollin' on those highways. Head straight north." In ten minutes they'd be alongside, Tom figured. If only he had a gun!

George pushed to a sitting position. "What's happened?"

"Here's what . . ."

The cars behind were gaining. "Any time now they'll get in range."

"Only two guns among us."

George reached in his pocket. "Naw, We got three guns. Since last week I been goin' prepared."

Red's eyes narrowed. "In a quarter of a mile they'll be alongside."

"Can't you go any faster?" Marge begged. Ross was leaning on her shoulder, weak with pain.

"She boilin' over as it is."

The lights from the rear threw full upon the dilapidated car; its occupants ducked as a shot sung across, splintering the wind-shield.

"Our one chance," Red swung up his gun. "Plug their tires."

His aim missed. Shouts from the rear, an extra spout of gas. Seth's rifle ripped about the dazzling monster bounding over the earth at them. Leaning over the side, George took aim. Tom pulled him back. "For Gawd's sake, keep out of sight. Give me that gun."

George's mouth was set. "Sorry, comrade, but I'm a better shot than you are." A shot whizzed past his ear.

A loud report, then another. The car behind staggered, leaped across the road.

"That time we got 'em."

"Both front tires, begorry!"

A crash. "The car behind—it's smashed into 'em!"

They drove on for another hour. "But I doan wanta go north," George argued, plead. "I ain't agoin' that's all."

"Drive on driver," Red spat over the car's fender. "Now, George, me, Marge, Tom, Ross 'n Seth here've taken a vote, 'n you gotta follow orders."

As sleeping fields and villages slipped past they sought to convince him.

"I know how you feel, buddy," Tom dropped a hand on his shoulder. "But you gotta see it our way. . . . How you'll be more use to the revolution—strung up or alive?"

"We ain't saved you tonight for nothin'?" Marge added. "We want you to go now so later you can come back 'n carry on the work with us. Lucky I grabbed the relief till." She shook the tin box. "Thar oughta be enough here to buy a ticket."

They drew up at the station. "Come on, comrade. When all's said 'n done—orders're orders. . . . It's only for a few weeks."

As the train pulled out, those watching it chug down the tracks breathed easier. "Wal, that's that. A close call." Tom started for the car. "Think we can make it back by day light?"

"We gotta get Ross to a doctor soon as we can. Reckon thar's one around here?" Marge asked.

"We'll see."

"Doan mind me. It's Tom I'm worryin' about." Ross pulled at his shoulder. "Tom, how 'bout your not goin' back for a few days? We'll drop you off somewhar with Seth along. You know how feelin's runnin' now."

"Nonsense," Tom answered, "it's no diff'rent for me than for Red or Jem, or any of you."

"You know it is too." Seth rejoined. "They're after you special."

"Suppose we take another vote?" Ross demanded.

Tom looked around. "If we did, boy, it'd be three to two. Marge 'n Red would vote my way."

Marge could barely nod. She daren't trust herself to speak.

The earth glided swiftly under them. The roads looked bleak, deserted. Slowly the day broke. What would it hold?

The doctor who dressed Ross's shoulder asked the boy many questions. Marge, who had gone in with him, felt relieved when they were again outside.

"I bet that old codger didn't believe a word we told him," Ross commented. "Wal, so long as he didn't call in the police, it's all right."

In the next town they found newsboys running through the yellowed streets, calling, "Ex-try! Ex-try! Police Chief Murdered by Union Red!"

Between them they mustered a few pennies and Seth ran over for a paper. "Gee whiz! Look at this." He handed it to Tom. Under the cross-page headline his own face grinned up at him, below it the caption: "Wanted for Murder of Riverton Chief of Police Anderson."

Following a lurid, inaccurate account of the night's happenings, the paper stated that "all the ring leaders of this gangsters' communist union have been rounded up and lodged in jail—except its most notorious one, Tom Crenshaw, who immediately fled to parts unknown. A nationwide search is being organized. Machines are patrolling every highway in the state on the look-out for the foul murderers of Chief Anderson."

"But you never even had a gun," Ross protested. "How could you've killed him? Everybody around the hall can testify to that."

"This is an old method, son," Tom answered him, "a way the American bosses use to get labor organizers out of the way. With the mill barons it ain't a question as to who killed Chief Anderson, but how can they best kill the strike."

"They hired first the bunch of hoodlums! Shootin' up our place, threatenin' women 'n chillen. We got a right to some self-defense, ain't we?" Red demanded.

"That's it," Tom repeated, "the workers' right of self-defense, 'n to a Union 'n better conditions."

As they rounded the next curve two police cars crossed directly in front of them. "Halt, or we fire!" Machine guns swung over the sides.

"Now, you sons of—, we got you."

Seth and Red looked toward Tom. "Lay down your guns," he told them, "we ain't afraid to go with 'em. The law'll be sorry it ever started this business afore it's done."

All were searched, handcuffed. The police whistled to find Tom un-armed. "Slick, ain't-cha?"

Marge, Red, and Ross they placed in one armoured car, two guards alongside. Tom and Seth they placed in the other. A plainclothes man climbed in beside the strikers' driver, pressing the nose of his pistol against his side. "You follow that car in front, 'n any tricks from you 'n—" he nudged the steel against the other's ribs.

A mile down the road, Marge, looking back, saw the car carrying Tom turn off down a side road.

"Whar you takin' my brother?" she demanded.

"To a safer place than Gaston County. His life ain't worth a farthin' if any of the mobs can get their hands on him...."

She struggled to get out. "Lemme go, I tell you." Red and Ross threw themselves against the door, fighting with handcuffed wrists. "You're lyin'! They're gona murder Tom."

The guards pinned them to the floor. "Try that again 'n we'll blast your dirty beans,—not exceptin' the woman's."

Later on one of them, eyeing Marge's drawn face, volunteered, "We warn't a-lyin'.... The State aims to do this legal."

At Morton County jail, the sheriff had Tom and Seth brought into his office. "They've sent you here for safety—till the trial starts. . . . Hardly think to find you in this out-of-the-way place. . . . Now, remember, not a word to the other prisoners. Your name here," he thrust a thumb at Tom, "is Henry Johnson. You understand? 'N I'll not allow a single paper or letters to enter the jail till after, so the men won't catch on."

Tom nodded. He understood all right. Or did he? Was it a trick or—?

The prisoners crowded together in one dingy, rat-infested room, put him through kangaroo court and charged him his last twenty cents. To no-one did he mention the strike. Seth was lodged on the floor above. Three days passed—a week. The prisoners grew glum, ugly. Why shouldn't they get their letters and papers. What had they done, they speculated, to get the sheriff's goat?

When Tom was called into the office they cast suspicious glances in his direction. Who was this guy, anyway; what was he doin' chinnin' with the sheriff?

The sheriff had called him in to talk about the strike. "You see," he cleared his throat, "you got a good break, bein' sent here. Over to Gaston they doan know this, but a lot of my folks've been mill people." He leaned closer. "I gotta lay low, you understand. But that was a swell strike you were leadin'. You say you didn't shoot Anderson? Boy, I'll give you all the protection this jail affords. . . . As I said, I gotta lay low. Though if it comes to that, let 'em take their old job. I feels with the common people."

Tom looked at him. The old fellow was a mis-fit, sure enough, over-looked so far by the clumsy machine of North Carolina politics.

"I bet," the sheriff told him, "thar ain't another sheriff in all the state that'd feel the way I do."

"I'm sure thar ain't." Tom replied. "'N if you're askin' me, if you mean what you say, you'll not be sheriff long."

When Tom was returned to the jail the prisoners crowded around him, grabbing for his hand. "I knew it all along," one old fellow said over and over. "I knew it all along." "You did like—" his mates joshed him.

"We snuck a paper through the bars from a kid outside—cost us two bits—but it was worth it," they explained. "Now, Tom Crenshaw, tell us about the strike."

They couldn't do enough for him. His twenty cents was returned, they treated him to 'baccy and told him their stories. "None of us here is really bad fellows," they explained, "you'll understand that. Just poor folks, with a li'l hard luck. Now me 'n that fellow thar, we were picked up for vagrancy. But how can you work when thar ain't a job to be had? 'n Frankie here, he's in for stealin' a mule to plow his land."

"But the mule was mine by rights, anyway," Frankie lumbered over, "the man what claimed it had cheated me double time over. He owned the land I was workin. So—"

"It's sure good to see the poor folks risin'. Let me outta here 'n I'll—"

One old inmate was disappointed. "So you really didn't kill that Anderson? He was an onery cuss, as ever ambled on two legs."

The men uncovered a hiding place in the rafters, "whar we'll hoist you, in case the kluxers come messin' 'round here," they told Tom.

Frankie produced a row of bottles. "Boy, if they come for you, we'll just greet 'em with a shower of these."

XXV.

Another Civil War

"THEY GOT US PACKED in here like sardines," Miz Crane humped her shoulders. "All our main pickets must be behind these here bars."

"The idea of chargin' a hundred people with shootin' one man. They must be crazy!" Dolly scratched her arm. Thar was somethin' in this jail besides folks!

"They ain't crazy," Marge answered, "they're after bustin' our strike."

"Let us outta here, they'll see who's busted!"

As news of the coming trial flashed through the country, angry demonstrations took place from Boston to California, spreading across the oceans to Tokio, Moscow, Berlin and London. In Paris, Mexico, and South America United States consulates were stormed with cries, "No more Saccos and Vanzettis! Set our comrades free!"

Mill workers gathered spontaneously on many hills to discuss what could be done. "Sure as anythin', if they try to go through with this," some of them stated, "we'll get down our guns 'n march on that county jail."

"Guess all of this'll get the Governor scared," Red grinned at lawyer Brandon, who had just told how telegrams and cables of protest were pouring in from all sections of the globe.

"If anything'll get you boys out, these mass protests will."

"You know." Phil ruminated, "afore this happened Chineese 'n I-talians 'n all like that were just chinks 'n dagos to me. Forriners that wore pigtails, say, 'n ate dead rats. But now, bearin' all you tell about how they're gettin' their heads cracked by the cops for tryin' to set us free," his eyes filled, "it sure makes a diff'rence."

"That's what we call working class solidarity," Jem took up the Daily. "Now it says here that more'n ten thousand mill workers in Shanghai made a demonstration for us this week. It says they got chillen as young as seven years in those mills that're owned by Yankee bosses. 'N nobody gets more'n a few cents a day for fourteen hours. Think of that! They got it worsen'n us. But they're helpen us."

"Boy, if I ever get outta here I'm gona helpen 'em too."

After several conferences the State of North Carolina decided to narrow its case to fourteen strike leaders. Tom, Jem, Marge, Carrie, Rose, Phil, Dolly, Red, and several others were held, the rest released.

Cables and wires continued to pour in.

Again the prosecution conferred. "Southern chivalry," they declared, "leads us to release the women in the case."

"I know their chivalry!" Marge retorted. "I've been visited with more'n seventeen years of it, eleven hours a day.... Southern chivalry! Look what it does for colored women!... The law thinks it's got a better case this way, that's all. But we'll show 'em yet."

Carrie and Marge found Ella May busy with Union and defence work. "Gee, it's good you-all are out. With the mill terror so bad, all but the nerviest are scared to speak out. You know mill folks ain't used to bein' organized, so a lot ain't learned yet what it means to stick.

"But nigh everybody'll help to get the boys out, 'n a lot are joinin' the Union on the quiet." The singing woman, as the workers called her, rested her brown arms on her hips. "Thar's a big outin' 'n meetin' for this Sadday, near Charlotte. It'll be nice you can come along."

"WE'RE LUCKY TODAY. Got somebody to drive us over." Ella May nodded to the truck-driver who calculated he "could leave off haulin' truck one day if it'll help the boys any."

"The other time I was in Charlotte I had to foot it." Lifting up her last child, Ella May climbed aboard.

As the truck jostled its tightly-packed load of men, women and children down the highway the hot air rushed down their throats, scorched their bodies.

"Anyways, heat or no heat," Ella May observed, "thar'll be a good turn-out."

"The mill men're sayin' they ain't gona let us have any more meetin's," somebody commented. "I wonder what that means?"

"Those yellow dogs can't stop us." Ella May folded her arms. "Watch thar, Elsie, doan let baby Ike lean over that-away. He might slip through, he's that skinny."

"What's that comin' up on us from behind?" Ole man Hollis squinted his eyes. "Look sharp, some of you young eyes, 'n see who-alls aboard."

"It's a comp'ny truck."

"I can see guns. 'N the boss-weaver from Corey."

"They'd not try shootin' in broad day-light!"

"Anyways, I wish we-all had some guns."

The truck behind thundered past, running across the road directly in the path of the other.

"Look out thar!"

The smaller truck swerved into the ditch, tumbling over on its side, scattering its occupants in the dusty bushes. As the strikers pulled themselves to their feet, rescuing their children, the company truck opened fire.

Ella May clutched at her chest. "They've shot me." As she fell baby Ike ran to her, crying, "Mama's hurted. Mama's hurted."

Her friends lifted her up. "I saw that skunk Heslop aim at her. Full in the chest."

The mill truck had disappeared down the road.

Marge held her friend's head in her lap while the men struggled to right the truck. "Hurry . . . hurry . . . for Gawd's sake, hurry." It was five miles to the nearest village, and not a farm house in sight. Before they could get her to a hospital, Ella May was dead.

"They killed our singin' 'oman," the mill hands said, "we'll not forget. They killed her a-purpose."

Dolly, Marge and Ross who had seen Heslop fire at Ella May went with their Labor Defence lawyer to swear out a warrant against him. Mr. Carpenter, one of the lawyers for Corey mills, however, defended Heslop and produced men who swore there had been shooting on both sides and that a stray bullet had hit the Wiggins woman. After a summary hearing the case was dismissed. "The mill killed our singin' 'oman," the word ran from hill to hill. "We'll not forget. They killed her a-purpose."

"I'M GONA FIND A WAY, honey," Marge told Elsie, "to have you-all live with me. We'll manage it somehow." Ike buried his head in her lap. Marge gulped. "I'll try to raise you the way Ella May'd want."

From Michigan came a letter from an iron miner's wife. "We'd like to give Ella May's children a home, and a working class training."

"That's kind. But we'd rather stay with you." Twelve-year-old Elsie clung to Marge's arm.

This was the last time she saw the children. While she was away collecting for the defence the Presbyterian Children's Orphan Asylum, under protection of the law, took the four wailing children to its headquarters in the southeastern part of the state. "We'll not allow those Bolsheviks 'n free-lovers to keep you." The thin-lipped matron sat very straight in her chair, cowering Elsie with her eyes. "We're goin' to give you a good Christian education 'n raise you as Constitution, law-abidin' citizens of this great state."

"You see, thar's nothin' more we can do," Lawyer Brandon explained to Marge, "you've no legal claim to the children, though every moral one."

"It's good as kidnappin'." Marge smoothed the letter that Elsie had sent her. "I bet they're mean to the chillen, 'n I know they teach 'em everythin' backwards to the truth."

She re-read the child's last sentence. "No matter what, I'll never forget what-all Ma fought for, 'n I'll learn Ike and Mary and Toby, too."

"You see what's happened over to Marion?" Binnie and her brother ran up to Marge. "Deputies shot down more'n a score of strikin' hands for picketin' the mill."

"Nobody except the deputies had guns or nothin'," Ole man Hollis joined in.

"Shot 'em down like dogs. Six dead 'n another dyin'." Ross' eyes blazed. "Ev'ry one shot in the back!"

Shuddering, Marge drew Binnie closer.

"It's cold-blooded murder. The mill hands what seen it happen are swearin' out warrants." Ole man Hollis cracked his knuckles.

"But nothin' 'll come of it," Marge predicted. "What come of our sweatin' out against the murderer of Ella May?... Naw, on mill hills thar's only one kind of justice—mill justice. I tell you, nothin' 'll come of it." And nothing did. Except, several weeks later nearly one hundred Marion strikers were read out of the mill Baptist church, on the charge of "riotin' 'n disorderly conduct" before the mill gates.

"ACCUSED, RISE 'N FACE your jurors," the judge commanded. Tom, Jem, Phil, Red, and the three other boys stood up. A hush went over the crowded court. Marge, sitting as far forward as she could get, raised a hand of greeting.

The trial did not develop just as the prosecution had planned. Every device known to the legal profession for prejudicing the jurors against the defendants was used, every possible bogey raised. Yet several of the state's witnesses, under fire of the defense, grew confused and openly contradicted their earlier statements, while Tom and his fellow-witnesses told simple, consistent stories that no amount of cross-questioning could break down.

The prosecution decided to play its trump card. The widow of Chief Anderson was brought into court, dressed in heavy black. She was escorted to a seat at the front by Park, one of the main witnesses for the state and recently appointed to the position of Chief of Police.

"Your honor, we beg to submit major testimony in this case."

A door to the left of the court room opened. Two officers shoved something before them covered with a black cloth. Dramatically the prosecutor tore the covering aside, revealing a wax image of the dead Chief Anderson, clothed in the uniform which he had worn the night he had been shot.

His widow shrieked, fainting into Chief Park's arms.

A juror bounded in the air, fell to the floor, yellow froth on his lips. The fright had driven him temporarily insane. For weeks he had to be kept in a padded cell.

Since eleven jurors do not make a jury, "Mis-trial" declared the judge.

A canvas of the jurymen by the defence revealed that a majority had been for acquital.

"At the next trial," Brandon remarked grimly, "the State plans to be more certain of its jury."

"GUESS THIS OLE LIZZIE'LL hold together till we reach Cleveland?" Jem inquired anxiously. He was jammed on the floor of the back seat, his long elbows and knees protruding over the doors at each end.

"I doubt it." Tom, busy at the wheel, laughed as he pressed on the gas. "We're apt to have blow-outs 'n engine trouble. But we'll get thar, all the same.... Somehow, today I ain't got a worry on me.... Boy, we're out at last 'n four months to give the bosses hell before the next trial starts."

"'N how we'll raise it!" Jerry, sitting beside Tom, hummed as the car rumbled noisily over the West Virginia roads.

> "Stand, Brother, Stand!
> Brother, Stand by Brother!"

"George 'll be thar, woan he?"

"Sure thing. All fired up to come South again. . . . You know," Tom shot a look over his shoulder. "This new Union center we're organizing at the Cleveland convention is gona be a big boost for our side."

Marge, sitting between Dolly and Nancy sniffed at the brisk air. The roadside was heavy with golden-rod; the rich greens of the maples and oaks, touched by fall's tingling fingers, glinted with the first hints of copper and red. Fall—it brought back the time Bob had come home from the war, and that last year she had lost both him and the baby. Fall!

Now—her brother to go on trial for his life, singing because his girl was coming back ... Ella May gone ... The strike called off ... The Union temporarily driven under ground ...

"Jem," Dolly giggled, "you sure whalloped that lady reporter one."

He shifted his knees. "I warnt aimin' to. I just—"

"What you-all talkin' 'bout?" Marge asked.

"I'll tell you. The day the boys got bailed out, you know how all the reporters come 'round, askin' questions. Wal one lady comes over to Jem 'n she says, 'I'm sure sorry you lost your strike.' I could see Jem hadn't been payin' her much mind till then, but at that he pricked up his ears 'What's that you say, Ma'am?' he said, so politely-like. 'I was sayin',' she told him, 'that I was sorry to see you defeated.'

"Wal, Jem just stood thar a minute, a-lookin' at her. Then he hoisted his trousers. 'Licked, ma'am?' he told her, 'why, lady, we just begun to fight!'"

Tom slammed the car wheel. "That's a good one! Jem, man, you're all right."

As the machine sputtered around the next hill, Dolly twisted her fingers. "Come to think of it, though—thar's a lot wonderin' what did we get outta all this?"

"Why, thar's a lot we got." Jerry looked around at her in surprise. "Everybody knows we won the five-hour cut in the work-week for all mills in Gaston County, with no cut in pay. That was one of the things we was a-strikin' for—shorter hours." The textile plants had announced this reduction in hours during the early part of the trial. "'N they let up on the stretch-out too."

"That's so," Dolly answered. "All the Gaston hills know they got us to thank for that. But—"

Jem humped his cramp shoulders. "What's more, we got our Union started, 'n we've learned better how to stick together, white 'n black. I set a store by that."

Tom had slowed down, listening carefully. "Nancy 'n Marge, what you got to say?"

The colored woman pursed her lips. "'Course it was a big disappointment, not to win all we set out for."

"What we did get, the price come heavy," Dolly threw in.

"That's the good truth," Nancy continued. "But the way I look at it, we could hardly expect to win everythin' the first time, could we?"

"If the other mills had come out, we could," Jem insisted.

"Wal, me 'n Jerry here figger it's like Uncle John said. Each time the mill folks gotta keep a-inchin' 'long 'n a-inchin' longer a bit more, till we get whar we're goin'.'"

"You know, that's kinda how I feel," Marge said. "The big thing to me is it showed the working people's power. Once we're organized, nothin' the mill men can do can stop us. . . . What's more, these weeks learned a lot of us whar we're headin'—what's our goal."

"That's the thing," Jem nodded. "Whar we're headed, 'n how to get thar."

"You see Dolly," Tom spoke over his shoulder, "no strike is ever lost. Sometimes the workers win all they went out for, sometimes only part. Sometimes the most they can do is stop the onslaught of their bosses, on their conditions 'n pay. But whatever the immediate results, in the long run every strike that unites the workers' ranks is a step forward for us. . . . Every strike is one link in a long chain that leads from mill slavery to workers' freedom."

A loud report. Nancy clutched Marge's arm. "Oh, Lawdy, who's shootin' now?"

Tom threw off the gas. "Just a blow-out," he announced ruefully. "Shell out comrades, 'n we'll jack her up." They had two more punctures before night-fall.

"This lizzie's shoes are worn as thin as mine." Jerry rubbed his knees, cramped with stooping.

"We'd make as good time walkin'," Jem declared, "'n save tempers 'n gas."

That night they camped along the road-side. Tom had them up at day-break. "Gotta get an early start, else we'll never make Cleveland by Friday. The old can's rattlin' like she had the plague."

"Maybe you knew Tom was a strong Union man," Jem teased, "but you never knew how strong before. Why he just can't sleep or let nobody else sleep till he gets to that convention!"

"What's the joke?" Dolly rubbed her eyes, plucking straws from her stockings and dress.

"Oh doan mind his tongue wagglin'," Tom hustled them along, "his brains ain't roused yet."

When, at last, the 1918 model limped into the city Marge viewed the sky-scrapers and dense traffic with amazed eyes. "Gee, Tom, it'll be somethin' to take over 'n run places like this!"

They pushed their way through the crowd milling around the entrance. Everybody, it seemed was shaking hands and exchanging greetings. "Hello there Bill! How's the Coast?" "Hey, Jack, you old switchman, you a delegate too?" "'N I told that cop, I told him ..."

George elbowed his way through. "Tom! Tom Crenshaw!"

"It's the delegation from the South!" Immediately the crowd surged around, hurrahing. The mill hands clung together, eyes dim. Beneath Marge's quiet exterior something bubbled, broke. "They're our kind. . . . We belong! . . . We belong!"

Tom edged them into the office. "Whew! Pretty hot reception for such a close day, eh? ... Say, George'll fix you up 'n introduce you around. I gotta run off for a couple of hours. Some friends arrivin' from New York—Marge'll tell you why. ..." With a grin he was off.

Several hours later he was back, an arm slung around each of his companions. "Marge—comrades—step around. I want you to meet my pals"—he gestured toward the tall Negro and the small girl with her wealth of black waving hair brushed straight back from her high forehead. "This is Fred—Fred Morgan. 'N this is Bess—" he added slowly, "Bess Crenshaw. When we go back they'll head with us—South."

MARGE, WAITING for the convention to open, alternately stole glances at Bess and gazed about the crowded hall. To think this red-cheeked girl, now her sister, had sat in the Soviet Council at Moscow 'n helped make laws for more'n two million people! Thar sure must be a lot she had to tell.

She'd never seen a hall so large as this. Tom said it could hold nigh a thousand people. The main floor was fast filling up, while the galleries, reserved for local workers, teemed with life. Marge watched faces of every cast and hue move down the aisles past her, seeking their places. Signs had been put up for each section. "Miners' Delegation," "Metal," "Auto," "Marine," and near where they sat, "Textiles."

Suddenly everyone was clammering to their feet, as the leaders marched on the stage. "That's Bill Foster, in the center," Bess whispered, "the leader of the Big Steel Strike of 1919."

Near the front some began to sing; rapidly the song spread the length of the hall.

> Arise ye prisoners of starvation,
> Arise ye wretched of the earth!
> For justice thunders condemnation
> A better world's in birth! ...

Marge, looking about to catch the words she didn't yet know, saw that there were many like herself, straining to learn. Others sung in deep, sure tones:

> We have been naught—
> We shall be all!

Clenched fists shot into the air: men, women and youth stood at attention as all joined in the familiar chorus:

'Tis the final conflict—
Let each stand in his place.
The International Soviet
Shall be the human race.

As reports and speeches followed one another through the long afternoon, the baby lying in the lap of the little woman on Marge's left threw itself bodily to and fro, gurgling at the ceiling. Tiring of this game, it began to whimper, fumbling for its mother's breast, pulling at her thin hair which she carefully smoothed again behind her ears. The woman bounced and whispered to it in some language Marge couldn't understand, meanwhile jotting down notes in a small book she carried. Catching Marge's eye, "Maybe you'd hold her or put down what the speakers say, for awhile?" she asked in broken English. "Baby's tired out. We traveled all night in a truck to get here, from Bentleyville, Pennsylvania. Fifty miners and their women... You see the National Miners' Union woman's auxiliary what sent me'll be expecting me to bring it all back. That's why I got to get it down in that book."

Marge saw much of Anna Mashenski and her miner husband, Fritz, after that. "How's it in the coal fields?" Fritz rubbed his empty eye socket. "It's rank starvation there. Our children no shoes, nothing. Men going below ground, risking their lives with only dry bread in their buckets. Since the war it's been hell to pay in the camps. The old union we fought for thirty years to build, smashed by the operators with the help of the Lewis gang. Think of it, drawing fifteen thousand a year out of us coal-diggers' dues, and turning traitors! Jesu, it ain't safe for him to show his fat mug near Bentleyville!"

"Looks like it's the same all over—wherever the A.F. of L. been—heartaches 'n sell-outs," Margie said. Anna looked up from her nursing child. "We were desperate when the new Union come. Now there's fresh spirit going through the coal-fields. The miners and their women are making ready to march again."

All the next day the delegates reported. "It's like a great movin' picture," Marge confided to Jem, "travelin' to ev'ry part of the country. . . . Look like I could see millions of lives pourin' into one common stream."

"Yeah, generatin' a power that nothin' can halt. . . . You guess Marge, we'll ever be able to take it all back, to the folks on the hill?"

"SO THAT'S HOW IT IS over thar, eh?" Jem stirred his glass of steaming tea. "I'd sure like to see that Russia."

Ed Benson, an old friend of Tom's, a former wobbly, who now worked in a Cleveland steel plant, had brought the southern delegation out to his place—"Where these two," he nodded at Bess and Fred, "can tell us all about it." Ed was a red-faced, hairy-chested man with arms that reminded Marge of sturdy oak trunks and a booming voice that startled her ears, accustomed to the soft drawl of the Carolinas.

"Think of mills workin' seven hour shifts," Jerry marveled, "'n wages goin' up 'stead of down!"

"'N no Jim-crow or boss-men to sass you 'round!" Nancy shook her head in wonderment.

"What I can't get straight," Dolly asked, "is whar all the money come from to build clubs 'n nurseries 'n things like that?"

Fred laughed. "Because the Russian masses had sense enough to drive out their Rockerfellers, Morgans, 'n Jenkins. Now, all the wealth they produce goes not to a small class of blood-suckers but for the common good. That's why they can plan out the best way to run things, and everybody have jobs 'n a good livin'. Give our Soviet Union a few more years 'n she'll show the whole world."

Marge sat with wide eyes. In that country, so Bess said, working women get two month's vacation with pay before 'n two months' after child-birth, free care at the hospital 'n all. ... If she had been there, little Bobby and Roberta'd not have died. ... If it had been that way here, her Bob would have gotten well. ... Some day life on Riverton hill would be like that. ... Folks like her running the factories, folks like her making the laws ...

"Tom, what you-all gotta see is the Red Army." Fred placed his tremendous hands, palm down, on the table (He's like his Ma, Marge realized, with his deep-set melancholy eyes, his ringing voice). "Thar's a sight to make your blood sing. ... Boys, let 'em try to start a war against her 'n—"

"You doan think?" Dolly was aghast, "they'd try to start another war?" Everyone drew closer.

"No doubt of it." Bessie's face darkened. "The signs are clear."

"War's a disease that breeds 'n breeds, so long as the greedy rule."

"It's the scramble for profits."

"'N it's allays 'rich man's war 'n poor man's fight,'" Jem drawled. "I know right well none of us what fought through the last one'd take up rifles for Wall Street again."

"But what of the younger men? What about them?" Bess demanded.

"That's what the Russian workers asked me, time 'n again," Fred said. "'When the bankers declare war, what will the American workers do? We know our European brothers will fight for—not against us. If they start a war, it'll let loose revolutions throughout Europe. ... But what about America?'"

"The answer to that," Tom looked around at his companions, "depends largely on folks like us. On how fast we organize. The workers 'n farmers of this country are still not waked up. Not more'n ten per cent have ever been in unions of any kind. The're doped on ev'ry hand. Until we reach them, what can we expect?"

"That's true." Fred said, "but now thar's the first signs of the sleepin' giant rousin' again. In 1919–21, as some of you remember, the workers here fought long 'n hard. But they got sold out 'n lulled back to sleep. Now they're stirrin' again."

"You can hear the first thunder claps," Tom exulted, "'n the smell of storm brewin' in the air."

"Our Riverton strike was a li'l cloud burst to what's ahead!" George drew in a generous breath. "By golly, let 'er come!"

"This fake prosperity can't go on much longer." Fred predicted. "Goods are pilin' up in the store houses, the people have no money to buy. The day of accountin' can't be far off. . . ."

Tom's eyes glittered. "When it does, more wage-cuts, speed-up, lay-offs. More millions on the streets. More farmers ruined, crops rottin' in the fields ... Then, hunger marches, bread riots, strikes ...

"... Revolutionary upheavals in the colonial countries ..."

"... A Soviet Europe ..."

"... 'N here at home the storm'll sweep from coast to coast!"

"Is that what you see ahead?" Dolly gripped her glass. "It's sure gona be hard goin's the way you talk. Year on year."

"That's it," Fred answered softly. "Hard goin's, year on year. Our generation's born to struggle. But the stakes, comrades—the stakes come high."

Marge could feel the lash of the wet wind, the tremor of rushing bodies. . . . She was riding the gale! Not swept along, but deliberately, joyously a fore-runner, a marshaller of the gathering storm.